SOUTHERN CHARM

SOUTHERN CHARM

Book One of the Caswell Chronicles

J. D. MORRIS

This is a work of fiction. Similarities to real people, places, or events are entirely coincidental.

SOUTHERN CHARM

First edition. March 8, 2021.

Copyright © 2021 J. D. Morris.

ISBN: 978-0-578-88987-0

LCCN: 2021907442

Written by J. D. Morris.

To everyone who believed, thanks for the support... To those who didn't, thanks for the drive.

I

Becca sat on the hood of Sam's old Chevrolet, watching as the wind rippled gently across the surface of Sardis Lake. She had no idea why, but there was just something about tonight that gave her a feeling of unease. It could have been chalked up to the fact that she and Sam had snuck out well past both of their curfews. It might have also been that the lake itself was supposed to be closed to the public at this hour of the night, which meant that they were technically trespassing at the moment. Whatever the reason might be, something was gnawing at the back of her mind and filling her with a sense of dread that the girl simply could not pin down.

A twig snapped somewhere off in the distance to the left of her and Becca felt herself jump, effectively pulling herself out of this internal reflection. She quickly spun around and looked out into the wooded area that surrounded the lake in the direction that the sound had come from. At first, she could not see anything besides the dense bank of shadows and fog that had drifted lazily up from the surface of the lake.

"Sam?" she called out. "Is that you over there?"

Becca saw nothing other than the motionless dark stretching out in front of her as she waited for her eyes to adjust.

"Sam?" she tried once more, garnering no more response than before. Just then, she felt the trees rustling overhead as the wind began to pick up around her.

"Samuel Ethan Potts!" Becca called again, using the boy's full name this time. "You get your sorry bumpkin ass out here, right now!"

At that moment, the rest of a low-hanging branch fell from one of the trees just as something else wrapped around Becca's waist and she let out a scream in the highest pitch she could reach. The girl thrashed about wildly, in a desperate attempt to free herself from this unknown assailant as she was lifted into the air. She kicked out toward her assailant and flailed her arms, unthinkingly, until her elbow finally made contact with something hard enough to warrant a shout from the other party.

"Christ's sake, Becca!" a painful shout in a familiar tone, followed by muffled laughter.

She whirled around to see Sam standing there, holding his nose and playfully glaring back at her.

He removed one of his hands to reveal a thin scarlet line trailing from one of his nostrils, where her elbow had successfully landed, down to his chin. "How bad does it look?"

"No worse than usual," Becca shrugged, to which Sam chuckled. "Just be glad it wasn't my heel."

"Trust me," Sam acknowledged, grabbing his crotch, "I am."

"Let me see," the girl said, removing her friend's other hand and tilting his head toward the lone street light on the ramp. "It doesn't look like it's broken. Not this time, anyway."

"Oh, gee, thanks! I'll take that assessment from the girl who barely passed her freshman A&P class," he joked. Noticing that something was off about her tonight, he asked, "What's got you so on edge?"

Becca shrugged, "I don't know. Something just doesn't feel right."

"Right," Sam gave his friend a sarcastic nod. He took his shirt off and used it to wipe the blood from his face. "Glad we cleared that up."

"I'm serious!" Becca protested. "Something is weird about tonight. I don't know what it is, but I just feel like we're being watched or something."

"It's the government," Sam replied in a matter-of-fact tone, nodding as he spoke. He pointed up into the clear, starry night sky. "They've got drones trailing us."

"Would it be too much to ask that you be serious for just one second of your life, Sam?" Becca scowled at his explanation.

"I'm not even joking!" Sam protested, though he couldn't help but laugh at her expression. "Someone's got to run the camera, after all."

It took a few seconds for the vulgarity of the joke to register and by the time it did, Sam had already sprinted halfway down the boat ramp that led out into the water. She took off after him, half laughing at his arms flailing about as he ran and half swearing at him for leaving her stranded on the bank.

"I'm going to kill you when I catch you!" she cried out.

"That would mean that you actually *could* catch me!" Sam called back, having already made it to the edge of the water. Becca silently cursed his Track and Field advantage over her as she ran along to catch up with him. Then, an idea occurred to her.

"You *know* you'll have to come out *sometime*, Sam!" she said, halting in her pursuit.

"Nope!" Sam smirked, dashing into the water. "I can stay out here until you get tired. I'm a fish, now, Becca!"

"Good!" the girl called down the way to him, laughing at how ludicrous her friend was being. "That means I get your dad's truck!"

Sam shrugged and let himself fall backward into the water with a satisfying splash. Becca closed the distance between the truck and the water as Sam proceeded to backstroke several laps, loosely and with graceful ease. She paused on the edge of the lake, staring out into its murky depths. Just then, the foreboding feeling she'd had just moments earlier resurfaced, deep in the pit of her stomach. She felt a chill go up her spine and could not tell if it was from the wind or something else.

"What's wrong?" Sam asked, ceasing his paddling to curiously view the trepidation on his friend's face. Becca stood there for a moment and shook off the cool as being nothing more than the breeze bristling the hairs on the back of her neck.

"It's fine," she lied. "Just a little cold, is all."

"I'm sure we can find something to do that'll warm you up," Sam grinned impishly, cupping his hands together just under the water's surface so that it squirted up in her direction.

"Not. even. funny," Becca felt herself flush deep red. She scowled and Sam stuck out his tongue playfully, before diving into the murk of Sardis Lake. He resurfaced a few feet farther away than he had been and continued swimming in circles with the disjointed grace of a frog.

"Come on in, scaredy-cat!" he called out to her. She still had not moved from her spot on the shore. "The water's fine!"

Becca stuck just her big toe in at first, shortly followed by the rest of her foot. Sam was right; the water did feel rather inviting and, somehow, warmer than the boat ramp she currently stood on.

The girl sheepishly waded out into the shallows of the lake, taking a sharp inhale as she hit a cold patch. She began paddling when she could finally push off and not touch the bottom of the lake. Same was currently ignoring her in favor of bobbing up and down a few yards further out, looking almost like a human buoy.

"Wait!" Becca called out as Sam noticed all the noise she was making and swam away. "I can't see that far out!"

"Don't tell me you're suddenly afraid of the dark, Rebecca Jane?" he laughed. "You think there's a shark out here or something?"

"Can't you just wait a second?!" she replied, not bothering with an explanation.

Becca paddled more furiously now, trying to close the distance between herself and Sam so she could give him a piece of her mind; or push him under, if nothing else. Becca submerged herself then, knowing that she would move faster in beneath the water than paddling on top of it as she had been. When she resurfaced, she wiped the water from her eyes with the back of her hand. Looking around, however, she was surprised to see that Sam was no longer where he had been just seconds ago.

"Sam?" she called out, knowing he wouldn't hear her if he was underwater. She tried once more, but there was no response as her voice echoed out over the vast seemingly vast surface of the lake. She felt something brush against her foot just then and instinctively jerked away, fearing it might be a snake. As she did this, a hand wrapped around her ankle and pulled her hard into the murky blackness. Becca did not even have a chance to suck air into her lungs before being pulled down and spat out water as she came back up. She kicked down and out behind her, making contact with something using all the might of her foot against the water tension.

"Dammit!" a gruff voice came from behind her. She spun around to see that it was Sam, once more. And once more, he was holding his nose and laughing in pain. "That's the second time you've tried to break my nose in the past five minutes, alone!"

"You could have drowned me, you jackass!" Becca snarled, reaching up to smack him in the back of the head. She had to suppress the urge to laugh at his misfortune. "I didn't mean to, Sam," she said, a bit more gently this time.

"Sure," he snorted, nursing both his injured nose and pride. "You'll have to forgive me if I don't believe you, Becks."

"You did it to yourself," Becca countered, her want to laugh being quickly replaced by a defensive rage. "Maybe if you weren't being such an asshole, it wouldn't have even happened."

"Oh, *I'm* the asshole," Sam chuckled, removing his hand from his face to reveal the damage that had been done by her heel. There was no mistaking that it was broken this time, as the bridge was all crooked now. "Remind me, again, how that is, Miss Furyfists?"

"Screw you, Sam," Becca glared now, splashing water in his face and not caring that he'd have to explain what happened. She started to swim back to the shore, finding that she no longer wanted to be anywhere near him at this point.

"And just where do you think you're going?" he laughed, watching her graceless struggle to put distance between them.

"*You're* taking me home," she called over her shoulder, spitting out water as she made her way back to dry land with some effort.

"Oh, *am* I?" Sam asked with a hearty guffaw. "I don't recall saying anything like that. Because I'm *pretty* sure this is the first I'm hearing about it. And I also don't recall agreeing to it."

"Fine! If you don't want to," Becca paused to look back, "then I'll just walk home!"

"At two in the morning from Sardis Lake?" he eyeballed her with mock fury. "Becca, you live all the way out in Abbeville. You'd get there faster if you swam across the damn lake!"

"So?" she snorted. "This'll just count as my cardio for the week."

"Wait!" Sam called out, fighting back his laughter, although not very well. "Becks, I'm sorry!"

The girl said nothing in response, so he let out a sigh. "If you really want to go, then I'll take you home."

"Thank you," Becca said begrudgingly, suppressing her rage until they were in the truck.

"That was the part," Sam explained, "where you were supposed to say 'Oh no, Sam. It's fine, Sam. I was just being a moody little asshat, Sam.'"

"I hope you drown, Sam," Becca mocked him with a scowl. She turned back to swim away, full-force now. Sam called after her, but she did not allow herself to pay attention to what he was saying.

Only once she had made it back to the shore completely did Becca glance back to see that Sam was, once again, nowhere to be found.

"This is getting really old, Sam!" she cried out then, feeling her anger rising to a crescendo inside of her. "Come *on*!"

There was no answer, just as had been expected. Then she saw a ring of ripples out toward the middle of the lake, where he had been just before she had turned her back to him. Becca smirked to herself and picked up a rock, tossing it into the center of the circle. "You think you're funny?"

Becca turned on her heel and started to walk back to the truck, where she could wait and drip dry on the hood. She had just barely made it to the Chevy and was readying herself to climb up when she heard the muffled sound of someone's voice behind her. She couldn't register what the other had been saying before she heard a loud splash. She spun back around and called out, "Sam?"

As she watched the seemingly still surface of the lake, she felt her heart hammering in her chest.

Sam had resurfaced at the sound of his name this time, only there was something very wrong with the scene. He was somehow standing limply on the water, despite the fact that he was much too far out for him to be able to touch the bed of the lake, even at his height.

As Becca stared curiously, she realized, with a swelling feeling of horror, that something was holding him aloft. She focused her gaze in the darkness and saw that it looked almost like some sort of tentacle, but Becca knew that couldn't be right. Sardis Lake was not, in any way, connected to any body of water that would allow something that massive or strong to make its way in.

"Becca!" Sam cried out, his voice cracking to reveal that he was in immense pain of some sort.

"Sam?" she managed, not fully processing what was happening before her. "What are you doing? What *is* that thing?"

"Becca!" he repeated her name, ending with a ragged gasp. "*Run!*"

The words had barely escaped his lips when the thing that had been holding him up smacked Sam hard onto the surface of the water. Becca felt her stomach doing cartwheels inside of her, but somehow she knew there was no time for her to get sick just yet.

She tried to move but found herself frozen to the spot by panic.

As she tried to make herself do something other than just stand there, Sam resurfaced once more and she could finally see the thing as it was wrapped around him fully this time. It looked like a tentacle in almost every aspect, but there was something deeply unnatural and unsettling about it. It was almost as if whatever it was was not truly belong in this world, let alone the lake.

Becca could see, even from this distance, that Sam's eyes were pleading with her to help him, but what could she do? She could not even bring herself to move from the spot where she was, glued firmly in place by fear. Becca was merely a spectator now, to what she was sure were her friend's last moments.

She felt utterly useless; powerless in the face of the thing that had taken hold of Sam and her terror.

"Sam!" she screamed, feeling her voice crack just as Sam's had moments ago.

The thing, whatever it was, seemed to be taking joy in the abject horror it was causing at this point. It jerked the boy back and forth violently and began squeezing his midsection. Even from where she was standing, Becca could hear the sickening and repeated cracks of her friend's ribs as they snapped under the pressure.

There was a sudden and brief pause then, and it was almost like the thing was trying to decide what to do next. Finally, it slammed Sam back down into the surface of the lake in three lightning-quick motions before he went limp.

Becca knew there was nothing she could do now. She watched helplessly from the bank as Sam's body went completely motionless and he was dragged under.

This time, there was no resurfacing.

Sam was gone.

As if being propelled by some external force, Becca felt herself running up the boat ramp and in the direction of the Chevy. She knew she did not have her license yet, but that was not high on her list of priorities, so she pushed it to the back of her mind. Becca sat in the driver's seat not knowing how, or even if she could, process what had just taken place and not having the time to do so. The girl was working on pure adrenaline at this point. Somehow, her hands found the key that had been left under the seat and stuck in the ignition, turning it over as soon as she could.

She could not even scream at this point. Even if she did, Becca was not entirely sure that she would have been able to hear it right now. The hammering of her heartbeat inside her ears seemed to drown out both sound and logic.

She shifted the old truck into gear and peeled out of the parking space, squealing tires as she did so. She was still unsure of exactly where she should be going at this time of night. The only thing she did know was that she had to get out of here. Her best friend was gone now, and Becca had no clue of what she should do as she followed the winding road back toward civilization in the vain hope that someone would be able to help her.

II

Remi was awakened by the sound of his phone vibrating on his nightstand. He rolled over to see that it was barely half-past two in the morning. Instinctively, he rolled back over and tried to ignore it the first time, assuming that it must have been a wrong number, being that it was so late.

The phone buzzed a second time. He guessed it must have been the same person calling back from before, so he ignored it again. On the third attempt, he picked his phone up and, though he did not know the number, something told him that it must be someone from work that was trying to get in touch with him. He groaned and picked up on the sixth long buzz, hoping the person on the other end would at least have a decent excuse.

"Mmmyellow?" he answered groggily, bringing the ball of his palm across the backs of his eyelids and yawning as he spoke.

"Caswell?" the voice on the other end was familiar, though Remi simply could not be bothered to place it in his current state.

"Speaking," he replied with another great yawn, fighting the urge he always had on his off days to hang up and roll back over.

"It's John," the man paused, clearly waiting for some sound of recognition from Remi. That recognition never came, so he went on, "Y'know? From the Coven?"

"Right," Remi answered, not caring who the man was or where he hailed from, though it *did* sound vaguely familiar. Then the sound of the heavy breathing in the silence on the other end of the line in the silence made it click. An image of the paunch clerk that handled incoming cases overnight at the Coven House of Oxford, Mississippi flashed through his mind.

"John," he groaned inwardly, knowing that a call from another Coven member at this hour of the night could never mean anything good. "What's up?"

"We have a bit of a situation here," John answered after a short pause.

"Could whatever it is not have waited until a semi-decent hour?" Remi asked, closing his eyes and pushing his face into his pillow once more.

"I know," John pleaded with him. "I really hate having to bother you, but nobody else answered."

"Can't imagine why," Remi chuckled to himself. "I would suggest that you speak fast, John. I'm about two seconds from passing back out."

"Okay," the other man spoke in a rush now, making his best attempt to keep Remi's attention. "So, apparently something happened earlier tonight out at Sardis Lake and now there's a girl sitting here. She's somewhat hysterical and looks a bit disheveled, but she won't actually tell us what happened. Or, rather," he paused, as if searching for a better word to use, "she can't tell us what happened."

"What do you mean 'can't'?" Remi asked, sitting upright now, genuinely curious. "And what do you mean by 'something'? She didn't tell you anything useful?"

"No," John seemed somehow irritated and apologetic simultaneously. "She started to tell us, but then she broke down sobbing. We were lucky we got the location out of her before that."

"So," Remi started, working slowly through his mental fog. "Do a transfer to OPD and have her put in solitary until she decides she wants to talk."

"Tried that," John explained. "They refuse to take her until we at least have a name."

Remi grunted, pushing himself back against the headboard and trying to think of another solution.

"So you mean to tell me that they won't take a Jane Doe?" he asked, not bothering to mask his annoyance, which was steadily mounting.

"Apparently not," the other man sounded exasperated. "Or, at least, not from us."

"Figures," Remi let out a deep sigh, trying to figure out what to do.

I just want to go back to sleep, he thought to himself.

"What about a Veritas Charm?" he suggested, though he was not sure that would work. If the girl was so hysterical she could not form coherent sentences on her own, there was no guarantee that the charm would be able to get anything more substantial out of her.

"That's the other thing," John said, somewhat absent-mindedly.

"John," Remi let his frustration be known this time. "I don't have the time or the patience for these partial stories. Tell me what you know. Now."

"The girl," he paused as if trying to find the correct way to explain it. "She's a Mortal," he finished and the word hung between lines like a solid force.

"Could you repeat that?" Remi asked for clarity. "I'm sure I misheard you."

"You heard right," John said. Remi had no idea how to respond.

There was no logical way a Mortal should have been able to *find* the Coven House, let alone make it inside. Sure enough, most of them knew roughly where it was located just from their history classes, but there were several Glamours around it to deter them. These stretched not only over the physical house itself but the grounds surrounding it to prevent this sort of thing from happening. There were numerous reasons as to why the girl should not be there, and just about as many questions as to how and why she had come to them. Yet, according to the man on the other end of the line, there she was.

"You still there, Caswell?" John's voice came through after a few long seconds.

"Yeah," Remi answered, unsure of what else he could say. "Just give me a minute."

He was on his feet now, moving around the room and gathering his belongings as the clerk remained silent on the other end of the line.

"What should I do?" he asked finally, just as Remi was pulling on his shoes.

"There's nothing you can do," Remi said, knowing that the simple clerks of the Coven were not trained on how to deal with Mortals in these types of situations.

"Just get me an interrogation room." he went on. "And have the girl wait in there. Hopefully, she'll be a bit more talkative by the time I make it up there."

"So you are coming, then?" John asked, sounding almost relieved to hear this.

"Do I really have a choice in the matter?" Remi sighed, more to himself than the other man. He looked longingly at his bed, mentally shaking himself. "Give me about an hour."

"An hour?" John seemed confused by this. "But I thought you lived just a few minutes away?"

"Yes," Remi agreed, before explaining, "The bars on the Square will still be letting out, and I need to get some sort of caffeine in me if I'm going to ask questions without snapping you or some panicky Mortal girl in half. They'd have a field day with that if it ever happened. Unless you'd prefer to be on the run from Mortals for the rest of your life?"

"Got it," John understood now. "I'll get everything ready."

With that, Remi ended the call and continued pacing around his bedroom. He felt dizzy and made his way hastily toward the bathroom to get sick in the toilet.

Before being woken up by the clerk from the John, the Coven clerk, Remi had spent his only night off in the past two weeks at a party hosted by a member of the Woodland Fae Court. He hated downtime and had wanted to let off a little steam before hitting the grind for another long block of days. Retrospectively, however, he thought that, perhaps, spending his free time getting covered in neon glitter and heaven-only-knows-what-else might not have been his shining idea of the year. He hadn't even really known the host, but was invited through another member of the Court and had politely, downed every single drink he had been served just like the champion that he was.

So many little, neon-green mysteries...

Remi was still not entirely sure how he'd made it back home afterward, and as he stood in front of the sink, assessing the damage of the night, he wasn't entirely sure that he wanted to know.

Remi was not an unattractive man. He was not overly muscular, but not slender either, falling comfortably somewhere in-between. He stood at just under six feet tall, which was good as he could generally find people in a crowded room. Since it was the middle of June and he was lucky enough to live in Oxford, Mississippi, Remi had managed to stay outdoors most of the summer thus far to combat his natural state of being as pale as the driven snow. This, however, brought out his multiple scars, making them appear whitewashed against his currently tanned skin.

There was a slight crook in the bridge of his nose; a reminder of an altercation he'd had during his Academy days, though he'd forgotten the details over the years. His hair was brown and severely unkempt, falling just past his pronounced jaw, and was constantly being pushed out of his eyes when he was working on cases.

All of those were ordinary features, however when compared to his eyes.

Above all of the other badges he had worn over the years, Remi was a Warlock. This meant that his irises, unlike those of Mortals, were iridescent; an evolutionary byproduct of the magic that coursed through his veins. He had heard of rare cases where a Warlock's eyes remained neutral and darkened like their Mortal counterparts, but that was a once-in-a-century sort of occurrence. In color, his were a silvery shade of blue. Like moonstone gems, just as all other Caswells before him.

Magical bloodlines had a way of strengthening themselves, with the more dominant traits overtaking the weaker ones. This meant that if a particularly skilled Warlock with green eyes had children with someone average and with brown eyes, the child would have green eyes as a mark of the stronger Magical blood.

Remi marveled at his reflection for just a bit longer, simultaneously making sure that he was done being sick from the Fae drinks he had consumed earlier, before grabbing his keys off the nightstand and making his way downstairs. He lit up a cigarette on the middle landing between the first and second floor and inhaled deeply, letting the smoke fill and burn his lungs.

If he was being forced to come into Oxford's Coven House on his *one* day off, he was at least going to get some tiny bit of joy out of it, even if that joy slowly killed him.

The girl was surprisingly young; much younger than Remi had been expecting on his way over here. She couldn't have been more than fifteen or sixteen if he had to venture a guess. She might have been beautiful under normal circumstances, but as she sat with her blonde hair in a tangled mess and with mud smeared all over her, Remi could not be sure. She was wearing oversized and tattered clothing that had clearly been soaked through and was only just now drying. Remi could tell that whatever had happened to her tonight had obviously left her extremely. He suspected the worst but did not want to verbalize it until he was positive.

He stood with his arms crossed over his chest and watched as the girl fidgeted in her seat. She would occasionally glance up from her hands, which were interlaced on the table in front of her, to the mirrored wall that separated her room and theirs. She would open her mouth a few times like a trout as if she was trying to form words. Inevitably, they simply would not come and the girl would resolve herself to staring back at her palms. Remi found it almost painful to watch but kept this bit of information to himself.

"How long has she been like this?" he asked, sipping his coffee and feeling the scalding liquid burn the inside of his mouth.

"A little over an hour," John informed him with a shrug. "Maybe two?"

"And she hasn't said anything this whole time?" Remi could not make himself look away from the trainwreck on the other side of the filmed glass of the observation room. "Other than where the incident took place?"

"She didn't even tell us that," John admitted. "It was just a guess based on the wet clothes and her being covered in mud. But I could be wrong."

"Maybe," Remi agreed. "But probably not."

He took another sip of his coffee and felt John fidget to his left. "How did she find us?"

"That's the thing," John said. "There's no way she should have been able to even find the House, let alone get inside. There's just no way."

"There are ways," Remi answered knowingly.

"Like?"

"She could have just been looking for help," Remi explained, "which is most likely the case. Our Glamours allow even Mortals to pass through if they are seeking assistance. She could have also been attacked by a magical creature, in which case the House itself would have made an effort to bring her here, even without her knowing it. Our enchantments only keep us in hiding unless our laws have been broken or we're specifically sought out by someone who needs our help for whatever reason."

You'd figure even a clerk would know such basic history, Remi thought to himself as he took another sip of coffee.

"Even a Mortal?" John had a puzzled expression on his face, to which Remi nodded.

"Didn't you pay attention in history class?" Remi cocked a single brow at the round man standing before him. "We learned about that on the first day."

"Honestly, I copied off the guy next to me and slept through most of that class," John seemed a little embarrassed.

"I know," Remi smirked. "I was the guy you copied off of. You're welcome. By the way, you snore."

A look of surprise crossed over John's face now and Remi had to stifle a chuckle as the other's face turned bright red.

"Guess that's why you're in the field and I'm stuck pulling graveyards here," he said.

Remi nodded a silent agreement, patting the man on the shoulder and moving past him into the room where the girl glanced up briefly, before fixing her gaze back to her interlaced fingers.

He took a seat in the chair directly opposite the girl across the metal table in the center of the interrogation room and kicked his feet up, leaning his chair back on its hind legs.

"I've got all night," he informed her casually. The girl looked up to meet his blue moonstone gaze but said nothing.

After about thirty minutes of nothing but the sound of the clock ticking away on the wall behind the girl, Remi got up from his seat. He had finished the last bit of his coffee and moved to the small pot in the corner of the room. As he scooped the grounds into the filter and filled the back with water, he could feel the girl watching the back of him.

"That's not the best view, just so you know," he attempted a joke, turning to lean against the wall as the machine on the counter percolated to life. "The back of me, I mean. It's not the best view if you're going to stare at me for a long period of time."

The girl quickly averted her gaze, despite the fact that she had already been caught.

Remi smiled; at least he had gotten a reaction. He stood there, watching to see if she would venture a second glance at him knowing that he had his eyes fixed on her now. He made a sharp, quick whistle when the coffee had finished brewing and the girl looked back over at him. He held up his styrofoam cup in a gesture of offering as the aroma from the fresh pot filled the room almost entirely. The girl began to shake her head at first, before pausing to reconsider.

"Good," Remi smiled with a nod of approval. "How do you take it?"

The girl opened her mouth as if to answer, but no sound came out. Remi nodded in understanding. He turned away and refilled his cup, splashing it with a single creamer, before preparing another for the girl. Remi brought it back and placed the lighter one across the table.

"Three creamers, three sugars," he explained. "You're still young, so I figure you're not bitter enough for black coffee just yet." The girl smiled, remaining silent as she brought the cup to her lips. Remi watched her, trying to piece her story together in his mind while she sipped. "Can I at least get your name?"

The girl pondered this for a moment, almost as if she was struggling to remember it. She was still clearly hesitant. Remi wondered if, perhaps, the enchantments of the House had brought her to them without her knowing what had taken place and she was still in too much shock to tell them that. He knew subconsciously that couldn't be the case, but stranger things had happened in his time here. He watched as the girl seemed to struggle internally a few moments longer with the decision, before finally answering, "Becca."

"Good," Remi smiled. "That's a start, at least. Now, I'm guessing you prefer that instead of 'Rebecca'?" The girl nodded and took another slurp of her coffee.

Remi pulled the box of cigarettes from the chest pocket of his shirt, putting one in his mouth and setting the box down onto the table.

"Mind if I smoke in here?" he asked. Becca made no inclination of either possible answer, so Remi assumed she did not mind. His hand fumbled to the same chest pocket and he let out a small swear as he realized that he had left his lighter in the cupholder of his Jeep.

Becca watched him curiously, slurping her coffee as he shrugged. Remi snapped his fingers and a small flame danced to life just in front of his face, causing the Mortal girl to jump and take in a sharp breath.

Remi brought his face closer to the teardrop-sized ball of fire, puffing a few times to light his cigarette before snapping his fingers again, causing the flame to disappear. He glanced across at Becca, who was now watching him intently and with very wide eyes. Whether the girl was entranced by the flame or his casual use of magic in front of her, he knew not.

"Would you like one?" he offered, and the girl declined with an almost disgusted shake of her head. "Good. Keep it that way."

Remi shrugged, more to himself than her, and stared up at the ceiling. He noticed immediately that this particular interrogation room, unlike some of the newer ones, did not have a fan. There were a few quick raps on the filmed glass that linked this room with its respective gallery, indicating that John was still watching them from the darkened side.

Remi twirled the fingers of his free hand and muttered, "*Nova Caeli.*"

There was a soft and immediate whoosh of air as his incantation made a focused vacuum above them. The smoke from the tip of his cigarette had previously been billowing upward to collect on the ceiling. As the two watched, that same smoke gradually dissipated into the cloud of fresh air that had been created.

Remi gave a quick thumbs-up to the man in the gallery, smiling to himself and feeling very much like a badass, magical Mariska Hargitay. He then turned his attention back to Becca. The girl stared at him, almost disbelievingly.

"What's wrong?" he stared back, curiously.

"How did you do that?" she asked timidly, almost as if she had never actually witnessed a Warlock at work so up-close before.

"You do realize what I am, right?" Remi furrowed his brows, watching the girl closely. She said nothing but kept her gaze fixed on him, as if suddenly cautious and curious of what else he might be able to do. The pair sat in silence for another half hour or so before Remi had an idea.

"Look," he began slowly, trying to think of what to say to make the girl talk.

"We can do this however you want," he went on. "I was supposed to be off today, so I really don't have anywhere to be or any plans to contradict that. It would be great if you could start with some explaining, but if not, that's entirely fine. I've gone days with no sleep for cases before, so I am perfectly prepared to just sit here and stare at you for the next three days."

"I know you're a Mortal," he explained, "so our Covenant prevents me from doing anything to try to piece your being here together without consent. I also gather that you're a minor, so I can't even get that form of consent without your parents being here."

He finished and the two remained in silence for another few moments, before the girl finally said.

"It all happened so fast," she spoke so softly that Remi had to lean closer just to hear her. "I'm not even really sure *what* happened to him."

"Okay," Remi nodded, listening intently now. "Let's just start from the beginning. Who is the 'him' you're referring to?"

"Sam," Becca answered, a shadow of fresh pain tearing its way across her face.

"Sam," Remi repeated. To clarify, he asked, "Okay, now is Sam a boy or girl?"

"Boy," she replied.

"Is this 'Sam' your boyfriend?" he asked. The girl shook her head, her face a mask somewhere between disgust and what-if. "Okay, so he's just a friend?" She nodded.

"Where is Sam?" Remi asked. "Did he come here with you?" Becca shook her head again and Remi noticed that she looked as if she was nearly ready to break down as she went silent again. He had another idea then, and quietly asked, "Becca, would you mind if I did something that might help you talk to me?"

"What do you mean?" the girl seemed almost terrified at the thought of what he meant.

"Just a little charm to calm your nerves a little," Remi explained. "I promise it won't hurt, and you'll feel a lot better. But I won't do anything if you don't want me to. And if you feel sick or anything, just let me know and I promise I'll stop it right then. Does that sound okay to you?"

The girl considered this offer for a moment, not knowing what this might entail for her before ultimately agreeing.

There was a harsh rap from the observation gallery and Remi shot a quick warning glare to John as he stood from his chair and moved around the table. He stood behind the girl and brought his fingers to rest on her temples. She tensed immediately but otherwise made no effort to protest.

"Okay," Remi explained as he imagined a blanket covering the girl's entire body. "You're going to feel almost like a tide is washing over you after I say this. I just want you to keep breathing like normal and just let it flow through you. Does that sound good to you?"

Becca nodded under his fingers and he spoke the charm, "*Quiesco.*"

Remi felt a rush of energy surge through his own body and into the girl. She became instantly relaxed, actually slumping a bit in the chair and nearly letting go of her styrofoam cup as the calming wave coursed through her.

"What was that?" she asked, after regaining herself and sitting upright once more.

"A Soul-Soothe charm," Remi explained, moving back to his seat across from the girl. "It will allow you to talk to me about what happened without getting overwhelmed with any negative emotions. After this interview is over, I'll remove it if you want, so you can feel however you think you should feel about tonight. Sound fair?"

"Sounds fair," Becca nodded, taking another loud slurp from her cup. "Your eyes look brighter than they were before."

"You've really never met a Warlock, have you?" Remi smiled at the thought of this. The girl shook her head and he went on to explain, "It happens when we use magic. Depending on what kind of spell we use and the intensity of it, they might shine like this for seconds or days. It all just depends."

"Cool!" the girl sounded genuinely curious about this newfound information. She seemed like she had a slew of other questions that she wanted to ask but didn't. Instead, she inhaled deeply and let out a great sigh, "Let's get this over with, I guess."

Remi nodded and went on with his questions, "So, Sam. Who is he to you?"

"My best friend since grade school," Becca answered with little hesitation. "Or," she paused, "at least he *was* my best friend since grade school."

"Was?" Remi repeated. "Why is he not anymore? Did something happen between the two of you tonight that you'd like to tell me?"

"Not *between* us," Becca clarified. "Something happened *to* us."

"If something happened to the two of you, then why are you the only one here, Becca?" Remi asked. "Did Sam decide to go to the Oxford Police Department?" Becca shook her head and paused.

As Remi watched, it seemed to him that she might have been replaying the earlier scene over in her head and still couldn't manage to wrap her head around whatever had happened.

"Becca?" he prodded. "Do you *know* what happened tonight?"

"Of course I know what happened!" the girl exclaimed, making Remi wonder if his spell had worn off so quickly in the face of a teenage girl's anxiety. Then she seemed to regain herself. "It's just," she paused, seemingly searching through her mind for the right words. "I don't know. It's like I was there and I saw it, but I can't really explain it."

"Take your time," Remi gave the girl a reassuring smile, hoping to instill some more confidence in her. "It doesn't have to be the perfect story. I just need to know what you saw."

He took a sip of his coffee and sat back in his chair, waiting and watching as the girl seemed to lose herself in the details of her mind.

"It's going to sound insane," Becca said finally, after about fifteen minutes of silence. "But just hear me out."

"That's fine," Remi shrugged. "I've always liked a good, unbelievable story." He added a smile at the end, hoping to nudge her further into telling him what had happened. Becca seemed like she was unsure how to take this, but went on explaining what had happened earlier that night.

To his absolute surprise, the girl left no single detail out. He found himself, on more than a few occasions, having to tell her to slow down while he took notes in shorthand so that he could make a file for the case later. As she went on in painstaking detail, Remi began to form a picture so clearly in his mind that he felt like he had been there to witness the scene play out first-hand. It was easy to see why she had ended up here; he expected the Mortal authorities would have laughed it off as some drunk teenager's pipe dream. Remi knew differently, however, from what the girl was telling him.

"So, what you're saying," he spoke softly and in a measured voice, reviewing his winding scrawl on the stenography pad after Becca had finished her retelling of events that had transpired. "Is that some sort of sea monster with tentacles attacked you and your friend while you were out at Sardis Lake. And that whatever this creature was, that it dragged your friend under and that's when you came here to find someone to help you. So there's a very real possibility that your friend never resurfaced." He paused to let it process a bit for her, before asking, "Does that sound correct?"

Becca nodded, hastily adding, "I know we shouldn't have been out past curfew. But we didn't think it was that big of a deal. I mean, we've done it sever-" she caught herself, then corrected, "We've done it a few times before. But nothing like this has ever happened."

"Becca," Remi gave her his best warm smile, despite the shivers creeping down his spine at her tale. "I've snuck out before, myself. I'm not going to get you in trouble for something like that."

An expression of unbridled relief spread across the girl's face, then Remi added, "I'm more worried about whatever it was that attacked you and Sam. The fact that you are the only one that made it out of that lake raises a lot of questions for me."

"Right," Becca seemed to be weighed down by the latter portion of Remi's statement, as her voice trailed off and her gaze became distant once more.

"But I'm going to do everything that I can to find out what really happened," he hastily reassured her. "I'll keep in touch with you about whatever I find out tonight."

"Tonight?" Becca asked disbelievingly. "You're going out there now?"

"Of course," he replied casually. "I need to make sure no one tampers with the scene, so I need to get out there before it opens to the public in the morning."

This seemed to do nothing more than agitate the girl, despite his carefully nonchalant tone. Remi could tell that his spell was slowly starting to wear off.

He stood from his chair and made his way around the table to stop behind Becca once more.

"What are you doing?" she seemed to be unhinging more rapidly with each passing second and she watched him with an accusatory glare that had not been there before.

"I just have a few more questions," Remi lied. "I just need you to stay calm. Is it alright if I do this one more time?"

Becca made no move to object but kept her eyes focused on him this time. Remi brought his hands once more to her temples and repeated his charm from before, "*Quiesco*."

This time, however, he focused harder for a stronger effect. Slowly, the girl's eyes rolled back into her skull so that only the whites were visible; an untrained person would assume she had expired, but Remi knew she had only fallen asleep. He cradled the bulk of her against him, shifting the girl's weight so that she rested her head on her crossed arms on the table in front of her. It was at this time that John burst into the room.

"What the hell do you think you're doing, Caswell?" he shouted, storming into the interrogation chamber as if someone had lit his rear on fire. The clerk was fuming.

"I guess I'm taking my tired ass out to Sardis Lake," Remi answered casually as if he hadn't just broken one of the Covenants.

"You know what I mean!" John let out a frustrated sigh. "She's not going to be happy about this."

"That's why you're not going to tell her until *after* I've gotten back," Remi said, and when John made to protest added, "Don't force me to Bind your tongue, John. I hear it's very uncomfortable for the afflicted party."

"Who are you taking with you?" the clerk quickly changed his line of questioning at the thought of Remi's idle threat.

"Taking with me?" Remi repeated, cocking a single eyebrow at the man.

"You're not going out there alone, are you?" John was in obvious disbelief.

"John," Remi gave the clerk a look that made it apparent that he was more than willing to make good on his earlier threat. "Do you really think anyone is going to answer their phone at four in the morning?"

"But we don't know what's out there," he protested, though it was clear that he knew Remi was right.

"Which is exactly why it makes more sense that only one person should go," Remi explained. "The larger the crowd, the more likely it is to be spotted by whatever it was that attacked these kids."

John was clearly still skeptical about the whole situation but made no vocalized objection to this logic.

"Should I request a transfer to the Mortals?" he asked, deciding it might serve him best to keep changing subjects.

"Some sort of tentacled monster attacked them from beneath a body of water that doesn't connect to anything but spillways and fisheries," Remi recalled the sleeping girl's claims. "Do you really think that the Mortals are prepared to deal with something like that?"

"Right," John agreed. "What should I do, then?"

"Call a Healer," Remi suggested without hesitation. "A female, if any are on call tonight."

The clerk gave him a questioning look and he went on, "Because you're going to get in touch with Becca's parents, and it wouldn't look proper for an underage Mortal girl to wake up surrounded by a group of male Warlocks, no matter how well-meaning the intent behind it might be."

"Right," John agreed a second time. "Should I try to contact the boy's family as well?"

"No," Remi shook his head. "Not yet. I don't want to worry them on the whereabouts of their son if there's any chance that this creature didn't kill him."

"Caswell," John made to object, but Remi cut him off with a quick glare.

"Don't," he said simply, holding up a single hand to prevent any further protest on the clerk's part. "If you call them at this hour of the night and all we have to offer them is 'Oh, something killed your son, but we don't know what it was,' they're going to think we did it. It's not fair to put them, or ourselves in that sort of situation if it can be avoided. Mortals love their evidence. It gives them a sort of closure that they wouldn't get otherwise."

John nodded silently, understanding that Remi was right.

"I'll get on that," the man said, not questioning his reasoning this time.

"Good," Remi nodded, wanting to be done with this conversation. "I've got an entire lake to sift through, now."

With nothing more than a curt nod, he left John to tend to Becca and her family. He hoped beyond all hope and against the knotted feeling that had begun to form deep in the pit of his stomach that the boy would simply be waiting on the bank of Sardis Lake to say this had all been an elaborate prank. But Remi knew better than that, by now.

III

Remi stood silently on the boat ramp that led down to the banks of Sardis Lake, cigarette hanging loosely from his lips as he surveyed the surrounding area. The early morning breeze had picked up by the time he had arrived, filling him with a chill and making him wish he had grabbed at least a light jacket before leaving his house earlier.

That's only something a sensible person would do, Remi thought to himself. *Far be it from me to be a sensible person.* He gave a low chuckle as the wind seemed to emphasize his point at that very moment.

He pushed his hair back and away from his face with a bit of effort as the sudden uptake of air had caused it to become more like a thousand tiny, bristled whips against his eyelids. The leaves in the trees on either side of him rustled as if anticipating his arrival. He took the last, deep drag of the cigarette he had been working on before letting the butt fall to the pavement. He stubbed it out with the toe of his boot and made his way closer to the edge of the water. Remi watched as the tide ebbed and crashed against the large stones that dipped off into the lake, wondering how the boats got past them when they were being lowered into the water.

Remi inhaled the dampness of the mid-June air, listening to the cicadas chirping somewhere off in the Mississippi night. This, when paired with the echoes of the waves moving rhythmically against the bank filled him with a sense of longing that he knew would soon be shattered.

He was very aware that he was being carefully watched by two of the Fae Courts, as this was one of the few areas where their domains overlapped. The Courts were not overly territorial when it came to these areas and each other. However, as far as their Queens were concerned, Remi as a Warlock was an outsider. Besides this, the lake was also a local hotspot for the Oxford Mortals being that it was the middle of a rather crispy summer. These things coupled together gave Remi the unshakable sense that someone's eyes were on him, though he did not know who. He took a moment to gather himself mentally before going on about his business.

Remi had been lucky enough to only have a limited number of dealings with the Fae and their Courts in an official sense to this point. He supposed that he could have probably listed off all of them in total on a single hand and still have fingers left over. While his own experiences had been decent enough, Remi knew that this particular magical race was not one to be toiled with lightly.

While the Fae had been burdened with the curse of not being able to lie, being that they were creatures of nature and lies were considered a manufactured concept, they found ways around it. Remi knew that the Fae clung to their secrets, even among themselves and their opposing Courts. When it came to it, they were perfectly capable of dealing in half-truths and ambiguous information that was, more often than not, misinterpreted by whichever party had the misfortune of crossing them. For this reason, many magical folks, especially Remi's fellow members of the Witch's Guard, tended to avoid having any contact with these immortals in any situation that could not be helped otherwise. This particular type of scenario was, of course, exactly the type that Remi currently found himself in.

Because, why not? he mused to himself. *Next time, you put the phone on silent and roll over like we practiced.*

Silently cursing his miserable luck, Remi swallowed against the lump of nerves that had lodged itself inside his throat. He took a few sharp breaths to ready himself and slowly waded out into the water, shoes and all, until he was hip-deep in the now-icy murk of Sardis Lake.

He shivered as the wind picked up, rippling across the water and causing him to wish he had waited until at least sunrise to do this.

Even though it was the middle of June, the water that had soaked through his clothes and hunting boots was just as cold as if he had taken a shower and stepped outside for a cigarette during a blizzard. His clothes clung to him, soaking up even above where he had stopped in the lake and revealing every indention of his body through his shirt and adding at least ten pounds to the weight he was already carrying himself.

Remi fisted his right hand over his heart in a gesture reminiscent of an ancient warrior's salute, speaking out into the lake that surrounded him and whatever else might be lurking and listening to his words.

"I, Remington James Caswell," he spoke his full name, as was the custom when addressing any of the Fae Courts and their Queens, "Warlock belonging to the Oxford Coven and member of the Witch's Guard, do so humbly request a temporary audience with the Court of Water Fae!"

Remi listened with bated breath as his voice echoed a few times out into the lake and around the woods surrounding Sardis, before eventually fading out. The only reaction this seemed to garner was a family of birds taking flight from one of the tree branches. As he heard a goose honk mockingly in the distance, Remi couldn't help himself from laughing at how ridiculous the scene might be to anyone who was watching. He waited silently, watching the moonlight dance off the mostly still water for what seemed like a brief eternity with no response.

Remi knew better than to call out a second time, as the Fae might view this action as an insult. Being that this was the Water Court in particular that he was attempting to deal with, Remi did not want to run the chance of them seeing his mounting impatience and drowning him before he could make it back to land. So he waited, constantly scanning the surface of the water for any indication that his request had been granted.

"Any time would be nice," he found himself muttering under his breath as he shivered once more in the suddenly breezy night. Just then, a distortion began forming in the middle of the lake. Remi watched silently, not knowing what to make of it.

What started as a few small ripples on the lake surface, soon joined together and deepened, forming a sort of hollow region in the center of the lake and pulling the water immediately surrounding it into its center. As the growing emptiness deepened, the wall around it began to churn in a clockwise motion, picking up speed as it did so until it had become a whirlpool that was easily large enough to sink a small barge.

Remi stared into the center of the opening and watched as several tiny clouds of glowing, blue orbs emerged from within its depths. These formless creatures floated weightlessly on the surface of the water around the mouth of the opening that had just formed. To Remi, it seemed like they were somehow dancing, despite their undefined bodies.

As the rest of them went about in their graceful motions, one of the orbs broke away from the main group and started gliding its way toward Remi. As the orb floated toward him, Remi found himself feeling slightly panicked, despite the beauty of it all. As the spherical being moved closer toward him, so too did the whirlpool. Remi had somehow become rooted to the spot, unable to move away in any direction. He did not know if this was due to his own internalized fear or some inherent enchantment from the creatures that were hovering so effortlessly above the whirlpool.

Great, he thought to himself. *So this is how it ends.*

Remi did not know how to react, so he waited silently for his inevitable and swiftly-approaching doom, knowing that no spell he could speak would save him from the incurred wrath of the Water Court. But even as the orb neared him, he became pleasantly surprised to see that his panic had been unfounded. The whirlpool quickly and easily engulfed him, filling Remi's ears with the deafening roar of a spillway, as the creature began swirling around him from head to toe. As it did this, Remi found that it was steadily reclaiming every last bit of moisture that had penetrated him and rejoining it with the water that twisted so violently around them.

When the process had been completed, the orb swirled around him playfully and let out a sort of sound that, to Remi, somewhat resembled a high-pitched 'mew'. It was almost as if the being was examining the very nature of him and liked what it had found.

Remi watched in awe as the sphere came to a halt directly in front of his face and glowed brighter than it had up until that point. As he stared, the thing began morphing, gradually taking on the form of a small girl with pale blue skin and silvery-white hair. He knew this to be a water sprite and, as she smiled at him, the girl took Remi's hand in her own, simultaneously sending static warmth and shivers throughout his entire body.

"Come, Caswell of the Witch's Guard. Our Lady would grant your request for an audience," the sprite informed him.

Despite the girl's young appearance, there was something of an authority in her voice that he had only heard from the immortal beings he had encountered.

"Thank you," Remi began, welcoming the cold mist of the whirlpool that was spritzed out from it every so often, "but how can I-"

Before he could finish this thought, the other water sprites, still in their spherical forms, swarmed around the two of them and began throwing themselves at the watery wall of the whirlpool. Remi was clueless as to how he should respond to this sudden onslaught from the creatures, so he simply watched.

At first, nothing happened and he remained confused. Then, as the beings continued, the water fell away, revealing a stoned archway that had been somehow etched directly into the very mouth of the still-swirling whirlpool.

"Do not fear, Warlock," the sprite said cheerfully as if this nothing was out of the norm for her. "Our Lady is well aware of the humans' unfortunate lack for water-breathing."

The girl let out a tiny, melodic giggle and Remi couldn't help but to join her. The other sprites, after having finished carving out the pathway, drifted up and affixed themselves to walls inside the whirlpool so as to prevent the remainder of the lake from crashing in on their work.

To Remi, it seemed effortless like they were merely holding back a low-hanging curtain.

Remi felt a gentle tug on his arm and found that he was being ushered through the stone archway by the lone humanoid sprite. He glanced down and was surprised to find that there was a set of steps leading straight down into the crashing waters. As they crossed the threshold, he caught himself looking back over his shoulder to witness as the path was gradually being reclaimed by the lake, step-by-step as they inched their way further into the stairwell.

Remi's gaze trailed down and he saw that water had begun forming in a neat circle just behind his feet, almost as if edging him forward. The sprite seemed not to notice any of this, however, as she floated gracefully to his left. She continued holding his hand to guide him and Remi could only imagine that this must seem so routine to a creature of her years by now.

"I just hope you know that I'm a terrible swimmer," he joked, but the girl did not respond in any way. He wondered if she had not heard him or if she was simply choosing not to acknowledge his remark.

Instead of a response, she lifted her free hand up and out in front of her. As she did so, Remi heard the low rumbling of the whirlpool outside crashing in upon itself while, at the very same moment, sconces all along the wall sprung to life. Each had been spaced at intervals along the cave that they were now standing in and were casting a pale, blue light over the path that stretched out in front of them. It was a soft glow, but it radiated just barely enough to illuminate the narrow corridor.

"Let us move forward, Warlock," the sprite said, freeing herself from Remi's loose grip and floating gracefully through the hollowed-out tunnel.

Remi instinctively knew not to answer or protest at the request. Not wanting to be swallowed up by the darkness and water behind them, he followed the woman, letting himself trail behind her just slightly enough. As the two of them moved along in silence, Remi could not help but be amazed at the structure of the tunnel itself.

The floor and walls seemed to have been carved into the very sediment under the waters of Sardis Lake, which would have been impressive enough by itself. The ceiling of the pathway, however, was the crowning feature in this hallway. It was completely comprised of water, besides a few bits of soil here and there where the corridor seemed to jut up over its boundaries in earthen waves. This reminded him of a Mortal aquarium he had seen somewhere years before on a field trip, although this was definitely more awe-inspiring.

He was sure it must be even more impressive during the day when the sun's rays glinted down through the depths, although it still managed to have a murky sapphire hue despite the sky above being completely dark when they had made their way through the archway.

While he had been staring up and marveling at the beauty of it all, Remi tripped over a rather large rock in the path and stumbled a few feet forward. He looked over to check if this misstep had been noticed by the sprite floating ahead of him. Though she said nothing, Remi did see a playful smile forming across her face. He could feel that his own was turning a soft shade of pink in embarrassment.

Remi tore his gaze from the girl now and focused, instead, on the sconces that lined the walls of this corridor. It did not take long for him to notice that the torches were not lit by actual flames at all. Instead, they appeared to be more like iridescent orbs of water, dancing very similarly to how the sprites above had first appeared. Remi smiled to himself, noting that as they passed by each opposing pair of torches, the accompanying 'flames' broke free from the sconces and floated up into the ceiling. It was there that he saw them rejoin with the lake.

He was amused at how closely he was being watched, despite having been granted an audience with the Water Queen, but he did not feel threatened by the onlooking members of this Court. They seemed to be playfully curious about him, more than anything else. He silently wondered if they watched all visitors this closely or if it was simply due to his status as one of the Witch's Guard that made them uneasy.

After what had only felt like a few minutes, they reached what seemed to be the end of the corridor. Remi gave the sprite a puzzled look, wondering to himself why she would have brought him to a dead end. He had been expecting to be led to meet her Queen and something about this abrupt and unforeseen enclosure along the pathway gave him an uneasy feeling. He swallowed against this and said nothing that would have given it away.

"Nice waterfall," he joked instead. "But where's the Queen?"

The sprite turned to face Remi then, examining him almost as if she was confused by his question.

"Do you not see it?" she asked. "Look closer, Warlock."

Remi gave her what he was sure must have been his most curious expression to date, but did as he was told, focusing intently on the end of the tunnel.

Though he could see a physical wall behind it, the cavern stopped short in the earthly hallway. It ended at a small waterfall that fell from the lake above them. Instead of filling the tunnel, however, it had been somehow charmed so that the water at the bottom dissipated in a sort of light mist and floated up in tiny clouds to be reclaimed by the lake above them. Noticing this minuscule detail gave Remi an idea that had not occurred to him before.

"It's a Glamour?" he asked, but the sprite simply smiled at the question. Remi could not tell if it was meant to be one of encouragement or a challenge to him, but he hoped it was the former. He furrowed his brow then and replied, "I don't think I'm strong enough to undo a Glamour created by the Fae by myself."

To this, the girl before him began laughing in the same musical tone she'd had in everything else up until that point and shaking her head in an almost condescending way.

"No, no, Warlock!" she laughed. "You are not meant to *undo* it; you are simply meant to go *through*!"

"But," Remi was just as confused as he had ever been, "there's nothing to go into except for a wall." The girl did not seem to have anything more to offer him, which caused him to wonder if this was some sort of joke that he was not quite getting.

"Look," he pleaded finally, "I've never had any dealings with the Water Court before this night. If I can't get in there, and I can't go back, then I'm stuck down here. Can you please help me, just this once?"

The sprite crossed her arms over her chest and stared at Remi then. It seemed as if she was silently weighing her options to help him or leave him down here to suffer whatever fate might befall him. Finally, after what felt like a brief eternity, she nodded, "Okay, Warlock. I shall help you, but it shall only be this once!"

"That's all I need," Remi bowed his head, grateful for whatever assistance the girl could offer him.

Remi stepped back then and watched in amazement as the sprite lifted her arm and submerged it into the water falling from the ceiling. She pulled a side of it back, giving the appearance that she was drawing a liquid curtain from a window. As she held it open, Remi peered inside and saw what looked to be a mirror image of himself staring back at him. Only, instead of the tunnel stretching out behind him, this reflection showed another scene entirely. Remi was slightly bewildered by it all and gave a quick glance over to the sprite that had led him here.

"I'm sure you will know where to go from here, Guardsman?" she smiled, watching as he pieced it together.

Finally, Remi nodded and stepped under the curtain of the waterfall, little droplets falling on the back of his neck like a soft drizzle of rain. As he did this, he felt himself being pulled in several directions all at once and had to fight against the urge to be sick. He knew that this was merely a side effect of using a portal to any particular destination for the first time when one did not know where they were supposed to be going.

He closed his eyes and felt himself being lifted by some invisible force, not daring to open them again until he felt that his feet were touching solid ground once more. Remi instantly checked behind him and saw the Portal he had come through. Seeing that he had made it through to the other side safely, the sprite let the curtain fall back into place and floated upward into the lake ceiling of the tunnel where she rejoined with her sisters.

Remi smiled and turned his attention back to the area that stretched out in front of him. To his surprise, he saw that he was now standing in the middle of some sort of antechamber. He wondered if the portal had brought him to the right place as this didn't seem to match the aesthetic of the previous corridor.

He looked around and found himself in awe of the structural beauty of the place, regardless of whether it was where he was supposed to be or not.

There were six marble pillars at intervals around the room, tapered at the ends and bulky in the center to give the illusion of being straight lines. These held up the ceiling of the room, which consisted of some other body of water. It was not unlike the passage that had brought Remi here, although this one seemed to be physically in another area of the world. The sunlight glinted down through the waves and cast hues of crystalline blue over the marble structures of the room.

Remi had the sneaking impression that wherever he was currently, it was somewhere far away from Sardis Lake and Oxford, Mississippi altogether. Knowing that the Fae Courts had no definitive physical location in the world, Remi dared not even venture a guess as to where that might be.

Looking around the room, Remi saw a handful of ornately decorated stone doors tucked away behind small waterfalls, just as the one that had brought him here. This made him instinctively wonder what other paths were hidden behind them. Each door was flanked by knights that towered above him.

Each of them wore a set of armor that seemed to have been carved straight from diamonds and glistened in the rays coming down through the watery ceiling. Though the Court guards stared blankly ahead, Remi knew that they were watching him just as closely as the sprites that had been masquerading as torchlights in the passage that had brought him here.

The floors were marbled as well, with small pools carved directly into it. It was in these pools that water cascaded from the ceiling and collected. There were four of them, each hosting a party of nymphs and naiads, all laughing musically. None of them seemed to notice the intruder gawking at them, nor did they seem to care. These pools together framed a set of stairs that led up, ending in a throne. Watching him serenely from this throne was the Queen of the Water Court.

She had been around for centuries and was possessed of immeasurable beauty, even by Fae standards, as she was a siren. Mortal and non-Mortal alike, who had set eyes upon her had sung many lengthy tales of their undying praise. It was those very tales that had labeled her the Lady of the Lake in the vain hopes of coaxing her out in their futile adoration.

Her hair was a pale blonde and was pinned back into an elaborate crown of waterlilies, besides a few ringlets that gently framed her face and collar. Remi noticed as the sunlight glinted off of it, there was a seafoam coloring to it, much like the waves crashing upon a shoreline. Her porcelain skin, where visible, glistened like the sun reflecting off the surface of the ocean. Her eyes were aquamarines that held every mystery of the sea; warm and inviting, yet dangerous and unpredictable.

Her lips were full and light pink, upturned slightly into a knowing smile as she watched Remi surveying the room between them. The Queen donned a silken toga with a bronze tidal clasp at the left shoulder, that gave her the look of a Greek goddess. The hem of the dress lapped around her ankles as she descended the steps from her throne.

Remi was unsure if this was how the Queen truly looked. He knew that certain creatures, such as members of the Fae, had Glamours in their very blood that made them appear more appealing to any who happened upon them. Even as he stood before her, Remi could not be certain if the Queen's beauty was a side effect of one such Glamour, or if the tales that had been spun about her over the years were simply true.

Nevertheless, he did not want to take the chance that she was some grotesque sea monster waiting to devour him. Remi fell to one knee and fisted his right hand over his heart, staring down at the marble floor so as not to offend her.

"Thank you for your time, M'lady," he addressed the Queen as formally as was possible without knowing her name. "It is a pleasure to be standing in your grace in your Court of Water."

To his surprise, the Queen laughed at how stiff his words sounded, though not unkindly.

"The pleasure is all mine, Guardsman Caswell," she spoke and her voice was like a song he could never grow tired of. "Although, there is no need for such formality. You are, after all, a guest in our halls and shall be treated as such." The Queen smiled and tilted her head slightly. "You may rise, Warlock."

Remi obeyed and took in all of her beauty for a second time, full-force.

"You may call me Rydia if you please," she requested. "Lady of the Lake is such a mouthful, would you not agree?"

She ended this with a melodic laugh, and Remi felt a sort of fire fill his veins that he was not accustomed to. While this was not an unpleasant feeling, it served as a reminder that he was dealing with a Siren and should be careful.

"Just a tad," he agreed, pushing down his desire and focusing on the task at hand with some effort. "I'm sure you must have grown tired of being reduced to an Arthurian legend over the years."

Rydia's smile faltered briefly and Remi suddenly found himself very conscious of the possibility that he had said the wrong thing. Just as quickly, the Queen laughed at this and clapped her hands together delightedly, filling the entire Court with the sound.

"Oh!" she exclaimed. "I was unaware that you Warlocks could read the minds of us Fae with such ease and prowess!"

Remi let out a silent sigh of relief, laughing along with her. "Not quite, although I wish sometimes that we could."

He looked up to the ceiling and could not help but ask the first question that popped into his mind, "Where, exactly, are we?"

"Why," Rydia sounded confused, "in the Water Court of the Fae, of course. Where else would we be, young Caswell?"

"Yes," Remi laughed at his own question, choosing to rephrase, "but where exactly *is* that, M'lady?"

"You mean that you came in through our portal beneath your Sardis

Lake and now you are wondering what body of water you currently stand under?" she watched him closely as if gauging his reaction.

Remi knew that the Fae had many secrets, even among themselves, that they were not always so keen to reveal. He found himself wondering if this was one such secret, but the Queen answered after only a moment's pause.

"Our Court is just as vast as the water that covers the world we live in, Guardsman," she explained. "Wherever that is, so too are we. This Court is nowhere, which allows us to be everywhere simultaneously. We are unbound by the laws of the world as you might know them. This allows us to be both inside and outside of your realm at our discretion."

Remi found her words somewhat foreboding but, upon seeing her guarded expression, knew better than to press the subject further.

"Right," he agreed simply, thinking it best to remain focused. "I'm sure you know why I have come here, then?"

Rydia nodded at the question, her smile fading only slightly, "Yes, Warlock. I am well aware of what brought you here. But I am just as unsure if this is what you will ask, as I am that I will have the answers you seek."

Remi nodded, knowing that this was the Water Queen's way of setting subtle boundaries. He knew he should take the hints and not cross them, if only for his own good. She could easily have him drowned simply for stepping foot in the Water Court, or she could have the guards throw him out back at the surface. The former would be a violation of several of the Covenants, while the latter, although inconvenient for questioning purposes, would at least let him live.

Remi did not find himself too wanting to find out which of these options Rydia might choose if he were to test her patience, as he was already breaking a few of the Covenants himself just by being here without permission from the Coven.

"There was a death on the shore of Sardis Lake," Remi began, "which is where your Court has one of its portals. Do you acknowledge this, M'lady?"

"I have never denied this fact, Guardsman Caswell," Rydia answered, her smile just as serene as ever. "Do not let consequence dictate which questions you ask on this night."

Remi nodded and swallowed against the dry lump that had formed in his throat already, "I'm sure you understand how it looks to someone on the outside, being that it was so close to one of your portals?"

"Yes," Rydia agreed, her smile unfaltering as she went on. "I am to understand that we of the water are being accused in this regard. Is that correct, Warlock?"

"No accusations are being made at this point, M'lady," Remi tried to sound confident, though he did not feel it. "Right now, I come seeking only the answers about this particular incident."

"You do not have to make the accusations to imply them, Warlock," Rydia replied calmly. "Although I am certain you meant no harm, I am sure you are aware of the penalties for such blasphemy."

"I am quite well aware," Remi spoke quickly, paying more attention to his words going forward. "But I will also make clear that I am here of my own accord. So even if I find something incriminating, there's no way I could use the information against your Court."

"A bold move on your part, young Caswell," Rydia seemed amused now. "Or, perhaps, foolish would be a better term to describe such a dauntless choice?"

"We'll see," Remi forced out a nervous laugh, not knowing what he had gotten himself into. "I'm just hoping for a lead in regards to the Mortal."

"Tell me what you know," Rydia coaxed, and Remi was instantly aware that all eyes in the Court were now fixed solely on him and the Queen.

He briefly recounted what the Mortal girl had told him, omitting everything that was not pertinent to the death of the boy named Sam, though he had a suspicion that the Queen already knew just what those omissions were.

"A tentacled monster in Sardis Lake?" Rydia asked, with a tone of mild disbelief. "That is unheard of, Warlock!"

"That's what I thought, as well," Remi agreed.

"Everyone knows that krakens prefer saltwater, not fresh," the Queen said matter-of-factly as if it was too preposterous to even be considered.

"I didn't know that," Remi admitted, having been caught slightly off-guard by the statement. "But that's not my point, M'lady. My point is that's what the girl saw, and I don't know what it could have been. Which is what brings me here, to your Court."

"Well, I know what it was not," Rydia seemed offended that Remi had to be informed of a kraken's water preference. "But I shall help you, nonetheless."

"And I do thank you for that," Remi inclined his head in a gesture of goodwill. "What do you think it could have been?"

"I do not *think*," Rydia replied simply. "I simply *know* it was no individual or creature from my Court."

"And how do you know that?" Remi asked, trying to relay his genuine curiosity.

"For the same reason the Woodland and Air Queens would know that none of their Court would do such a thing," she explained. "To take the life of another creature is an unnatural act for our elements. Being that the Fae are creatures charged with the preservation of Nature, it would be a sin to do such a thing, regardless of what the circumstance may be."

"What about Fire Fae?" Remi asked the only logical question he could think of in the moment.

"It is possible," Rydia mused. "Although highly unlikely that they would be so foolish to bring any of their internal conflicts so near the domain of another Court unless provoked. As we have done nothing thus far to garner this sort of reaction, I doubt it was even them."

"Fair enough," Remi said, going along with the reasoning. "But then, who?"

"I do not know," Rydia replied, "as I was not there to see for myself."

"Then there's no way to find out?" Remi let out a hopeless sigh, unable to stop himself.

"Not quite," Rydia gave him a knowing smile.

"What does that mean?" he was confused.

"We have our ways, Warlock," she said, turning away from him to face the pool that was nearest the steps that led up to her throne. "Come," she gestured for him to follow and began moving toward the pool.

As the two of them walked along, the Fae that had been lounging in the marble bath relocated themselves to the surrounding area as a sign of respect for their Queen.

As they reached the pool, Rydia turned to face him and Remi felt the fire in his veins once more. He averted his gaze and found himself glancing at her feet. Although the Water Queen had legs, he noticed that they were covered with flesh-colored scales that glistened silver in the light as she moved.

"Are we going for a swim?" Remi tried to be humorous, but the joke fell flat.

"You must peer into the water for the answers you seek, Warlock," Rydia's tone was a gentle warning that she was not amused.

Remi followed her instruction, moving his gaze to the crystal-blue nothingness of the marble pool. To his right, he felt Rydia lift her hands so that they stretched out in front of her at chest level. He took a glance over to see that her palms were open, facing down toward the pool. He looked back at the water just as it began lapping around in a clockwise motion, slowly picking up speed until it was at a point that Remi was sure it would splash out onto the floor around it.

To his surprise, the water began shifting from a magnified image of the bottom of the marbled basin and into a scene that Remi had only just imagined during his interrogation of the Mortal girl earlier.

He, as well as everyone else in the Court now, was currently staring down into Sardis Lake at dusk. He saw Becca sitting on the hood of a beat-up, red Chevy while a raven-haired boy called out for her to join him.

They all watched as the short horror scene played out, Remi looking up only briefly enough to see Rydia's impassive face staring down. There was no sound from the members of the Court as the boy named Sam was dragged under multiple times and Becca ran away screaming into the night. Then the tentacle rose one last time snapping the boy's spine in half like a chopstick, which the girl, thankfully, did not see. Remi felt himself caught in the overwhelming wave of dread as the scene froze like this, as if suspended by some sadistic film viewer.

He looked up at Rydia, whose face had not changed during the entire ordeal.

"What *was* that?" he asked in disbelief, not entirely sure what he had just witnessed.

"Look closer, Warlock," Rydia answered, ignoring his question.

Remi obeyed and forced himself to peer back into the water of the pool just as it began moving forward again.

A second tentacle shot up from the water, grabbing the boy's lower half while the first clung to the top of him, and Remi noticed something he had not before. There were no suction cups or other things that would mark these as any sort of living creature. In fact, they actually looked more like sticky, black tendrils than tentacles, altogether. The closer and longer he chose to stare at them, the more perplexed Remi became.

Whatever they were, the things were slowly and methodically pulling both halves of the boy back into the murky depths of the lake as the scene suddenly seemed to change perspective. It was almost as if they were all watching a movie where the camera panned out to reveal the bigger picture for the audience, although the boundary of the image itself did not seem to widen.

Remi's eyes trailed from the ends of the things holding the boy up to their source, searching for some sort of creature or sign that could explain this to him. Then he saw something he had not been expecting at all.

At the opposite end of the tendrils that were slithering away from the husk that had formerly been Sam, there was a human-sized mass beneath the surface of the water, just where it got too dark to see.

Almost as if sensing the combined gaze of the Court upon it, the thing turned its head and Remi felt almost as if it was somehow watching them, despite this being a recollection of something that had happened hours before.

This did not seem to matter to the creature, as it continued staring.

Suddenly, the scene blurred, as if it had been covered in ink, and a menacing growl tore through the Court, bouncing off the walls just as two glowing amber eyes filled the pool.

Remi's blood went cold and he looked quickly to Rydia, hoping that she had some sense of what was going on, but she appeared to be just as lost as he felt.

The Queen clapped her hands together with authority and a thunderous boom that echoed through the chamber. The water instantly rose up and out of the pool like a pillar before crashing down back into the basin, obscuring the image.

The scene shifted quickly as a peal of snarling, inhuman laughter hung in the air.

No one spoke for a few seconds until the demonic voice had subsided.

Finally, Rydia turned to Remi with some effort, her face having grown pale during what felt like a fully-fledged altercation.

"I trust you have what you came for, Warlock," she said in a voice that made it abundantly clear that tonight's interrogation had effectively come to an end.

Remi nodded his silent agreement at the underlying statement, though he was shaking all over from the shock of what he had just witnessed. There was no denying it to himself or anyone else. It wasn't just any creature that had killed the Mortal boy. It had been a Warlock.

But who? he wondered to himself, trying desperately to piece the bits of information he had together.

"Before you go," Rydia's tone seemed to be cautioning him for his journey ahead, "I must show you one more thing."

IV

The man moved through the woods that sat on the edge of the lake with the same effortless grace of a shadow, his cloak not even making a sound as it billowed behind him. This skill had inherently been acquired through decades of keeping himself in hiding from those who had misunderstood what he had been trying to do so long ago.

Though it was no longer required because of this thing of second nature, he used a Glamour of Concealment; lest he get careless with his footsteps and be seen. That was the one thing the man could not afford just yet.

He knew what had to be done this time and there could be no mistakes of any kind if there was any chance of accomplishing his end goal.

The breeze rustled gently through the canopy of trees above and behind him, almost as if watching his movements and propelling him forward. He took comfort in that thought. If no person would have agreed with him, at least the elements were on his side.

The man had just reached the edge of the final row of sprawled oaks when he saw the creature. She was a slight woman with skin that was a pale, iridescent blue, dancing about on the surface of the lake, purifying the areas where the Mortals had been just hours before with her touch. She sang as she did so and the man felt a tug at his heart, for what he knew what must be done.

No, he pushed the futile emotion away and stared at the beautiful creature before him.

If he were to be successful tonight, there could be nothing of regret left within him. This was not simply a thing for sport; he sought to better the world with this ritual and rid it of its affliction. There was no reason for him to feel remorse at something so beautiful.

It is not a meaningless death, he reassured himself. *It is simply an unknowing sacrifice. They will thank me for it later.*

Almost as if sensing his mournful gaze upon her, the naiad froze in place, her toes just barely skimming the lake's surface. Her eyes briefly scoured the woods where he had paused, locking with his own in an instant. This broke the man out of his reverie.

He could feel his heart leap several times in his chest and swallowed against the dryness that had overtaken his throat. It was too late for him to turn back now. Though he wore a Glamour to conceal himself from any potential Mortal stragglers, the Fae and animals in the small wooded area could easily see through such a charm.

The two stood there for a small eternity, simply taking each other in. One was lamenting to himself what must be done; the other, simply curious about the potential new friend.

The man took a cautious step forward and the naiad visibly tensed. He held this position for a few seconds, willing her to come closer.

The creature stared at him for what seemed like hours, though they were mere seconds. It was apparent that she was taking him in, unsure of this stranger's nature and intent. She quickly relaxed when she saw his glowing irises, marking him as another part of her world. It was clear that she saw him as less of a threat because of this.

If only she knew, the man thought to himself, inching closer to the water spirit.

She spun around gleefully, causing the water beneath her to ripple only just slightly. She let out a giggle, as many of the youngling Fae tended to do when they were excited. The melodic sound drifted through the air like a weightless kiss.

She beckoned him closer and the Warlock went, keeping his actions reserved for the time being. He let himself inch ever closer to her until he could feel the shallow waves at the rim of the lake lapping at his boots, trying to get in. The Warlock lifted his arm toward the creature and held it out for her to examine. She tensed briefly before bringing her face down near his outstretched hand, very much like a dog might inspect a stranger before allowing them to stroke its fur.

The Warlock felt the water Fae let her guard down and took a deep breath to calm himself. In a move like lightning and before the naiad could do anything to stop him, he brought his hand down and clasped it tightly around her throat.

The girl let out a shriek that echoed briefly throughout the area around them, making the Warlock silently grateful that no one was around at this hour, before it caught in her throat with a gurgle of spit and blood. Even in dying, the naiad's voice was like a song that was becoming morphed, shifting from rhapsody to ballad.

He squeezed tighter as the girl tried to pry herself free, clawing in futile strikes against his hand and scratching away pieces of his skin.

The Warlock steeled himself, watching as the blows came at him increasingly slower and further apart until eventually coming to a halt altogether. He watched as the light drained from her, extinguishing the shimmering light that every one of the humanoid Fae seemed to possess. The girl's eyes slowly glossed over and froze in a haunting stare at his face. This was the last thing she would see in this lifetime.

The man lifted his free arm and, with his wand, made a thin slice across the girl's throat just under where his hand was placed. There was a sharp intake of breath from somewhere in him as he watched the scarlet trail gently across her collar bones. His heart sank in his chest at the knowledge of what he had done, but he knew he must not let himself become bogged down with feelings of remorse just yet.

He stayed his grip on the girl so that she would not fall, which was surprisingly easy as she seemed to weigh no more than a droplet of water. With his other hand, he stowed his wand back into his robes and pulled out a small glass vial, uncorking it and placing the rim at the bloody pool that had formed on the girl's chest. It took only a few seconds for the life essence of the naiad to fill the container before he replaced the stopper.

The Warlock gave the girl a single, sorrowful look. He finally allowed himself to lament over the life that he had stolen from something so beautiful and innocent; something so pure when compared to the other vile creatures of this world.

It is those creatures that I shall purge, he reminded himself. *That is why it must be this way.*

He finally relinquished his hold on her and let her body glide gently back into the water with an almost silent splash and a thud as her lower parts sank to the bottom. The lake welcomed her like a mother might welcome a child returning home, waves lapping over the girl almost like arms.

The Warlock stood and watched as the girl's body dissipated, reminding him of seafoam. She was gradually becoming one with the lake and nature as was customary when a Fae reached the end of their life cycle. He took solace in the knowledge that the circle would continue, with a new naiad spawning from some stream in another part of the world. One to take the original's place and who would have no memory of what had befallen her in this previous life.

The girl's physical body had just finished remerging itself with the lake when the man heard the rev of an engine and the squeal of tires. Though the sound was distant, it was growing closer with every second. The man knew he did not have time to duck back in the trees for risk of being seen by the vehicle's headlights, as he could no longer keep his Glamour of Concealment intact with his mind in such a chaotic and emotional state.

So he leapt forth into the lake, coming down just past where the naiad had fallen. He remained with his head above the surface just long enough to see the truck come skidding to a halt on the pavement. He floated there for a moment longer and watched as the boy got out and made a beeline for the trees, followed shortly after by the girl who remained by the truck.

The Warlock covered his mouth with an unspoken charm that would allow him to breathe underwater and allowed himself to sink into the dark depths of the lake, unbeknownst to the Mortal couple. It did not take long for the two of them to leap in. He saw the boy splash around with the same effortless ways that a fish might take. The girl, however, was not far after him.

In all of his years, the man had never quite understood how or why the Fae were so willing to sit idly by while the generations of constantly-spawning Mortals continually came so near to one of their portals and polluted it just by *being*.

It is disgusting that they do not get rid of this nuisance, he was slowly becoming enraged just thinking about it.

He would not stand for such defilement, even if the Fae seemed to be unbothered by such an act of treason as was the desecration of their home.

The Warlock did not have to wait very much at all, as he quickly saw the boy wading farther out and then swimming until the boy was nearly just above him. He reached into his robes once more and retrieved his wand, gripping it tightly in his hand and smiling gleefully to himself as he aimed it directly at the boy; the girl would have to wait for now, as she was only just coming away from the bank.

He felt the rush of his spell at work as smoky, black tendrils erupted from the tip of his wand under the water. They pushed their way up against the undertow and toward the unaware Mortals. The man watched with a reserved sort of satisfaction as the billowing, formless structures twisted themselves around the boy's body, solidifying at once and pulling themselves so tightly that they crushed his ribs.

He watched the boy struggle in vain against the force of it as the girl made her way out, not knowing that her friend was dying under the surface of the water. The Warlock let the tendrils carry the boy close enough to the girl so that she was forced to watch as he tried to grab at her heel for help. The girl jerked her foot away and there was the sound of her shouting above the water.

The man's tendrils lifted the boy high above the water and heard him yell for help, to which the girl did nothing more than shriek in horror. He brought the boy crashing down and willed for the tendrils to tighten, to which they obliged. He did this a few more times as the girl swam swiftly away, before finally giving a sharp tug, effectively severing the boy's lower half from his torso.

The Warlock watched as the tentacles brought both halves into the lake before dismissing them. He watched as the boy's body sank slowly down, staining the water red as he fell. All the while, the tendrils dissipated until they had become nothing more than inky-black muck in the water. The man swam away, laughing to himself as he made his way back to the surface and the surrounding woods, knowing that the Mortal girl was long gone by now.

He took one final look behind him as he reached the shore of the lake. Upon seeing that no one else was around, he ducked back into the safety of the wooded area.

He tugged at the air and willed a flower to form in his hand. The Warlock tossed the water lily into the lake in exchange for the life of the naiad that he had just taken, before turning back toward the trees and walking away. He would leave nothing for the boy. He had no time to waste on a life that meant nothing.

There was work to be done this night, and he had only just begun.

V

"Tell me again," Sylvia Ashcroft said, "why, exactly, you need access to the Archives?" Sylvia was the Arbiter to the Oxford Coven, which meant she was in charge of everything that went on both inside and outside of the house when it came to the Warlocks. She mainly dealt with the leaders from all the races to ensure that things remained civil between the Mortals and non-Mortals in the area. She also supervised the Witch's Guard, which were a sect of magical knights that served as a police branch for the Coven.

As the Arbiter, it was Sylvia's duty was to act as the final say on all things that went on when it came to the Oxford Coven. Beyond that, she also served as a judge when it came to the rogues that were brought before her when they had broken any rule of the Covenant. Barring anything too serious for her word to be final, she was still required to answer to the Magisters on the High Coven for things that might affect Warlocks and other non-Mortals outside of her charge.

Remi had made it out of the Water Court not long after the scene in the basin. He and Rydia had gone for a further round of questioning in which the Queen had informed him of the naiad that had been killed just moments before the boy named Sam had been attacked. He had made some promises on behalf of the entire Oxford Coven and, if he did not want to incur the wrath of a Fae Queen and her loyal subjects, aimed to keep at least most of them. Only now, he was at risk of being on the wrong end of Sylvia's ire.

Currently, he sat in a high-backed, leather chair across from his Arbiter in her office. He had been trying to convince her to grant him access into the Coven's Archives with no luck. He needed to look for something that might give him a clue as to who the Dark Mage was or, at the very least, what they might be planning by murdering twice in one night in the same spot.

"I've told you everything I know," Remi repeated for what felt like the hundredth time since he had sat down in the office.

He had already recounted the story of what had transpired the night before in the Water Court at least three times since he had gotten back and was tired, whether that had to do with the lack of sleep or the repetition, he knew not.

What Remi did know was how difficult it would be to get him access.

"I know you've told me," Sylvia agreed with that fact. "But why can't you just look at the books offered in the regular library on the first floor?"

Getting into the Archives was usually very difficult, as it held not only the entire history of the Oxford Coven, but *all* Warlocks. Remi knew the likelihood of a unanimous vote of agreement between all five Magisters based on a hunch from a single member of the Witch's Guard with no physical evidence to back it up was slim at best. He also knew the chance had to be taken if he wanted to find out just who this mysterious magical assailant was.

"I don't even know that looking through those musty, old books will be of any help," he admitted, now. "It's just a feeling that I have."

"A *feeling*?" Sylvia repeated, giving him a look of skepticism. "That's all you've got for me, Caswell? A *feeling*?"

"Well," Remi admitted, "I have the word and testimony of Queen Rydia. It would be solid enough since the Fae can't lie."

"Yes," Sylvia agreed. "But since you ventured into a Court without my knowledge or consent, we can't use anything you found out last night." Remi watched as his Arbiter's shoulders slumped in defeat. "I wish you would have just waited and come to me with this beforehand,

Caswell," she went on. "At least then, we would have some form of documentation backing this theory of yours."

As she pressed her fingers to her temples and rubbed, he could not help but notice how worn the position had left her.

When Sylvia had first taken up the mantle of the Oxford Coven's Arbiter, no one thought it would be a long-term governance for the woman. Her husband, Franklin Ashcroft, had served for thirty years before she had taken on the role. He had done many things for this branch of the Coven and had been widely respected as one of the best Arbiters to serve by both Mortals and non-Mortals. He had done many things for both the treatment of Warlocks, as well as the overall betterment of the local community.

After his passing had left a vacant seat, there was no one immediately available to step into the position. There had been no election for her, as the Magisters had simply appointed her until one could be held to elect someone to take his place. Having been by her husband's side throughout his entire tenure, it seemed the best option under such short notice. That had been five years ago, and there were still no signs of any election proceedings to date, as far as anyone could tell.

In just that short time, Remi had watched along with everyone else as Sylvia had gone from a relatively attractive woman with looks that could have easily put any vintage Hollywood bombshell to shame, into an increasingly gaunt being that barely resembled what she had once been. She was now little more than the ghost of a human.

Where once there had been enough charisma to sway any room in her favor, there was now only worry. Her hair had gone from bouncy and blond to straw-colored and greying. She had no time for makeup now, so the lines on her face were worn in its stead. Even her once-bright, glowing peridot irises had almost fully glossed over and collected bags beneath. Looking at her now, Remi couldn't help but feel sorry for the woman who had once been Sylvia Ashcroft.

She continued massaging her temples in the vain hopes of ridding herself of the headache in her own high-backed chair.

She did not even bother to look at him as she spoke this time, "Come on, Caswell. You've got to give me something more than 'just a feeling' to work with if you expect any of them to go for it."

"I don't have anything else to give you," Remi replied, before adding, "I mean, I could give you some fabrication, but I'm pretty sure that would be deemed as unethical if they were to find out."

"Who said they had to find out?" Sylvia gave a wry smile then. "Go ahead; try me."

Remi cocked a single eyebrow to question this decision but otherwise did not object.

"Well," he thought about how to word it to sound official, before proceeding. "There's no knowledge of any magical families with amber eyes, rogue or otherwise, in the surrounding area. It could just be an undocumented mutation in an already existing line, but we have nothing further to go on. If we don't find out who this is, then they could kill more Mortals or other creatures. And then we might have a war on our hands between Warlocks and whatever other future victims."

He paused then, feeling odd for having come up with a lie so quickly off the top of his head in front of the Arbiter. "Does that sound like something they'd go for?"

Sylvia shrugged, "It's better than nothing. I'll send the paperwork for a grant as soon as I can get it filled out. What will you do if they turn your request down?"

"We'll cross that bridge when we get there," Remi admitted. "I'm sure you can use some of your pull to make sure that we don't have to worry about that, though."

He gave the Arbiter a sly smile, to which she frowned slightly.

Sylvia did have *some* pull among the Magisters, as she had married into the Ashcroft line. This meant that her sister-in-law, Dahlia, was on the High Coven. Other than that, there was her brother Virgil, who had recently taken up the seat after their father had passed away a few years ago. Even if she couldn't manage to convince the other Magisters, Remi was sure that if she could at least get those two to side with her, then the others might be more willing to agree.

"I can try, Caswell," she replied now. "But I make no guarantees."

"I don't need a guarantee," Remi smiled. "I'll come up with an alternate plan in the meantime."

"Please do," Sylvia did not sound relieved.

As Remi stood to leave, she stopped him just as he reached the door.

"Hold on, just a moment, Caswell!" she said and he turned on his heel to face her.

"What is it, now?" Remi turned back to face the Arbiter, albeit slightly begrudgingly.

"This arrived just this morning," she replied, indicating a manila folder in front of her that he had not noticed before. She held the item up in front of her and gave him a questioning expression. "Would you like to take a look?"

"Not really," he answered honestly, longing desperately for his bed. "Can't someone else do it?"

"They could," Sylvia replied. "But then, how would I get my kicks, Caswell?"

Remi sighed, knowing there was no use in arguing, and pushed the thought of more sleep out of his mind for the time being. He came back to the Arbiter's desk and reached for the file, opening it and giving her a confused look as he skimmed the pages.

"You want me to investigate property damage?" he asked. "Isn't that generally something the Mortals take care of?"

"It is," Sylvia admitted. "But take a closer look at the details."

Remi did and found himself at an even bigger loss as he read the multiple accounts from people that had been there. All seemed to corroborate with each other and Remi wondered if it might not be some sort of scam on the part of the Mortals involved.

"They all saw a man dressed in a black cloak?" he asked, to which Sylvia nodded. "Halloween isn't for a few months," he went on. "Do you think it could just be some sort of prank?"

"Could be," Sylvia shrugged. "But we both know that's not how they'll see it if we decline to at least send someone to investigate."

"They'll see it as a coverup," Remi finished for her. "But it happened around the same time I went out to the lake. I definitely didn't hear any explosions. I didn't even see any officers anywhere near there. When I came back through."

Sardis Lake was just a few miles away from the University of Mississippi's airport for private jets. Since he had to pass by there on his way back to the Coven House, Remi felt almost certain that he would have at least seen the blue lights if something this big had taken place in such a short window of time.

"It could have happened after you entered the Court," Sylvia suggested with a shrug. "Could have happened before John even called you after the girl arrived. That time stamp on there might have just been when the file was made by whatever officer they had on the phones last night."

"Right," Remi agreed. "But I still don't see the point of me going if they've already cleaned everything up, other than to save face and keep them from coming for us."

"That's exactly why you're going, Caswell," Sylvia explained. "I know it's highly unlikely that you'll actually find anything, but it'll serve to calm their nerves and keep them from tying up our phone lines with accusations and threats. Can you just do this one thing without being contradictory?"

"Yeah, sheesh," Remi gave an offended look. "I'll look into it, lady. Calm down."

The Arbiter said nothing, but gave a menacing glare that Remi could feel was meant to be the end of the conversation. If he had managed to get any amount of decent sleep, he might have taken the opportunity to ruffle her feathers a bit more. Presently, however, he was too tired even for this.

The sooner you get done, the sooner you get to enjoy your day off, he told himself.

"I'll let you know what I come up with," he said aloud. "If there's anything to be found, I'll be the first to bring it to everyone's attention."

"Good," Sylvia snapped. Then, in a gentler tone, "Thank you, Caswell."

Remi inclined his head and tucked the file under his arm, turning on his heel to leave the office for a second time.

The scene was much worse than Remi had initially anticipated on the drive over. He had at least expected that the majority of the damage would have been cleaned up by the time he arrived but as he could see now, he had been severely wrong in that assumption.

"You the one from the Coven?" an officer came toward Remi as soon as he had made it through the mandatory screening at the front of the building. He could tell from the man's uniform that he was from the Oxford Police Department. Remi gave a silent nod to the man, not sure if he would be welcomed to look around or made to answer for the damage.

"Finally!" to Remi's surprise, the officer sounded almost relieved. "We were all beginning to wonder when someone was going to show up." He let out a laugh and gave Remi a slap on the shoulder before handing him a pair of latex gloves. "The bulk of everything is over here, if you want to come have a look."

"Were there any casualties?" Remi asked, pulling on the gloves and knitting his fingers together so that he could have a better grip. "I know there were some injuries, but have you heard any updates on those officers?"

"It wasn't just officers," the man said. "A few civilians were trying to board that jet over there," he indicated an overturned private liner. The thing seemed to have had its wings burned off, as the one that Remi could see from where he stood had a tower of black smoke billowing out from its edges. Several fire engines surrounded it and were spraying water that just barely reached the flames that licked around it.

"But, no," the man beside him went on. "There weren't any critical injuries. Everyone should be making a full recovery by the end of the week."

"You're sure about that?" Remi gave the man a disbelieving look. "That looks pretty serious from what I can tell."

"It looks a lot worse than it is," the man explained. "It's almost like whoever it was didn't have any intentions to actually kill. It was almost like he was making a show out of it all."

"You were here then?" Remi asked, filing this bit of information in the annals of his mind.

"Not until after everything had gone down," the officer admitted. "I came in when the fire guys got here to put everything out, so I missed the action."

"Is there anyone here who actually *did* see what happened last night?" Remi asked, to which the man started to shake his head.

Then, he seemed to catch himself and exclaimed, "Wait, I think Jeff might have been here then! Do you want to talk to him before you start looking around?"

"Yes," Remi replied. "I'll wait here while you go find him." The officer gave him a curt nod before darting off in the opposite direction. Remi watched the man's back until he could no longer see it, before pulling out a cigarette and lighting it.

He inhaled a few times while he waited, figuring that it would take a while for the first officer to find the man known as Jeff. He had just finished smoking and let the butt fall to the ground when the man reappeared, leading another, slightly older officer behind him.

"Found him!" the younger of the two said once they had reached Remi. The Warlock inclined his head to welcome the new man. "Would you like to go to check out the scene, now?"

"I'll take over from here," Jeff said, holding up his hand dismissively. The younger man seemed visibly hurt by this, but followed the order and walked away in the direction the two had just come.

"I take it you're here from the Coven?" the older man addressed Remi now, who nodded. There was something in his voice and Remi could not tell if it was exhaustion from being on the scene for so long or a general disdain toward him. He knew that most of the older Mortals were somewhat wary of having to work with the Witch's Guard, or any Warlocks, on certain issues, but he did not want to say anything if this was not the case.

"Yes, sir," he said. "I understand that you were one of the first officers on the scene last night. I had a few questions for you if you don't mind?"

"Go ahead," Jeff replied, motioning for Remi to start walking toward the wreckage of the private jet. "What is it you needed to ask, Mr. -?"

"Caswell," Remi answered. "And I was just wondering what, exactly, it was that you saw during the attack?"

"What do you mean?" Jeff asked as they moved along. "Are you having doubts that it was one of your people who did this?" The tone he had taken on the last part of his comment irked Remi.

"First off, sir, let's be clear about one thing," Remi said, trying to sound as dignified as possible. "Even if it was a Warlock that did this, it was not one of *our* people." The man said nothing to contradict him, and Remi went on, "Secondly, the file that we got did not mention any incriminating details to suggest that this *was* a Warlock, other than the fact that they were wearing a cloak. Which, let's be honest, could have been anyone playing dress-up, as I'm not sure any of us have actually worn robes to a battle in centuries."

He watched as the man folded his arms in front of him, almost as if waiting for Remi to finish his monologue.

"Now," Remi went on, "if you could give me a little more to go on, that would be very much appreciated, sir."

"Look down, Mr. Caswell," Jeff had formed a condescending smile now and Remi felt a crunch just under the sole of his boot.

He moved his foot to the side to see that they had stopped in a patch of grass that had been littered with metal jackets from several bullets. Remi knelt and picked one up, noting that it had to have been fired from a far-off distance, as there were no casings anywhere to be found.

"These look like semi-automatic rounds," Remi said, squinting confusedly at the Mortal officer. "But if this is where they all landed, then why is there no blood?"

"The bastard blocked them all," Jeff let out a bitter chuckle as he said this. "Right before he flipped over several of the squad vehicles. I just work here as security overnight, but last night I felt like I was an extra on the set of a freaking Hollywood movie!"

Remi considered this for a moment, before finally saying, "That's not possible. I only know of a handful of spells that would be able to deflect a bullet. And even then, it usually doesn't work. Especially not on this many of them at once. Are you sure it was just one Warlock?"

"It was dark," Jeff noted. "So it's possible there could have been more than one, but it was *definitely* a job done by Warlocks."

"What makes you so sure about that?" Remi asked, pulling a small ziplock bag from his pocket and placing the metal jacket inside to take back to the Coven House for analysis. Upon seeing Jeff's suddenly quizzical expression, he explained, "We can try to perform a Trace on it. Maybe find out what spell was used and what kind of wand it came from."

"Would you be able to find who this guy is from that?" the man asked, seeming genuinely impressed by this idea.

"Maybe," Remi shrugged. "It's a long shot, but if we can find that much, we can figure out which Warlocks own those types of wands and narrow our search down."

"I never knew that was an option," Jeff mused. "Of course, I've never really had to work a case with any of y'all before this."

"Most Mortals don't," Remi admitted, explaining, "We generally don't use that type of analysis anymore, but since we don't have anything else to go on right now, it's really our only option."

"I see," Jeff nodded. "Well, are there any more questions you had?"

"Yeah, actually," Remi said. "Why would he attack the airport? I mean, if he didn't kill anyone, then what's the point? Was he jealous of someone's jet?"

"I think it was just a display of power," Jeff guessed. "Or it might be a distraction from something else. I don't think this will be the last we see or hear from this guy. I just don't know what else he could possibly be planning while we investigate this."

"Do you really think this could just be some sort of distraction? Like maybe there was something else happening last night that he didn't want us to see?" Remi asked the questions, then something clicked in the back of his mind and it suddenly dawned on him. "Did you happen to see which way he came from?"

Jeff shook his head and explained, "I was watching the front door by the time he had made it here. Most of the first responders didn't even get here until he had already done his damage and left." Seeing Remi's defeated expression, he asked, "Why? Is there something else that happened last night?"

Remi knew he shouldn't lie, but he also hadn't made a case on the two Mortal teens from the previous night. So he also knew he should not reveal too much on a case that was still under the jurisdiction of the Oxford Coven.

"No," he said, finally. "I just figured if we knew where he came from, we might have something more to go on."

"Makes sense," Jeff agreed with the logic of his explanation. "I wish I did know where the bastard came from, so we could go find him and bring him in."

Remi gave the man a reassuring look for a brief moment, before turning to leave.

"Where are you going?" the Mortal officer asked. "Don't you want to look at the jet?" Remi shook his head, holding up the bag with the bullet before storing it in his chest pocket.

"This should be all I need," he explained. "If it's the same guy that did all of this, it looks like this should be plenty enough to get me the information I need to find him." The man seemed disbelieving, but understanding. "Carry on, Jeff. Thank you for your time."

Remi turned back the way he had come down and heard something that sounded like metal creaking a little further down the tarmac. He spun around to see that the Mortals in the fire engines were hauling tail away from the overturned jet and he could see why. The flames that they had been trying to spray down had only grown higher in the short time he had been chatting with Jeff and were now spreading to other parts of the liner, growing white-hot in their intensity.

He heard them shouting out something, but couldn't quite make out what it was from where he stood. Then, with a sound so booming it seemed to suck the noise out of the air around it, the back end of the jet exploded in a cloud of flames, sending shrapnel all around as it did so. Remi looked to see that no one had been hit at first, but there were bits and pieces of metal that had been sent higher into the air that were coming down all over the place.

"Everyone move!" he shouted out, pulling his wand from where he had tucked it inside his boot. He pointed it at the area where the most metal seemed to be concentrated and shouted, "*Levis!*"

A ring of white light shot forth from the tip of his wand, covering everything that was hanging in the sky from the explosion and holding it aloft. Using both of his arms to pull the weight, Remi guided the cloud of metal pieces over and away from the group of Mortals that would have been crushed by the falling debris. When he had rested everything safely on the ground, he glanced to see the majority of them were now staring at his glowing blue moonstone eyes.

"Get that cleaned up," he said simply to Jeff, tucking his wand back into his boot and walking away for a second time. Once he had made it back to his Jeep and hopped inside, he pulled the manila folder from the passenger seat and opened it. He grabbed a pen from the glove box and jotted a few quick notes of what he had learned from Jeff. Reaching back into the glove box and pulling out a paperclip, he pinned the small bag with the bullet fragment to the top of the folder before closing it. He lit up a cigarette and cranked the vehicle, putting it in gear so he could head back to the Coven House and inform Sylvia of what he had found.

"What's this?" Sylvia asked as Remi tossed the folder in front of her on the desk. She opened it and saw the metal jacket that he had pinned inside at the top of it. "Is that a bullet?"

"It is," Remi replied, then clarified, "At least, it's a piece of one. It was left at the scene of the attack last night."

"So this was a Mortal shooter?" Sylvia furrowed her brow, not making the connection.

"No," Remi explained. "I need that analyzed. Apparently, the guy that was responsible for the attack deflected a full round from multiple semi-automatic rifles from the OPD without getting so much as a single scratch on himself."

"You're joking?" Sylvia seemed genuinely shocked by this assessment. "There's no way that could have been a single Warlock!"

"That's according to one of the officers that was still there from last night," Remi informed her. "He told me what he saw, and I have no reason to not believe what he's saying."

"Very well," the Arbiter observed. "I'll have it examined and let you know what they come up with. What are you doing the rest of the day?"

"Hadn't made any plans," Remi admitted. "Probably going to go enjoy the rest of my day off. Why? Did the High Coven come to a decision about granting me access into the archives already?"

"Not yet," the woman behind the desk replied. "I'll let you know when they give me an answer, Caswell." She paused and Remi saw the beginnings of a plot forming across her face.

"Oh, no," Remi said, waving his finger accusingly in the air as if it would save him from whatever she was about to suggest. "Do *not* give me that look, right now! That is *not* a look you should be giving me right now."

"What look?" Sylvia played coy as a smile grew on her face. "I have no idea what *look* you're talking about."

"What do you want?" Remi sighed, knowing she was about to ask him to do something he would hate.

"Just a small favor," she beamed sickeningly. "Before you object, I think you should know that if you manage to do a satisfactory job, it might get this request for access granted even faster."

"Go on?" Remi lifted a single brow. He was at least slightly intrigued now and Sylvia knew it.

"My nephew is visiting for the summer," she said, and instantly, Remi heard himself groan. "He's thinking about transferring to our Coven and I need someone to show him around town."

"A babysitting gig?" he grumbled as he spoke, longing to be back in his bed to sleep the remainder of the day away. "That's worse than an escort mission in a game," he said, then to the Arbiter's confused look, waved his hand dismissively, not having the desire to explain what he meant. "Keeping in mind that I've only had, *maybe* two hours of sleep at best, what's in it for me?"

"That depends," Sylvia seemed to ponder the question briefly. "It's Dahlia's son. And you're wanting something from the High Coven for one of your cases. I'll let you weigh that out for yourself."

"Where is the little scamp?" Remi did his best fake smile and bent over as if expecting a small child to materialize out of thin air to greet him. What he got instead, threw him off, if only momentarily.

"I'm not a 'scamp'," a voice drifted from the shadows in a corner of the room behind Remi.

He turned to see a man, about his height, stepping into the light that was coming from the window behind Sylvia's desk.

The Arbiter's nephew was a few years younger than Remi, maybe in his early 20s. Remi imagined he must be fresh off the heels of his Academy training. His raven hair fell in loose curls around his face, ending at his angular jaw and giving him the appearance of some sort of fallen angel, Remi thought. His skin had an olive tint to it that gave Remi the impression that he was at least some part Italian.

Remi had to stop himself from voicing his discontent, because although the boy did not appear overly muscular, his shirt seemed to be at least two sizes smaller than it should be, giving the impression that he was bulging out of it. Remi imagined he could take him, but was far too tired for a confrontation.

The thing that stood out the most against his other dark features were the man's emerald eyes, which were currently darting around the room as he fidgeted nervously, clearly uncomfortable with being so obviously sized up by a stranger.

"Finn Ashcroft," he said finally after he was sure Remi had finished assessing him. "A pleasure, I'm sure."

Remi did not acknowledge him at first but instead turned back to face Sylvia. She was the pair of them with a smile plastered on her face, clearly amused at the interaction.

"Are you sure no one else can watch Huckleberry over here?" he asked. "I would really like sleep."

"You *do* realize that I'm right here?" Finn said, to which Remi eyed him and gave a dismissive shrug. "And it's *Finn!*"

"I'm sure there must be at least a good handful of people around here that are quite a bit tamer than I am," he said, having turned back to the Arbiter. "Wouldn't want the sweet prince to get that gorgeous mug all scuffed up in the field."

"I'm positive there are," Sylvia admitted, raising a single brow before adding, "I also said 'someone capable'."

"You *also* said 'keep him out of trouble'," Remi noted.

"I never specified that," Sylvia said.

"I know you," Remi scowled. "It was heavily implied."

"I'm old enough to take care of myself, Aunt Syl," Finn piped up from behind Remi. "If he doesn't want to do it, I'm sure I can manage by myself."

"See?" Remi smiled hopefully. "He doesn't need a chaperone. That means I'm free, right?"

"That fact was never in question, Caswell," the Arbiter laughed. "I said you're doing it, so you're doing it; whether you want to, or not."

Remi groaned and she added, "Do you want access to the archives, or not? Because I don't have to send this request."

"Fine," Remi huffed and glared. "But I'll just go on record as saying that this is entrapment and I have no intentions of enjoying a second of it."

"That makes it even better for me, then," Sylvia grinned impishly, lacing her fingers in front of her as she watched the two of them.

Remi turned to the other man with a sour look on his face and extended his arm, "Remi Caswell. Finn, you said?"

"Yeah," he replied, shaking Remi's hand. "Ashcroft. My mother is a Magister, but you don't have to treat me any different from anyone else here."

Remi found himself with an urge that he could not resist upon hearing this and jerked his hand back, shaking it like it had been set on fire.

"Oh!" he shouted dramatically, making both Finn and the Arbiter jump with a start. "Prince Ashcroft graced me with his presence! He touched me, a lowly plebe! I'll never wash this hand again!" Finn scowled at him, to which Remi laughed indignantly, "You're just another random joe to me, don't worry. You drink?"

"It's not even noon," Finn said.

"That wasn't the question," Remi replied. "I've got a clock on my phone. I asked do you drink, not do you get hammered before lunch."

"Yes, I drink," Finn answered. "Why?"

"Because we're going to the Square," Remi replied. "The best way to show you everything that is wonderful and messed up about this town can be done in a single afternoon on the Square. You game?"

"I'm game," Finn nodded and the two glanced around to gauge the Arbiter's reaction.

"Does that sound good to you?" Remi asked.

Sylvia threw her hands up dismissively, "Sounds perfectly reasonable to me. I just don't want a repeat of your last trainee; we still haven't heard back from her."

"Last trainee?" Finn repeated. "What *last* trainee?"

"Don't worry about it," Remi shushed him, ushering him out the door of the office. "Those drinks aren't going to down themselves."

Autumn's Bloom was unlike most of the other bars in the area. Where they were mostly long, wooden boxes with terrible songs playing over a sound system with broken speakers, this one was more decorated and calming. The floor was a dark-stained wood and the barback was bright orange like California poppies. The bar itself was made of a polished, wooden slab that had been placed on top of black iron, giving it the appearance of flowers in a cage.

This bar was one of only a handful of Fae-owned businesses inside Oxford city limits. Even out of these, it was the only one to boast a location on the town's historic square. Fae generally preferred not to have dealings with Mortals unless there was no way around it. Unlike the rest of her brethren in the area, however, Vesna seemed to openly welcome the opportunity.

The hole-in-the-wall was the only place in town where the Mortals and non-Mortals seemed to come together and join each other in drinks and patronage.

There had once been a case against it in the Mortal courts to have it, along with every other magical business, removed from the city of Oxford altogether. The basis of this particular case had been that anything non-Mortal was a hazard to the sanctity of the community. This frenzy had been stirred up by a local alderman after his underage daughter had been caught frequenting the bar by a local reporter.

Being that it was her establishment, Vesna had gone to trial in the Mortal court and brought it to everyone's attention that the Fae had been in Oxford long before even the first Mortals had laid claim to the land. She had then stated that even the Warlocks had arrived not long after them in the attempt to create a Coven in the area. This had been implied that the non-Mortals were simply being civil by allowing them to stay in the area. She had also pointed out that if her bar had not been there, that the girl would have found another place in which to do her unsavory deeds.

The judge had, luckily for everyone, agreed with her about teenagers being inherently mischievous when it came to the law and age restrictions.

Remi had been too young to pay attention to the details all that much. What he did know is that it had been a landmark case in the Mortal courts, especially for the 80s, as it had been one of the first that had favored any magical creature without the High Coven getting involved. That was the type of power that Vesna had.

Now, as Remi and Finn entered and made their way to the stools, Remi noticed that Vesna herself was present today. This was odd to him as, even when she was present, she was usually locked away in her office taking care of bills and other miscellaneous tasks of the sort. He took a quick glance around and saw, as he had imagined, that all Mortals in the building, male and female alike, were watching every single move she made. The men seemed to be lost entranced, while the females that were with them appeared to be more envious. Remi could not say that he particularly blamed either group.

Being a Woodland nymph, Vesna's skin had a slight green tinge to it that was offset by her blood-red hair, giving her the appearance of a living rose. Her lips were a soft pink, like the petals of a daisy. Her eyes, much like Finn's, were emeralds; although hers had a more natural, earthy quality to them. When she leaned close enough, Remi caught the faintest hint of honeysuckles in a spring meadow breeze.

Despite being known as a businesswoman to the Mortals in the town, Vesna managed to remain cemented as leader and Queen of the Woodland Court.

Remi liked to imagine that her seemingly effortless duality had to do with the fact that, out of all the different types of Fae, those in the Woodland Court were the ones most commonly associated with Mortals throughout. He could never be sure if this was out of sheer curiosity, or if they were gaining knowledge to use against them as blackmail later.

Seeing him and flashing a smile, Vesna waved him and Finn over.

As the pair reached the counter of the bar, Vesna beamed once more. "The usual?" she asked then as if she had just noticed Finn, added, "Who's the new guy?"

"My latest charge, as per the Arbiter," Remi answered, referring to Finn. "Better make it two today."

Vesna nodded with a knowing smile, then to Finn, "How about you?"

"Tanqueray, thanks," Finn replied. As Vesna set three highball glasses on the counter and began pouring, he looked at the cream-labeled bottle of the amber liquid that Remi had chosen as his poison. "What is your 'usual'?" he asked.

"Jack Honey," Remi answered. "Although I have been known to frequent the British staple from time to time. Amy Winehouse, Adele, and a broken heart are usually involved in those decisions, though."

"More like a bruised ego," the woman behind the bar chuckled as she topped the glasses off and returned the bottles to their rightful places.

"Noted," Finn smirked as Vesna pushed the drinks across to them. Remi took his first one and downed it in a single gulp, to which Finn followed suit. "I'll take another."

"You don't have to keep up with me," Remi laughed. "I don't need your aunt blaming me for your liver failure."

"I'm not new to this, Caswell," Finn retorted as Vesna handed him his second glass.

"It's been a while since we've had another Ashcroft in here," she noted, making Finn's eyes widen out of sheer curiosity.

"How did you-" he began, but she stopped him with a raised hand.

"I know my Warlocks," she chuckled. "I'm not as young as I look."

"Right," Finn said a bit wistfully, before glancing around the rest of the bar behind them. "Is it always this busy here?"

Vesna shook her head before answering, "Orientation week; incoming freshman and their families all packed into this tiny town until Sunday, and the bars get hit the hardest."

"Come on," Remi gave him a pat on the back and handed Vesna his debit card. "Start me a tab."

He nodded over his shoulder to a narrow, wrought-iron staircase that spiraled up to the second floor. Finn followed and the two ascended, making their way out onto the balcony overlooking the streets of the Square and taking a seat at one of the few available tables.

They sat in silence for a few moments, nursing their drinks and watching the Mortals in the crowd bustling about below them.

"So," Remi started after a few minutes had passed. "What brings you to Oxford?"

"Nothing in particular," Finn said. "Family, change of scenery... Several things, I guess?"

"Which Coven are you originally from?" Remi asked.

"New Orleans," Finn replied. "Joined them after I finished the Academy."

"You want to transfer from that House to Oxford?" Remi shot him a disbelieving look. "Why would anyone want to do that?"

"It's where my Academy was," Finn answered, before taking a sip of his drink. "I just joined up after I finished, but that was three years ago. Eleven years in one place just gets stale."

"Makes sense, I guess," Remi nodded, taking a swig from his own glass. "Is that where you're from?"

"Nah," Finn shook his head. "I grew up in Salem with Mother. When my powers manifested and I was old enough, I had the option of any Academy I wanted with her being a Magister. I never really had any intention of staying there."

"Why didn't you just go back home after your Proving?" Remi asked.

"It's bad enough having a parent looking over your shoulder under normal circumstances," Finn chuckled. "I'm sure you can imagine how intensified that feeling is when that parent is on the High Coven."

"I feel that," Remi agreed, pulling a pack of cigarettes from his chest pocket. "You smoke?"

Finn shook his head in refusal and Remi shrugged, snapping his fingers and lighting the tip on the small flame that jumped to life in front of him. He inhaled a few times before waving the flame away.

A girl at a nearby table to his right began coughing profusely, to which Remi turned and smiled. She looked shocked to see his moonstone-ringed pupils, which made Remi chuckle to himself before muttering, "*Nova Caeli.*"

The breeze that had been blowing around the balcony seemed to focus on the area immediately around him now, carrying the smoke billowing from his cigarette away from them. He watched as the girl, along with her parents, stood and moved to a table on the other end of the balcony and began shooting menacing glares in his direction every few seconds.

"How did you do that?" Finn asked after Remi had taken a few drags.

"Do *what*?" Remi asked, exhaling and propping his feet up on the railing.

"Casting without saying anything," Finn specified. "I've heard of it, but I don't think I've ever actually seen someone do it; let alone, do it so casually."

"Oh, that." Remi looked down at his lit cigarette and back at Finn, before musing, "I guess it just takes practice. I don't really think about it, anymore. It just kind of happens at this point."

"Can you do others or just that one?"

"Maybe? I've never really had the need to try any others, but I'm sure I could if I were to concentrate hard enough."

"Fair enough," Finn mused.

"Back to you," Remi veered the topic back on course, as he was not particularly fond of talking about himself. "I know your mom is one of the Magisters, but what about your dad? I don't think I've ever heard anyone mention him."

"You probably won't," Finn said glumly. "As far as everyone is concerned, I'm a product of a single person."

"Oh?" Remi raised a single, curious brow. "A scandal among the High Coven?"

"Not exactly," Finn chuckled. "He's a Fae. That's about all I know, really."

"A Fae?" Remi said, feeling a bit disappointed. "I was hoping for something a bit juicier than that."

"Well, it was the early 90s," Finn shrugged. "People didn't look so fondly of interspecies relationships back then. And with her being a Magister, it had to be covered up."

"I see," Remi nodded. Deciding it was best to move away from his current line of questioning, he asked, "Well, do you have any questions for me?"

"I'm just curious about the last trainee Aunt Syl mentioned," Finn laughed, to which Remi grumbled.

"If you really want to know," he began, "it was completely out of my control. She had worked a few cases with me for about a week. We both had a Saturday off, so we went to a party that this Woodland guy was throwing for the fourth of July or something. I can't remember exactly what the occasion was. But anyway, I tell her when we first go in, 'Stay away from the green drinks'."

He paused for dramatic effect, taking a drag of his cigarette before continuing, "What is the first thing the kid does? Goes straight for one of the drink tables and downs three of them before anyone can stop her like she hadn't been warned beforehand."

"What happened then?" Finn was giving him an expression somewhere between concern and hilarity.

"What do you think happened?" Remi asked as if it should have been obvious. "Nothing at first. She kept saying she was fine and that she had no idea why I was so worried. Then her eyes rolled back in her head and she was on the floor, foaming at the mouth and twitching just like she'd been hit with a taser at a disco."

Remi paused and finished his drink and cigarette, waving one of the waitresses over. "She was in the infirmary for about three weeks after that," he went on. "I think she went up to New York when she finally recovered. Haven't heard hide nor hair from her since then."

"And yet," Finn smirked, "Aunt Syl left me in your care."

"Your potential funeral," Remi shrugged as the waitress came to take their glasses for another round.

"So, what is it that's so great about this town?" Finn asked after she had walked away. "You mentioned that I could see everything I needed from just one afternoon on the Square. Well, we're here, but I haven't seen anything to sway me in either direction."

"Well, look down there," Remi said, tilting his head to indicate the streets below. Finn did as told and he went on, "That's probably one of the best things I can say for this town. With it being a small town with such a large college, it's probably one of the most diverse places you're going to find around here. And everyone gets along for the most part."

"I feel like there's a 'but' somewhere around here," Finn noted, causing Remi to glance over at the family of Mortals that was still staring him down like he had gotten sick on their shoes.

"That," he said. "Even with all the strides we've made in the past few decades for fair treatment of Warlocks and other magical creatures, you get people like that. The ones that think you're beneath them just because of what you are, despite being in a Fae-owned bar. Because they're Mortal. And even with all the squabbles they have amongst themselves, if you're not Mortal, they'll all unite against you before they tear each other apart."

"That's nothing," Finn shrugged. "New Orleans has a pretty big Klan presence. You think they do terrible things to other Mortals? You should see what happens when they get a chance to 'purify' a Warlock."

"Noted," Remi said, feeling a chill run down his spine despite the warm breeze of the balcony.

Just as he was about to light another cigarette, the waitress that had taken their glasses had reappeared. Remi took a quick look at her face and saw that she was clearly trying to remain calm, though he was unsure what might have been the cause of this.

"What's up?" he asked, shooting a glance to Finn, who was already on his feet.

"The two of you are needed downstairs, immediately," the girl leaned down to whisper in his ear.

Remi shot up, trying not to draw the attention of anyone around them. Luckily, they were all too wrapped up in their own conversations to notice.

He and Finn made their way back downstairs, where Vesna was waiting at the foot of the stairs.

"Follow me," she said, quietly enough so that only they would hear. The two exchanged confused glances before following her to the back of the bar and out of a door that Remi assumed was where the employees entered the building.

"We have to move quickly," Vesna went on as they walked down the alley and across the street. "Go ahead and call your Arbiter. Have her send a van and a clean-up crew immediately."

"What's going on?" Remi asked, fishing his phone from his jeans pocket and dialing the number. "Do we need Healers?"

"No," Vesna sounded grim. "It's too late for that now."

"What do you mean?" Finn asked, looking just as puzzled as Remi felt.

"You'll see," she said, hastily leading them past the buildings across the street from her bar.

They were in one of the few free parking areas on the Square, where most of the employees that worked in the shops and bars left their cars before work. About midway down was a pair of dumpsters, surrounded on three sides by a low brick wall. It became clear to Remi as they moved along that this was where the Woodland Queen was leading them. Once they got there, it did not take long to see why.

"They're on the way," Remi said, hanging up with Sylvia. "How long has she been here?"

"No clue," Vesna replied, staring down at the girl. "Had to be sometime after we closed last night. She wasn't there when we brought our trash out." Remi and company looked down at the pavement, each with a look of disgust mixed with something else.

Tucked behind the larger of the two dumpsters, hidden almost completely from any potential gawkers, was a body. Though the rest of the body was obscured, the foot that stuck out was too freshly manicured and too well-maintained to be mistaken for a man's.

"What do you need me to do?" Vesna asked, turning away and looking almost like she wanted to get sick.

"Are any of your girls from last night here today?" he asked, his brain kicking into investigative mode. The Woodland Queen nodded.

"All but one," she explained. "She won't be in until later on tonight."

"Good," Remi said, then to Finn, "Question each of them. See if they noticed anything or anyone suspicious last night or first thing this morning."

"Right," Finn nodded. "If not?"

"Them," Remi indicated the building closest to them. There was a group of workers from the restaurant huddled on the stairs that descended from the back door, smoking cigarettes and watching the three of them with obvious curiosity. "If anyone saw anything last night, it would be them. In fact," he paused to consider, "do that now, before you go back into the Bloom."

Finn nodded and walked away. Remi and Vesna watched as he made his way to the Mortals and began pointing behind him to the dumpsters, having retrieved a pen and pad from somewhere on his person.

"How long do you think it will take for them to get here?" Vesna asked, referring to the crew that Remi had requested from Sylvia.

"No clue," he shrugged. "Could be ten minutes, could be an hour. You know how these weekends are."

"I don't know which is worse in this town," Vesna chuckled, though the sound fell flat. "Orientation or home games?"

"Did you see that before?" Remi asked, suddenly noticing something he had not earlier.

"What?" Vesna gave a confused look.

"Her skin," Remi said, moving to kneel down on the side of the dumpster. "It's flaking off. It looks like ashes."

"A Vampire?" Vesna had gone from perplexed to concerned. "Is she alive?"

"No," Remi shook his head. "Definitely dead. But someone left her out here, I'm guessing with the expectation that the sun would get rid of any evidence before someone found the body. We need to cover her before that happens."

"We shall use Nature," Vesna agreed. To Remi's puzzled expression, she lifted her hands above her, netting her fingers together.

Remi watched as vines on the lower half of the surrounding brick wall began snaking their way upward and over, twining themselves around each other in a way that mimicked the pose that Vesna held. He had not noticed the vines at first, but now they had become a naturally-occurring latticework.

While it was impressive, Remi noted that there were still tiny rays of sunlight peeking through the interlocking plants. He moved his own hand across the area, imagining darkness threading itself through the cracks that had not been already filled with leaves.

"*Umbra*," he said, and the space in front of them was draped in a curtain of shadows, enveloping the girl and shielding her from any further sun exposure. Her skin immediately stopped flaking and the cracks seemed to become less pronounced in the shaded area. He turned to the spot where Finn had been conversing with the Mortals of the restaurant and saw that neither the younger Warlock nor the others were still there.

"Guess he finished with them," Remi mused.

"I shall go check on his progress," Vesna answered the unasked question, to which Remi nodded thankfully. "You remain here and see what you can gather before your people get here."

Without another word, the Woodland Queen made her way back through the parking lot, crossing the street, and walking back into the alley that led to the rear entrance of Autumn's Bloom.

Remi turned back to the girl that was lying on the pavement behind the communal dumpsters. He grimaced as he knelt, getting to work trying to piece her last few hours together.

VI

The Dark Warlock made his way along the trees that lined the paved road, taking solace in the fact that few Mortals were on this side of the town unless they lived in one of the houses. He had only just begun his work for the night and could not be bothered with unnecessary casualties. Although, would anyone *truly* consider a Mortal life lost a *casualty*? They were clearly the lowest species known to exist on this planet so if one were to cross his path, surely they would not be missed by anyone of importance.

He laughed to himself at the very notion of someone missing a Mortal as he came to a cross-section in the road.

Seeing that no one was around, he walked across, stopping only at a gate in the wire fence that split the path in front of him from the rest of the area. He stared up and saw that it was only a few feet taller. He imagined could have very easily been scaled if he chose to do so.

That would make me but little more than a common thief, he shuddered to himself at the very notion of it.

The Dark Mage lifted his wand from beneath his cloak and pointed it at the oversized padlock. The thing had been chained to the gate, keeping it closed in an obvious and futile effort to keep undesirables from crossing through the fence. He spoke the words of the simple unlocking charm and watched as the thing fell to the ground with a clang that was muffled by the grass, soon covered by the chain that had held it in place.

Smirking to himself at the simplicity of these Mortal contraptions, he pushed the fence open and strode through with ease. As he made his way across the man-made pitch, he noticed the large brick tower looming over it all to his right, tucked neatly between the rolling hills. In the darkness, the spire atop the building blinked a bright red every so often, as if it were a beacon of some sorts.

Seeing the gargantuan metal tanks with their wings spread out to the side, he supposed that the building must be some kind of communication tower for the Mortals, though he knew not what sort of messages they would need to relay.

Deciding that it was not important enough for him to ponder, the Dark Warlock made his way across the open, mostly-empty field. It felt as if he were being propelled forward in a singular direction by some unknown force.

Perhaps, it is merely the night willing me to finish the work I have started, he mused to himself with a smile.

As he reached the halfway point in the field, there was a sudden and deafening roar behind him as one of the steel eagles came to life. In that same moment, the Dark Mage was thrust into a blinding white light that came from somewhere atop the signal tower, near where the communication antenna had been bolted in place.

"Hey, you! Down there!" the voice echoed around him from every direction. "You can't be down there!"

The Dark Warlock felt a menacing grin etching its way across his face as the opportunity had presented itself to him so eagerly. His grip tightened around the hilt of his wand and he aimed it in the direction of the spotlight initially, then thought better of it.

If I get rid of that first, how will these Mortals see what glorious destruction I am capable of? He posed to himself, quickly readjusting his wand to point at the roaring engine of the mechanized dragon to his immediate right on the tarmac.

"Drop your weapon!" the Mortal voice called down to the Dark Warlock just as he spoke the incantation. He watched as the flames roared to life, effectively exploding his target.

Instantly, what had been little more than a nervous curiosity merely seconds ago erupted into complete and utter chaos. The alarms sounded as Mortals shouted in fear and confusion. Off in the distance, he could hear the wails of local police sirens echoing through the night.

The Dark Warlock watched as the door of the jet flew open and the emergency slide was thrown out, enabling the handful of panicked passengers to tumble down onto the pavement below.

He waited until they had all made it out safely before casting another charm at the jet and sending them all flying as the second explosion consumed what was left of their trophy.

These Mortals do love to flaunt their money, he laughed openly at them now as they ran like ants.

He noticed the blue lights sweeping over the landscape as Mortals fled the scene in every direction. He turned to see the several law enforcement vehicles that had already made it onto the scene.

"Drop your weapon and put your hands in the air!" a feminine voice pleaded with him from a speaker that was located atop one of the vehicles. "This doesn't have to end badly for you if you just cooperate with us, sir."

The Dark Warlock smiled menacingly and turned to acknowledge the direction the voice had come from. He stretched his hands above his head and let the Mortals think they had won for a brief moment, waiting until he heard a sigh of relief from the projecting end of the speaker. With that, he determined that it was the leftmost of them.

"Good," the voice sounded almost relieved at this gesture. "Now, just drop your weapon and we can end this whole thing."

But why would I want to end such a fun game so early? the Dark Warlock thought to himself.

With a lightning whip of his wrist, he flicked his wand at the vehicle, launching it high into the air behind it with the weightlessness of a child's toy.

The Mortals reverted back to their original state of frenzy and quickly began shouting orders at one another.

He watched as a handful charged toward the overturned vehicle to retrieve their fallen comrades. The rest drew weapons of their own, each focusing their crosshairs on his lone figure in the dark. He held his wand in front of him just as he heard the hammers thundering through the night as the men fired.

The Dark Warlock let out a whole-hearted and terrifying laugh that would send shivers down any sane person's spine as, one-by-one, each metal jacket from each individual bullet hit his invisible barrier and fell to the ground just before him.

A few of the Mortals who were close enough to notice lowered their rifles, while those beyond the second line remained oblivious to this feat and continued their fruitless storm of bullets that would never touch him. It did not take much longer for even those men to catch on and bring their own weapons down to their sides, masks of horror stretched tightly across each of their faces.

It was abundantly clear to him that these Mortals, ants as they were, had never been pitted against a god such as himself.

They will all soon learn why gods were meant to be worshipped, not challenged, he laughed to himself.

Keeping his wand steady in front of him, he brought the tip down and, without so much as a flick of his wrist, he sent a wave of force that lifted the remaining cars simultaneously and tossed them past where the first had landed as lightly as if they were pebbles. Some landed on their roofs, while the rest simply barrel rolled until they were in an upright position again.

There were no explosions, no Mortals in any of them, no unnecessary destruction. This would not be a massacre; merely a fractional display of his power.

The Dark Warlock twisted his wand over in his hand and focused on the weapons that the Mortals clutched to in an effort to maintain some semblance of order over the chaos he was so easily plunging them into. He pulled back hard and wrenched the things from each Mortal's hand, disarming them and letting the contraptions fall to the ground in a useless heap of scrap.

Then, in a gesture reminiscent of a bygone era, he tucked his wand into the chest of his robes and raised his hand to the rim of a hat that was not there and tipped his head.

"Good evening to you all," he said in a voice amplified by an unspoken charm. "But I really must be on my way."

The Dark Warlock turned on his heel and began to walk away, noticing only after a few steps that he remained bathed in the unforgiving white light of the communication tower. He reached back into his robes and pulled his wand out one last time, aiming it at the flames that were still raging from the engine of the metal bird. He pulled that same fire directly to the spotlight that hung so high above them all, where it wrapped slowly around the oversized lantern.

With one final, unspoken charm and a last wave of his wand, the flames were amplified. It looked very much like a phoenix rising from its ashes as the bolts holding the thing in place were melted away. With nothing to hold the actual bulk of the spire in place, it began slowly creaking forward and pulling away from itself. The wires were burned away in seconds, hastily dousing the light.

As he strode away, he could hear the low creak of the iron caving in upon itself and the Mortals shouting amongst themselves to get out of the way. There was an almost deafening boom as the spotlight fell to the ground from the top of the communication tower.

That will do for tonight, he thought to himself, making his way across the remaining expanse of the tarmac and emerging himself into the small thicket of trees that obscured it from the road in front.

He knew the Mortals would not strike out against him again until they had a more thought-out course of action. That hesitation would give him just the amount of time he needed to finish his work.

The girl was on the playing field when he found her. The Dark Warlock watched her for a time before he spoke. She was methodically lining up several black-and-white checkered balls in a neat line in front of her, before furiously kicking each of them into a net at the opposite end of the agroturf with the inner bend of her right foot.

As there was no one else around, he gathered that she was not playing for points. He surmised that she was practicing for an upcoming game or something along those lines.

"Are you going to tell me why you're watching me," the girl began without looking at him as she collected the balls for a third time. "Or are you just going to sit there like a creep all night?"

The Dark Warlock found himself laughing more at the sass than the girl's insolence.

"How long have you been Turned?" he asked, to which the girl rounded.

"What did you say?" she spat then, rounding on him as if she had been insulted. "Who are you and what do you want?"

Even from his position in the darkness of the cloud-filled night, the man could see the blood-rimmed irises that marked the girl as a Vampire. He smiled, more to himself than the girl as he rose from the seat he had taken on a nearby metal bench.

"I'm sure you don't need me to repeat what I said," he replied, casually striding toward her. "As for who I am and what I want, well... Those are both really nothing to concern yourself with, as you won't be leaving this place tonight."

"That so?" the girl snorted at such a bold accusation, assuming he was just some cocky, old geezer that she could easily overpower. "And just how did you come to that conclusion?"

"Easily," he replied as he closed the distance between them in a few short steps. "I always get what I want. And tonight, what I want, happens to be you."

"I'm not interested," the girl said, smiling to reveal her descending fangs. The Dark Warlock glanced down just briefly enough to see that her manicured nails were poised to strike as well. He chuckled to himself and the girl glared, "Find something funny, old man?"

"Not *funny*, per se," the Dark Mage replied with a dismissive wave of his hand. "Simply that I do enjoy a challenge. But I assure you, that won't help you much."

Without another word, the girl tried for a preemptive strike, but he was too fast for her. He had already turned the phrase over in his head several times and as the girl made a lunge for his face, it was pulled back and snapped by an invisible force.

The girl let out a beastly howl of pain and brought her other arm, only for it to meet the same unseen wall and be dislodged from its socket at the shoulder.

"You think this will stop me?" she roared in anger, lunging forth with her entire battered body. She was thrown back as she hit the invisible barrier that shielded the Dark Warlock.

"Such vigor!" he shouted excitedly. "Your blood will do quite nicely for the ritual!"

"What do you want from me?" the girl asked, coughing up blood as she lay sprawled on the grassy field.

"I've already told you what I want," he whispered, kneeling down and bringing his face so that it was less than a breath away from the girl's. "And I never answer the same question twice to the same person."

The Dark Warlock felt the girl tense her neck beneath and jerked back just in time to see her jaw chomp down on the air where his face had just been.

"I will admit that you have charisma, child," he laughed. "But that will not help you in this scenario, I'm afraid to say."

The girl's eyes met him in abject horror just as his next unspoken charm wrenched her fangs from her skull and the blood began pouring down her lips. The Dark Warlock watched as the crimson liquid dripped from her jaw as she howled in a mixture of tortured pain and fear.

"Go rest, child," he said in his most soothing voice. "This shall all be over for you, soon enough."

Reaching into his cloak, he pulled out his wand and an empty phial; the second one he had used on this night.

With his wand, he spoke the words of power and watched as a thin scarlet line formed. Removing the stopper from the phial, he followed suit with the Vampire's blood just as he had done only an hour ago with the water spirit out at the lake.

After he was certain that he had collected all of the girl's life essence, the Dark Warlock resealed the cork in the bottle and made to leave. He had just reached the end of the pitch when he heard the sirens off in the distance. Although he was sure they were responding to the scene he had caused just moments earlier, he rounded on his heel, thinking it best not to leave the body in such plain sight.

The Dark Mage knelt down and collected the deceased, tossing her over his shoulder like a heavy, burlap sack of dead weight. He was still not strong enough to apparate to his destination, so he would have to carry the girl until he could find a spot to drop her off.

He spoke the concealment charm and shrouded himself and the body in a cloak of night before making his way from the site, the girl's dislocated limb banging against his back the entirety of the trek.

VII

It had not taken Remi very long to gather what little evidence he could from the body of the girl, nor had it taken long for the crew Sylvia had sent over from the Coven to arrive on the scene to detail the area.

Judging from her skin tone, she was some sort of Latina. She might have been Puerto Rican, but he was unsure, as most of her once-tanned skin had flaked off to the point that she was barely recognizable. What little had not been turned to ash in the sunlight was too little to decide the exact ethnicity the girl had been.

From what he had gathered, the girl had been a little more than a Fledgling. This meant that she was still a relatively young Vampire when compared to the others in the surrounding areas. This also meant that she had recently gone through the process of having been bitten and Turned. This much was not difficult to piece together since her skin had been in the middle of ashing over and flaking away.

One detail that Remi had found beyond disturbing, was the fact that she had been left in such a mangled position. Her left wrist had been completely snapped as if someone had bent it back until the bones inside had cracked and then continued twisting until the bone had stabbed through her skin. Her other arm had been pulled entirely from its socket, though still inside the skin, and left to hang haphazardly at the girl's side. Remi found the seemingly abandoned placement of her odd since whoever or whatever had done this had gone to the trouble of prying her fangs from their place inside the top of her mouth.

The only thing that seemed abundantly clear to Remi at this point, was that whoever had left her like this had been unsure of just how far they should go to make it look like an accident. Some of the injuries had been done almost intentionally, while others had seemed a bit more reserved. They had also left her body in a heavily trafficked area of town but taken the time to hide her behind a dumpster as if they had not wanted her to be found immediately.

It simply did not make clear sense to Remi, as just when he thought he had pinpointed a particular motive, another detail threw him in a separate direction entirely. He wondered if the girl had been attacked and overpowered, as most of her wounds seemed to indicate an intense struggle on her part.

"Find anything?" one of the crew members asked him, pulling him out of his internal questioning. Remi turned and held out a wallet that he had found tucked underneath the girl's body.

"Just this," he said, looking down at the blood-caked item. "Not sure if it's hers, but it seems like it would be our best bet."

The man took it from his outstretched hand and opened it, picking through the contents until he found an identification card. "Analisa Valasquez," he read the name, before tucking it back into its slip. "I'll have it sent to OPD along with the body. They'll want to look over it to catch anything we might have missed."

"Don't trust us to do our job without supervision?" Remi chuckled, pulling a cigarette from the pack in the chest pocket of his shirt.

"You know the Mortals," the other man shrugged as if he had accepted the hassle many years ago. "I'll have them contact you if they come up with anything."

"Don't bother," Remi shook his head, lighting the cigarette in what had become his usual fashion lately. "Have them contact the Arbiter first. It might not even be the same girl, but if she wants me to look into it, I will. Otherwise, I'd be glad to have one less thing on my plate to deal with."

"Right," the man nodded as if he understood, before tucking the wallet under his arm and following the rest of his crew to the van. They wasted no time in pulling away from the scene and the Square altogether.

Remi took a brief glance behind the dumpster to make sure that they had not missed something in their haste to get away from the prying eyes of the nearby Mortals, before turning toward the alley that had brought him here.

"*Lux*," he muttered under his breath as he began walking away, feeling the static charge through him as the Cloak of Shadow he had cast dissipated behind him.

It did not take him long to get back across the street and down the alley. He came in the staff entrance of Autumn's Bloom, where he found Finn sitting huddled over a glass at the bar. The young Guard seemed to be in deep conversation with Vesna.

"I knew him in passing," the Woodland Queen was saying in a hushed manner, polishing a glass as she spoke. "I did not know him personally, as he was not a member of my Court."

"What was he like?" Finn seemed very excited. Remi was unsure if he should interrupt the conversation just yet, so he stood in place for a few seconds and waited. Whatever she was telling him seemed to be important and he listened intently as Finn spoke in a slightly exaggerated whisper, "What did you hear of him?"

"He was reckless and foolish to do what he did," Vesna said. "Only a Fae with those qualities would have relations with a Warlock of such stature with all of your Covenant laws that forbid such things."

There was a finality in the Woodland Queen's voice that Finn did not seem to notice in his drunken state, as he seemed to be readying himself to ask another question.

"Find any persons of interest while I've been out there?" Remi interjected himself, coming out of the shadows before Finn could dig himself any further into his hole of annoyance with Vesna. The pair of them turned to see him framed in the doorway from the light of the sun setting behind him in the back alleyway.

"No, unfortunately," Finn gave a look of defeat and turned his gaze down, focusing intently on the glass in front of him.

"How did you fare, Guard?" Vesna asked, though Remi had a sneaking suspicion that she could already read the answer on his face.

"Found a wallet with her name," Remi answered with a shrug. "They'll take it to the Mortals to put out a found person's report on her. May be able to find her family, at least. There wasn't much to go on as far as finding out who did it."

"Then you think it's a person?" Vesna suggested, to which Remi shrugged again and shook his head in an unsure manner.

"No way of telling just yet," he admitted with a sigh. "I think whoever or whatever it was had the capacity to think like a human. Might have been a Warlock, might be a Fae. There's no way to know until they finish examining the girl's body, though."

"Oh, I see," the Queen said, setting the glass she had been polishing upside down on her side of the counter and moving to the register. "That's unfortunate."

"Tell me about it," Remi agreed. "How much do I owe you today?"

Vesna handed him his card and shook her head, "I'll pick up your tab today since you didn't get to enjoy yourself as you wished."

"Well," Remi took his card and tucked it back into his wallet. "Thank you for that, M'lady."

He reached into his wallet and pulled out a fifty-dollar bill, placing it in the tip jar at the edge of the counter with a wink. Vesna nodded her approval, knowing that she would divide it evenly among the other girls who had worked that day. He wanted to ask what she and Finn had been discussing but felt something in the pit of his stomach telling him that it might have been a subject that was a bit too personal for him to get into just yet.

"I'll get him out of here, then," Remi said, looking at the other Warlock teetering on the bar stool.

"Yes," Vesna followed his gaze. "I think that would be for the best."

Hearing the two of them referring to him, Finn took the glass in front of him and slammed back the remainder of his final drink, pushing the emptied highball across so that Vesna could take it away. He then stumbled to his feet, only to be caught by Remi under his arm.

"Thanks for that," Finn said, with only a slight hiccup.

"You are beet red, kid," Remi laughed, grabbing the wrist of the arm that Finn had draped across the back of his neck. "We're going to my house first."

"But we have to go tell Aunt Syl what we found," Finn slurred his words, blowing his whiskey breath straight into Remi's face.

"Yes," Remi agreed. "I'll deal with her eventually, but we don't need her killing me when she sees you eight sheets to the wind."

"It's only three sheets," Finn protested with a pronounced wave of his free hand. "The phrase is 'three sheets to the wind'."

"No," Remi countered with a chuckle. "It's eight. I counted them."

Without another word, Remi half-walked, half-carried Finn out of the bar, with the younger Warlock hiccupping with every other step. As the two made their way back across the street and into the free parking area for a second time that day, a voice behind them made Remi give pause and turn back to see what was the matter. It was Vesna chasing after them.

"What's up?" Remi asked, clearly confused as he thought he had retrieved all of his belongings before leaving the bar.

"Nothing of importance, Guard," she smiled, before explaining, "I only meant to ask that you join me back here later tonight."

"For?" Remi prodded, unsure of what she could possibly want to see him alone for.

"You shall see when you return, Guard," Vesna replied.

"I can't tonight," he explained, shooting a quick, indicative glance over at Finn. "I'm stuck babysitting the Arbiter's nephew."

"I was not meaning to exclude him," the Woodland Queen chuckled slightly. "I would encourage him to join us. He might learn something."

"Sure," Remi answered, knowing it was best not to protest a Queen of the Fae, even if there were several witnesses. "What time did you have in mind?"

"Does two o'clock work for you both?" Vesna asked. "That should give your charge time to sleep off some of his poison. It would also give me plenty of time to get rid of any unwanted eyes."

"Sure," Remi nodded, feeling uneasy about what she was asking. "Two works. We'll see you then."

"Splendid," Vesna said, turning back toward her bar. "I shall be waiting for you to arrive." She glanced back at Finn briefly, before adding, "Sober by then, hopefully."

"I'll work on that," Remi laughed, turning back toward his Jeep and opening the door for the younger Warlock to crumple into the passenger seat.

"What was that about?" Finn asked, only half-conscious by this point.

"Looks like we're pulling a graveyard shift tonight," Remi replied, then added, "You puke on my seat, you're paying to have it detailed."

It seemed like he had barely blinked before they were back up and getting ready to make their way back to Autumn's Bloom to meet the waiting Woodland Queen. In reality, however, the pair had slept well over eight hours.

After they had gotten back to Remi's house to rest, Finn had gotten sick in the downstairs bathroom, before passing out clutching the seat. Remi had taken to the couch just outside the door, just to make sure that the other did not choke on his own bile in his stupor.

Remi had called the Arbiter to let them know what had happened and get her approval before taking off again. He did not need, nor want another ear-full from her for meeting with the head of another of the Fae Courts without permission again. She had given in, on the stipulation that he report back to her first thing in the morning with their findings.

Once he had shaken Finn awake from his huddled position on the bathroom floor, the two had made their way back out to the Jeep and went to grab a bite to eat from the gas station before driving back across town to the now-empty town square and Autumn's Bloom, where Vesna awaited their return.

Though Remi had only had a few drinks before being called to examine the girl's body earlier, paired with his recent lack of sleep, he felt like he had been steamrolled several times over. From the look of him, he could not imagine that Finn felt much better in any sense and, quite frankly, could not blame him one bit.

"Did she give you any idea of why she wanted us back here at this ungodly hour of the night?" Finn asked, chugging the last of his energy drink as he silenced his phone and slipped it into his back pocket.

"Not a clue," Remi replied, following suit with his own phone and flicking his cigarette onto the pavement.

The pair left the Jeep and walked directly across the street from the free parking area and down the alleyway that led to the rear entrance of Vesna's bar. Neither of them knew exactly what to expect from this meeting. By the look of things, it seemed that the Woodland Queen had shut down early for the night.

There was not a single soul in the building when they entered now, not even the staff. As they came inside, the Queen stood and turned to greet them.

"Welcome, Guards," she beamed, filling Remi with a mixture of warmth and dread so that he was unsure of which instinct he should trust at this moment.

"Hello, Vesna," he replied. "Or M'lady? I'm not sure how to address you in this circumstance."

The Woodland Queen surprised him with a casual shrug, "Whichever you would prefer. My Court is not nearly as formal as the others, I am sure."

"M'lady, it is," Remi said, not wanting to offend as he did not want to turn a warm welcome to an icy front when it came to a being who controlled nature itself. "I'm assuming you didn't invite the two of us back for cocktails after dark, then?"

"Not quite," Vesna chuckled, more to herself than them. "At least, not tonight, I'm afraid."

It was then that Remi noticed that she had ditched her usual working attire in favor of a shimmering, floor-length gown the color of bark with a plunging neckline that revealed her navel.

Remi felt himself blush slightly and averted his gaze. He focused instead on the man beside him, only to find that Finn was staring at her full-on, his mouth gaping in awe at the Nymph's beauty. Her rose-colored hair had been pulled back by a crown of interwoven thorns, with antlers that resembled a stag. Her face was shadowed over and it was this particular detail that struck a chord of trepidation within the pit of Remi's stomach, as he was so accustomed to her bright personality behind the bar.

Vesna looked every bit as severe as he imagined the Queen of the Woodland Fae should look when dealing with matters that were not regarding Autumn's Bloom.

"Follow me," she said after she had given them ample time to compose themselves once more. The pair of Guards immediately snapped out of their dumbfounded states and obliged, following Vesna into a small room just behind the counter. It was easy to figure out that this room must be her office, where she handled affairs regarding business.

"You brought us here to do payroll?" Remi joked and, to his surprise, the Queen genuinely laughed in response.

"Not tonight, Warlock," she said, closing the door behind them and locking it. "Perhaps another time."

She moved to stand beside a full-length mirror in the far corner of the room and looked back at them.

"So, we came here to stare at our reflections?" Finn asked, but Remi had seen one before and knew what the thing was before Vesna had a chance to contradict the other man.

Remi stared at the mirror, admiring its clawed, golden feet that held it in place. It did not have borders on any other side of it aside from these at the bottom, which further assured Remi of what it was.

"That's not just a mirror," he said, to which he saw Vesna was nodding in agreement. "It's a portal."

"Is it?" Finn breathed out heavily, making it clear that he had never seen one in person before. "Really? But, why is it here in your office?"

"I had always wondered how you got back and forth between here and your Court so quickly," Remi mused aloud, to which Vesna chuckled and nodded.

"Now you know, Guard," she said. "That information does not leave this room, however. As I am not too keen on the idea of my resources being used by your Coven so freely as they tend to do."

"But, Aunt Syl wouldn't do anything like that without your permission," Finn chimed in, to which Vesna simply snorted.

"It is not your aunt that concerns me, young Warlock," she explained. "But I have grown accustomed to the fact that your High Coven enjoys adding to its Covenant laws, so long as it is beneficial to your people. Do you understand?"

"We do," Remi answered for both of them before Finn could object. The other glanced at him and Remi shot him a look of warning. He seemed to pick up on this, as he remained silent. "Now, why is it that you've brought us here tonight, M'lady?" Remi went on.

Rather than answering, Vesna raised her arm in front of the mirror. When she moved back, it was revealed that they were no longer looking at a reflection of the office they stood in, but a heavily wooded area that Remi was unfamiliar with. The surface of the portal rippled as if to remind them that it was only a gateway into the new area, and in no way physically attached to the room the three of them were standing in.

"Enough talk, Guards," Vesna seemed to be growing impatient, although her voice maintained its soft regality. "We waste valuable time that could be spent elsewhere, attending to more pressing matters."

Without another word, Remi and Finn watched as the Woodland Queen stepped over the claw-footed threshold of the portal and into the wooded area beyond. The mirror seemed to ripple intensely as she immersed herself into it, but did not shatter as Remi had expected. Instead, it simply expanded to take in Vesna's full form, before reverting to its original dimensions.

"Have you ever used one of these before?" Finn asked in a slightly timid voice.

"What?" Remi smirked. "You're afraid? I figured you'd have more experience than I did with all the Fae that live down in New Orleans."

"Just because they're there, doesn't mean they're any more willing to share their secrets with us," Finn said, to which Remi shrugged in mild agreement. "Oldest first, I suppose."

"That's not how this works, kid," Remi shook his head. "Get in there."

Finn made a scoffing noise of protest but otherwise did not object as he went ahead.

Remi watched as the younger Warlock fell through the Portal's mirrored edges, landing face-first on the padded dirt of their destination. Vesna was already standing there to collect him, and the two waited patiently for Remi to follow suit. He gave one last glance at the door of the office to make sure that it was securely bolted and, upon seeing that it was, stepped through the shimmering gateway one foot at a time, just as the others had.

He thought it felt like running through a tall field of grass in the summer. Remi could feel the glass pushing back against him slightly, but it took minimal effort for him to break through to whatever specific place it was that Vesna had opened the portal to. He reached the other side with only slightly more composure than Finn had, but not quite the dignified air that the Woodland Queen seemed to possess.

"This looks familiar," Finn mused as he stood and brushed himself off. "But I don't know why."

"I know what you mean," Remi agreed, only half paying attention. He spun around slowly, taking in the scenery as he did so.

Unlike the Water Court, which had looked more like a sunken, ancient temple, the Woodland Court was more like an open forest. There were a few platforms made of leaves and twined branches connecting throughout the canopy overhead. He could just barely make out the few humanoid outlines that were standing on these platforms. He thought they might be sentries of some sort.

Remi noticed some of the shadowy figures darting swiftly through the treetops, obscuring the night sky only briefly as they moved along. He imagined that it must be trailing them as if the two Warlocks might be potential threats for the Woodland Queen. He felt only slightly uneasy, but they seemed to be more cautious of the pair than genuinely threatened. At least, that was what he hoped.

Remi credited this heightened feeling of being watched to the fact that he and Finn were standing below with Vesna, who was the Queen of whatever Fae might be above them. Where the Water Court was made almost completely of marble, there seemed to be no other structures of any kind in this wooded area aside from these platforms and the trees themselves.

He looked behind him in the direction that they had come and was somewhat surprised to see that there was absolutely no indication of the portal or the office room they had just been in. It seemed to have been swallowed up by more trees and Remi briefly wondered how they would get out of here if things turned sour.

Also, unlike the Water Court, there were no visible guards stationed anywhere that Remi could see. Even the ones he knew were directly above them somehow blended into their surroundings. He made a quick, sweeping glance around and saw that there were no other Fae around other than Vesna. He had heard that there were those Woodland Fae that could take on the shape of animals. Although Remi wondered to himself if Vesna's Court guards were merely some of these bestial Fae or if they were simply more forest-like than the Queen herself. Either way, he couldn't help but be filled with a sense of unease in this new place with only Finn and the Woodland Queen to keep him company.

"They are around," Vesna said with a knowing smile, almost as if she had heard his thoughts somehow. "Most of the subjects in my Court choose to remain in their natural forms unless it is otherwise needed. Especially when in the company of strangers with such distinct eyes."

"'Natural forms'?" Finn repeated, to which the Queen nodded.

"Yes, Guard," she confirmed. "Whatever makes them most comfortable; for some, it is that of a doe, while others are content to be a bushel of roses. Still, some of the more inquisitive of my people choose to remain as human in an effort to mimic and study those that roam about so freely in the world. Who am I to tell them what is best for them?"

The words seemed to resonate with something in Remi and he found himself nodding in agreement.

"I wish the Mortals could understand that," he said aloud before he could catch himself, though he had not meant to.

"Yes," Vesna said watching him with eyes that were not unkind and smiling serenely. "Don't we all? Alas, they go to war with themselves for that very same reason, be it pigment or ideas. So how can it be expected of them to accept those who are so obviously different from them?"

"Fair point," Remi sighed and none of them said anything for a few minutes as they moved along until they reached a small clearing in the center of the woods.

"What is that?" Finn asked hesitantly, indicating a mass of lumps that had been covered in a thick brown cloth that Remi had not noticed before.

"Sadly," Vesna answered, gazing down mournfully, "it is why I have asked you both here tonight."

The Woodland Queen knelt then, drawing back the cloth just enough to reveal the face of a young woman. Had Remi not known better, he would have almost mistaken her for simply having been asleep; but he did know better. He felt a shiver run down his spine but remained silent out of both respect and curiosity.

Even though there was a smile on her face as she stared up at the starry night sky with closed eyes, Remi had seen enough faces like that to be sure that the girl was not just asleep.

"You brought us here to examine another body?" Finn asked, obviously feeling just as confused as Remi felt at that moment.

"No, young Warlock," Vesna shook her head as her gaze remained fixed on the face of the deceased Fae girl. "I simply asked you both here to talk and to bear witness to our ritual."

Finn made a quizzical glance over to Remi, who was just as clueless given their current situation.

"Just watch," the Queen said calmly. "We shall speak afterward."

Remi felt a hot, wet blowing sensation on the back of his neck then, and turned to see a large stag staring at him. It was easily twice his height and seemed to be built almost like a Clydesdale with antlers that matched the ones in Vesna's crown. If they had not been in the

Woodland Court, it would have seemed very much out of place. Here, however, the creature seemed to belong. Sensing that the creature was waiting for something, Remi tapped Finn on the shoulder and the two of them stepped aside to let the great stag through.

The pair watched as the creature lifted Vesna's hand with its nuzzle as a form of greeting, before moving on to pull the remaining cloth from the Fae girl's body.

Remi saw, with a tight feeling in his chest, that she was clutching a bouquet of lilies with a single bloom of wisteria in the center of them. He knew these flowers were meant to represent mourning and rebirth and found himself wondering why the Queen had chosen these in particular.

"How did this happen to her?" Finn asked, but Vesna held up a hand to quiet him.

"Watch," she whispered, kneeling down to touch the girl's forehead.

The two Warlocks did just that, both of them in silent awe as the girl floated weightlessly up until Vesna could guide her to rest on the rack of the deer. The Woodland Queen then snapped her fingers and suddenly, what had once been a dark area of the woods was illuminated in a yellow-green light. Remi looked up to see that this effect was caused by a cloud of what appeared to be fireflies and glowing luna moths.

Remi felt goosebumps forming on his arms and the back of his neck. He assumed that the moths were simply disguised members of the Woodland Fae, and there were so many of them that had come to pay respects to their fallen sister. He found himself unable to speak as he was enveloped in the soothing glow that emanated from the throng as a whole.

A few of these Fae-moths landed on the prongs of the deer's antlers and fluttered, almost like they were readying themselves for something as the fireflies hovered lazily just below as if waiting. It seemed as if all of the creatures around them were stirring and working in unison toward some common goal, but Remi found himself unsure of just what that might be.

Finn turned to him then, making like he wanted to ask him something. Remi simply put his index finger over his own mouth and pointed from his eyes to the scene that was unfolding before them.

The younger Warlock looked like he wanted to object, but said nothing.

The two of them watched as Vesna took a few steps forward until she was standing in the very heart of the clearing and lifted her arms high above her head.

"One of your sisters has fallen," the Queen seemed as if she was addressing an audience that Remi could not see. "Help me send her from this world so that she can greet us once more."

Once more? Remi thought to himself, but he did not dare speak for fear of drawing the ire of the entire Court.

As he waited for some sort of response from whoever Vesna had been talking to, he saw some of the lower hanging branches from the trees seem to bend down. He was not entirely sure if these were members of the Fae in disguise or simply the trees themselves bending to the will of the Woodland Queen as the vines had earlier that day. He watched silently as the branches began scratching at the ground just in front of her.

In a few minutes, it became clear that the trees were somehow managing to dig a hole into the floor of the clearing.

Remi stared onward in muted anticipation as the dirt started piling up on the side of the indentation which was soon large, deep, and wide enough for an adult person to fit into.

The trees reverted to their original positions, standing tall in the forest to shield the scene from any unwanted eyes. Vesna turned to the deer that was holding the girl in its antlers and kissed the creature on the cheek. This seemed to be a signal of sorts, as the stag moved forward so that its front hooves rested on the edge of the freshly-made hole in the forest floor.

"It is time," Vesna said quietly, to no one in particular.

Remi looked over and saw that Finn seemed like he was almost ready to burst with questions but before he could speak, the luna moths began to stir and flutter from the antlers they had been resting on up until this point.

The iridescent moths began swirling about in the air just above the stag like a small cyclone, landing once more on the girl in tiny clusters of green wings.

Remi and Finn paid careful attention as the creatures began fluttering their wings with fierce intent and lifting the girl's body as though it was no heavier than a feather. The fireflies were quick to cradle her underneath so as to make the burden easier for the others.

The Fae disguised as insects quickly floated the girl down and over the empty grave. Slowly, they all lowered her carefully into it, swirling out in unison after they had successfully reached the bottom. They then began hovering over the dirt that had been moved to the side in mounds.

It was at this point that the stag let back its head and let out a loud, whistling grunt that echoed around the forest a few times before dying out.

Remi heard the heavy hoof beats as four more stags of similar stature and build joined the first, placing themselves at differing intervals around the grave mounds. The leader of the deer stomped its front hooves on the ground in front of him as if to gain their attention. Indeed, the others seemed to watch him intently as he began pushing the dirt into the hole with his snout.

The first deer did not need to look up, as Remi felt the creature was sure that his comrades would follow suit.

Just as he had suspected, when Remi turned, he saw that the others were doing just as they had been instructed to until the dirt was completely back in its original spot, albeit with a few more lumps; this was quickly remedied by the stags stomping on the ground to pack the dirt back into place as tightly as they could manage without opposable thumbs.

When they had completed their task, the first deer made a second grunting noise to signal dismissal to his friends before turning back to Vesna. The Woodland Queen stroked his muzzle, almost like a horse, before giving him a peck on the snout and sending him away. She then turned to the watchful Warlocks and smiled.

"It is done," she said simply.

"What will happen to her?" Remi asked, thinking back to the comment about the girl greeting them once more. "Will she somehow be revived by this?"

"Not revived, no," Vesna replied solemnly. "But she will be given new life."

"What does that even mean?" Finn seemed to be even more confused now than he had been prior to the burial. "If she is given new life, does that not constitute as a revival?"

"Not quite, Warlock" Vesna explained. "When a Fae within my Court dies, they are brought to me so that I may welcome them into the next life. They are then reincarnated as a flowering tree, from which more of my Court are formed when the blooms reach maturity. It is not a common occurrence as we are immortal beings, but it is a burden that I bear in the highest regard as their Queen."

"I didn't know that the Fae could die," Finn verbalized what Remi had been thinking.

"True, we are immortal," Vesna echoed, going on to explain, "However, there are ways in which we can die; not that your kind need any further knowledge on that front." Her tone was calm, but her words had an edge to them that Remi imagined must be surely broader than just he and Finn.

"What happens if a Fae who dies is not brought to you for this welcoming into the next life?" Remi asked, remembering the scene he had witnessed in the Water Court with Rydia.

"I do not know," Vesna answered, a forlorn expression having spread across her face. "It has never happened in my time."

"What about the naiad from the lake?" Remi asked before he could stop himself, indicating the girl that was now under the forest floor. "What is *supposed* to happen to her when she dies?"

"I am not sure," Vesna replied thoughtfully. "I do not know what happens to those of the other Courts once they have fallen. Even we have secrets amongst each other, as I'm sure you understand even as a member of the Witch's Guard."

"Why bring us out here just to witness you performing your burial ritual for some random Fae from another Court?" Remi asked, sounding more agitated than he had meant to. Vesna did not seem to notice this slip-up.

"To assure you that despite this one man," she explained, "that there is no ill will between your Coven and any of the Courts in this area."

"You think our suspect is somehow connected to the Oxford Coven," Remi said, and though it had not been a question, Vesna nodded in response.

"Given the circumstances," she began, "and the location of the two most recent murders, I think it would be foolish and wishful thinking to assume otherwise, young Caswell."

The Woodland Queen finished and her words hung in the air like a suddenly tangible realization that Remi had been pushing to the back of his mind until that point.

He inhaled, readying himself to contradict her, but could only muster a sigh, "I don't have enough evidence to agree or disagree. All I can do at this point is hope."

"Then we shall help you find whatever evidence it is that you need," Vesna said, coolly. "And in doing so, whoever this dark one is so that he can be brought to justice before your High Coven, as well."

"Is that all?" Finn asked, an edge to his voice that Remi had not anticipated. "No claim to his head or anything like that once this is all over with?"

Vesna smirked then, "Though it would be an acceptable form of repayment, it is not required, young Warlock."

"Thank you, M'lady," Remi interjected himself quickly before Finn could open his mouth again. He had no desire to deal with an angry Woodland Queen in her own Court, surrounded by her subjects.

"It is well, Guard Caswell," she nodded. "Although, I will remind you that if he is not stopped soon, so many deaths will disrupt the natural order of things. Were that to happen, it would surely doom us all. Death has always been a patient mistress, Guards, but even She does not take kindly to being overwhelmed in such a destructive and careless way."

Remi had heard Death personified many times throughout the years from several different sources, but something about the way the Woodland Queen said it as if she had an intimate knowledge of the being unnerved him.

"I hope it does not come to that, M'lady," he swallowed against the lump that had formed in his throat.

"As do we all, Warlock," Vesna's tone was both somber and menacing. It sounded very much like a warning, he thought. "As do we all."

Remi felt the chills run down his spine as the nymph's words hung in the air. She nodded her chin in the direction they had come, revealing that the portal was now there waiting for them once more. From this side, it appeared as merely a shimmering, gold tear in the otherwise calm air. He grabbed Finn and turned to leave the forested Woodland Court behind, knowing that its Queen had her watchful gaze trained on their backs the entire way.

VIII

Remi was awakened the next morning by the feeling of his phone vibrating underneath him. He had managed to roll over on top of it at some point during his fitful sleep.

He had dropped Finn off at his hotel room after leaving the Woodland Court last night and come home to crash on the couch, having not had the energy left to make it all the way up the stairs to his bedroom. He was lucky that the shorts he usually slept in had already been downstairs so that he did not have to sleep in his uncomfortable jeans.

For someone who had never so much as set foot in any of the Fae Courts, Remi had managed to visit two of them in the past forty-eight hours, and only one of those had been by invitation from the Queen of said Court herself. It was exhausting and he secretly hoped it would not become a regular occurrence on this, or any other, case.

Remi answered the phone on the sixth vibration to hear Sylvia on the opposite end, telling him that his request for access into the archives had been granted and that she would be eagerly awaiting his arrival at the Oxford Coven House.

He thanked her, assuring the Arbiter that he would be there within the hour before hanging up. He stretched and rubbed the backs of his hands across his eyelids, dislodging the granules of sleep that clung to the inner corners before rising and making his way to the kitchen.

Remi grabbed the empty coffee pot from the counter, filling it and pouring the water into the back of the machine. He did not even bother to measure the grounds, opting to guess what looked like his usual preferred strength instead. He drew the curtain and opened the half window just above the sink to let the light in as the machine behind him began percolating.

This was one of Remi's favorite times of the day. When he first woke up, there was no one else around who would require anything from him. There were no expectations this early in the morning and he found it nice that he could just be alone with his thoughts.

Remi pulled his phone from the pocket of his shorts and began checking his emails and texts, thankful that the Mortals had at least mastered technology over the years since they did not have magic of their own. Seeing that there were no important updates from anyone he cared to respond to this early, he set his phone on the counter and grabbed his mug from the cabinet.

He poured the freshly-brewed coffee into the first cup of the day and pulled the milk from the refrigerator. He then added just a splash before returning the carton. He imagined a small twister inside the mug and watched as the two liquids blended together.

Hmm, Remi thought to himself, thinking of Finn's question yesterday. *There's another one I didn't even think about.*

Remi took the first sip of his morning fuel as he rounded the corner back into the living room, retrieving his cigarettes from the shirt he had been wearing last night and making his way outside. He stood on the back patio, letting the sunlight warm him and everything else as it tried to wake the world up.

Remi stood there for a few minutes, alternating cigarette inhalations and sips of coffee as he listened to the Mortals around him getting a start on their own days. He remembered it was Tuesday as he heard the yard workers two houses down and smelled the freshly cut grass. Knowing that they would probably be knocking on his gate within the next few minutes, he went ahead and pulled the lever, cracking it open for them.

He had just thrown his butt against the fence when he heard his phone vibrating on the counter. He went back inside to grab it before making his way back to his seat on the patio to answer it as he lit a second cigarette.

Remi had never seen the number before, so he answered in a quizzical tone, "Hello?"

"Hello?" the voice sounded familiar. "Is this Remi?

"This is he," Remi felt himself making a face as he tried to figure out who was on the other end. "Who, may I ask, is calling?"

"It's Finn," the voice answered.

"Oh, hey bud," Remi said as it clicked for him. "What's up?"

"Hey," Finn sounded somewhat flustered on the other end. "Look... Do you know the bus schedule, by chance?"

"Bus schedule?" Remi asked. "Like the O.U.T. lines?"

"Yeah," Finn confirmed. "My internet isn't working on my phone and I don't know what stop number to punch in on the information line thing."

"Kind of," Remi said, trying to remember which lines went where. "Where are you trying to get?"

"The Coven House," Finn replied, sounding more than a little embarrassed. "Or at least close enough where I can just walk the rest of the way."

"Oh," Remi chuckled to himself. "Well, are you ready now?"

"Yeah, kind of," Finn said. "I still have to grab a quick shower, but it shouldn't take me that long to get dressed afterward."

"How long do you think it'll take you?" Remi asked, ashing onto the stone beneath him.

"Probably about twenty minutes," Finn replied. "Why?"

"Okay," Remi said. "Just get ready and I'll swing by. I'm heading that way in a minute, anyway."

"You don't have to," Finn objected, clearly too proud to take a handout, even when it was offered.

"Nah, kid. Save your bus fare for another day."

"Thanks, man," Finn sounded relieved. "Just let me know when you're close and I'll meet you outside."

"Cool, cool," Remi said, flicking his second butt against the fence and making his way back inside. "Do you like coffee?"

Remi and Finn walked into the Coven House and made their way directly toward the staircase at the center of the first floor, where the Arbiter's office was located.

The Oxford Coven House was, on the outside, one of the oldest buildings in Oxford itself. Before the Warlocks had purchased it, it had been a two-story, antebellum-style home. This came complete with a wrap-around porch and alabaster pillars at intervals around the house, which held up a balcony that surveyed the grounds. There was a wall of oaks that obscured them from the Mortals on the other side of the high, wrought-iron gate and provided a natural shield before their barrier had even been applied.

The house itself was white, with royal blue accents to give it a regal sort of look. The shudders were always open, giving the illusion that one could look directly into the house, but it was so heavily Glamoured so that no prying eyes could see what the interior truly looked like.

There was a huge maze out back with a stone garden at its center where important ceremonies, such as inductions into the Oxford Coven, were sometimes held.

The house had itself been abandoned sometime shortly after the burning of the Historic Square in 1864, no doubt by a family of Mortals seeking to preserve their well-being. After the first Mortals had moved out, the entire estate had been reclaimed by the city for tax purposes, where it was eventually purchased by the High Coven in the hopes of establishing a presence near the state's university. While the thought of having Warlocks so nearby after a disaster had made some of the town's Mortals uneasy, the mayor at the time had been so willing to secure funds to rebuild things, that he had not batted a lash or offered it a second thought.

While the exterior of the house and the grounds had been left similar to their original state in an effort to appease the Mortals on the historical society, the interior had been heavily Glamoured to increase space. This was required in most of the buildings that became Coven Houses to make room for the constantly growing and changing needs of the Warlocks inside.

The first floor was set up similar to every office that Remi had ever set foot in, complete with cubicles and several desks where the lower-level Warlocks milled about. These clerks took care of the paperwork and other secretarial duties that none of the others had the time to do. Sometimes, this was strictly between other Covens and occasionally it was with the world outside.

Above that, was the Arbiter's office. Since the office itself was too small to take up an entire floor, the reading library was on the opposite side of the landing. It was constantly being updated and housed every volume imaginable. This included such classic literature as 'Pride and Prejudice' and 'The Picture of Dorian Grey', to the more modern things like 'The Book Thief' and the entire 'Harry Potter' collection. Remi was fairly certain that he had seen at least a few religious tomes from the various Mortal faiths among the vast shelves as well, but he could not imagine anyone making the effort to read through them all in their spare time.

The third floor was where the Healers worked in the House's Infirmary. This was located just below the training barracks, ironically. The training barracks was where Warlocks could practice new spells without fear of destroying something, as the Glamours on that floor were specifically cast to withstand as much damage as a direct blast from an atomic bomb in case the Coven ever found themselves under attack from the Mortals. Although, Remi had read about a case before that particular Glamour had been placed, in which a Warlock had blasted himself straight through the floor and into a bed in the Infirmary below.

The fifth floor was the highest Remi had ever been in his time with the Coven, as it served as the judicial floor where rogues were brought when they had broken the Covenants. The sixth floor was a sort of dormitory used for housing any visiting Warlocks. While it was mainly used for Healers and members of the Witch's Guard who were passing through, its sole purpose was intended for wartime. This being the case, it was always ready to accommodate at least 1,000 other Warlocks without extra enchantments. While he could not recall it ever having been used during his time with the Oxford Coven, Remi was glad to know that the House would be ready, should the need ever arise.

The seventh floor of the house was a kitchen and dining hall, though it was seldom used as most people simply went out for their meals. Above that was the chapel, which is where a Warlock who wished to join the Witch's Guard underwent their Proving ceremony. The ninth floor had been Glamoured to resemble an open courtyard. This had been done so that if any rogues escaped from the tenth floor and made their way down, they would think they had made it out of the house for a short time before they were recaptured.

The eleventh floor was the Magister's hall, complete with a courtroom and separated dormitories of its own. This type of floor was in every Coven House on the off chance that something happened to the High Coven in Salem, the Magisters could travel to any other Coven House around the world and be prepared on short notice.

Above them, was the Hall of Mirrors, where portals that had been seized over the centuries were hung. Remi was pretty sure that none of them were still active, but just knowing they were all there in a single area of the house sometimes gave him the creeps if he let himself dwell on the thought for too long at a time.

The thirteenth and topmost floor in the entire house was the archives, which is where the entire history of Warlocks was said to be contained.

Remi and Finn walked under the crystal chandelier that hung in the center of the first-floor ceiling, just above the grand oak staircase. They made their way to the second-floor landing and the Arbiter's office. It was situated to the right of the main stairs, with another set across the landing that spiraled upwards and onto the higher floors.

The pair entered without knocking, knowing that Sylvia was expecting them. Just as anticipated, the Arbiter was sitting at her desk. She was huddled over several stacks of papers and seemed to be flipping through them rapidly as if she had recently lost something important.

She looked up at the sound of the door closing behind them. "Good," she said. "I was wondering when you would get here."

"Sorry," Remi shrugged. "Late night last night." He thought it best not to let the Arbiter know he had been to another of the Fae Courts without Coven approval. Finn seemed to pick up on this specific omission and remained silent, sipping his coffee from the tumbler Remi had brought for him when he had picked him up.

"I was starting to think you had fallen back asleep after I got off the phone with you earlier," Sylvia said, rising from her seat and smoothing her skirt before moving around the front of her desk.

"As tempting as it was," Remi admitted, "I had to go grab him before I came in."

As Finn made to object, Sylvia reached onto the top of the stack and pulled off two sealed envelopes, handing them to Remi. The first had an image of a woman with tiny, crescent-shaped wings holding a full moon with her right hand and a wand with the other. He had seen the emblem only once before and knew that the red wax was the standard seal of the High Coven.

The other had a similar, although slightly less ornate seal of two wands crossing themselves over an outline of the state of Mississippi in blue wax that he knew came from somewhere within this Coven House. He took the one from the Oxford Coven and broke the wax, pulling out a neatly folded piece of parchment, skimming over the contents of the letter.

"Well, that was faster than I was expecting," he said, looking up. "Are there any links to that brand of magic that we know of?"

"As of now," Sylvia replied with a grim expression, "no. But they will continue looking into it."

"Looking into what?" Finn asked, seeming a bit confused.

"A case I had to go investigate yesterday," Remi explained. "I brought back a piece of evidence for the Coven to Trace, but it's coming up inconclusive with anything that we have on file." He turned to Sylvia then, "Have they contacted any of the other Houses? Maybe they have a rogue in their records that matches up with this guy?"

The Arbiter shook her head, replying, "They've called all of the Houses in the immediately surrounding states. None of them have anything that we can use."

"Well, let me know if they do come up with anything," Remi said, turning to leave.

"What about the other letter?" Finn asked, obviously curious about why he would have an envelope addressed directly to him from the High Coven.

Remi stopped in his tracks and broke the wax seal of the second envelope, skimming over the contents of the parchment just as he had the previous.

"An hour?" he asked disbelievingly. "What am I supposed to do with an hour?"

"What do you have to do with an hour?" Finn asked, still puzzled.

"I know," Sylvia pursed her lips together. "It's the best I could manage under such short notice, Caswell. To be completely honest, they didn't even want to grant you that much time."

"Did you tell them-" Remi began, but the Arbiter cut him off.

"Yes," she said with a nod. "I told them everything I could without mentioning you venturing into a Fae Court by yourself with no prior sanction from the Coven."

Remi felt his cheeks getting hot and was not sure if it was anger or embarrassment rising to the top. It felt as if he were being scolded by a mother for something he had no control over.

"Well," he thought, weighing his options aloud. "What if I can't find anything useful in an hour?"

"Then we're out of luck and have to backpedal right back to square one," Sylvia crossed her arms and let out a heavy sigh.

Remi gave an exasperated sigh of his own and turned to Finn, "I hope you can read faster than you drink. We're going into the archives."

"We'll see," the younger Warlock laughed.

"No," Sylvia said shortly. "*We* won't be finding anything. Read further. That paper grants you access, Caswell; you, *alone*."

Remi groaned as he reread the letter, in greater detail this time, until he saw the line that the Arbiter was referring to.

"You all really hate me, don't you?" he asked, feeling almost defeated before he had even begun. "You all have seriously gotta be shitting me!"

"I know," Sylvia shook her head and threw her hands up in an exasperated fashion, "I tried, Caswell. I really did."

"I'll be back in an hour," he said, accepting that there was nothing more to be done at this point. Then to Finn, he added, "Hold my drink and watch me fail."

Finn laughed and took the cup from Remi's hand as they exited the office.

The archives were located on the topmost floor of the house and after ascending thirteen flights of stairs, Remi found himself cursing the Coven altogether for not having at least one elevator in the entire building.

This is why no one escapes the top floor! he thought to himself. *Their legs are complete jelly by the time they would make it out of this place!*

"You're carrying me back down, kid," he said aloud to Finn. "You have an hour to decide if that will be bride-style or piggy-back."

"What if I don't wait for you to get out of there before I duck back down?" Finn laughed at the idea, clearly enjoying seeing how rapidly Remi was melting in front of him.

"Have you ever been stabbed to death with a spoon, Ashcroft?" Remi glared at the younger Warlock. "Because that's *exactly* how you get stabbed to death with a spoon."

"One," Finn laughed as he spoke, "I can't say that I have. Two, you don't have a spoon."

"That you *know* of," Remi mumbled to himself.

The pair reached the final landing in front of the archives and Remi felt the burn in his calves and hamstrings as he stood still. This was one of the few points in his life where he reflected on his smoking like a freight train as a potentially poor life decision on his part.

"Halt!" a voice seemed to boom throughout the entire house, leaving Remi's ears ringing after. "What business have you here, Proven Ones?"

Remi looked around and saw a hulking figure in black robes standing just beside the entrance to the archives and found himself questioning how he had missed such a towering man before he had spoken. He gave the impression that he had been expecting them, while also making Remi wonder if this new man would let them through. As Remi thought of how best to answer, he could feel himself being watched.

He held up the letter that Sylvia had given him downstairs as if it was a pass, "I have been granted access to enter these halls by the Five Magisters of the High Coven."

Remi spoke with a level of authority contrary to what he felt as a tingling sensation ran its way down his spine.

There was a long pause, followed by a cold laugh, and then, "That is for me to decide. Your High Coven has no more dominion over me or my halls than they have over the Mortals, though I am sure they would love to believe otherwise."

The figure pulled back his hood with gloved hands, revealing a bald head and the burly neck of someone that could easily snap the two Warlocks in half with brute force if he chose to do so on a whim.

Remi saw that the man wore a silver necklace with a pair of two serpents biting each other's tails, with a blood-red ruby pendant fitted into their center. His eyes were milky-white and shining, making Remi wonder if he was blind even as they scoured over him, seemingly searching for something within his very soul.

"You seek knowledge, Proven One," the man spoke before Remi had even formed the thought to ask. Remi noticed quickly that although he had heard the voice, that the man's lips had not moved.

"To be honest," Remi began carefully, "I'm not sure what it is that I seek."

The corners of the man's lips turned upward, but remained shut as he replied, "If you do not know, then why do you seek entrance into my Halls?"

"You keep saying 'your halls'," Finn noted, confirming that Remi was not the only one hearing the man's voice in his head. "These are the Coven's archives. Are you even a Warlock?"

As Finn asked, Remi noticed that though the man's eyes held the same iridescent quality as those of a Warlock, there was something inherently different about them that he could not quite place.

"I am the one who will ask the questions, young Ashcroft," the man's voice and expression were completely stone, making Remi immediately hopeful that Finn would not push the boundaries.

"I didn't mean any offense," the younger Warlock offered quickly and Remi was relieved to see that the robed man's expression seemed to ease, even if only slightly.

"I am Pendragon," the man informed them. "I am beyond your understanding. I am both the Guardian of these accords and the Halls themselves. I am as much one of your kind as I am greater. I am both a prisoner of time and free from its callous bindings. I do not owe any answers to your Coven, yet I am all of them at once. We are many and we are one."

Pendragon finished his self-introduction and Remi felt both queasy and calm, not knowing which of the two he should pay attention to. "I am Pendragon," he repeated. "State your claim, Proven One."

Remi was a ball of nerves at this point, not wanting to anger the Guardian of the Archives, but not knowing what to say at the same time.

"I want answers," he said finally, in a tone that managed to be much more reserved than what he felt. "If that means venturing into your halls to find them, then so be it."

He watched as Pendragon gave him an icy smile, "Be careful of what you wish for, Caswell of the Witch's Guard."

There was a sound like shattering glass behind the man and Remi noted that the iridescence of the doors had dissipated in that same moment.

"Watch the time, Proven One," the Guardian said, almost like a warning. "It gets away far too easily. We would not want you to be bound inside like so many of those before."

Remi felt his stomach knot itself together almost instinctively, but he simply nodded in understanding before making his way to the doors that would lead him into the archives.

As soon as he had crossed the threshold, Remi heard the doors close behind him with an authoritative thud. He found himself immediately being plunged into an overwhelming bank of shadows that was so thick that he could not even make out his hand when placed in front of his face. It was far too dark for Remi to see anything, so he pulled out his phone to use it as a light. This would serve little purpose, as the screen seemed to become taken over by the dark even as he tried to open the flashlight app.

So much for that, he thought to himself, tucking the thing back in his pocket.

Remi tried to push down the cluster of nerves that had formed in the back of his throat and found himself struggling for the Latin word for 'light'. It seemed that even his thoughts had been overtaken by this sort of magical fog that permeated throughout the room.

I guess I'll just spend my entire hour in this one spot, he thought to himself with a harsh chuckle.

Remi closed his eyes and took a deep breath, calming and centering himself. This simple act seemed to help him push through it and he muttered, "*Lux*."

Instantly, pedestal torches roared to life in bright, blue-white flames and Remi felt himself jerk back instinctively, surprised by the effect his incantation had caused.

"Not quite what I intended," he mused aloud to himself. His gaze darted around the room as far as he could see and Remi was impressed by the grandeur he now found himself in. "But I'll take it."

There were shelves upon shelves of books, large and small, that towered above him in every direction like skyscrapers. Even the pillars that held up the ceiling, which he could not even see at this level, had shelves wrapped around them from the floor and going up. Remi found himself wishing he had the ability to freeze time just to sit in this room and flip through each and every one of them.

He knew, however, that there was a task at hand that he only had an hour to complete. On top of that, he did not want to test Pendragon's warning of being trapped in here.

There was a circular desk only a few feet ahead of him, where all of the shelves seemed to meet in the center of the room. Remi hastily made his way toward it, hoping to find something there that might guide him in his search.

When he had reached it, Remi found that there was nothing else on the desk but a small clock and some hastily scrawled notes. Remi wondered how long these had been here and then shuddered at the thought that the owner of them had not made it back out. He glanced at the face of the clock and saw that it was somehow still ticking.

He briefly wondered if this was some sort of enchanted clock or if it had simply been left there recently. Remi did know that the archives had several entrance points throughout the various Coven Houses and pondered if someone else might have been in this area just before him.

The hands told him that it was now seventeen minutes past ten. If he only gave himself forty-five minutes to look, Remi figured that would give him plenty enough time to make his way back to the desk and find his way out of the archives. Then he had an idea!

Remi held out his hand and said, "*Filum.*"

Instantaneously, a thin, golden thread materialized in the center of his outstretched palm. Remi searched for one end of it and once he had found it, he tied it to an outcropping sliver of wood at the edge of the desk.

Holding the line loosely so that it could unfurl itself, he picked up the clock and started to walk toward one of the shelves immediately to his right. Remi did not know exactly what he might be looking for, but as he trailed along the shelves, he scoured the titles and hoping that something would jump out at him.

After a few moments of skimming over the book spines, Remi had resolved himself to head back toward the desk and try a different section when he heard a skittering behind him. He laughed at the thought that even such a heavily Glamoured place might have a problem with mice when he heard something else that sent shivers through him.

There was a second sound of something moving swiftly across the floor, only this time it was accompanied by a laugh. For him, this wasn't just any laugh and he wondered if perhaps the Glamours might be playing tricks on him somehow. Remi had heard it several times before in his life and even in his dreams and knew that he must be hallucinating it now, even as it echoed throughout the towering shelves around him.

"Who's there?" he called out, but there was no response. Without thinking about it, he tightened his grip on the clock and the magical rope and began heading in the direction he had last heard the disembodied laughter. As he moved forward, he would hear the scuttling sounds every so often and turn himself in that direction. He silently cursed himself as he went along through and in between the shelves, because what if this was some sort of monster that the archives had as a defense mechanism. Granted, he had never heard of anything like this, but there was always that possibility and he should know that by now as a member of the Witch's Guard.

But what if, he wondered against himself. This seemed to be just enough reason for him to keep trekking along to find out what had made that sound.

Remi had been going for what felt like a few minutes with no sound and had resolved to follow the thread back in the direction he had come from when he heard the sound and the laugh a third time. Suddenly he was running that way before he knew what he was doing. He could hear the gears inside the clock rattling in one hand while the string trailed loosely behind him in the other.

As he sprinted, he could feel the whoosh of air where the shelves broke apart and branched into others. He did not care about his initial purpose anymore. There was something else in here with him and he had to see what it was for himself. Remi listened carefully for the source of the laugh, turning to follow in whatever direction the thing had moved, not knowing what would be waiting for him when he found it. The thing seemed to be playing with him at this point.

Remi knew who the voice belonged to, but he fought the idea of it back as the very notion of this being that person was impossible. He wondered briefly if there wasn't something or someone in here messing with him. Maybe it was a spirit that had become trapped and now used people's memories against them. Perhaps it was the archives themselves making sure that no one got out once they entered. He questioned if the High Coven knew this and that's why they were so selective of who they granted access to, but he imagined there was another reason behind that.

Remi's mind was racing and he was becoming increasingly fed up with this game of cat-and-mouse that this invisible being seemed to be playing with him.

"Where the hell are you?" he paused his search long enough to call out. He heard his voice echo around a few times in the shelves surrounding him, but otherwise, there was no response.

As Remi was resolved to turn back and follow the thread, there was a loud thud, followed by the voice. This time, it was calling his name. Every hair on Remi's body stood on end as if charged by the same sort of static that came clung to the air when a Warlock used magic. He stood there, motionless as the countless emotions washed over him.

"Remi," the voice was barely above a whisper, but he heard it just as clear as if it were yelling out to him. It repeated and Remi could tell that it was close. He listened again and determined that it must be on the opposite side of the shelf to his left. He doubled back, having seen a gap only a few feet behind him as he had been chasing the voice.

Remi moved now with a speed that even he had not known he possessed. His lungs were on fire, but he did not care about that right now. He needed to find out who or what the voice belonged to before he could focus on anything else.

He rounded the corner and his jaw immediately hit the floor in shock. Remi found himself at a complete loss for words, unsure of exactly what he was looking at.

There was a solid, dark mass standing only a few feet ahead of him in between the dimly lit shelves. He looked down and saw that there was a large book lying open on the floor. He assumed this falling tome was what had caused the thud he'd heard as the thing in front of him seemed to have no distinct features to boast. As Remi neared the mass, careful not to move too fast and alert the creature, it rounded on him. As it did this, Remi watched the thing change gradually from an amorphous blob into what resembled a woman's figure.

The being moved closer toward him and Remi could see now that it seemed to be comprised almost entirely of stars. It was as if he was looking through a telescope with a human-shaped shutter capped onto its end. Remi felt a chill forming deep inside of him, starting with his bones until it filled him completely. He stared at the thing, not fully knowing how to process this.

This was nowhere in the work manual, he thought to himself. He wished there actually *had* been some sort of hand guide that could tell him what to do in this situation. *Is it some sort of undiscovered Fae?* he wondered, as that seemed like it would be the most logical explanation for this primordial deity that stood before him.

As the being moved closer, he could see his breath coming out in tiny puffs just in front of his face and noticed how the temperature had suddenly taken a drastic plummet between this shelf and the last. He was utterly perplexed by just what he was looking at.

Sure, he had been unsure of exactly what he had been expecting to see, but even he knew that this had not been anywhere on that list of possibilities. The thing inched ever closer toward him, and he felt himself faced the complete deterioration of a fight or flight plan. Remi could not decide if he should run in the direction he had come in an effort to preserve himself, or stand there and cast at the mysterious creature until it was no more.

Before Remi had the chance to make up his mind, the being was upon him, lifting its arm.

"Remi," her voice sounded sad this time. As the galaxy-comprised woman cupped his face with her hand, Remi felt all warmth instantly flee his body.

Remi felt a spark as it made contact with his skin, then he watched in abject horror as horizontal slits formed in her face and opened to take him in. He struggled to catch his breath, which had left him, and fight back the tears that were stinging against the backs of his eyes. Suddenly, it was his own blue moonstone gaze that had been mirrored back at him, shimmering even brighter than the nebulas that could be seen on the rest of her.

The spectre wiped away the single drop of liquid betrayal that had escaped down his cheek and said his name one last, sad time. Then just as suddenly as she had materialized before him, she was engulfed in a light so bright that even with his eyes closed, Remi could feel.

When he reopened them, his vision had gone spotty. He felt like he had just witnessed the death of a star. He leapt to his feet and searched the narrow passage between the bookshelves desperately for any sign of the being, though he knew he would not find any such thing. The woman was gone now, leaving Remi to collapse on the floor with his back pressed to one of the beams separating the different shelves.

The tears came openly now, landing on the stone floor and brushing away the dust that had accumulated from centuries of other Warlocks before him. He found himself tossing aside the thread and clock he had managed to hold up until this point as his head reeled. Remi's mind was suddenly teeming with unanswered questions and conflicted emotions.

"Every time," Remi laughed bitterly, staring at the cold ground beneath him. He focused on the marks his tears had left in the dirt and punched out at the stones, just wanting to feel something that he knew he could wrap his head around.

Pain, he muttered to himself as the impact sent shockwaves up through his arm to his brain.

Remi could feel time slipping away from him, but could not bring himself to do anything about it for a few minutes after such a trying experience. He felt shaken and wondered why she had appeared to him like this after all these years. Surely, she had some sort of plan other than effectively rattling him.

I doubt she found me just to help me sift through old tomes.

Finally, after what felt like enough time, Remi forced himself to his feet. He walked over and knelt down over the book that had been lying open a few feet away. He attempted to pick it up but found that it was too heavy to even budge. He placed his hand on the cover and focused his energy, "*Responso gravitas.*"

He lifted the now-weightless volume with ease this time and muttered, "*Denseo.*"

The thing instantly became smaller, shrinking until it was roughly the size of his phone. He hastily tucked it inside his jeans pocket, moving to retrieve the clock and thread only to find that neither was where he had left them. Remi felt his veins turn to ice as the panic set in.

Did they disappear when she did? he thought to himself. He remembered the static charge he had felt when her hand had come into contact with his skin and shuddered. *Did she undo my spell?*

Remi reached into his pocket only to find, with a mounting feeling of horror, that his phone had disappeared as well.

"No!" he shouted at himself, almost as if to keep his terror in check. "I will *not* be trapped here!"

He thought frantically for something that would get him out of here without having to blast down the walls and risk it being ricocheted from the Glamours. Then he had it, he shouted, "*Volantes Oculum!*"

He had a brief glimpse of the spiralling shelves as if he was looking down on them from somewhere above, before being snapped back into his own head.

Remi ran now, knowing he had only moments before he found himself locked somewhere in-between the untouched pages.

"You look like you saw a ghost!" Finn had been sitting on the steps just before the landing.

Now, he jumped up when he saw Remi, drenched in sweat and doubled over, wheezing from the unexpected jog he had just completed. He tried to catch his breath as the doors to the archives closed themselves behind him with a grim finality that could be heard even through the ringing in his ears.

Remi felt the static charge in the air as the Glamour was put back into place and choked back bile, not wanting to give whoever might be watching the satisfaction of seeing him heave on the floor.

"You found what you were searching for, Warlock?" Pendragon's voice behind him was cold. There was also a sly edge to it that gave Remi the impression that the Guardian of the Archives knew exactly what had just transpired, despite his current incapacity to form a coherent thought.

"And then some," Remi answered simply, hearing an edge in his own voice that he had not anticipated.

Pendragon's blank, white eyes flashed briefly and Remi was sure the Guardian was about to send him into whatever oblivion he had just narrowly escaped. Then Remi watched as the corners of his mouth turned upward into a grimace of a smile.

Remi and Finn exchanged brief glances of concern before turning away. The younger Warlock draped Remi's arm over the back of his neck while tucking his own arm around the other's waist. Both descended the stairs in an awkward, but hasty manner as Pendragon's harsh laughter echoed through their minds for the first few flights down.

IX

After Remi and Finn had reached the bottom of the stairs, Sylvia had been waiting for them just outside her office. She had taken one look at Remi and the way he was being held up by Finn and ordered both of them to take the rest of the day off, saying that she did not want to see either of them until lunch the next day.

It was still midday by the time they had left the Coven House. Traffic was backed up all along the streets of Oxford as incoming students and their families attempted to make their way around. Remi was almost positive that there was a wreck somewhere further up. Since they were just coming to a bend in the road, there was no way to be sure of this, however.

"I wish they would just go ahead and make it mandatory that these kids take the buses until they learn how traffic is supposed to flow all around town," Remi said.

He had let Finn drive after they had left the Coven House and instantly curled himself into a ball in the passenger seat. He still had an overwhelming feeling that he might heave out the window at any given moment. He rolled the window down to let some fresh air in and sparked a cigarette with a weak snap of his fingers.

"What happened in there?" Finn asked finally, having avoided pressing him during their entire journey down and out of the house. "You look like someone punched you in the stomach with a sledgehammer."

"Didn't they?" Remi chuckled coolly, not wanting to share his experience with anyone else just yet. He looked distantly out the window as he took another drag of his cigarette. "Anyway, it doesn't matter. I just need some food in my stomach and I'll be fine."

"Chicken soup?" Finn suggested. "Do you want me to stop at a store and pick some up once we get moving?"

"No," Remi made a disgusted face. "I meant sushi. If I call an order in now, it'll be ready for pick-up by the time these godforsaken people get out of the way."

Finn laughed as if this was the most absurd thing he had ever heard, but made no other outward objection.

"Just drive straight until I tell you to pull over," Remi directed as he pulled up the number on his phone.

The two of them got back to Remi's house after about thirty minutes of bumper-to-bumper traffic. Remi had ended up getting sick out the window, much to the honking dismay of the cars behind them. It had relieved some of the pressure that had been building inside him and he had felt fine afterward.

"Is it always like that?" Finn asked, placing the bags on the counter in the kitchen.

"No," Remi shook his head. "But remember how Vesna was talking about orientation week at Ole Miss?" Finn nodded, an expression of vague recollection across his face. "*That* is what she was talking about."

"And it's worse on game weekends?" the younger Warlock asked, almost disbelievingly, to which Remi snorted.

"Stick around, kid," he laughed. "You'll see why I take off every Grove weekend and keep my happy ass locked up in this house." Remi turned and opened the fridge, leaning in and calling back over his shoulder, "What do you want to drink?"

"Surprise me," Finn said, adding, "Nothing with alcohol."

Remi laughed and grabbed two cans of soda, tossing one to the other man.

"So, what did you get?" Finn pulled up a chair while Remi pushed himself onto the counter and crossed his legs, placing his drink down beside him.

"You were there when I ordered," Remi gave him a confused look. Somehow, his phone had made its way back into his Jeep before they had even left the Coven House.

"I meant from the archives," the younger clarified, to which Remi gave a nod of recognition

"Oh, yeah!" Remi exclaimed, feeling only slightly foolish for having forgotten so easily. "This."

He reached into his pocket and pulled out the book that he had charmed to fit inside the palm of his hand, placing it onto the counter between them. Finn stared down at it with a furrowed brow.

"You managed to get access into *the* archives and all you came out with was a pamphlet?" he asked, clearly confused as to what made this thing so special. He glanced at Remi as if he had gone completely mental. "Are you sure nothing happened up there?"

"It was roughly the size of Connecticut when I found it, okay?" Remi frowned, waving the latter comment away. "I just, for some odd reason, didn't think that would fit into my pants without a little Vaseline. Call me crazy."

He leapt from the counter then and grabbed the book, taking it into the dining room where he put it on the table. The table creaked and Remi, remembering how old it was, thought better of this. He took the book a second time and moved into the living room, setting it on the floor and moving the coffee table to the side with his leg.

"What are you doing?" Finn came around the corner, staring from the book to Remi and back.

"*Dissuo*," Remi spoke, making a sweeping motion in the air just above the book. The two watched as the volume gradually expanded and became heavier, Remi's previous charms having been undone.

"Looks like we're eating in here, then?" Finn asked.

Remi stared down at the dusty tome, wiping the cover with his foot so that his sock became covered with the grime that had been obscuring the title.

"'*The Complete and Unabridged History of the Coven*'," he read aloud, feeling the words escape his lips almost like an incantation that had been charged with some sort of dormant power.

"Oh, good!" Finn said from the kitchen with mock enthusiasm. "Just what I've always hated; history." He rounded the corner, carrying the boxes of takeout and drinks into the living room and setting them on the coffee table.

"Well," Remi said, flipping through the first few pages. "*Unabridged* explains why it was so heavy. I remember hearing about these kinds of books that are specifically charmed to update themselves on particular subjects. I wonder if this is one of those?"

He reached toward the coffee table and pulled out a hidden drawer, taking out two stenography pads and pens. He handed one to Finn and said, "Hope you didn't have anywhere to be tonight?"

"I'll cancel my dates," the younger Warlock laughed.

"We've been at this for hours, man," Finn yawned from his sprawled position on the floor. Remi peeled his gaze away from the book in front of him, rubbing the backs of his hands across his eyelids. He glanced up at the clock to see that Finn was right. Indeed, they had been working at piecing this puzzle together since sometime just after lunch and it was almost midnight now and they were seemingly nowhere closer to being done.

They had finished all of the food, downed several sodas and pots of coffee, and smoked through at least a pack and a half of cigarettes each. Remi had the smallest inkling that they had not even scratched the surface of what they might be looking for. He started to wonder if maybe they were simply overlooking some important detail, or if he had grabbed the wrong book in his shaken state.

"Maybe it's time for a break?" Remi stretched from where he sat on the floor, hearing every bone in his back crackle with the motion. He flipped the ear of the page down to serve as a marker and slowly rose to his feet, his legs weak and tingling from such an extended period in a crossed position.

He walked over to the window by the front door and opened it in the hope that some of the smoky air would flow outside. He flipped the switch to turn the fan on and made his way to the kitchen to repeat the process with the windows on that side of the house.

Remi checked the time on his phone again and found himself in a mixed state of fury and exasperation. They had spent most of the day pouring over the pages of the tome and still somehow had nothing to show for it.

"What do you want on your pizza?" he asked as Finn rounded the corner. The younger Warlock shot him a quizzical look.

"You're hungry?" Finn asked with a raised brow. "We *just* ate!"

"Nine hours ago, kid!" Remi laughed, lighting another cigarette, more out of habit than the desire to smoke.

"It was not nine hours," Finn said, a bit disbelievingly just as his stomach growled. "Everything," he corrected, laughing at himself.

"Cool, cool," Remi said, stepping out onto the back patio. "Call your aunt."

"Why?" Finn asked. "We haven't found anything important."

"To tell her that," Remi replied. "Tell her that we haven't found anything in this book, but that we're working on it. Just keep her updated so she's not on my ass in the morning, would you?"

"Right," Finn said, grabbing his phone from the counter and heading into the living room to make the call.

Remi turned back to stare up at the stars as he placed the order, finishing his first cigarette and lighting another with the cherry. When the call was over and he had been given the arrival time, he shifted his gaze to the moon. Finn came out and lit up his own cigarette.

The pair of them said nothing for a while, before Finn finally asked, "Isn't it strange living so close to so many Mortals?"

"What do you mean?" Remi asked, having never really thought about it.

"I guess it wouldn't be here," Finn said, more to himself than Remi. The younger Warlock seemed almost as if he was searching for the correct words to use. "It's just... Back home, we're all kind of sectioned off into districts. I don't know if that's the city planning or if it's just personal prejudice between all the different races down there."

"What do you mean?" Remi asked, having not been old enough to notice anything like this when he had been to New Orleans himself. "I'm not sure I'm following."

"Well, I mean," Finn seemed to wrack his brain for the words to explain. "You've got your poor Mortals in the Ninth Ward and your rich Mortals in the French Quarter. Then you've got the Warehouse District where most of the Vampires hang out. The Lycans usually end up in Esplanade and the Fae are kind of all over, depending on which Court they're a part of."

The younger Warlock seemed to think on this for a few moments before adding, "The Warlocks usually just stick to the Academy in Gentilly or the Coven House in Holy Cross."

"It's just all very deliberately sectioned off amongst all the races," he went on with his explanation. "While here, it's more of a melting pot where everyone kind of interacts with each other. It might not always be in a positive way, but it's more common here. Maybe just because it's a college town, though."

Finn paused here, as if trying to not lose his train of thought.

"During the day," he said in closing, "everyone pretty much plays together all nice-like, but when the lights go down or something important is on the table, it gets pretty cut-throat around there. It's just not like that here. I was just wondering if you had noticed, but I guess you wouldn't have if you've never been anywhere else."

Remi nodded as slowly, Finn's ramblings started to piece together enough for him to get the gist of what the younger Warlock was saying. He shrugged and lit another cigarette before answering.

"It's still sectioned off here," Remi replied. "It's just less noticeable to an outsider, like yourself, who's only here for a visit. Which might be, like you said, because it's such a popular college town. Don't get me wrong, there are still shitty people everywhere you go. But here, it's more of a monetary thing. Money talks, and if you've got that in this town, you're all the better for it."

Remi inhaled deeply before continuing, almost as if using the cigarette as philosophical punctuation on his words.

"The thing about the Mortals here," he continued his explanation, "is that they're generally too vain to notice anything that doesn't immediately concern them in some sort of way. You'd be hard-pressed to find a Mortal in this town that gives two shits about anything you do, as long as you don't bring Ole Miss into it. And if you do manage to find one that doesn't fit that description to a T, nine times out of ten, they're only lying to save face in a public setting."

Almost as if to reiterate his point, over the fence, his neighbor called out a loud 'Hotty Toddy!' at the mention of the Mortal university. This was followed by a drunken whoop and the chanting of the college's battle anthem. Finn jumped slightly and Remi laughed.

"Like that, I mean," Remi paused to inhale and gather his thoughts. "Here, the Mortals' main concern is the students and the college. As long as you don't mess with either of those things, it doesn't matter who you are, they generally don't mess with you. Their laws govern them, our Covenant governs us. It's a mutually peaceful cohabitation. I don't really know how else to describe it."

"Live and let live?" Finn suggested, to which Remi nodded. "I guess that would make sense. Seems like it works fine so far." He flicked his cigarette out and Remi followed suit, both of them heading back inside.

Remi checked the clock on his phone, announcing, "Fifteen minutes to kill. What should we do, kid?"

"I guess we could knock out a few more pages?" Finn offered. He made his way into the living room and Remi watched as a look of confusion spread slowly across his face. Remi rounded the corner to follow his gaze, which had landed on the book that was still open on the floor between the couch and the coffee table.

"Did you change the page when you called your aunt?" he asked and Finn shook his head.

Remi glanced over to the window and could see that the wind outside was blowing the curtains up. He looked back at the book and could see that the wind seemed to be trying to blow to the next page. There seemed to be some sort of invisible force holding it in place for some unknown reason, which he found this strange. He had removed the only two charms he had placed on the book earlier before they had even started taking notes.

From where he stood just behind Finn, Remi could see that the swirling script at the top of the page read *'The High Coven: How Seven Became Five'*.

Remi quickly pushed past Finn and crossed the room to close the window. He grabbed his pen and pad before resuming his position in front of the open volume.

"You ready to take some notes?" he asked and Finn gave a disjointed nod before joining him on the floor.

Remi turned the page and began reading, pausing on the first line.

"What is it?" Finn asked, poised to jot down any information that might be relevant. "What does it say?"

"Apparently in the weeks following the end of the Salem Wars," Remi spoke as he read the first few lines of text, "when the original High Coven was put into place, there were initially seven members."

"Seven?" Finn gave him a face as if he was sure he had misheard.

"Yeah," Remi reread. "I guess it makes sense. They were just coming out of a war and needed solidarity. Seven is the strongest prime number when it comes to building a Circle. Besides thirteen, but most decent Warlocks avoid having that many in a Circle because of its ties to dark magic."

"So you think it's plausible?" Finn asked, making notes as they talked. "What else does it say?"

"Since there was no time for an official election to be held to decide which Warlocks would serve as the original Magisters, they just selected the strongest living families that hadn't been tried to take the seats," Remi said, skimming over the details.

"How did they select the 'strongest' families, though?" Finn asked. "Or does it say?"

"It doesn't," Remi flipped through the pages, trying to make sure he had not missed a passage somewhere. There was nothing to be found in the script to reveal how these ancestral Warlocks had gone about shaping the future for them all.

Remi thought about it for a moment, neither him nor Finn speaking while they both tried to guess how the original Magisters had made up the High Coven. He could feel something at the corners of his mind, almost as if he had heard something about this during his years at the Academy.

Finally, after a few more minutes of rummaging through the annals of his mind, he stumbled on something and tugged.

"Natural selection!" he shouted, startling Finn in his excitement. The younger Warlock gave him a puzzled expression, to which Remi began explaining, "You know how magical bloodlines work, right?"

"Vaguely," Finn furrowed his brow, seeming lost.

"Well, when Warlocks have kids," Remi stood and took his pad, feeling like a professor as he drew makeshift diagrams as he explained, "the strongest bloodline naturally takes over. The weaker one just sort of fortifies whatever those dominant traits might be. It's why all of this family has a certain eye color, or why that family has a natural affinity for a specific element. I mean outside of marriage into the family, of course."

Remi quickly retrieved his pack and lit a cigarette, inhaling deeply as he went on with his explanation, "It's why certain Warlocks can use a spell and start a raging forest fire, while another Warlock can use the exact same spell and barely light the wick on a candle."

Finn examined Remi's poor artistic skills and nodded along, "I guess that would make sense. Just pick the ones that have been 'fortified' over several generations." He paused to mull it over before squinting.

"But, wait," he said. "How would they know something like that back then? If there hadn't been a High Coven up until, when, 1693? If it wasn't in place up until that point, then how did they know? There wasn't even a registry until, like, 1702. And the colonies weren't as interconnected back then, so how could they be sure that those seven Warlocks were *the* most powerful to serve as Magisters?"

"I guess they were just making a wild guess and hoping for the best,"

Remi suggested. "Or maybe, they figured that it would sort itself out later on down the line?"

"We see how well that worked out," Finn smirked. "But if it started out with seven, then how did we get to a point where it was only five?"

Remi shrugged and began speeding through the lines of the next few pages, not bothering to stop and look at the diagrams that had been presented as they were repetitive to the point of absurdity. Not seeing anything of note, Remi was about to flip back to the original page when something caught his eye. His gaze had shifted, landing upon a section titled '*Downfall and a New Order*'.

He glanced up at Finn to see that his interest had been piqued by this section, as well.

"What's that?" the younger Warlock asked just as someone knocked on the door, making them both jump. Remi looked out the window to see the shining beacon of a pizza delivery car.

"Food's here," he said, absently marking his place and standing.

"Caswell?" the girl read the ticket off to confirm, jumping slightly when she looked up to meet Remi's shimmering blue gaze.

"That's me," he answered in his deepest Southern drawl. "What?" he flashed a grin. "We've got to eat, too."

"It'll be thirty-four, ninety-five," the girl handed him the ticket to sign. "I just guess I wasn't expecting one of y'all to be in this neighborhood. I thought you guys all lived in that big house on the edge of town."

"We have the option," Remi admitted, signing the ticket and adding the tip. "But most of the others snore in their sleep. And I'm just not about that communal bathroom life."

The girl laughed somewhat nervously, "Same!" She glanced down at the ticket and back to Remi with wide eyes. "Are you sure?"

Remi nodded, "Have a good night."

"You, too! Thank you!" the girl called back as she practically skipped out to her car.

Remi pulled the boxes inside to a questioning look from Finn, "How much did you give her?"

"What?" Remi shrugged, skirting around the question. "I scared her.

I left her a little extra so they wouldn't blacklist me and deprive me of pizza. Because that would be a tragedy that I am just not prepared to deal with at this point in my life. Never you mind how much that might have been, kid."

Finn cocked a single brow but said nothing more about the subject.

The pair laughed as Remi sat the boxes on the coffee table. He opened the topmost one and the steam billowed up directly into his face, along with the aroma of all that had been melted into the cheese. He grabbed a slice and slid back on the carpet to continue his perusal of the volume at his hip. He quickly found his place and went back to reading.

"It says that, apparently, there was discord among the original Magisters from the start," he read.

"Oh, yeah?" Finn said around a full mouth. "Like what kind of 'discord'?"

"Chew your food, kid," Remi scolded. "I'm not doing a Heimlich on this carpet. You're just going to have to die if you start choking." Finn stuck out his tongue, which was covered in half-eaten pizza, and Remi turned back to his reading.

"*Apparently,*" he went on, ignoring the younger Warlock's sounds of mock gagging in the background, "none of them could agree on how to go about bringing harmony to the people. One thought that all Warlocks should be militarized, while another thought the peaceful route was the way to go. Then another thought Mortals should be held accountable for the deaths of so many Warlocks and made subservient to us, while another thought that we should all work together as equals. One even thought the two groups should avoid each other at all cost."

"Can't blame them on those mixed feelings, really," Finn mused and Remi nodded his agreement. "But seriously, how could they get anything accomplished if none of them could agree on the simplest of things?"

"Well," Remi read further, "that's where the modern power structure comes into play." Finn switched his slice to his other hand so that he could write as Remi spoke.

"The Magister," Remi went on, "that thought everyone should be ready for war left voluntarily and formed the '*Praecantr Praesidium*', which later came to be known as the Witch's Guard. That original founder is the one that came up with the Proving ritual for anyone else who wanted to join them."

"Nice," Finn said, making a note of it. "They must have been pretty powerful to even think of something like that for new members."

Remi nodded, going on to explain, "The one that thought that Mortals should bend down to our will ended up taking their cue from them and established the '*Magicum Medicus*', which later became the Healers."

"That's a decent point, I guess," Finn noted. "So they thought a strong defense was necessary. That's reasonable."

"Not quite," Remi gave him a grim look. "While the Warlocks that became the first Healers were genuinely dedicated to learning how to repair broken bodies, the former Magister that had formed the coalition was later found to have been doing experiments in secret with the bodies in the morgue. Experiments that have since been outlawed."

"Oh! And so the plot thickens," Finn glanced up from what he had been scribbling. "Does it say what kind of experiments he was doing?"

Remi skimmed over the page but saw nothing overly detailed about what the Warlock had been doing in the morgue. He shook his head and shrugged, grabbing another slice from the box and offering another to Finn.

"Well," Finn said, taking another slice and thinking aloud. "Does it at least say who these original families were? I mean, maybe that's what we're supposed to be finding. Maybe we're supposed to be looking for whoever those original Magisters were, or at least the ones that left. Maybe that's our clue. We already know who serves on the High Coven now, but if your natural selection theory is right, then the High Coven could have changed hands several times over by now. Maybe we're supposed to find out who was there first and try to locate those families?"

"Yeah," Remi spoke as he flipped through the tome of magical history, searching for names. "But how would that help us now? This was over 200 years ago!"

"Look," Finn said, his tone suddenly serious. "You saw the same thing I did when we came back in. Someone or something wanted us to see this specific chapter of that book for whatever reason. Now, I don't know what, exactly, you saw in those archives, but clearly, someone is trying to guide you in a certain direction. This might not be pertinent to this particular investigation, but it's definitely some kind of lead. And that means it's definitely something that we need to check out."

Remi was genuinely impressed with the younger Warlock now.

"And here I was thinking you were just some rookie who was still wet behind the ears," he jested, giving Finn a look of approval, which the other shrugged off dismissively.

Then Remi found it; a hexagram with two circles drawn around it. There were glyphs and symbols all over the page, both inside the circles and in the corners of the page itself. Inside the circles, at each point of the star, were small colored dots. Out to the side, copies of the dots had been placed into a list with names scrawled out beside each of them in a beautiful, swirling script.

"This is it!" he shouted excitedly at Finn, who had leapt from his seat on the loveseat to join Remi on the carpet in front of the large book to see for himself.

"Ashcroft," Finn read his own last name, next to a dark green dot that was clearly meant to match his emerald eyes.

Remi looked over the list of Magisters' names as Finn copied the list in his notes. Baylin was next to a dark blue dot and Remi imagined the glimmering sapphires of a faceless Warlock.

Wrenn was an amethyst; Buckingham were rubies. Henderson was peridot, which reminded Remi that this had been Sylvia's maiden name. Then he saw something that surprised him and made him chuckle.

Below the first five names was the surname 'Caswell' in the same scrawling ink. Directly out to the left of it, where there had been a color to match the others, was a silver crescent moon; to the right was what looked like a downturned sword.

"I guess the Caswell eyes would have been kind of difficult to find a color for back then," Finn mused aloud. "But does *that* mean what I think it means?" He indicated the symbol of the sword beside the name.

"Maybe?" Remi was just as clueless as the other. Neither was entirely sure whether to accept or deny this potential legacy with what they had just read about the original High Coven.

"I always thought you had a penal code sort of look about you," Finn joked, but Remi was too preoccupied with his own thoughts to notice or retort.

He was staring at the line beneath his own last name.

Where there should have been a final surname to tie the story altogether, there was only a charred mark. It was as if someone had purposely tried to burn the very memory of the name from history completely. He wondered briefly if it had been another Warlock or the book itself trying to cleanse its own timeline.

To the right was a staff entwined with two serpents that Remi knew to be a caduceus, universally meant to represent schools of medicine even in Magickal society. To the left of the scorched parchment, as he had expected, was a golden orb staring up at him, just as mockingly as the amber Warlock's eyes it was meant to represent.

"At least we have something to go on," Finn tried to sound optimistic, but Remi suddenly felt too heavy to acknowledge the positive sentiment.

"That's not promising," he said in a hollow voice that didn't even sound like his own.

As Remi stared down at the page, he came to the grim realization. The hollow feeling in the pit of his stomach that made him imagine that his intestines were in tangles, was something he would have to get used to until this case was closed.

Rather than driving Finn back to his hotel room or calling him a cab, Remi had let him take over the spare bedroom upstairs just across from his.

"You can borrow some of my clothes for a shower until we can get you checked out later," he had told the younger Warlock, who had given him a strange look. "What? I need you nearby in case we get a lead in the middle of the night."

When Finn had tried to thank him and offer some form of payment for letting him stay there, Remi had turned it all down. "It's nothing," he had said. "It's just more convenient for both of us like this. That way, we only have to leave from here for whatever, instead of me having to drive halfway across town to pick you up or drop you off."

"Fair enough," Finn had said. "But be warned, I sometimes I walk around in the buff."

"Fair enough," Remi had mimicked. "But be warned, I see any dangly bits, I cut it off. Good luck explaining that one to the Arbiter."

X

The Dark Warlock stood on the sidewalk in front of the house, cloaked in shadows and waiting for his opportunity as the Mortals moved in droves around him, unaware of anything that might have been out of place.

He had never understood their culture, but as he watched them now, he was both mesmerized and baffled by them.

He watched as young Mortals of all genders, shapes, sizes, and colors moved hastily down the street, dressed like they were going to some sort of commoners' ball or another unimportant affair. As he listened to the multiple conversations being had, the Dark Warlock became even more confused by it all. The majority of them seemed to be talking about going to a library.

Why would so many of them get all spiffed up just to go study? he wondered to himself. *Curious creatures, these Mortals.*

The Dark Warlock waited, unmoving for what seemed to him like hours while the bulk of the crowd filed itself down toward their late-night study like the herd of cattle they were, leaving only a few stragglers behind. Now was his chance.

He moved like a shadow under the cover of night. Where the artificial moons of the lantern posts illuminated the path, his Glamoured cloak of darkness kept him concealed. He reached the steps of the building where an intoxicated Mortal of maybe twenty years leaned against one of the great stone pillars for support.

The boy hiccupped and heaved into a nearby bush as the wind picked up.

Just as he regained himself, the wind whipped one of the banners of the house against a window, causing a whiplike crack to echo throughout the nearby area in front of the house. Whether it was coincidence or his intoxication, it was at that moment that the young Mortal locked eyes with the Dark Warlock, causing all remaining pigmentation to drain from his face.

The Dark Warlock smirked to himself, his grip tightening around the hilt of his wand. He would have left the boy alone, but he could not afford to take the chance of being exposed this early in his plan.

He lifted his wand in the boy's direction, secretly basking in the Mortal's fear.

"*Discedo Vita*," he spoke, feeling the static of the spell course through him. In that instant, the boy's eyes glazed over as his spirit was effectively severed from his body.

The husk of him collapsed on the stone of the steps and the Dark Warlock's nostrils flared as he sucked in the remnants of a life left behind.

Before one of the odd, directionless Mortals could notice, the Dark Warlock flicked his wand at the door of the house.

"*Recludo*," he whispered, rotating his wrist as if turning a key. There was a slight click as the door unlatched itself and creaked open for him to enter. The Dark Warlock wasted no time and pushed through the door, making his way upstairs to where the boy slept.

There was no one else in the house at this time of the night as most of them had left with the crowd earlier. For this, the Dark Warlock was silently thankful; more Mortals meant a more senseless waste of life and he saw no need for that on this night.

It took no time for him to ascend the staircase and find the boy's room at the end of the hall. He entered the room and stared down at the sleeping lump of flesh, sickened by the very idea of this mistake of a creature. The entirety of the room smelled like a wet dog as the boy tossed and turned in a feverish state, no doubt dreaming of chasing bones and burying them.

The Dark Warlock gagged silently, choking back his own bile as he watched the sweat dripping from the pores on the boy's ebony skin. He heard a clammer outside as someone discovered the corpse of the Mortal he had left on the steps of the house.

The Dark Warlock wasted no time in uncorking the glass phial, knowing that the finders would be storming the house in no time and waking the sleeping dog in the bed beneath him. He sliced across the boy's throat as he slept, letting the crimson dribble into the tube just as he had with the others. The boy did not even open his eyes as his life force left him and his dreams were effectively ceased.

The Dark Warlock could feel himself becoming suddenly giddy in the moment. Everything was nearly ready for him to complete his plan and bring about a new order to this forsaken world. Now was the final hour, when he could let them see his work.

He had been too careful with the others, hiding the bodies as if in fear and knowing that they would deteriorate within a certain amount of time before they could be found and traced back to him.

This one would be special; this one would be an invitation of sorts.

As the Dark Warlock stared down at the dark-skinned corpse, a thought occurred to him and he knew what else he had to do before the boy's death was noticed.

He tucked the phial in the chest of his robes and muttered the incantation, feeling the rope manifest itself in his free hand.

He had barely managed to cover the boy in his Glamour of shadow just before the door was thrown open by Mortals looking for the culprit responsible for the corpse downstairs.

XI

Remi woke up the next morning to the sound of rain on the roof. He stretched in his bed as he heard thunder rumble somewhere off in the distance, debating to himself whether or not to get up or roll back over and sleep a few more hours. He had always loved sleeping in late on days when it was storming outside, not wanting to get himself caught up in the downpour until he absolutely had to.

He listened upstairs and, upon hearing no sign of Finn being awake and roaming about, decided to roll back over. Remi had only just closed his eyes to doze back off when he felt his phone vibrating somewhere underneath him. He lifted himself to fumble around inside the cushions of the couch before retrieving it and falling back into their welcoming embrace.

The caller ID announced that it was Sylvia Ashcroft. Remi checked the clock at the top of the screen and saw that it was only half-past seven in the morning. He silenced the call and placed his phone on the arm of the couch, rolling back over until the time was a bit more decent.

Two seconds later, his phone was vibrating again. He groaned to himself, figuring that the voicemail would pick it up and the Arbiter would call back later and she did. Two more seconds after the last call had dropped, his phone was vibrating again.

Remi grumbled to himself again and picked up on the third vibration.

"Caswell," Sylvia's voice came through before Remi could speak. "We have a problem on our hands."

"Good morning to you, too, Sylvia," Remi's voice was gravelly and his throat felt scratchy.

"Have you seen the news?" the Arbiter did not waste time on pleasantries, which was unlike her.

"Not really," Remi replied jokingly. "I don't get the greatest reception in my dreams."

"So was I," Sylvia's informed him through what sounded like gritted teeth. Her tone had an edge to it this morning and Remi knew it would serve him better not to test her patience with his usual banter. "Until the Chief of the Oxford Police Department woke me up."

Remi knew immediately that something was seriously wrong. The Mortals generally never interacted with Warlocks, at least not willingly. Even then, it was usually not unless there was no way for them to avoid it.

"Are you there?" Sylvia asked after a moment of silence on his end. "Caswell?"

"Yeah," Remi choked out. "Just trying to wake up." He grunted as he moved to his feet.

Remi flipped on the TV and immediately muted the blaring volume so as not to wake Finn upstairs. "What station should I tune it to?" he asked, bringing his voice to little more than a whisper.

"It's already national," Sylvia's voice was grim and to-the-point.

"Shit," Remi said absentmindedly, not knowing what to brace himself for as he flipped through the channels. Until he landed on one of the big Mortal networks, where it all became immediately clear.

The scene was torn; one part complete and utter chaos, the other seemingly hopeful. There were several small groups of Mortals huddled around in prayer circles across the screen. The image shifted to reveal others breaking into shop windows on the Square and fighting in pits with Mortal officers from both the city and county departments.

The contrast in itself was enough to let Remi know how dire the situation already was, but the next scene had him fighting back nerves and silently thanking the universe that Sylvia had called before he'd had a chance to eat anything.

A bulletin ticked its way slowly across the bottom of the screen while the brand logo for the University of Mississippi flashed in the top right corner opposite the anchor's head, warning that the images to follow were graphic and not suitable for any young viewers.

Remi knew that school had been out for the Mortals for almost a month, but imagined this must be in case there were any younger children home and awake at this hour. Even though it was summer, he knew that some parents were still working and readying their kids to take to daycare programs.

Just as the bulletin had finished making its way across the third time, the scene shifted and became shaky. It was almost like someone was constantly moving the camera to get a better angle.

Remi did not need the woman's commentary to know that this was somewhere on campus. He had been in this area before, but could not quite place it until he saw the James Meredith statue. Remi could barely make out anything else about the statue except the head, due to the mob of Mortals that had swarmed in droves around its base for some reason. Whatever was going on was happening in front of the college's library.

Remi turned the subtitles on and read along as the script began making its way across the screen to block out some of the images and instantly felt his stomach turn itself inside out. As if to punctuate the words currently on-screen, the person behind the camera finally managed to elevate themselves and get a better angle at that very moment. All at once, it was revealed that a body of a man was dangling from the statue. Both had been attached at the neck in a grisly fashion by a doubled noose.

The man looked almost grey and Remi was unsure if it was the overcast weather or something more sinister, but it was obvious to tell that the body was that of a black man. That detail, paired with the fact that James Meredith had been the University of Mississippi's first black student to enroll back in the 60s, had Remi feeling like he had been punched in the stomach with a power drill.

"Sylvia, with all due respect," he managed in a voice that was barely more than a whisper, "we have a lot more than a 'situation' on our hands."

"Get Finn," she said calmly, making Remi wonder how much longer she'd had than him to process the information. "Both of you need to be ready for anything. Get here as soon as possible. Take the back roads, because there's no way you'll get here with traffic as heavy as it is on top of this. It seems like every Mortal in the town is either touring the grounds on campus or rioting in the Square."

"Have they targeted the Coven yet?" he asked, though he was not entirely sure that he wanted to hear the answer to that.

"Just get here," she said in a flat tone that let him know this would be her final word on the subject.

With that, the Arbiter hung up the phone, leaving Remi to feel immediately glad that he had let Finn crash there the night before.

Remi went straight to the kitchen and threw himself into overdrive with his morning rituals. He started the coffee maker, lighting a cigarette as he did so. He then jogged up the stairs, two at a time, heading straight for the spare bedroom where Finn was asleep and blissfully unaware of their current state of affairs.

Remi went in without knocking to see that Finn had kicked off all of the covers and opened the window at some point during the night. There was a small amount of rain that had been blown in and soaked into the carpet. He smiled to himself, almost not wanting to wake the other Warlock but knowing that it must be done.

Remi shook the younger man awake in a light manner, so as not to startle him and risk getting decked. He had done that to someone himself once before and still had yet to hear the end of it. He chuckled to himself, thankful that the comment last night about sleeping in the nude had been an idle threat.

"What is it?" Finn shot up immediately, obviously not expecting to have been woken up. "What's wrong?"

"Calm down, kid," Remi said, suppressing a laugh. "We have to get ready quickly. There's a closet in the bathroom. Get a shower, find something easy for you to move around in. I'll meet you downstairs in about fifteen minutes. I've got the coffee making now."

He turned to leave, then paused in the doorway and glanced back. "Do you happen to have your wand with you?"

Finn said nothing, but nodded, his face an odd mixture of puzzled concern.

"God, you're tiny," Remi laughed aloud, coming downstairs and placing his dueling equipment on the counter. "I don't think I've been able to fit into that since fifth year."

Remi adjusted himself and his clothes so that he could move easily without his jeans chafing and pinching him, just in case he had to run. He then grabbed his leather bracers and strapped them onto his arms, before buckling the holster on his left thigh and tucking his wand into it.

"It's a bit snug," Finn admitted, squatting and leaping a few times to adjust himself. "But that's easier for me to move in than something baggy getting in the way, like everything else up there."

"Did you find your wand?" Remi asked, pouring himself some coffee and splashing it with milk in his usual fashion.

"Yeah," Finn replied, indicating a hilt sticking out over his right shoulder.

"Overhanded," Remi noted, raising a single eyebrow and not taking his eyes off the hilt. "That leaves your body open to attacks, you know."

"Only if I'm slower than the attacker," Finn gave a cocky grin and Remi could not help but let out a small snicker.

"Come on, kid," he said, twisting a lid onto his thermal mug before grabbing his keys and heading out the door.

Remi had to park at the health clinic when they arrived because there was no way he could maneuver his Jeep through the crowd of Mortals that had swarmed outside the Coven House.

There were too many of them standing around for him to count. Some of the officers he knew from working with them on cases before. Remi could see that they were making an effort to disperse the mob with little luck. He imagined that Sylvia had called the Mortal officers shortly after hanging up with him so they could have someone posted outside the Coven grounds before the riots had gotten any worse.

He could tell from here that most of the crowd was made up of civilians, all of which were steadily trying to break through the wrought-iron gate that was situated just between two of the towering oak trees that served as a physical property line to the house.

Remi puffed away on his last cigarette and watched silently as television crews from all of the Mississippi stations pulled over on the sidewalk and began setting up their cameras, covering them with clear tarps so that the now-torrential rain would not affect the machinery.

"If this is us, I'd hate to see what campus and the Square look like right now," Finn mused. Remi had filled him in on the gist of the situation during the ride over, having figured it was best for him to be somewhat prepared for what they might be heading into.

"How good are you at combative spells?" Remi asked, striking up another cigarette out of habit as he watched the scene play out before them. He took a sip of his coffee while staring at the continually gathering Mortals.

"Decent, I guess," Finn replied, tearing his gaze from each of the different camera crews to look over at Remi.

"Defensive? Non-verbal?" Remi asked; Finn nodded to both. "Good. I want you to be ready for anything out there. I don't know how many fights you've been in if any, but I'm here to tell you that these Mortals are vicious. That stuff I told you last night about how they generally didn't bother anyone as long as you left their school and their kids alone? Well, someone has done both of those and we're in the South. This was a race crime and now, they're pissed. And most of them have guns."

He took a deep drag of the cigarette before going on, "I don't want you doing anything that is going to cause any long-term damage. You know that the Covenant strictly forbids that sort of magic unless absolutely necessary, so you only incapacitate them and move on."

"This isn't my first riot with Mortals," Finn pointed out but agreed.

"Let's go," Remi said in a somber tone. He downed the last of his coffee and took the final drag of his cigarette before flicking the butt out the window.

"*Apsque*," the pair said in unison. The air around them charged as invisible bubbles formed over each of their heads to shield them from the downpour.

The two got out of the Jeep and as soon as they shut the doors, the Mortal camera crew that had been standing nearest to them made a beeline straight in their direction.

"Can you tell us what, exactly, is going on here?" the woman thrust her microphone into Remi's face so hard it hit his teeth.

"No comment," he pushed the speaking stick out of his face and spoke directly to the woman. He did not like dealing with Mortals on the best day, especially reporters, but knew he must maintain his composure if they were to have any hope of moving past the throng of people blocking their way.

"How about you, dear?" she ignored him and shoved the microphone into Finn's face, though not as vigorously. "Do you have anything to say about the body found this morning on Ole Miss campus?"

Finn hesitated, shooting Remi a brief glance before parroting, "No comment, ma'am."

They made to move past the woman and heard her tell her cameraman to follow them. This caused Remi to turn on his heel and let his blue moonstone eyes bore into the man.

"If you don't want to replace that camera today, I would suggest that you stay back here where it's safe," he muttered, turning his gritted teeth upwards into a fake smile.

The anchorwoman made to object, but the man with the equipment seemed to have gotten the point and did not pay her any attention.

Remi turned back toward the gate and started walking, Finn following closely behind.

"Do you think they'll listen?" the younger Warlock asked.

"She might not," Remi admitted. "But most of them seemed to have more sense than she did. They should at least stay out of the way for now."

"Hold it!" a staunch, bald Mortal with a thick, grey mustache blocked their path. "Stay back! There's nothing to see here!"

"We work here," Remi informed the man. "Can you tell us what's going on, sir?"

"I didn't ask who you were, son," the man ignored Remi's question. "Y'all ain't got no business here, now git!" Remi felt Finn tense slightly beside him but remained calm.

"This is our Coven, sir," he offered. "The Arbiter is expecting the two of us."

"Well, howdy doo!" the Mortal feigned an exaggerated interest in the comment, before laughing it off. "I don't care if ye got an appointment ta see the Queen o' England fer tea. I said ya ain't gettin' in thur, and I meant it. Now git out o' here!"

Remi could see that the man was trying to get a rise out of either of them, but he kept his cool.

"May we speak to your commanding officer?" he asked, physically biting his tongue after he had spoken so that he had something to focus on.

"I am the only commandin' officer you gone see, boy," the man said and Remi was glad his teeth were holding his tongue, as he had to fight to keep a straight face at the absurdity of this Mortal.

"I'm sorry, sir, but we have a prior engagement. Come on, kid," he said to Finn, moving to get around the man, but finding himself blocked.

"Did I say y'all could move, boy?" the man shouted and Remi could suddenly feel the barrel of a gun at his back. He instantly froze and swallowed against his own mounting fear and agitation, not wanting to give the man a reason to pull the trigger. Finn was looking at both of them, mouth and eyes suddenly wide in a mixture of shock and disbelief.

Remi could hear the feet of the news crews stomping toward them now on the rain-slicked pavement. He shifted his gaze just past Finn to see that several of the Mortals in the crowd had heard the shouts of the man, causing them to turn out of curiosity. Some of those to turn around included most of the other officers, who were staring at their peer in abject horror.

"Sanders!" one of the younger city cops yelled. His eyes were widened and his expression told Remi that he was clearly trying to process what he was seeing. "What in the *hell* are you doing?"

"He's got a weapon!" the Mortal behind Remi lied to save face and he could hear Finn let out a sound of disgust. "I told you to put your hands above your head where I can see 'em!" he shouted at Remi, jabbing the barrel deeper into his back for punctuation.

Remi obliged, while Finn and the Mortals kept their gazes locked on him.

"Sanders!" the other officer repeated. "Put it down!"

"He tried to attack me!" Sanders yelled back a second lie.

"No, he didn't!" Finn shouted and the remainder of the crowd that had not yet turned stopped what they were doing to pay attention now.

"It seems we have a stand-off between one of the protesters who, just moments ago, declined to comment on the state of the situation," Remi heard the same female anchor talking callously in the nearby distance, "and an Officer Sanders of the Oxford Police Department."

"On the ground!" Sanders growled at Remi.

"Look, I don't want any trouble," Remi assured the man behind him. Catching Finn's attention with ease, he mouthed the words *Don't move*. Finn gave a curt nod, so as not to alert the Mortal that was currently threatening Remi.

"I said *on the ground!*" the man repeated, jabbing the gun into Remi's back once more. This opportunity was just what he had wanted.

Remi pushed himself into the barrel slightly to give himself better momentum. In a single motion, he spun in and toward the Mortal while bringing his left arm under the man's in an upward and circular motion. Clamping his own hand tightly to his chest, he simultaneously brought his right elbow down hard on the man's gun arm to lock the wrist holding the weapon to his chest with the full pressure of his forearm so that if the Mortal were to attempt to fire, he would be aiming at himself.

Remi then quickly shot his right arm over Sanders's left shoulder and gripped it, pulling him toward him while kneeing the man in the groin. The man let out a yowl of pain and tried to pull his presently immoveable wrist from Remi's clenched bicep, which loosened his grip on the gun. Remi wrenched the weapon out of the Mortal's hand and pointed it at the man's head.

"Please, don't hurt me!" Sanders pleaded, throwing his hands up in front of him in a defensive stance. Remi could see that his once cocky demeanor had now been replaced by fear. Remi glared and aimed the gun into the empty air and releasing the magazine so that it fell out at his feet, before tossing the cleared weapon onto the pavement to the right of him. "Oh, thank you! Thank you!"

Without another word, Remi reared back his casting arm and punched the Mortal in the temple, instantly knocking him unconscious. He was disgusted enough that he wanted to kick the unconscious man while he was down but refrained as there were too many witnesses. He turned to see that all eyes were still on him, most of their mouths hanging open in what seemed to be disbelief.

"Where did you learn to do that?" Finn whispered, to which Remi glared unintentionally.

"Required Mortal training class from the Academy," he said, much more calmly than he felt after having a loaded gun stabbing him in the back. "Grab the gun," he told the younger Warlock, then to the officers, "We're going to bring his weapon to you all to hold onto until he wakes up!"

The young officer who had been walking toward Sanders before gave a single thumb up in agreement for all of them. They were all still watching him carefully, slack-jawed at what they had just witnessed.

In his peripheral, Remi could see Finn bending down to retrieve the weapon just as the sound of a gunshot tore through the rainy morning.

Remi quickly shot a concerned glance at Finn, who was now holding the discarded gun out in front of him by the back of the barrel where the hammer was so no one would mistakenly think it was him that had fired.

Remi checked the crowd, who were all glancing around to see who had fired the initial shot but not seeing any clear culprit. Then he saw it and his heart skipped a beat. The gates that kept the Coven House's pathway sealed off from the rest of the town were slowly creaking open.

"Someone stop them!" he shouted, but it was too late. Whoever had fired had clearly aimed at the lock on the gate. It was now thrown open and the Mortals were flowing freely into the grounds of the house. The Mortal officers searched him as if for approval, to which Remi shouted, "Go after them!"

"*Posuit en auto*," Finn said and the gun faded away, transporting itself to the Jeep. It only took a second for the weapon to disappear, after which the two Warlocks charged for the gate.

Remi took the lead with Finn remaining close behind. He was almost sure that the news crews were not far behind them. Up ahead, Remi could see the officers running to catch up with the Mortals from the crowd but since they had a head start, he knew that they would not be caught until they reached the entrance courtyard.

It did not take long to reach the front door of the house and even as he ran, Remi could see other Warlocks filing out of the entrance to stand at the top of the stairs. The Arbiter was at the forefront of the Coven group, making him imagine that they had either heard the gunshot that had broken the gate's lock or had been watching it unfold on whichever station of the crews behind them was already broadcasting live.

As the Mortal mob reached the entry pavilion of the Coven House where the gravel path snaked tightly around a stone fountain, they all stopped together as if they were waiting for some sort of signal from someone in their midst. There was yelling and throwing of rocks. Remi knew that still, somewhere in the group, was an active gun.

"No violence unless absolutely necessary," Remi said quietly to the Mortal officers as he and Finn caught up to them. "Nothing lethal, period. But if you see the one with the gun, you take that bastard down at all cost."

The officers did not seem to mind that their orders were being given to them from a Warlock, even if that same individual had knocked their commanding officer unconscious just seconds ago. Most of them nodded in agreement before fanning out among the crowd.

"What do you want me to do?" Finn asked, his emerald gaze darting around and searching for any sign of the Mortal that had broken through the front gate.

"Get to the front," Remi said in a hushed tone. "Same rules apply to you especially. Neither of us is going to want to deal with the High Coven after this." Finn agreed as he spoke. "If you somehow get caught in the crowd, you send up a flare and I'll come to you. Our main priority is protecting the Arbiter and the Coven. Let the Mortals deal with their own people unless you absolutely know there's no way around it."

Finn gave one final, curt nod before pushing his way into the thick of the crowd. Remi kept his eyes on the other Guard for a few seconds until he became lost within the sea of Mortals. He placed his hand on the hilt of his wand and followed suit in another direction, ready to defend himself at any given second.

Outside the gate, Remi had counted what looked less than a hundred Mortals. The crowd he saw now, however, could easily range somewhere in the low thousands. This made him wonder if they had somehow multiplied during the jog toward the house, or if more of them had simply been waiting for the distraction of the earlier gunshot. He pushed these thoughts to the back of his mind as he shoved through them, elbowing his way toward the front and apologizing when he got a rude glance from any of them.

"Please, leave!" Sylvia's voice rang out above them and Remi knew that she had amplified it to be heard over the white noise of so many people speaking at once. "We have no qualms with any of your kind, nor do we wish to!"

The crowd surged angrily, jostling Remi about like the shifting tide of an ocean. The collection of voices deepened to the point that he could only make out a few sentences in his immediate vicinity.

"Our *kind*?" one man spat in disgust. "Like we're less than you damn Shiners?"

"The hell does this *hag* think she is?" another female voice chimed in with the man.

"Y'all know she talmbout us normal folks!" a second man laughed. "Damn Shiner don't know who pays the rent on this here place. Y'all know that's where our taxes is going!"

Remi ignored them, knowing that they were just spewing nonsense at this point.

"Naw!" the first man said in genuine disbelief. "You ain't serious?"

"Like a heart attack!" the man lied. He went on to boast, "I used to work at the courthouse, so I seent where them checks was going!"

Remi tucked his head down, hoping that he could get out of the way before these Mortals noticed his blue moonstone eyes as the man spouted more falsehoods than he cared to count.

"Just like a damn Shiner!" the woman shouted behind him. "Trying to tell us to get out of her yard that *we paid for!*"

"Damn right!" the lying man shouted, having made himself furious with his own tall tales.

The volume increased again, drowning out even those nearby voices as Remi continued to push his way through. Then it dawned on him that while this was, indeed, a race war it didn't seem to be the kind that he had been prepared for. This was followed shortly by the horrifying realization that someone had brought this problem straight to the Coven's front door.

Remi kept shuffling through the Mortals with even greater haste now, his gaze fixed down at their feet and hoping that no one would see his glowing eyes. He had never before been so ashamed and frightened at the same time before.

He had read enough on Southern Mortal history to know what they did to people who were different from them.

With a mob of this size and tensions this high, he found himself not wanting to find out what might happen if it could not be brought under control. There were grunts as Remi pushed through, searching desperately for any sign of weapons and excusing himself when he found any of them impassable. In the back of his mind, he hoped that Finn had at least made it to the front of the crowd by this point.

"Excuse me," Remi said as he reached what felt like the hundredth Mortal in the past few minutes alone as he had been dancing through the individuals.

This man did not move and Remi shifted his gaze up from the feet to see a behemoth of a Mortal, easily three times his size. The man saw his eyes and gave Remi a silent look of disgust, but laboriously stepped to the side.

"Who is you think you pushin', bruh?" a scrawny, black man, no taller than Remi's chest, shouted. He turned and pushed against the silent hulk, who did not even budge. The crowd immediately around them openly guffawed at the ridiculousness of the shorter Mortal.

"Sorry, man," the titan apologized, still moving aside for Remi to pass. "Ain't no room for folks to get by."

"Oh," the smaller of the two yelled up at the other. "Yo ass *gone* be sorry!" Remi felt his heart leap up into his throat as the Mortal pulled a gun and waved it in the larger man's face.

The women who had just laughed at the spectacle began screaming in terror, while the men ducked out of the way behind them. Remi had to give credit to the handful that tried to pull the women out of harm's way.

Suddenly, there was a large space around them all and Remi felt his pulse quicken as adrenaline began pumping through his veins. The bear-like man knocked the other Mortal to the ground in an uncharacteristically fluid motion as quick as lightning, crushing him with the full weight of his body.

There was a shot fired somewhere into the distance and the gun was thrown, landing a few feet from Remi. He lunged for it, his body moving of its own volition now. As he straightened, there were more shots fired, followed by screams coming from every direction within the crowd. Remi could not be sure if it was the officers or more civilians displaying such force at this point.

All immediate gazes were fixed to him as he held onto the weapon the minuscule Mortal man had tried to use, but no one seemed to have the capacity to move. Then a single man shouted, "That's the Shiner from out there! Somebody get him!"

The crowd surged in, mounting on top of him before he could reach for his wand. During this, the gun was pried from his grip. Remi's right arm was quickly pinned behind his back and he felt it snap almost instantly as he was thrown to the ground and someone's knee came down between his shoulders. A single hand knotted itself in his hair, pushing his face down into the gravel. Remi felt the blood trickling down his brow like sweat and tasted its coppery tinge in his mouth.

He tried to break free, but the grip tightened against him and he felt a sharp pain that shot up and through the pinned arm. He heard it crack this time and knew immediately that it had been broken.

Where are the officers? Remi wondered to himself. *Or Finn?*

He heard a gun go off somewhere close-by and instantly felt a stabbing, white-hot pain just below his knee. His vision suddenly became hazy and he knew that he had been hit, whether by a stray bullet or deliberately, he could not be sure in his current position.

Remi found it odd that he was still being held down when he was clearly not capable of shooting anyone.

Then, just as a grim thought occurred to him, the full weight of whoever was holding him down came crashing onto him, pushing him further into the rocks.

Remi's head was suddenly free and he craned his neck over his shoulder to see the large man from earlier lying on top of him now, unmistakably dead. White spots began to dot themselves throughout his vision as Remi realized that he was slowly being crushed by the now-eternally sleeping giant.

Remi somehow managed to worm his hand under the man's stomach, searching for the hilt of his wand and hoping he could reach it before he passed out. He became somewhat fearful that he would not be found until he had already been totally flattened. He felt the pommel with his fingertips just as a shot went off immediately above his head. Remi's ears were ringing as a bullet casing fell to the ground just in front of his face.

His body moved now, purely on impulse, leaving him little time to question if this was due to fear, adrenaline, or a combination of the two.

"*Depello!*" Remi heard his voice muffled through the ringing as if he were shouting from underwater.

The weight of the man was lifted and shoved away from him and Remi sucked in a sharp, deep breath. Whipping his wand from its holster, he gave thanks to the universe that the man had not broken his casting arm. He rolled over and found himself staring right at the hooded owner of the gun.

The Mortal had a bandana pulled up over his face, giving the impression of some sort of old-fashioned bandit outlaw.

Remi flicked his wand, not even bothering with a verbal incantation, and the gun was sent flying. The only visible part of the man's face was his eyes and they were currently widened in surprise as Remi aimed directly at him now, shouting, "*Praecipito!*"

The Mortal was plunged face-first into the gravel by the unseen force of Remi's jinx, knocking him unconscious with the impact as his head bounced off the rocks. Remi pushed himself into a sitting position to survey the Coven's entrance pavilion. His ears were still ringing but even that sound was gradually subsiding, only to be replaced by the swelling roar of the pandemonium that was still happening all around him.

While it had quickly dispersed after the initial gunfire, there were still enough Mortals on the grounds to be considered a tangible threat.

Remi saw that more Warlocks had come from inside the House to join the fray and that the local officers had called for backup. He was glad that the two groups were so immediately identifiable because now was no time for second-guessing.

He looked to the front steps and saw that Sylvia remained with a handful of other Warlocks, ensuring that no one could break through the last line of defense. The Arbiter's blonde hair whipped around her face in the breeze as she kept her wand steady, maintaining a protective barrier. Sylvia met his gaze and called out something to him.

"What?" he yelled back, still unable to fully hear. Sylvia shouted again and this time, he could tell that she was searching for someone. Just as Remi pushed himself to his feet, a bright crimson globule shot high into the sky above everyone.

Finn, he thought to himself.

Sylvia saw this sign of distress and made to shout something else but Remi was already on the move, running headfirst into the bedlam and slipping on the mud a few times as he went along. His broken arm slapping against his side absently with each stride. He could feel that he was soaked and figured that his Umbrella Bubble charm must have popped at some point during the chaos.

It took next to no time at all for him to find Finn in the crowd. He was surrounded on all sides but seemed to be holding his own pretty well against the Mortals. They ebbed and flowed around him collectively. Remi watched the young Guard as he seemed to almost dance around them all with a certain grace, casting charms and jinxes.

It was almost like watching a painter throwing paint onto a blank canvas. The Mortals that had been moving as a single unit fell individually as each cast from the Warlock's wand connected with them.

Remi was just wondering how he had managed to hold them off and send a beacon up for help when Finn's emerald eyes connected with his through the rain.

The younger Warlock shot him an obviously relieved grin just before he was taken down from behind.

"Hey!" Remi shouted and the hoard of Mortals that had been gradually encroaching on Finn rounded, turning their attention onto him. Remi made an upward sweeping motion with his wand, shouting, "*Aliquot Procul!*"

Those in the front of the group that had set their sights on him were sent flying through the rain, over and above their cohorts. Remi whipped his wand back down with lightning speed, "*Flagrum Ignis!*"

A fiery chain erupted from the tip of his wand, burning despite the downpour. He quickly brought it across, scorching several of the second-tier Mortals.

Those remaining looked hesitant, shooting each other glances as if they were generally unsure of whether to charge forward or run away.

"Come!" Remi goaded, burning with a furious rage that had replaced any adrenaline or fear from earlier. He lifted his weapon to the sky, shouting as he did so, "*Tempestas!*"

Lightning shot from his wand into the heavens and he sneered like a feral beast as the Mortals searched the clouds. Remi could feel them, swirling and darkening even without taking his attention away from his targets.

"I said *come!*" he shouted again.

Almost as if to punctuate his words, there was a deafening clap of thunder. The ground beneath them shook as a bolt struck just behind Remi, seeming to respond to the one he had cast and sending static through his entire body.

"Come at me, you *pigs!*" Remi literally spat the words at the terrified bunch as they clamored over one another in the opposite direction. "You *can't* outrun this!"

The mosh became frozen in place as the light drizzle that had already been coming down for most of the morning became so torrential that it was difficult to even make out his wand in front of him. Remi had called for a typhoon and now all of the Mortals were watching him, officer and civilian, like he was some untamed deity bringing forth divine retribution.

They had all become suddenly too fearful to move and Remi felt oddly satisfied by this notion. Mortals and Warlocks alike had all stopped fighting and were now watching him in alarmed unison to see what he would do next.

"*Conquiro!*" he shouted. There was an instantaneous clap of thunder, followed by several bolts of lightning. Remi had charmed them to seek out each of the Mortal civilians that was holding a weapon, which they did.

He watched as several hazy figures in the distance were struck and thrown to the ground before going on with his response to their incursion.

"If you do not wish to join your fallen brothers," Remi called out, letting his voice be carried by the wind, "then you will leave this place at once! And you will not return!"

Many of the Mortals shared timid glances, seeming genuinely unsure if the offer was a hoax, while others took flight immediately.

"*Fulmen*," Remi whispered, calling down another single bolt that made up the minds of the remaining people. He watched as the Coven House's grounds cleared all at once, feeling himself presently drained from the several powerful spells he had just cast.

"*Serenitas*," he choked out just barely before falling to his knees in the wet grass.

He could feel his vision spotting over as the weather righted itself, the sun piercing through the clouds that were rolling away just as quickly as they had rolled in.

Remi looked up just briefly enough to see the remnants of his funnel cloud being blown away before letting his head lull down to his knees, no longer able to keep it aloft.

He sat like this for a few extended moments, catching his breath as officers and Warlocks surrounded him.

"The kid," he whispered breathlessly. "Get him into the House."

Two of the other Warlocks ran off to grab the unconscious Finn just a few yards away. "The guns," he choked out, thankful that a few of the Mortal officers understood and went to collect those that had been struck down with his spell.

"The bodies," he managed to issue a final, vague command and those remaining went about gathering those that had been lost in the chaos that had ensued, leaving Remi alone and soaked in the mud of the grounds.

"Are you hurt?" Sylvia Ashcroft was suddenly at his side.

"I'm fine," he lied, grimacing as the pain finally cut through his facade and washed over him completely now.

"Get him to the Healers!" she beckoned to some unseen party behind her as the spots in Remi's vision grew to the point where he no longer knew who she was talking to. He heard the Arbiter calling out a few more commands that quickly became too muffled and distant for him to comprehend.

Suddenly, there were arms wrapped around him on either side, pulling him to his feet.

"I'm fine," Remi protested weakly. "Really, I am."

He tried to take a blind step, having forgotten the gunshot wound under his knee. Instantly, the white-hot pain seared throughout his entire body, just as fresh as when it had first happened now that adrenaline was no longer surging through him and serving as a cushion for the pain.

Without another word of protest, Remi succumbed to his wounds and let himself be taken in by the darkness.

XII

The Infirmary of the Coven was a quiet, grey stone room with twenty cots. Though it did not receive a fraction of the traffic that the other areas of the house averaged, it could be Glamoured to provide more space if the need arose. There were full-length, Palladian windows at different intervals between the beds, some of them leading out onto small balconies where patients who were staying for an extended period could enjoy a bit of fresh air without having to venture downstairs.

There were nightstands to the right of each bed, topped with water pitchers for any potential guests and privacy curtains on the off chance that the beds were at full capacity, as they were now. On the opposite side of each cot, there were medicine cabinets and sinks with copper basins for when bandages needed to be changed on some of the larger wounds that came through.

At the far end of the room, there was a storage pantry where the Healers mixed herbs from the medicine garden into poultices, salves, and potions for whatever they might need. The shelves of this room were filled to the brim with everything from cures for the common cold, to solutions meant to nullify the effects of Vampirism before a victim Turned.

Remi had thought that the Infirmary itself smelled like fresh linens and wondered if this was from the bedding in the room or some sort of Glamour that had been placed to keep it from smelling like sickness and old blood.

He had been drifting in and out of consciousness for a few hours after he had been brought back by the Healers, until they had finally given him something to keep him out. Now he was awake with his eyes closed as he listened to people shuffling around him, working on other patients.

"The bullet went straight through," a Healer was saying somewhere near Remi's bed. "We gave him something for the pain, but nothing was severely damaged. It should be healed up by tomorrow morning."

"That's good," another answered, sounding like they were standing on the opposite side of him. "And the arm?"

"Probably going to be in that sling for a few days," the first replied. "We reset the bones and mended what we could, but," they paused, as if checking to make sure that Remi was still asleep. "It was pretty messed up. Almost all of the bones from the elbow, down were shattered completely. Everything above that was just fractured. As long as he doesn't use that arm for the next few days, though, it should be fine."

"You realize that's a member of our Witch's Guard?" the second asked, making Remi smile to himself that his reputation seemed to precede him.

"Doesn't mean it'll heal any faster," the first retorted. "I still don't see how he cast that damn tornado out there. Poor sap's lucky he's not dead from a spell of that magnitude."

"Yeah," the other agreed, glumly. "What about the Mortal?"

"Headshot," the voice was grim and matter-of-fact. "DOA. The family is coming by later to collect the body." Remi felt his chest tighten but remained in character just in case they were still standing over him.

There was a clicking of heels on the stone floor and the conversation came to a complete halt. Then Remi heard the distinct voice of the Arbiter just at the foot of his bed, "Is he well?"

"This one's probably going to be out of commission for a few days, at least," the first Healer answered. "But most of his injuries were only flesh deep."

"I see," Sylvia's tone was flat. "And what of my nephew?" There was a pause as if neither of the two knew how to break some bad news to her. "What's happened?" her voice was concerned, yet also demanding.

"He's still under," the second Healer began quietly.

"He sustained some pretty heavy blows to the head at some point during the commotion," the first explained. "There were also at least ten stab wounds to the ribs and chest area of the torso."

"And?" Sylvia's tone was harsh as if she was not in the mood to be spoon-fed the story. "What is it the two of you are not telling me?"

"We've sedated him just enough to stitch up his wounds," the second took over, pausing as he searched for the right words. "His vital signs have been on a steady rise, but something's still wrong that we can't quite place."

"Meaning?" the Arbiter's tone seemed to be growing more impatient as the conversation went along.

"Well," the Healer said, hesitantly. "To put it simply, he should have been awake by now."

Remi remained still and silent but opened his eyes just enough so that he could watch the three figures at the foot of his bed. It was a hazy image, but he could still make out the shapes through his lashes.

"Is there anything that can be done?" Sylvia asked. "Perhaps you simply gave him too much of the belladonna. Maybe he's just having an allergic reaction to something."

"That's not possible, Madame Arbiter," the first Healer's voice was frigid and harsh, and Remi imagined he must have been offended by the accusation of an error on his part. "The only time I administer more than the required amount of something is when the Arbiter has sentenced a rogue to death by lethal injection. As you did not wish your nephew dead, I did not administer such a dosage."

"We've done all we can, Madame Arbiter," the second Healer sounded more understanding. "It is up to him to bring himself out of it now."

There was a long silence at this point, in which the Healers exchanged looks of concern while Sylvia seemed to run through the gamut of every possible emotion. Her expression finally came to rest on a ghost of a smile as she glanced further down at what Remi could only imagine must have been Finn's cot.

"He attended the Academy in New Orleans," she half-whispered. "Did you know that? Seven years in one of the most dangerous cities, as far as Mortals go. Stayed in that city since he was thirteen. That's where he made it through his Proving because he wanted to join the Witch's Guard."

The Arbiter gave a mocking laugh now that left Remi with a hollow feeling in his chest. He felt himself shiver, even beneath the heavy white linens of his bed as she went on, "He comes here for three days because he wants to transfer to a new Coven. And now he's a brain-dead vegetable in my Infirmary. Dahlia is going to have a field day with me when I have to go break it to her."

There was another grimacing laugh and Remi was glad that no one was focused on him at that moment.

The Arbiter's heels clicked softly away, before stopping as she reached the door. She glanced back at the two Healers, who were still in fixed positions at the foot of Remi's bed.

"Have Caswell meet me in my office when he wakes," she called back. Remi heard the door shut and then a brief silence in the room. He closed his eyes back fully until he was sure that the Healers had left the room as well. Remi used his left arm to push the sheets back as he saw that his right was in a sling, made of a single white sheet, that had been wrapped behind his neck.

He glanced down to see that he had been stripped of his jeans and that his left leg had been wrapped tightly with gauze strips just below the knee. Though he could not immediately tell the severity of the wounds, as he stood and put his full weight on it, Remi winced as a shockwave of new pain was sent through him.

He resolved himself to only use this leg to balance, as the pain seemed to be emanating from where the bullet had gone through.

Remi grabbed a pair of cotton shorts that had been left folded on the bed next to his, struggling into them and coming to the realization that he might actually have to listen to the Healers this time. Pushing the thought away and leaving the shirt on the bed as he did not feel like fighting with it as well just yet, he limped down the row of cots in the direction he had seen Sylvia look just seconds ago.

He had always hated being in this part of the Coven House any longer than he absolutely had to be under normal circumstances and as he hobbled along, he saw two things that cemented this feeling in him. The first was a giant set of unmoving lumps on top of several beds that had been pushed together to make a makeshift table, each of them covered in individual sheets.

He knew what it was under the linens, but felt himself shudder internally at the very idea of so many deceased and quickly expelled the thought from his mind.

He swallowed against the lump that had solidified itself against the back of his throat like a tumor of guilt and blind anticipation, searching along until he saw the second thing that made him want to flee the Infirmary and everything it stood for in his mind.

Finn was lying in another of the cots, completely unmoving and seeming almost as lifeless as the corpses that had been neatly arranged on the opposite wall. The young Warlock looked just as peaceful as he had that morning when Remi had gone to wake him up, almost giving the impression that he was merely sleeping.

Remi knew better than to think that from what he had just heard from the Healers.

He moved to Finn's bedside and gazed down at the Arbiter's nephew, unable to keep himself from wondering if he'd even be in this cot if they had not been paired with each other for the past three days.

"I don't know you that well, kid," he admitted aloud. "But I know you're pretty damn strong. And if you don't wake yourself up from this, then that would be a lie. And I'm not the biggest fan of being made to look like a jackass, even if it is only to myself. You got through your Proving. I know that means you can get through this."

Remi smiled at how foolish and sentimental he sounded, having never seen himself as that type of person. He found himself silently grateful that no one else was in the room to hear him talking to the unconscious Warlock. Then he felt almost simultaneously guilty as he realized that there was no one else that could come spend time with Finn while he was here.

Dahlia Ashcroft was a Magister and the High Coven was all the way in Salem, while the Arbiter was surely already dealing with the aftermath of this recent string of murders coming to the Mortal public's attention and was likely too busy to stick around in the Infirmary until it had died down.

Remi remembered then that Sylvia had mentioned wanting to see him when he woke up.

Remi turned away, limping slowly back down the row between the beds and out of the Infirmary. He made his way down toward the Arbiter's office one floor below, wincing internally with each new bit of pressure he was forced to put on his wounded leg.

Wake yourself up, kid, he thought to himself, hoping Finn might somehow hear him as he hobbled along. *Or I'll have to come in and wake you up myself.*

When he had finally made it down the stairs and into the Arbiter's office, Sylvia was propped against her desk watching a television set that was hidden in an armoire off to one side of the room. Remi's gaze travelled to the screen, where it fixed itself and he watched as a video of the earlier events play themselves out again.

There was a brief recap of everything he had already seen earlier that morning before he had left his house. Then, there was an image of him and Finn declining to answer any comments from the female anchor that had been outside when they had pulled up.

These were followed by his stand-off and take-down of the belligerent officer and the sound of the first gun being fired. He watched as they charged up the path that brought them to the front steps of the Coven House. Then, the screen split into several smaller ones and he could finally see what all had unfolded while he had been on the ground.

One of the angles continuously switched between different pairs of

Mortal officers as they moved through the mob that had been formed outside. A second had somehow managed to get to the front, where it panned over the faces in the crowd before coming to rest on Sylvia and the other Warlocks that had defended the House itself from being ransacked.

Another of the screens was focused on Finn as he made his way through the sea of Mortals and eventually began defending himself. Remi had not realized just how adept the younger Warlock was at casting up until that point. Even now as he watched, it was almost impossible to believe that so many spells were being thrown from a single Warlock's wand in such rapid succession. He watched in silent amazement as every Mortal that came up against Finn was either sent flying or knocked straight to the ground and left unconscious.

Then, there was the crew that was focused on him. From the angle, Remi supposed that they had followed him into the crowd and remained behind him as he pushed his way through. He felt slightly ashamed of himself that he had not been watching his own back better, but he had been too focused on burrowing his way through the Mortals without being noticed that he hadn't had the mental capacity to spare.

He watched as the tiny Mortal had fired shots and sent everyone into a panic. He watched as the Mortal behemoth had taken him down with ease before being shot. Remi felt his heart catch in his chest. He knew had been there when it had actually happened, but there was something almost surreal about witnessing it over again from a third-person perspective.

Remi took an overall look at the other screens and saw everyone else reacting to the sudden pandemonium. He saw the officers from the Oxford Police Department pull out taser guns and start shocking people into submission. He saw the Arbiter's group throw up the barrier and begin casting stunning charms into the crowd.

He watched as Finn cast at least ten stunning charms in rapid succession before throwing up a beacon charm into the sky and returning to the business of keeping the Mortals at bay. The younger Warlock moved in such fluid motions, that Remi almost missed it even then.

Then his gaze went back to his own little box, where he watched himself running across the grounds towards Finn. He watched as the younger Warlock let himself become distracted for just a second, before being overtaken by the Mortals that had been encroaching from the rear. Remi felt the same fire in his stomach that he'd had hours earlier as he watched himself kick into overdrive.

He felt the static charge of each spell a second time as he repeated them in his head. He watched himself knock back the Mortals that had piled onto Finn, before taking out several of his own. Then everything became almost too blurry for him to see, as the rain quickly became a monsoon. He heard his threat to the Mortals and watched as a few of them ran away in fear. He felt a victory deep within him now as he watched it back. Then he saw the bolts of lightning come down and the sky clearing and knew that it was over.

In hindsight, he supposed he should consider himself lucky that the weather had already been overcast. Otherwise, he might not have survived the spell.

As he continued viewing, he saw the last scene of Mortals fleeing in terror and the lightning strikes against those who had been carrying guns during the onslaught playing out again, although this time was from a much shakier camera angle. Then the reporter was talking directly to the camera from behind a desk in whatever studio Sylvia had it turned to. There was a picture of the first Harry Potter movie poster off to the side of her head and Remi had to stifle a laugh as he read the headline, '*Warlocks: Harmless Magicians or Destructive Menace?*'

He heard the woman ask if Oxford's Coven had gone too far, before promising an in-depth interview with one of the victims from yesterday's attack on innocent Mortals. Remi felt himself become instantly disgusted.

It was at this point that Sylvia finally took notice of Remi standing in the doorway and quickly turned the set off, pressing a button on the underside of the desk to close the cabinet doors so that it looked like an ordinary armoire once more.

"Not our finest moment," he mused. "I'm sure the High Coven has already been blowing up our phones while I've been upstairs?"

"No, surprisingly," the Arbiter moved to take her seat behind the desk. "Not yet, at least."

"You're letting them into the House?" Remi asked, surprised that she had been so agreeable to something so brash this soon.

"Not that I'm aware," Sylvia's lips were pursed together in a tight, thin line.

"But that's where all of the 'victims' are," Remi said. "Upstairs in our Infirmary." Sylvia said nothing and Remi put the pieces together. "A hit piece to make us look bad."

"Precisely," the Arbiter replied, clearly furious at the news outlet. "Which makes our job that much harder, Caswell."

She sighed heavily and Remi could see just how increasingly worn she was becoming under all of the stress lately. He couldn't honestly say that he blamed her, as he was beginning to feel that way himself and imagined it must be amplified many times over for her.

"I'm almost certain that I'll be getting a call from the High Coven any moment now, breaking all ties with this branch of the Coven until this is all sorted out," the woman said, wearily.

"They would do something like that?" Remi sounded almost shocked but had somehow expected something just as drastic in retaliation for today's events.

"I don't know if they will," Sylvia admitted. "But I know they have in the past with other Houses. That's one of the reasons we have so many Laws in the Covenant that protect Mortals."

"Do they think that would really solve anything with the Mortals?" Remi felt anger simmering deep within his chest, threatening to bubble over at any second. "Do they really think that the Mortals will see them any differently than the rest of us just because they distance themselves from the problems facing one of their own Houses?"

"I don't know," Sylvia replied earnestly, throwing her arms up in clear defeat. "I'm not sure of anything at the moment!"

"I'm sorry," Remi said, feeling somewhat guilty for how distraught the Arbiter seemed now. "I never meant to-"

"No," Sylvia cut him off by raising a hand. "You did what you were supposed to do. Your number one priority as a member of the Witch's Guard in a situation like that is to ensure that no harm comes to the Coven, be that the house itself or any of its members. That is exactly what you did and, for that, I can only be thankful."

Remi felt a bit of blood rush straight into his cheeks as he couldn't recall another time where the Arbiter had never so praised him before, especially not in front of him.

"Are you well?" she changed the subject.

"Yeah," he replied, a bit informally. He took a brief assessment of himself now that he had a moment. "I mean, well enough, I suppose."

"If you need some time off after today, I would completely understand," Sylvia offered. "I know spells of that magnitude can take quite a toll on a Warlock, both mentally and physically. I've even seen instances where an ongoing spell like that has completely drained whoever cast it before they could stop it. I'm actually surprised you didn't kill yourself out there today, Caswell."

"I've seen Warlocks kill themselves trying to toast bread," Remi tried to lighten the mood of the conversation. "Besides, if I died this early in the game, that would make too many people happy. And we both know that I'm just too damn spiteful for that."

When he saw that the Arbiter still had her concerned peridot eyes fixated on him, he added, "Look, I'm fine; honest. I just need to throw myself into this case to get my mind off of all this stuff that's been going on lately. Finding the rogue bastard or *bastards* that are responsible for all of this will make me feel a whole helluva lot better. Then we'll talk about me taking some time off."

"You're sure?" Sylvia asked, raising a single, disbelieving brow at him.

"Positive," Remi replied with a wink and the universal hand signal for 'okay.'

The Arbiter gave him one final look of trepidation before moving on, "Well, I'm glad to hear that. Now I have a more pressing matter. Caswell?"

"Yeah?" he asked, giving her a curious stare.

"Where is your shirt?"

Remi glanced down and suddenly felt a flush of his cheeks as he had opted not to grab the matching top to the pants he was wearing before he had left the Infirmary.

"I didn't want to fool with it, honestly," he replied with an absent shrug which sent a tiny wave of pain through his arm. "Anywho," he grimaced as he changed the subject, "what have you got for me?"

"Two things, actually," Sylvia replied, clearly making an effort to ignore his painful expression. "The Oxford City Morgue just contacted me about one of the bodies they received from us. There is a woman by the name of Valerie that wishes to speak with you personally about her findings."

"Am I supposed to know who that is?" Remi asked, giving a puzzled look. "I don't think I know anyone named Valerie, but I'll look into it. What's the other thing?"

"The Mortals are almost done with their investigation of the campus crime scene," she replied. "I figured that you might want to get down there and meet with them to see if they found anything we can use. You can take your pick of which one you want and I'll give the other to someone else."

"I'll take both of them," he said. "I'll head over to campus first and see if I can catch them before they leave."

"You sure you're up to it?" Sylvia asked. Remi gave a single-shoulder shrug, being careful not to move the injured arm this time.

"I need to go to that crime scene," he informed her. "There are some things that the Mortals don't search for when they're cleaning, and someone is obviously trying to make us look bad. So I'm almost positive there's something down there that they missed." The Arbiter seemed to be going along with his logic so far. "And if someone specifically asked for me," Remi went on, "then it might be a trap. On the other hand, it could be a lead or, at least, a connection. We need all of those two that we can get in the Mortal world, so I don't have the option to ostracize them on that off chance."

Sylvia had just finished agreeing with him for the final time when the phone rang. They both stared at it warily.

"That's probably Dahlia, now," Sylvia sighed and something clicked in the back of Remi's brain.

"When you're done with her," he spoke slowly as the thought formed, still a bit hazy in the foggy corners of his mind. He imagined this effect was from whatever painkillers the Healers had administered to him while he had been unconscious. "Go ahead and cancel Finn's hotel room and send for his things." There was another ring and a quizzical look from Sylvia. "He'll be staying with me when he wakes up."

"If I'm still in a position to do so after this," the Arbiter smiled at him warily, "I will do that."

She picked up on the third ring and Remi turned to limp his way out of the office.

The Mortals stood in the rain, each of them donning black ponchos with their hoods pulled up to conceal their faces. Remi was surprised that the weather had not let up in the hours since the showdown on the Coven grounds. In fact, it seemed to have gotten worse since he had been in the Infirmary, which made him glad that he'd had a spare cap in the back of the Jeep.

He could have almost sworn that he had seen the sun peeking through the clouds before he had passed out earlier, but that could have been chalked up to his imagination and exhaustion. It could have also been just plain, old Mississippi weather. Either way, presently, the rain was coming down in buckets.

As he made his way toward the small group, it became increasingly apparent that they were already packing everything up for the day.

Remi made his way up to the one that seemed to be in charge of the others and held out his left arm. Out of habit, the man held up his right but upon seeing that Remi's was in a sling, adjusted himself awkwardly to meet the shake.

"Remington Caswell," he introduced himself. "I'm from the Oxford Coven. Mind if I take a quick look around?"

"Fine by me," the officer shrugged. He was a rotund, older black man with a greying beard and looked almost as tired as Remi felt. "We were about to be heading out, anyway. You do whatever you need for your folks."

Remi tipped his hat in thanks and the two of them turned to watch as the noose was lifted from the James Meredith statue. He imagined that the man's body had been one of the first things that the first responders had removed from the area after arriving on the scene.

"I heard what happened at y'all's House," the man spoke without looking at Remi, choosing to stare at the other members of his crew as they put the rope into a heavy, plastic bag.

"I'm sure," Remi answered hesitantly. "It got pretty bad out there today."

There were no more words exchanged for a few long moments as the cleanup crew from the Oxford Police Department finished packing up their tools and the evidence that they had gathered. When it seemed to be done, the man turned to Remi and peered deep into his blue moonstone eyes with an intensity that made the Warlock almost uncomfortable.

The man broke contact only to glance down at his arm in the sling, before bringing his gaze to rest once more on Remi's face.

"I just want you to know," he said carefully and thoughtfully. "I want all of y'all to know that we ain't all like them what showed up today."

Remi was unsure why the man was telling him this, as most Mortals he had dealt with seemed to avoid contact with Warlocks at all cost. Although Remi felt that there was a genuine sort of sentiment about his words, he could not tell if the man was speaking as a Mortal or as an officer. Remi had no clue how to respond at first, so he decided to take a wild guess.

"It's fine," he replied awkwardly, feeling as if he was suddenly speaking for an entire group of people. "Neither are we."

The man tipped his hat slightly, and Remi imagined that he must have given an acceptable response as the man walked away to rejoin his team. He watched as the officers got into one of the vans and they all pulled away, leaving him to figure out what exactly he was here searching for in the first place.

Remi turned and made his way purposefully toward the statue. His leg was still throbbing from the bullet that had gone through earlier, but even that was already starting to subside.

He hobbled around the base of the statue, searching intensely for even one thing that seemed to be out of place. This was made difficult for the fact that it had been raining most of the day. All of the traffic through this area of the school after the body had been initially found did not help matters, although the inclimate weather did seem to be serving to keep most of them at bay now. This, paired with the fact that most of the classes today had been cancelled in the wake of everything, meant that campus was practically a ghost town at the moment.

Remi had circled around the base of the statue for at least fifteen minutes and was finding nothing that appeared to be out of the ordinary, when he finally noticed something peculiar. On the pavement just in front of the information plaque, were a few droplets of blood that had somehow dried on the concrete. This gave Remi pause, as the man had been lynched and he was almost certain that it had been raining constantly since he had been woken up by Sylvia's call.

How long had this kid been up here? he wondered to himself. *How long afterward did it take them to find him?*

He took out his phone, snapping a photo with the camera and sending it to the number he had saved as Sylvia's cell, though he rarely used it. He hastily locked the screen and shoved the device back into his pocket, not wanting the rain to mess up the screen while he waited for a response.

Remi went on scouting the immediate area, gradually expanding his field of view until he reached the patch of grass directly in front of the statue. He could not remember the last time he had been on campus when it was so devoid of people it was now, but appreciated how much easier this made things as he would not have to deal with prying eyes.

Remi saw no other traces of blood and figured that the Mortals must have cleaned up everything else that had been left as evidence. He turned on his heel to leave, resolving himself to wait until they had finished with their initial autopsy of the body when something glimmered in the grass and caught his attention.

He turned his head up toward the sky, ensuring that there was no sun poking through the clouds or lamps along the walkway that might have come on at some point. Even with the rain having plunged the campus into almost total shadow, it was too early for this. He wondered if perhaps they were simply on timers.

Nevertheless, as he confirmed neither of these things to be the case, he headed in the direction he had seen the light being reflected.

Remi struggled to keep his balance as his leg throbbed from the sudden constriction of his blood vessels as he knelt down to examine whatever this mysterious object might be. Even this simple act proved to be difficult, as he could only lean toward one side to catch himself with a busted arm in a sling.

He pulled out his phone a second time and snapped another picture, sending it as well before he went to remove it from the ground. Lying in the grass as if it had been tossed carelessly aside by someone who did not know what it was, there was a long, black stick with a hilt. The grain of it was very straight and the wood seemed to have an almost golden quality about it, causing Remi to question where it had come from.

The wand was roughly the length of his forearm and the slick quality of the wood that had been used jumped out at him, as most of the trees at the university were ordinary oaks. There was what appeared to be a hexagonally-cut garnet set into the base of the grip. From there, a silvery filigree of ornately-drawn fleur-de-lis patterns wrapped around the hilt, giving the tool an air of importance. It was clear to Remi that this was not just anyone's wand, but whoever that might be was anyone's guess at this point.

He reached down to pick it up from the grass and immediately regretted this action.

As soon as the skin of his fingertips made contact with the infernal shaft, an image of intimately familiar and sinister golden irises flashed through his mind. He was instantly and violently thrown back by an invisible force as the same familiar demonic chortle he had grown accustomed to at this point filled his head.

Remi writhed around on his back, feeling like his arm had been broken once more as his elbow had been one of the first things to land on the unforgiving pavement. He let out an almost bestial growl as the white-hot pain surged furiously throughout his entire body, causing a few tears of rage to well in his eyes at his own foolishness.

He laid like this, letting himself become increasingly soaked until the pulsing had gradually subsided to a manageable, yet constant, throbbing in his arm and leg.

He slowly regained his footing, standing back up to fish a handkerchief from his now-wet back pocket. Keeping it tucked skillfully between his fingers and the wand he had found as a makeshift shield, he picked the thing up a second time. He was careful not to let the dark object touch his bare hand this time as he did not want a repeat occurrence.

Feeling somewhat defeated and slightly vulnerable now, Remi began limping along the walkway back to where he had parked the Jeep. He had what he had come for now, and that was enough for him.

He crawled into the driver's seat and wrapped the handkerchief more tightly around the wand, before laying it down on the passenger seat. He stared down at the thing with a certain feeling of resentment as he lit a cigarette and pulled his phone out of his pocket.

Surprisingly, it had not been damaged in the fall. He unlocked the screen a third time and opened his contacts, pressing the icon for the Arbiter's direct office number.

"Hello?" Sylvia answered on the second ring.

"Did you get the pictures?" Remi asked, not bothering with an introduction.

"Caswell?" she asked, to which he confirmed. "Yes, I got them, but what does it mean?"

"Not sure," Remi admitted. "How long had it been raining this morning before you called?"

"I believe it started close to midnight last night," Sylvia replied, sounding unsure. "Maybe an hour or so after."

"So that means that someone killed this kid last night, with enough time for the blood to soak into the concrete and dry," he inhaled deeply, not liking the way things were piecing together for this particular case. "Then they hung his body up to make it look like a common Mortal hate crime before it rained."

"That makes sense," Sylvia went along. "But who's wand is that?"

"Could be who we're looking for," Remi kept his answers short, not wanting to worry the Arbiter until he had more to go on. "I'll bring it in for examining."

"Right," Sylvia agreed. "Where are you now?"

"Just leaving Ole Miss by the library," Remi replied, cranking the Jeep finally and shifting it into reverse. "I'm about to head over to the Department building to meet whoever this Valerie person is."

"Sounds good," Sylvia said with slight hesitation before adding, "Be on your guard, Caswell. Come see me as soon as you get back."

"Will do," Remi said, ending the call and flicking his final ash and butt out the window. He glanced down at the wand once more, hoping that he was not walking straight into another trap that had been set for him, before letting off the brake and following the road that would take him away from campus.

"I'm here for a meeting with someone named Valerie?" Remi asked the secretary at the front desk. The woman, who donned a less-decorated version of the uniform every other officer wore, looked up from her computer screen with a quizzical expression.

"We don't have a Valerie that works here," she said. "Are you sure you're not looking for the county building up down the road?"

"Are you certain?" Remi asked, positive he had requested the correct name. "I believe she wanted to see me regarding an autopsy that she just finished."

"Oh!" the woman shouted, recognition dawning across her face. "The girl that plays with the bodies downstairs!"

"That would be the one, I'm afraid," Remi let out a half-hearted chuckle. He already felt uncomfortable with the description the woman had given but did not want her to know that. He imagined that he could very well be walking into a trap, but he knew it had to be done.

"Just have a seat right over there," the woman instructed. "I'll page an officer up to escort you down there."

Remi obeyed, taking a seat on one of the bench-style chairs just inside the front doors of the building. He suddenly felt very much like a criminal waiting to be processed as he listened to the buzzing sound as the Mortal called for someone to escort him to the morgue on her intercom.

He glanced up at the clock on the wall behind the bulletproof window of the reception desk, telling himself that he would simply come back another time if five minutes had passed

"I just don't see how she does it," the woman continued talking, making Remi feel even more uncomfortable. He cocked a single brow. He had meant it as a question of why the woman was talking to him, but she seemed to take it as an invitation for conversation and went on, "Playing with those bodies down there all day. Like it's a hobby or something. It gives me the heebie-jeebies just thinking about it!"

Remi said nothing but nodded politely as the woman went back to doing whatever she had been working on before he had come in. He glanced over and saw that the current project was filing her nails and laughed to himself.

The reinforced door that led to the offices in the building opened and an officer peeked his head around the door. "Here to see Val?" he asked, to which Remi nodded.

"I guess?" Remi hesitated, feeling every bit of how on-edge he was in this place.

"Well, you can follow me," the man said, extending his hand. "I'm Davis."

"Remi," he answered, shaking the Mortal's hand and not feeling the need to be formal. He hoped this would not take that long.

"She told me to be expecting somebody for her," Davis informed him. "She just didn't mention that it'd be a Warlock."

The Mortal laughed then, revealing his perfectly white teeth. The man was handsome and friendly, and Remi found himself suddenly very aware of how scraggly he must look at that very moment.

"Is that going to be a problem?" he cocked a single brow and silently laughed as Davis held his hands up at his chest as if to tell Remi to wait. He enjoyed making Mortals feel uncomfortable in social situations. "I'm sure I can manage perfectly fine without an escort if it's going to be an issue for you, Officer."

"Oh, no!" the man exclaimed. "I didn't mean anything like that! Just trying to make small talk, and we don't get very many of you guys around here is all." Davis laughed a bit nervously and Remi swore he could see the faintest line of sweat beads forming on the other's head.

"Let's just go, shall we?" Remi's reply was short. He secretly enjoyed it when Mortals were nervous around him.

"Right," Davis nodded, holding up a handful of manila folders. "Let me just drop these off real quick and we can head on down."

The man walked ahead, stepping briefly into one of the offices to hand the folders off to someone else, before starting down the hallway. Remi followed behind, trying to avoid the accusatory glances he was receiving.

The pair went through another steel door and the man glanced back at Remi.

"I really didn't mean anything by that, back there," he repeated. "I've actually got two Warlocks married into the family."

"It's cool," Remi chuckled uncomfortably, searching for any sign that they were near their destination. He really hated being forced into situations where he had to come up with small talk.

"Yeah," Davis seemed oblivious to his eyes darting around the corridor and continued blathering on. "One's an instructor at the Academy up in Memphis and the other's a Healer in this Coven."

The Mortal paused in the middle of the hallway, his face suddenly lighting up like he'd gone through some sort of major epiphany during the short stroll. "You might know him!"

"If he's a Healer, probably not," Remi shook his head and watched the excitement fade from the other's face. "I generally try to avoid the Infirmary at all cost, unless I'm nearly dead and someone drags me in there unconscious."

The two shared a glance at Remi's arm in its sling and back at each other, laughing at the irony of the statement. "Exactly," Remi said, relaxing for a moment.

"What even happened?" Davis asked. Then as if the realization of it had suddenly bulldozed him mid-sentence, "Oh! You're him!"

"*Him?*" Remi instantly tensed once more. "What 'him?' Who's 'him?'"

"You did that- the- that tornado! That was you" Davis seemed almost giddy, like he was meeting a celebrity. "And that lightning that took all those guys out at once! And, dude," the man giggled then, throwing Remi off. Remi had never actually heard a full-grown, adult man giggle before that. "What you did to Sanders... Legendary!"

"Seriously?" Remi furrowed his brow disbelievingly. "Do you guys not like him, or something?"

"Let's just say that it's not the first time something like that has come up with him," Davis had lowered his voice.

"Gotcha," Remi nodded in understanding, feeling somewhat like a gossipy teenage girl.

"How do you even do something like that?" the officer asked, before slapping his palm to his face. "Right. Magic. Duh." Remi chuckled at the man's reasoning process. "Seriously though, you should come out with us sometime," Davis went on. "You were a beast out there. You're a damn legend around here."

"Is that why they were all staring?" Remi asked aloud without meaning to. Davis shrugged, almost like he knew the answer but did not want to say out of politeness. Remi decided to leave it be. "I might take you up on that after this thing heals up," he said, indicating his arm in its sling.

Davis nodded in agreement and pulled out a small notepad from his chest pocket. He scribbled his name and number down and handed it to Remi, who tucked it into his jeans.

"I'm serious, man," the Mortal said. "Hit me up."

"Will do," Remi lied, knowing the other would not notice.

"Well, here we are!" Davis announced in a grand voice.

They had come down two long hallways and flights of stairs and were now standing in front of another steel door. Davis opened it, holding it for Remi to walk through first.

Remi instantly felt the icy wind of the short corridor pierce through his still-damp clothes and silently cursed himself for not thinking to grab a jacket from the back seat before entering the building.

"Someone out there?" a female's voice called out curiously from an open door a little further down on the right.

"Visitor's here, Val!" Davis called back. He turned to Remi and tipped his head down as if to say goodbye before returning the way they had come.

"Valerie?" Remi asked, his voice echoing along the hallway as he made his way down and towards the door where he had heard the woman's come from.

"Remington Caswell, I assume?" the woman called, as if to make sure that the Coven had not sent someone in his stead. "The Warlock, correct?"

"That's me," Remi confirmed. "I was told you had asked to see me?"

"Right," the woman seemed pleased by this information. "Do come in, won't you? We have much to discuss." Remi did as he was asked, not knowing what to expect as he crossed the threshold of the doorway.

The room was small and Remi found that he was immediately filled with an overwhelming sense of claustrophobia at the thought of being so far beneath the surface in such an enclosed space. There was an office, roughly the size of a janitor's closet, just to the left of the door. In it, he saw an out-of-date computer and two filing cabinets that were much too large for the tiny room taking up most of the space within.

The rest of the walls were covered, floor-to-ceiling, with square, steel refrigerator-style doors that Remi could only assume must each house cadavers that had yet to be examined. There was a large surgical light fixed to a metal arm that hung from the ceiling in the center of the room. Beneath that were two examination tables, each with a body lying on it.

Between the two slab-like tables, was a woman with silver hair that had been braided and fell just below her right breast.

She wore a form-fitting black, knee-length dress under her lab coat. Her skin was abnormally pale, especially beneath the scrutinizing glare from the halogen lights overhead. But above all this, it was her eyes that struck Remi more than anything. They were a light brown shade with a deep-red circle directly around the iris that gave them an almost magenta hue.

"A Vampire?" Remi was somewhat taken aback by this discovery. "In a Mortal police department?"

"You're surprised?" the woman gave a sardonic smile, cocking a finely-plucked eyebrow at him as he stared.

"How did you-" he began, then paused. "Do they know?"

"Davis does," she informed him, a bit too matter-of-factly for Remi's liking. "The rest remain blissfully ignorant. As long as they don't have a reason to actively have any dealings with the 'corpse girl', they generally choose to stay as far away from this place as they can."

"I wasn't even aware that the OPD had a medical examiner," Remi mused aloud, which was true as he could not remember the last time he'd had to come to the building for anything other than transfer files in recent memory.

"Most don't," Valerie admitted with a casual shrug. "They know they have to elect a coroner every few years, but even that escapes most of their knowledge. He is usually on-scene during investigations. If he deems it necessary, the body is sent here for me to examine. If I can't find the cause for someone's death, then we send it to Jackson to the state examiner."

"Does that happen often?" Remi asked, suddenly very fascinated by this discovery for some reason.

"It used to before I got here," Valerie gave a soft smirk. "Of course, I'm a bit more competent at my job than the Mortals that came before me."

"How long have you been here?" he asked, feeling caught off guard that he had not known or even heard about her up until this meeting.

"Long enough to make an acquaintance," she replied, somewhat dodgily. "Not so long that it arouses anyone's suspicion."

She placed a hand on her hip and Remi saw that her manicured nails had been filed to a point. He briefly wondered if this had been done purposefully, or if it was a result of her Vampirism. Either way, he took it as a warning not to ask too many questions.

"But we're not here today to talk about me, Warlock," her voice was like a deadly silk. "I hear you have a few open cases on your hands at the moment, and I figured that you might want to be the one to see this before I have to send my reports off. Once I do that, the families are free to come collect the bodies for funerals and other such things."

"How did you know that I'm tracking rogues?" Remi asked, to which the woman gave a chilly and monotonous guffaw.

"I'm over two centuries old, child," she replied, eyeing him like she could easily destroy him. In his current state, he did not find himself wanting to test this unspoken threat. "You think I haven't made at least a few connections within that time?"

"Fair enough," Remi smirked.

He walked toward the two slabs and saw that these were, indeed, the bodies he had been expecting. One was the Vampire girl that had been left behind the dumpster at Autumn's Bloom and the other was the man that had been hanging from the James Meredith statue earlier that morning.

"What, exactly, am I supposed to be seeing here?" Remi asked, a bit cluelessly.

Valerie said nothing at first, pointing to the necks on both bodies. Remi took a closer look and saw that each had been sliced open. He had missed this detail before on the girl in his haste to get the body removed from the sunlight.

"So they both had their throats slit," Remi said grimly.

"Yep," Valerie said, almost too cheerfully for his liking. "But," she went on, almost as if she was excited to be sharing her findings with someone else, "there seems to be more to it than that, Warlock."

Remi watched curiously as Valerie switched on the surgical light overhead and pulled it down, focusing it on the man's throat. "Notice anything particularly unusual about the wound?"

Remi stared down for a few moments before shaking his head, to which Valerie let out an almost frustrated sigh.

"This man was hanged!" she exclaimed, to which Remi gave a quizzical look. He was clearly not piecing information together quickly enough for the Vampire's liking. "Even if he had been hanged after his throat was slit," the woman explained, gesturing animatedly with her hands as she spoke, "his neck would still have been bruised in the process. Notice anything missing around that big gash on his neck?"

Remi examined the man's throat once more, this time bending down to get a closer view of the area. After a few moments of making sure before he answered, he replied hesitantly, "But this man doesn't have any bruises. How can that be possible if what you say is true?"

He removed his gaze from the man and focused once more on Valerie, who was grinning wildly and revealing her fangs. Remi assumed it was from the sheer excitement of sharing her findings with someone else, but something about the woman's unhinged expression paired with the almost sinister lighting of the room gave him an unsettling feeling in the darkest pits of his stomach.

"His body appears to have been drained of blood completely before he was put up on that statue," Valerie explained, emphasizing that he had been hanged after whatever else had been done to him.

They both glanced briefly to the girl on the other slab in front of them.

"What about her?" Remi asked, more out of compulsion than genuine curiosity at this point.

"It's very hard to tell with her," Valerie explained. "With her being where the sunlight could get to her, even indirectly, that would have dried up the blood in her veins long before the skin started to flake away. Especially with her being a Fledgling, there's no definite way to know. Just her youth would allow the process to speed up exponentially, even had she not been drained beforehand."

Remi felt himself shiver involuntarily at the use of the word 'drained', as if the two had merely been tools that needed to be emptied after they had been used. He shuddered at the thought as Valerie's voice trailed off.

"But even if you aren't for certain," he mused aloud, "you do have a reasonable suspicion."

"But why would someone drain two seemingly unrelated people of their blood?" he went on. "What purpose could that possibly serve?" He paused and narrowed his eyes, but Valerie seemed to have read his thoughts even before he had fully formed them for himself.

"There are no bite marks anywhere on either of the bodies," she shook her head as she answered. "And those slices are too deep and wide across for either of them to have been made by a Vampire's nail. For one of us to get that deep, it would have taken chunks out of the neck."

There was another involuntary shudder on Remi's part at the use of the word 'chunks'.

"Then what?" he asked, his mind suddenly racing and trying to make any connections between the two bodies lying in front of him. "A Lycan wouldn't have drained the blood, but you say it couldn't have been a Vampire. The Fae haven't directly killed any outside of their own kind in centuries and they generally police their own when there's been a violation of the Covenant. And I just don't see any reason for a Warlock to have done this, besides to throw us on some kind of wild goose chase."

"Have you ever heard of *'Sanguis Veneficarum?'*" Valerie crossed her arms and stared at him as he tried to form coherent reasoning behind it all.

Remi had heard the term used before, but he could not remember exactly where or when that had been.

"I don't -" he started to answer, then the realization hit him with a startling force. He had seen it somewhere in the book he had taken from the archives just a few days ago.

"Blood Magic?" he guessed, unsure of it even as he said it. Valerie nodded and he suddenly remembered that the book had mentioned one of the original Magisters of the first High Coven conducting 'experiments' and being cast out for this reason.

This is it! Remi thought to himself, feeling somewhat excited. *This is the lead I've been waiting for!*

Remi could barely contain himself now as he waited for the woman to continue with her explanation. He had been trying to make sense of it all since the night Becca had stumbled her way into the Coven House.

"You said you were how old?" Remi asked, piecing it together in his mind as he went along. "Over two centuries, right? Did you ever hear anything about the original High Coven?"

"I've heard several things about them in my time," Valerie replied in a guarded tone now. "But I was dealing with my own demons back then, so I couldn't be expected to keep up with all of their internal struggles."

Remi instantly felt his heart sink as she spoke and realized that, even if she was truly as old as she said, that was still almost 200 years between the appointment of the first Magisters and her Turning. Then the woman added, "I will say that I did remember enough about them to ask for a Warlock named Caswell."

This admission had Remi's heart hammering so loud in his ears that he was certain the Vampire could hear it just as well as him. This thought was answered by a sly smile from the woman, making him question if it was true or if she was somehow reading his thoughts he was having to himself.

"Do you remember any of the other names?" Remi could barely contain himself by this point, feeling his knees becoming almost weak with anticipation.

"Let's see," Valerie answered slowly, seemingly thinking back to what he was sure must only feel like a few days for an immortal creature such as her. "There were your ancestors," she ticked each name off in her head and on her fingers as she spoke.

"The Ashcrofts, Wrenns, Baylins. The Buckingham line, I knew quite well," she paused and gave a slightly impish grin as Remi guessed what that might have implied. "Then there was the," another pause as she tried to remember. "Hendersons? Yes, that sounds right."

She counted out the names on her fingers, repeating them to make sure she was remembering all of them. "Who am I forgetting?" she asked, more to herself than him.

Valerie seemed flustered at this point, as if the final piece of Remi's puzzle was just on the tip of her tongue, but she could not quite find out which way to turn it to fit. Finally, after several repetitions, she let out a frustrated sigh of defeat, "I just can't remember what that last name is for some reason!"

Once again, Remi felt his heart sinking low within his chest. The trail had gone cold for him just as quickly as it had heated up.

"It's okay," he lied, more to himself than Valerie as what little hope he'd had was slowly and effectively dashed against the rocks. "You tried, at least."

He stared at each of the bodies, then back to her as he tried desperately to think of something else that might take his mind off of the fact that he was no further to a lead now than when he had come in. "Do you mind if I ask you a few other questions as I leave?"

"So long as they don't incriminate me," the Vampire shrugged casually, moving around the slabs with the bodies and gesturing for him to follow her into the small office at the front of the room.

They went inside and took a seat at the desk as Remi tried to work things out into a tangible line of questioning in his head. "How old were you when you were Turned?" he asked, finding himself suddenly very interested in her history. It was almost as if something divine was telling him that this was the best course of action currently.

"Come again?" Valerie cocked a single brow at him.

"Well, it's just," Remi paused, thinking of how to go about saying it delicately. "Most of the Vampires I've come across are... look younger, physically speaking..."

"You're asking why I still look like a 43-year-old woman instead of some twenty-something with perkier tits?" she asked, not unkindly. "I told you I was dealing with some things back then."

"Sorry," Remi felt himself become instantly flushed and hot.

"It is simply a matter of pride," Valerie explained. "For most of them that get Turned in their prime, they either had no control over the situation or they were just so vain that they searched for any way possible to not grow older as far as their looks. Me? I've never had a problem with the idea of aging. I never found the stigma that most of the others around me did."

She paused here and her voice trailed off, almost as if she were being haunted by some old memory caught in the back of her mind that Remi could not see. "But I was deathly afraid of dying," she went on, laughing at her own ironic turn of phrase.

"When you live long enough," Valerie explained looking off in a forlorn sort of way, "in a time where you have to watch helplessly as your parents, then your husband and children and everyone else you love die right in front of you from a disease as common back then as the cold is today, it frightens you. It shakes you to your very core that you might not see any of them again. It becomes a very real possibility that you never want to face."

She took another brief pause here and let out what seemed like a regretful sigh before finishing, "So you seek out the only solution that you can think of to stave off that dark reality for as long as *humanly* possible."

Valerie's gaze was fixed loosely on Remi, but he felt as though she was staring straight through him at something he knew would not be there if he were to turn around.

"Lacunae," she let out in a breathy voice and Remi felt a mixture of confusion and sorrow as he watched a single tear of blood escape from the Vampire woman's eye.

"I'm sorry?" he asked, trying his best not to come across as inconsiderate.

"The name I couldn't remember," Valerie explained with a quiet air of certainty. "Lacunae; that's the final surname of the original Magisters."

Remi said nothing as he felt his heart swelling to its capacity within his chest. He was almost certain that it would burst forth from the sheer amount of excitement.

XIII

"I need to get back into the archives," Remi said to a skeptical Sylvia. She eyed him curiously as she considered his most recent request.

He had rushed from the morgue to tell the Arbiter every bit of information that he had gathered from his visit with Valerie and now stood in her office. He had briefly explained to her that he had found what he was looking for as far a lead, but that he still needed to do more extensive research before he could continue with his current investigation and was now awaiting her decision on the matter.

"And while we're at it," Remi reached into the lining of his rain jacket and pulled out the wand. He had wrapped it up entirely in the handkerchief so that he wouldn't accidentally touch it when he reached for it. "I need this Traced as soon as they can get to it."

Sylvia had sat through most of it, her face an impassive mask that he could not read. Remi stared at the Arbiter, trying to figure out what was going through her mind. She crossed her arms and leaned back in her seat, staring down at the wand he had placed there as if it were a foreign language that she was attempting to decipher.

"I honestly don't think they'll go for it a second time so soon," she said carefully, a weighted tone to her voice as she referred to his second request for access. "Especially after that scene this morning. They're not too pleased with how we handled things."

"What did they say when you spoke to them?" Remi asked, glancing at the rotary-style phone that sat on the edge of her desk.

Sylvia shrugged at the question. "Surprisingly," she raised a single eyebrow, "they only sent a letter of warning. That wasn't them calling when you left. It was the Mortals' mayor."

"Seriously?" Remi was slightly shocked to hear this. "What could he possibly want from us?"

"He wants us to issue a public apology," she began, clearly disgusted by the very thought of this. Remi could not blame her, as he hoped he had somehow misheard her. "To both the group that stormed the grounds and to those that were taken into Oxford Police custody."

There were a few seconds of silence as she allowed Remi to process the bit of what she had just said. Neither of them said anything during this time, as if they were both waiting to see what the other's reaction would be.

"He also," Sylvia went on finally, speaking as if each individual word were a chore for her, "expects our Coven to agree to making reparations to the families that lost people during said storming of our grounds, as well as the family of the officer you knocked unconscious during the struggle." She paused to look at the notes she had taken during the call before proceeding, "A Mortal by the name of Sanders? Sound familiar?"

"Unfortunately," Remi spoke through gritted teeth, wishing desperately now that he had kicked the man when he'd had a chance to. "What did you tell him?"

"I told him that we would consider his demands and get back to him within the next twenty-four hours," Sylvia informed him, lacing her fingers together.

She glared at Remi, clearly just as annoyed by the situation as he was. He imagined that she could almost feel the boiling anger rising off his body as he bit the inside of his cheek so hard that he could taste blood.

"And?" he prodded, focusing on the self-inflicted pain coming from his mouth. "Surely, you're not considering it?"

"I am," Sylvia said weightedly and almost as if she was bracing herself for impact in a collision.

"Why?" Remi shouted suddenly and without intention, leaping to his feet. Then, taking a deep breath to compose himself, he sat back down and tried for a calmer tone, "Why would we ever consider doing something like that?"

"It's the lesser of two evils," Sylvia explained, sounding like she was trying for some level of diplomacy in the matter. "Sure, we'll lose some money and look weak. But if we don't do this, then we risk angering more Mortals in the long run. Can we really afford to do that at this point?"

"I agree," Remi nodded. "But we've both seen how Mortals work. If they think they can get something out of someone, they will all bum-rush the doors and start making demands like petulant children. Not all," he admitted, giving a measured one-armed shrug, "but the vast majority of them."

"I agree with you, Caswell," Sylvia sighed, staring at him as if she was searching for answers that he did not have. "Trust me, I do. But what other options do we have here?"

"I haven't the foggiest," Remi thought about it. "What about the officers that shot? Are they being held to the same accountability that we are?"

"None of them fired," Sylvia shook her head. "All of the shots came from within the crowd from the Mortals that broke through the gate."

"Any of the camera crews catch anything?" he asked hopefully, remembering how many news outlets had sent people to collect video of the incident. "Surely one of them must have something we can use to prove that we aren't the ones who put those Mortals in the Infirmary like that. They seemed to keep up with us pretty well from what they showed on the news."

"If they did, they aren't sharing it," the Arbiter pressed her lips into a thin line, conveying how annoyed she was by the whole situation.

"Well, can the Mortal authorities not do anything about that? I mean, they're all in cells at the prison. Surely, something can be done about it." Remi protested, then realized what the issue was. "They can," he said, putting it together, "but they won't until we agree to their terms. Right?"

Sylvia did not speak but averted her gaze confirming his suspicions. He let out a frustrated groan.

"Is he awake yet?" Remi asked after a brief moment of tense silence, trying to change the subject to something that would make him less miserable.

"Not yet," Sylvia shook her head, understanding that he had been referring to Finn in the Infirmary. "Nothing has changed as far as I'm aware."

"Did you send for his things?" he asked, tilting back in his chair to stare at the ceiling of the office.

"I have," Sylvia assured him. "They should arrive within the next few minutes."

"Is it too late to just have them sent to my house?" he asked hopefully. "Spare key is under the mat. Back door is unlocked if they can't find it."

"I'll arrange for that," Sylvia agreed to this in a muffled voice and Remi could hear her exhaustion that matched his own. He righted himself in the chair to see that her face was currently buried in her hands.

"I'm going to go sit with him," he said, rising to his feet and turning toward the door. "Just let me know whatever you decide to do in regards to the mayor," he finished with his back to the Arbiter. "And go get some rest. We both need it."

Sylvia nodded and said, "I'll have the guys take a look at the wand before they leave. Maybe they'll find something we can use before we have to deal with the Mortals."

Remi gave a half-hearted thumbs up over his shoulder as he made his way out of Sylvia's office and toward the staircase that would take him to the Infirmary, yawning several times along the short walk between floors. He did not think that he had ever felt more drained in his entire seven years with the Witch's Guard than he did in this moment.

Remi sat in an uncomfortable wooden chair at Finn's bedside in the Infirmary for what seemed like hours, watching the younger Warlock closely to make sure that he continued breathing. He swore to himself that he had seen the other's eyelids fluttering to open on more than one occasion, but after the third time, assumed that it was just him following something around in a dream.

The sun was only just beginning to set when Remi had come in, casting one side of the room into a hazy orange shade. It had finally stopped raining at some point while he had been in Sylvia's office and now he sat staring at the sky as it gradually shifted from a greyish-blue haze to a rose-colored wonder as the sun sank.

He had pulled the privacy curtain forward around them and listened as family members came to collect their perished loved ones. There were sobs from some and shouts of resentment, while others reserved themselves to a stoic acceptance of what had taken place. The ones who had been struck down by his spell that morning had all been taken to the Oxford Police Department and thrown in cells, where they awaited their individual trials. Remi secretly wished that they had been left for the Coven to deal with, but he knew that the Mortal authorities would never have allowed that, even with them being attempted criminals.

This was one of the worst parts about the job, Remi thought. He had always hated dealing with families of those caught in crossfires of devastation and generally avoided it whenever possible. He was secretly glad that the Healers were there to offer whatever solace could be had to the families this time because he was not sure that he would have had the energy to do it himself.

Remi found himself staring at the curtain and listening as one-by-one, the beds on the other side of the room were made vacant once more. He counted silently to himself as each group left.

Eight, he told himself after the last family had made their exit. *Eight less Mortals in the world.*

He felt a burning resentment toward the ones that had caused their suffering. This quickly mixed itself with a bubbling remorse at their loss, until he was left with a simmering stew of raging misery that he did not have the first clue of how to deal with.

Remi got up and peeked around the edge of the privacy curtain and across the way, seeing that there was still one body that had not been claimed as of yet. He could tell from the outline of the covers that had been drawn over him that it was the mammoth of a Mortal that had fallen on top of him during the initial altercation.

He glanced down at his arm in its sling and felt a brief pang of hatred, which he quickly bridled, feeling guilty for having had it in the first place. He knew that the Mortal had only been trying to protect those around him, most of whom Remi could only assume had been friends of his within the community. While the Mortal *had* broken his arm, Remi couldn't fault the man for that in all honesty.

After all, he thought to himself with a pang of remorse, *this arm will heal.*

Remi did not expect that he Mortal would suddenly wake up and pull back the sheet that had been thrown over him to conceal him from the rest of the room. He had only been doing something that had felt like the right thing to do at the time, and now he was a corpse lying in a bed because of it while no one came for him.

Remi felt suddenly hollow at the thought that he had not been able to prevent this. Then he felt himself becoming furious at the Mortal officer who he had taken down just before the first shot was fired. After all, if Remi had not had to deal with him, the other officers wouldn't have been distracted enough to allow the crowd to break through the front gates of the Coven House in the first place.

He clenched his free hand into a fist of rage just in time for a petite, older woman to peek around the curtain. She was the color of mocha and Remi instantly found himself wondering why he had never seen her in the House before. He let his hand open and stared at her curiously.

"Excuse me, young man," she spoke and her voice was even tinier than she was. "Do you happen to work here?"

The woman adjusted her horn-rimmed and bedazzled glasses then and Remi could see then just how devoid of color her rheumatic eyes were. He chuckled within himself as it finally occurred to him that she was not a Warlock at all.

"Is this y'all's hospital?" she asked, leaning heavily on her cane. "I was told that I could pick up my baby here."

Remi gave a puzzled look, which the woman did not seem to notice as he moved closer to her. She barely came up to his chest in her hunched position. She seemed to finally gather this and had to adjust herself to look up at him.

"Oh! You a tall one!" she laughed heartily as she craned her neck up and Remi was compelled to bend down to make up the difference.

"Ma'am," he began, peering around the room to see that it was momentarily empty. "Yes, ma'am. This is our hospital, but I'm afraid you're mistaken. We don't have any babies here."

"This the magic house, ain't it?" she peered up at him quizzically.

"Well," Remi began, hoping desperately that someone else would come in to relieve him of this conversation at any second. "Yes, ma'am. But-"

He was about to make another protest when the woman turned to see the body that had been thinly veiled by multiple white sheets.

"Oh, hush ya tawkin'!" the Mortal woman exclaimed. She had a thick drawl that seemed to get even more prominent when she got excited. "Now I know he in here! I been knowin' what he sleep like for a past thirty-eight years."

Remi gave the woman a puzzled look, imagining her to be some senile old crone when it dawned on him. He felt his chest tighten as he finally came to the disheartening realization that she was the person that had come to claim the last man's body.

"Only problem I gots now's, he done got too big fah me tah carry!" she laughed at the dilemma. She moved closer to the bed and smacked the limp foot that was under the sheet. "You betta wake up, here, Jermaine!"

There was no response.

Remi watched helplessly as the woman tried and tried again, on different lumps under the covering, until she finally reached the top of the sheets.

"Jermaine Octavious Pegues!" she shouted one final time, wobbling slightly on her cane as she did so. "You bettah gon' get yo butt out o' that bed this instant!"

The woman reached up to pull the sheet back from the head of the bed, but Remi's hand instinctively jerked up to stop her. He did not use force, but rather simply blocked her from pulling her own hand back. She seemed to get his implied meaning and unclenched the corner of the sheet that she had been holding onto.

As he steadied the woman, she tilted her head up to gaze into his blue moonstone eyes as he searched for some sort of consolation to offer. He could see the tears threatening to spill over her knowing cheeks and felt his heart breaking for this Mortal stranger as she whispered, "I reckon that mean he not gone wake up, is he?"

Her voice was sad and broken, but she somehow still managed to wear a defiantly strong smile across her face.

"I'm sorry, ma'am," Remi repeated his earlier sentiment, not knowing what else there was for him to say. The woman waved the comment away like it was a physical thing.

"It be fine, baby," she said, patting his hand and turning her attention back to the body of her Jermaine. "I done outlive err'body else. I guess it make sense I outlive this last one too. Last grandbaby I had left." The woman let out a heavy sigh that revealed her weary spirit. "I just always hope to myself that I be off to see the Good Lord first, 'fore this one go, too."

As he listened to this Mortal woman talk about being the last one in her family, he thought back to his earlier conversation with Valerie and the alternative she had taken. The difference was that this woman sounded almost ready to go, whereas the Vampire had sought a way to avoid her fate.

"But now," the woman went on, almost happily, "that just mean I ain't gotta wait on nobody else when I get where I'm going."

There was a certain serenity in her voice and words, whereas Valerie's had taken on a sort of distant longing for something she would never have again under normal circumstances.

"Can you help me get him out to the car?" she asked. Then, seeing Remi's arm in a sling, let out a hearty guffaw. "Well, I guess not!"

"I can," Remi replied, although he was not exactly sure how he was going to manage this feat.

"All by yourself?" the woman gave him a dubious stare. She seemed simultaneously impressed and concerned for his back.

"Maybe not," Remi admitted, feeling his cheeks go slightly pink. "But I can find someone to help us. Are you parked out front?"

"No, sir," the woman said. "But I'll run out there and have the deacon pull up close to the door."

"Sounds like a plan," Remi flashed a smile and the woman turned to leave with a determined look on her face. He watched until she was completely gone, noting just how fast she moved despite her cane.

When the woman had rounded the corner fully, Remi took a final, apologetic glance at the Mortal. He was wondering exactly how he would go about getting him down three flights of stairs by himself when two of the overnight Healers walked in. They gave Remi a unified expression of confusion when they saw that he was standing beside the bed of the final Mortal.

"Help me!" he pleaded, quickly explaining the situation to them.

The three of them watched as the Mortals drove away in a car Remi could only describe as a white hearse, before turning to head back into the house.

Remi made his way back up the stairs ahead of the two Healers, not stopping until he had reached Finn's cot again. He did not sit down this time, choosing instead to remain standing at the foot of the bed. Silently, he willed the younger Warlock to wake up as he watched him.

"You can go home, Caswell," Sylvia's voice behind him made Remi jump. He had not heard her click into the room and as he turned to address her, he could see why. Much to his surprise, the Arbiter had donned a fuzzy, grey dressing gown and slippers to match. She was now staring lazily at him. Remi had to stifle a laugh, which made the woman glare.

"Don't you say one word," she said, pulling her hair back into a tight bun as she did so.

"Wasn't planning on it," Remi sucked his lips in between his teeth and bit down, laughing out through his nose.

"It's late," Sylvia made an effort to ignore him. "Everyone is exhausted after today and I don't see him waking up any time soon. Go home, Caswell," she repeated. "I'll keep an eye on him and call you if something changes drastically."

Remi glanced from the Arbiter to the catatonic Finn and back again.

She's right, he thought to himself. That spell he had used this morning to scare the Mortals away had very nearly done him in completely.

To be honest, Remi was legitimately surprised that he had only been out for a few hours afterward.

As he stared at Sylvia, he realized that even though he was feeling utterly drained from all that had transpired, she did not look to be in much better shape. He watched the Healers come in talking amongst themselves and felt a certain sense of unease that he could not quite seem to shake in the pit of his stomach.

After the attack this morning had left so many Mortals dead and so many others injured, he was now unsure if the house could withstand another possible wave so soon after. The Mortals had broken through the front gate using guns in broad daylight and there was still a cloud of unrest hanging over the entire town. The purple sky outside the windows should have been a calming thing, but peace was the one thing that Remi did not feel at the moment.

Remi knew that the Arbiter was more exhausted than anyone and that if something were to happen, that the Healers were mostly trained in specialized restorative magic.

"Caswell?" Sylvia's voice broke him out of his doomsday thought bubble and he glanced back at her, a grim expression on his face.

Remi focused directly on the air just above the linens of Finn's cot, whispering, "*Prospicio Defensiva.*" An orb of blue-white light, roughly the size of a basketball, sprung to life at the foot of the bed.

As it floated in midair, a handful of feathery tendrils sprouted from either side of the being and began shifting around each other almost like they were reaching out for something, giving it the appearance of slithering wings. The Sentinel awaited further instructions that Remi never gave. Instead, he turned to a puzzled Sylvia and smiled.

"You should get some sleep, as well," he yawned. "He'll keep an eye out for the both of you."

"Good night, Caswell," Sylvia smiled, before quickly adding, "Oh, wait just a moment before you leave."

She materialized an envelope from somewhere in the pockets of her robe and handed it to him. He looked down at it and saw that it had the same seal of the Oxford Coven as the one he had received yesterday.

Remi did not respond, giving a final look to the spherical creature as it hovered over Finn's feet, ready to spring into action at the first sign of danger. The dim, grey walls of the room had been cast into its serene, bluish-white glow that seemed to radiate a restorative energy.

Remi tipped the brim of the hat he had been wearing all day to avoid the rain and turned on his heel, walking out of the Infirmary.

"Good night, Arbiter," he called back gently. "I'll see you both at the crack of noon."

The Dark Warlock stood in front of the simple, red-brick house and waited, just as he had so many times before this night. He could feel his skin crawling with anticipation as he readied himself to test his power without his wand.

While the few Mortals had been nothing more than a bit of collateral damage along his path to greatness, they had provided him with the extra boost of energy that he needed to rid himself of the wooden affliction that had plagued him since being freed.

He had always hated the impracticality of such trivial toys, viewing the infernal contraptions to be more hindrance than help. However, he had been forced to hide behind the slender piece of yew-wood, having been too weak to cast even the simplest of charms so soon after his stasis without aid.

As he watched the boy through the windows, the Dark Warlock felt the magic surging within him; coursing through his veins like a divine beast waiting to be loosed upon the unsuspecting world.

Several of the lamps overhead burst at that very moment, sending a shower of sparks down upon him as if to punctuate his inner thoughts.

Soon, he chuckled to himself. *Very soon.*

The boy, clearly having seen the show of lights, peeked his head just beyond the threshold of his doorway. The Dark Warlock watched quietly as the boy's pale silvery-blue eyes darted around the street like a chameleon. Seeing that nothing was the matter besides the lack of lamps, the boy took out a small straw and sparked the tip of it with a quick snap of his fingers.

So casual, the Dark Warlock smiled to himself. *Yes, he will do quite nicely.*

He watched as the boy inhaled from the thing in his mouth, making the tip burn ever-so-slightly brighter. He exhaled a cloud of smoke that wafted just overhead like hazy tendrils. His arm had been bound tightly to his chest in a plain, white cloth for some reason that was beyond the Dark Warlock. He felt it showed just how truly weak the creature before him was.

The boy's moonstone eyes had suddenly stopped their frenzied pattern of searching the street and froze intently on the Dark Warlock's feet. He stared deeply at that intuitive gaze that was now positively fixated on him.

He followed the boy's line of vision down to see that someone's Familiar had plopped itself down just in front of him and was currently purring up at him, longingly

Does he already know that I am here? the Dark Warlock wondered to himself, before quickly pushing the thought away. *If he knew, then surely he would have attacked by now.*

Chalking it up to nothing more than coincidence, he knelt down to stroke the creature under its chin. Black as the night sky itself and just as mysterious, the Familiar purred loudly at the first contact of his hand.

The Dark Warlock stayed like this for a few moments, only turning his attention back to the boy just in time to see him discard the burning straw and retreat back into his house. He righted himself then and gave a final, gentle nudge to the shadowy being with the toe of his boot.

"Go, now," he whispered, to which the thing gave a lazy harumph. "You must go back to your master."

The cat gave one last, audacious sneeze before turning and stalking away with its tail up in the air as if it had been insulted by the very idea of menial servitude.

Now, the Dark Warlock smirked, *it is time for the hunter to become the prey.*

He moved across the street like a shadow, robes billowing behind him in an unfelt wind, stopping just outside the front door of the house and placing his hand on the knob. He turned.

Remi tossed himself awake around three that morning. It was pitch-black in the room and he could vaguely feel that he had sunken down in the pillows just a bit too far for his liking.

It had been a fitful night thus far, as he was used to sleeping on his side. He knew he was going to have to find a way to cope with it for the time being, because he could not lose hours of sleep each night over the next however-long-he-was-forced-to-be-in-this-cast while he waited for the bones in his arm to mend themselves the rest of the way. He knew the Healers had done all they could do and that the rest would be up to his own body to fix.

To be completely honest, Remi could not even fully remember having made it upstairs after his last cigarette. As tired as he was, he imagined he had zoned out on the middle landing or ascended altogether half asleep. He was still bone-weary, but he knew that nature was not one to leave voicemails.

Remi threw back the covers and limped to the bedroom. Not even bothering to turn on the light, he moved strictly by muscle memory at this point. As he heard the echo of water on water, he debated with himself.

On the one hand, he would be more likely to hear his phone if Sylvia called if he were to hobble his way downstairs to finish the night on the couch and let himself be uncomfortable. On the other, he would get a deeper sleep if he stayed up here in his bed, which is what he desperately needed after the past few days he'd had.

Remi flushed with a sigh, resolving to stay upstairs at least for one night. He hoped that the Arbiter would take his joke about sleeping till noon seriously and, also, that nothing would change in Finn's condition during that time. He washed up and limped back into the bedroom, crawling back into the fortress of comforters and cushions he had made to fight his instincts to roll over onto the injured shoulder.

He actually could not wait until he got to the Infirmary in the morning. Remi had heard the Healers say that his leg should be ready for the field by then, but they had tied the bandages around the wound so tightly that he was having more issues moving it than the one time he had been forced to wear a cast from his toes to his groin for a week.

He had just readjusted himself so that the wounded leg was slightly higher than the rest of him when he felt an overwhelming sense of panic wash over him like the shower he so desperately needed.

Remi bolted to an upright position against the pillows and searched the room.

Did I close the door earlier? he asked himself. After all, he had not remembered making it up the stairs, so there was a heavy possibility that he had.

Even so, he was almost certain that it had been only slightly ajar just moments ago when he had gotten up to stumble into the bathroom. He waited for his sight to adjust in the dim light of his room and felt the dread intensify.

Now I know that I've never had that! he exclaimed inside his head, as he tried to keep his breathing level and remain calm.

Just a few feet from the door that he couldn't remember if he had closed, was a long, black robe that he knew did not belong to him. It seemed to be propped against the wall on some sort of coat rack that Remi was absolutely certain that he did not own.

As Remi stared at the figure, trying to discern where it could have possibly come from and why it was now standing in his room, he heard a low rumbling sound. Remi listened closer and thought that it sounded like some sort of feral beast, albeit one that he had never heard before.

Remi found himself frozen in place as the guttural sound grew louder and louder until it had become a palpable force pressing down on him in the darkness of his bedroom.

His bed began shaking at that moment and Remi could see now that the robe had started billowing wildly in the corner where it stood. He glanced quickly from the door to the window to see that it, indeed, remained bolted shut.

The growl, as it grew in volume, was slowly beginning to sound more human; a blood-chilling laugh. The voice became recognizable. It was just as familiar and demonic as the first time Remi had heard it during his visit to the Water Court.

He reached for his wand beneath the pillow where his head had been resting moments earlier. It was in that same second that the amber eyes shot open, glowering at him like a warning of dark events yet to come.

Then, all at once, it was gone

The Dark Warlock snarled in pain as the Familiar lunged straight at his face, taking a piece of him in its claws as it flew past him. The creature stared up at him, purring as if it had done nothing wrong. He could not truly fault the creature if it wanted to play; that was only natural for it, after all.

He reached down to stroke it once more and resume his work when he noticed what he had not before. The Familiar shared the same silvery-blue, moonstone eyes as the boy upstairs inside the house.

Surely it is not his! he thought to himself, with a certain alarm forming within him.

Before he could think on this any further, the creature sat on its hind haunches and stared up at him curiously. He continued to watch as gradually, the Familiar shifted forms from that of a simple, domesticated house cat to one of a more womanly figure.

Surely this cannot be! the Dark Warlock exclaimed inside his head. *She cannot be here!*

The woman seemed to be comprised of nebulas and stardust completely. She stared at him accusingly with those same, righteous moonstone eyes he had grown so accustomed to during his incarceration.

No! he shouted at the woman through his mind, knowing that she would hear him if she was truly who she must be.

Leave this place, the woman's voice echoed in his mind calmly. *And do not return until the time is right.*

The words were at once soothing and seemed to serve as a warning against whatever plans he might have been hoping to carry out on this night.

There is no way, he thought to himself. *This is simply a trick of my mind.*

He resolved himself to this belief and made to enter the dreams of the boy once more before he felt a searing hot pain run throughout his mind and body at once. He writhed in agony on the stones in front of the boy's home as the woman's voice echoed in his head.

I told you to leave this place, she spoke calmly. *You chose not to listen, so now you must suffer once more.*

No! he shouted at the woman, knowing that she would not hear his pleas. *You cannot do this to me!*

The last thing the Dark Warlock saw before he was banished back into his own home was the silvery-blue moonstones of the galaxy-clad being staring down at him with a feeling he knew from somewhere. Was it pity?

Remi shot straight up, drenched in a pool of his own sweat. He had, apparently, crashed on the couch the night before. As his heart hammered against his ribs and he tried to steady his ragged breathing, he thanked the universe and whatever deity might have been listening that the scene that had just played out had only been a dream.

Dawn was just breaking outside his living room windows and he let himself sink back against the armrest, feeling like nothing could harm him in the daylight. Then he noticed that the front door had been left wide open.

I know I didn't do that, he thought with a sudden panic rising back in his chest.

Remi instantly found his wand and gripped it tightly. He walked over and closed the door, locking it before checking the house. He checked the half bathroom downstairs and saw that no one was there.

He turned the corner into the dining room and checked the laundry closet and pantry. He glanced out the back window and decided that no one was downstairs.

Having secured the first level of his house, he moved upstairs to the bedrooms. Remi checked the spare bedroom that Finn had been in only a few nights before and saw that it was empty, before moving to his own. He grabbed the knob and instantly felt a static chill move up his arm and back down through his spine.

Remi shuddered as he turned and pushed against the door. He instantly noticed that the robed figure was not in the corner where it had been in his dream. He opened the closet and saw that it, much like the rest of his home, was empty.

Feeling somewhat relieved that he had not found anyone else, Remi grabbed a pair of jeans and a clean shirt. He walked into the bathroom and turned the shower on, letting the steam fill up the room entirely before he undressed and stepped in to clean off.

After he had showered, Remi made his way back downstairs and went about his normal morning rituals, opening the back door before lighting a cigarette. He started the coffee and remembered the envelope that Sylvia had given him the night before.

He went into the living room and grabbed the envelope and his phone from the coffee table, before coming back into the dining room. He took the seat nearest the door and opened the letter, pulling out the folded parchment that had been tucked inside.

Remi read over the first few lines and felt a hard lump forming in his throat. Apparently, when they had Traced the wand he had given the Arbiter upon his return, they had also re-Traced the piece of the bullet that he had brought in a few days ago. Both items had matched, although the Coven still did not have any record on who the Warlock might be in either case. To Remi, this was both a good and bad thing.

On the one hand, that linked two of his cases together. On the other hand, the fact that there was no way to physically Trace the rogue Warlock meant that there was still no way that Remi or anyone else could find him until they had more to go on. And who knew how many more people might end up dead in that time?

He let out a frustrated sigh and sat there for a few moments in silence, letting his thoughts race while he finished his cigarette.

He was in such deep concentration that he nearly started out of his chair when his phone rang and could not resist laughing at himself as he reached down to retrieve the device. He stared down at his phone confusedly, as this was a number he had never seen before.

Remi answered, only half expecting to hear another demonic laugh on the other end. Much to his relief, the voice was that of a familiar woman and though he did not know how she had come across his personal number, he was grateful that this was not who he had expected.

"Is this the Witchguard known as Caswell?"

Remi had made it back to the Oxford Police Department in what he imagined must have been record time. It was early enough in the morning that there was nearly no traffic on the roads.

The majority of Mortals that had influxed into town over the past week for orientation had already left. Those few who remained were there purely to enjoy what the town had to offer on the weekends.

He had only been caught behind a single University Transit bus after leaving his house. Luckily, the route went straight while he had gone left. Other than that, there were only a handful of people making the trek to work before nine on a Saturday morning.

"That was fast," Valerie noted, looking up as Remi entered the morgue for his second time in the past twenty-four hours. The Vampire woman was standing in front of what appeared to some sort of optical microscope, which had been attached to a projector that was focused on a dry-erase board at the far end of the room.

Upon first inspection, Remi noticed that there were no cadavers on the slabs in the center of the room this time around, for which he was grateful. He also noticed that Valerie seemed to be adjusting the lenses on the turret to bring something into view. He watched the image on the board as it went from blank, white slate to a brownish, hazy blob.

"What is that?" Remi asked, joining her as she tried to bring the slide into focus.

"That," Valerie answered, glancing up briefly to see the unclear projection, "is nothing."

She fiddled with the knobs a bit more until, finally, the slide came into view. "This," she said, stepping back from the microscope, "is what I wanted you to see."

"What, exactly, am I looking at here?" Remi asked, feeling just a bit ignorant as he squinted at the image that had been cast through the projector.

"Something that I discovered shortly after you left yesterday," Valerie responded, a grin already forming on her face as she prepared to explain. "This," she said, "is a sample of human skin tissue taken from a Mortal."

Remi must have made a face, as the Vampire hastened to assure him that it had been taken from one of the bodies that had already been sent off to the coroner's office in Jackson.

"Okay?" he drew the word out, feeling slightly confused, as he had not been expecting a biology lesson this early in the morning on a Saturday. Remi watched intently as the mortician pulled the first slide out of the diaphragm and replaced it with another.

"This," she said, adjusting the knob to focus the lens much more quickly than she had before, "is a tissue sample taken from the man we viewed yesterday. Notice anything different?"

Remi stared at the second slide, unsure of what he was seeing, but feeling like it was somehow not right.

"They're almost nothing alike," Remi guessed, his cheeks flushed as he stated what he imagined to be obvious. "This one looks like the cells are pulling apart more. It's almost like they're tearing at themselves to break free from one another."

He glanced over to see that Valerie was staring at him intently now, and wondered how long she had been in this position.

"Shouldn't they be more similar than this?" he asked, to which the woman beamed readily.

"Before I answer that," she said, removing this slide as well, "I have just one more sample for you to see." She placed yet another slide onto the stage and brought it into focus just as she had before with the other two.

Much to his confusion, Remi saw the same image as before, only slightly darker this time.

"Is this from the same person as the last one?" he asked.

"No," Valerie informed him. "This one was taken from a *living* specimen." To what must have been Remi's horrified expression, she quickly added, "*Willingly* given, solely for examination purposes. Before you get any ideas that I've broken the Covenants, Warlock."

"Haven't you?" he asked, a sly grin forming on his face.

"Not in this century," the Vampire's smile gave him the feeling that he did not want to know any further details and the two laughed together briefly, although Remi's was slightly more timid.

"What kind of person was this particular sample provided from?" Remi moved on, starting to get a clue into what she was trying to show him.

"A Lycan," Valerie's magenta eyes flashed briefly as she said the word, and Remi was unsure if this was for dramatic effect or a common blood hatred.

"Are you implying what I think you are?" he asked, to which the Vampire shrugged casually.

"I'm simply presenting you with facts, Guard," she said. "I imply nothing. Whatever you choose to do with those facts is entirely up to you after you leave this place."

"Might I ask how you came across this particular bit of information?" Remi asked, finding himself very curious about this new discovery from the Vampire woman.

"I had to clean up everything after examining the bodies yesterday so that the families could come pick them up and collect their things," Valerie said, flipping the switch to turn off the microscope.

She pressed a button on a remote to turn off the projector and walked to the wall beside the door and turned on the main lights.

"A bit of water got on the boy's arm," she went on, "and that's when it occurred to me that things might not be as they seem. I've been around long enough to know what a wet dog smells like, and I can say that it is not one of my more preferred odors in this world, Caswell."

"I have another question," Remi said, thinking back to the letter linking two of his cases. "The Vampire girl and the Lycan... Is there any chance that they were murdered by the same sort of weapon?"

"It's possible," Valerie mused aloud at this new proposal. "I can't say what sort of weapon was used to actually *make* those slashes across their necks, but I *can* say that they are very similar wounds. I can also say that the fact that both happened so close together and in the same town, it's almost too coincidental to not believe that they must be connected in some way."

Alarm bells went off in Remi's mind as his thoughts were sent into overdrive. The letter this morning had confirmed that the rogue who had killed the Lycan boy and blown up the jet on the airport strip had been connected. The amber eyes flashed through his mind and he connected the hanged boy with the floating body of the naiad that he had seen in the Water Court with Rydia and her subjects.

He could feel himself getting simultaneously excited and ill at that moment, finally piecing everything together in his head.

"So," Remi spoke slowly, drawing the word out as he tried to conceal his emotions from the Vampire woman that was staring at him with a puzzled expression. "This suspect has attacked a Fae, a Vampire, and a Lycan so far. If the pattern goes on like this, then that would suggest..." his voice trailed off and Valerie picked up where he had left off.

"There is no suggestion about it, Warlock," she said in a no-nonsense tone. "What I *would* suggest is that you get back to your Coven with this information. You need to figure out a defense strategy and put it into place as soon as you can. Your people are clearly the next on the list."

Remi knew she was right. He quickly said his goodbyes and bolted out of the room and up the stairs, ignoring the curious stares from the Mortal officers as he ran down the various connecting hallways and out into the parking lot.

Remi sped to the Coven House, taking most of the turns in town on two wheels. In hindsight, he took it as sheer blind luck that the roads were still relatively empty enough that he did not crash his Jeep into another car.

Once on the grounds, he came skidding to a halt just outside the front door and leapt from his seat. He ran up the steps and inside, taking those of the grand staircase two and three at a time. He did not care in the least that most of the Warlocks in the House were staring at him as if he had suddenly gone stark, raving mad.

Remi burst through the doors of the Infirmary just in time to witness his Sentinel spring to life. The thing changed from a miniature, glowing ball of light into an ethereal, winged humanoid figure with bluish-white flames where its eyes should be and an expression as unreadable as stone.

Most of the Warlocks around froze in their movements as, at first, the Sentinel did nothing but remain in place. Then, just as suddenly as it had taken on the form of this ghostly knight, the being materialized a lance of the same fashion as its body, hurling it directly at one of the Healers.

It looked very much like an avenging angel during this act, with its translucent wings flaring out behind it as if to shield those Remi had charged it with guarding.

The man had been coming toward Finn's bed with a syringe clutched in his hand and as the Sentinel's weapon pinned him to the wall on the opposite side of the Infirmary, he let out a wounded and otherworldly howl that echoed throughout the room.

"Caswell!" Sylvia shot to her feet, her face a mask of clear fury. "What is the meaning of this?" she shouted.

Remi did not respond to her, instead making his way directly toward the pinned Healer. He immediately wrenched the syringe from the man's hand and shoved it in his face.

"What's in here?" he spat accusingly at the man, who reached up, ignoring his accuser and trying desperately to pry the Sentinel's ethereal lance from his shirt. "*What is in this needle!*" Remi repeated, but the man was too preoccupied with his attempt at escape to notice.

As the man writhed against the wall, Remi saw a brief flash of amber in his eyes, before they returned to their original onyx. There seemed to be a glazed-over quality about them even now, in the man's panicked state.

"Check this, now!" Remi shouted, handing the syringe off to another of the curious-looking Healers, careful not to let any of the dark purple liquid escape from the tip of it.

The man grabbed the item from Remi's outstretched hand and ran off to the storage pantry to figure out what the contents were.

"Caswell!" Sylvia repeated, coming to join him in front of the struggling Healer. "What are you doing?"

Remi did not answer the Arbiter this time either, instead turning to his awaiting Sentinel.

"*Exauctoro*," he said and the whole of the room watched as the seraphic knight, as well as its weapon, dissipated before them.

Turning back to face the man just as he fell to the floor, no longer pinned to the wall by the Sentinel's lance, Remi said, "*Subvolo*."

The Warlock was lifted into the air, where Remi guided him to a nearby cot and placed him onto it, still kicking out at them the whole time.

"*Adalligo*," Remi said, and the man was bound to the bed by an invisible force.

"What are you *doing*, Caswell?" Sylvia was beyond furious now. "You cannot bind any other Warlock in this House without prior consent from your Arbiter, which I have not given you!"

Remi looked at her fully then. He still did not answer, but she could see the pleading nature in his moonstone gaze and instantly understood. The Arbiter gave a curt nod and stepped back only slightly enough to not be directly in the way. Remi placed his left hand onto the bound Healer's temple and whispered, "*Veritas.*"

He was treated with a flash of the same glowing, golden irises that he had become all-too-familiar with during his most recent nightmares. Remi jerked his hand back and screamed to the ceiling, "Dammit!"

His voice echoed around the room several times as if he had amplified it with another charm.

"What is it, Caswell? What's wrong?" Sylvia asked, giving voice to everyone's obvious concern that Remi seemed to have finally snapped under the pressures of his position within the Witch's Guard.

"Lockdown," he replied, quietly. Then to the Arbiter's confused expression, he unintentionally spat, "Lock the House down!" He was running full-throttle now and feeling more than a little buzzed from the rush of pure adrenaline that was currently coursing through his veins like a drug.

"I want this whole place on lockdown," Remi explained, this time a bit more calmly than he felt. "Every single Warlock here needs to be checked. No one leaves, no one comes through those gates. We are on high alert; code red! Our most immediate defenses have been breached!"

"What are you talking about, Caswell?" Sylvia shouted, her apprehension rapidly multiplying. "What is it that you saw?"

Just as Remi made to answer, the Healer that had taken the syringe came running back up the path from the Infirmary's storage cabinets. All attention was now on the man as he delivered the news that Remi had already been expecting, "This was a lethal dose of nightshade. If anyone would have taken it, they would have died within seconds. This is one of the things we give to the rogues that have been sentenced to death by injection."

Sylvia was just as pale as the sheets on the beds now, realizing that Remi was just as sane as he had ever been before this moment.

"What are you all waiting for?" she asked, shakily. Then, when no one did anything, she put the full authority of her position as the Coven's Arbiter behind her voice, shouting, "You heard the man. *Move!*"

Everyone in the Infirmary jumped into action and Sylvia grabbed the Healer that had just spoken by the collar of his scrub shirt.

Through gritted teeth, she whispered harshly, "If anyone so much as comes within three feet of this bed," she pointed to the one that held the sleeping Finn, "then you take them down at all cost and you come find me immediately. Do you understand?"

The man nodded just as rapidly as if his head were on a spring on the dash of someone's car. The Arbiter unclenched her hand and smoothed his shirt back into place before looking back to a speechless Remi, "Let's go, Caswell."

"Madame Arbiter," the Healer she had charged with guarding Finn called out after them. Sylvia turned with a questioning expression and he went on, "What do you want us to do with him?"

Sylvia looked down at the Healer that had tried to kill Finn with the nightshade, before focusing back on the man who had asked the question. "You throw that bastard in the dungeons and I'll deal with him later," she answered coldly, flashing an icy glare to match. "And if he tries to fight you going up there, then you have my full permission to toss him over the railing and make sure he hits the bottom."

The Arbiter turned without another word and moved with great haste from the Infirmary and onto the stairs, Remi struggling behind her to keep up with the pace. They began heading straight up instead of to her office as Remi had expected.

"Hello, Arbiter!" Pendragon's voice echoed through Remi and Sylvia's minds as he materialized. He sounded almost cheerful for some reason, which made Remi curious and uncomfortable. "How long has it been since our last meeting?"

"Not long enough," Sylvia replied shortly, making it abundantly clear that she had no time or patience for pleasantries and conversation. "This Warlock needs access into your halls once more."

"I see," Pendragon's milky-white eyes flashed just briefly enough for

Remi to notice. "But where is the Proven One's note of authority from the Magisters on High that your kind so highly regards, O' Great Arbiter Henderson?"

The Guardian's voice was sickly-sweet now as a smile scraped its way across his face. Remi found it odd that he used Sylvia's title with her maiden surname, but said nothing to point this fact out to either of them, figuring it would be best discussed at a later date.

"I do not have the time nor the patience for debates and decisions to be made on behalf of those in my own Coven, Guardian," Sylvia spoke calmly, but Remi could still feel the static charge in the air just as if she were suddenly casting an intensely powerful spell. "I am the authority in this House and we need answers now!"

"It seems that you have finally grown a backbone in this position," Pendragon replied, his smile no longer seeming disingenuous. "You are no longer the timid mouse of a Henderson Warlock that I once knew. This pleases me greatly." He paused then, almost seeming to debate with himself in his own mind. Finally, "Very well, Lady Arbiter. Your Proven One may acquire that which you seek."

Remi tried to share a glance with Sylvia at that point, which she ignored, focusing only on the Guardian and the door to the archives he watched over.

"Thank you," Sylvia said curtly, before turning to Remi.

"You may pass, Warlock," Pendragon's voice was aimed at Remi, though he continued staring at the Arbiter.

"How long do I have this time?" Remi asked, remembering the strict constraints he had been placed under the last time he had been up here.

"As long as you feel is necessary, Proven One," Pendragon answered, finally tearing his gaze away from Sylvia long enough to acknowledge Remi standing behind her.

"Meet me downstairs when you find whatever it is that you needed," Sylvia instructed, then with a pat on his uninjured shoulder, she added, "Good luck, Caswell."

Without another word, the Arbiter left him to once more venture back into the archives that he had now come to dread.

XIV

Remi walked through the threshold to the archives for the second time in the past few days and was slightly taken aback to find that entire room had changed. There were no longer spiralling shelves of volumes stacked upon each other. This time, the space seemed to be much more condensed than it had been before. Whereas before, the shelves had seemed to stretch on infinitely past Remi and he had wondered if he would ever find something he could use, now there was only a single blue-flamed torch sitting beside a circular desk in the center the center of the room.

The desk, which had been there during his initial visit, had been empty aside from the clock. Now it was overflowing with several stacks of thick, leather-bound tomes that covered every bit of its mahogany surface. Remi heard the sound of muffled footsteps behind him and turned to see Pendragon's hulking frame striding toward him in the dimness.

"How are you-" Remi began, but the Guardian held up a hand to cut him off.

"I can manifest both inside and beyond these halls at any given entrance point, if I so choose," he said, his lips noticeably moving this time as he spoke.

For some reason, this detail was more unnerving to Remi than his unattached voice bouncing around inside his head at the top of the stairs had been.

"Manifest," Remi turned the word over a few times, to which Pendragon gave a wry smile. "So you really are just a physical representation of these halls, then?" The Guardian gave a slight tilt of the head and Remi stated his most obvious observation, "Everything here has changed."

"Yes and no," Pendragon answered. "You must know that these books were here last time, as was the desk and the torch," he explained. "However, as you did not know who or what you were searching for in a more exact sense. The archives responded accordingly by offering you an endless wealth of knowledge, of which you took only a single book. As you return this time, you have a clearer picture in your head. These halls oblige that request with a more concise selection of titles."

"But that's just the thing," Remi objected thoughtfully. "I don't know what I'm looking for."

"Perhaps you do not," Pendragon seemed almost animated as he spoke now, as opposed to the stoic form Remi had grown somewhat accustomed to. "But I can safely presume that your thoughts are more focused this time around, rather than the jumbled mess you brought in with you last time."

"So," Remi considered this for a moment. "The archives are sentient, aren't they? They can read my thoughts?"

"I suppose one could make that observation," Pendragon nodded thoughtfully. "They are a living thing, as are many of the volumes upon their shelves, which are now hidden from your blind view. Whereas your common library just floors below us is updated manually by the appointed clerks, the archives are as boundless as the Warlock's thirst for knowledge who enters its halls. It cannot know exactly what you seek, but it can adjust itself accordingly to better fit whatever needs you may have, Warlock."

"I never knew that," Remi observed, having only just gained entry into the halls a few days prior. Then a thought occurred to him and he asked, "But what if I still can't find what I'm looking for?"

"Not many do," Pendragon answered Remi's first comment, though it had not been meant as a question. "That is why so many have been lost in these halls and so many more choose to fear them because of that unanswered longing. As for finding what you are searching for, Warlock, the archives will help you if you trust them to do so."

"I guess that would explain a lot about why the High Coven let so few in here," Remi mused. "But how will I let the Archives know if it's not what I'm looking for?"

"Open the pages to find out?" Pendragon smiled fully for the first time, throwing his hands up in a suddenly quizzical manner. "Hopefully now that you have a better understanding of how the magic inside these halls works, you can make quicker work of things than your previous venture."

Remi did not know why, but he preferred the daunting manifestation of the Guardian that stood outside to keep Warlocks out. Perhaps it was the simple fact that this helpful version of the being was such a stark contrast and seemed so out-of-character from what he had experienced before.

Remi pushed the thought away and glanced briefly at the desk, littered in its various tomes. He turned back to ask another question, only to find that Pendragon was no longer there.

Great, he thought to himself. *He can disappear just as fast as he manifests himself.*

There was a faint sound of a familiar voice laughing in a mocking and playful tone. Remi found that he could not help but join in as it echoed throughout both the halls and his own mind.

He crossed the room to the desk and began his search, opening the first of the thick volumes. He shuffled through each of them, quickly skimming over the pages and trying desperately to find something, anything, that he could use.

Whenever he found a shred of something that he thought might be useful later, he would jot down short notes onto a pad that had been sitting on the desk. Each of the books that he had taken notes from, he would place off to the side. Almost as if knowing when he found nothing useful in a book, it would disappear just as quickly as he had placed it onto the desk. There were also a few books that he never got to open as he moved along because they would vanish before he reached them. It was almost as if the magic within the room knew that there was nothing worthwhile to him in these select books and got them out of the way beforehand.

On the other side of the spectrum, as he worked and formed more precise and coherent thoughts in his search, the archives would provide him with new volumes on the desk in a separate pile from the rest. Remi repeated the process until there were almost no more books left on the desk for him to read through except for those that the archives had deemed necessary to his plight.

Remi checked the time when he had finished gathering his notes and was making ready to leave, shocked at how long he had been in this place. Three hours had already passed since he had first entered the archives and all he had to show for it now were his barely-legible, handwritten scrawls and three small books.

One was a history of magical families, several of which matched up with the list of original Magisters he and Finn had seen before. The second was an old alchemy book, in which someone had already taken several of their own notes in the margins. The pages themselves contained page-fulls of theories, applications, spells, and recipes that Remi had never even heard of before.

The last was a slightly thicker volume than the other two, as it had been devoted solely to the history, spells, and multiple 'beneficial' and 'practical' uses of Blood Magic. He kept this one tucked beneath the others, as he could already imagine the looks he would get if any of the other Warlocks were to see the title that had been so boldly emblazoned across the black leather in its scrawling, scarlet script.

Other than these, he had a few notes of his own in the pad that had come from all of the other books that the archives had provided him with. Before he went home to review them himself, he wanted Sylvia to take a look for herself on the off chance that he had missed anything in his haste.

"Caswell!" the Arbiter leapt from where she had been seated behind her desk. She seemed simultaneously relieved and surprised by his arrival in her office. He imagined she had expected him to be occupied in his search for at least another few hours.

Immediately, Remi could sense why she had given this reaction, however. The very air in the room felt heavy and charged with tension.

Two service members dressed in well-tailored, expensive black suits moved from where they had been perched by the door to block his path. The men wore earpieces and sunglasses, despite there being little to no light in the office. Remi supposed this was to hide their eyes from any potential threat. He had done it himself on multiple occasions on the off chance he was in a more crowded area and needed to scout for dangerous things and people without being noticed, but he could not be sure if this was the Mortals' reasoning. He did not particularly want to know, either.

Remi shuffled himself just enough so that he could peer around the taller of the two men. He instantly felt both of them tense in front of him, as if readying themselves to take him down before he could make a run for it.

"Stand down," said an unfamiliar male voice from one of the high-backed chairs in front of the Arbiter's desk. The men did as instructed, moving back to stand on either side of the door to bar anyone else from entering the office. "Come in, won't you, son?" the voice went on.

Remi watched as a wiry and somewhat disheveled-looking older man stood from where he had been seated and turned toward him. He knew the man immediately to be Mayor Kensington, the most recent elected official of the Mortals.

He wore a white, button-down shirt tucked into his jeans. This was paired with cowboy boots and a green, tweed jacket with leather elbows sewn on. It was a look that only older Oxford Mortal men thought could be pulled off successfully and made Remi immediately and overwhelmingly untrusting of anything the man might have to say.

As Remi remained unmoving and stoic at his place just inside the door, the mayor adjusted his thick, Coke bottle glasses to get a better look at the intruder.

"You're the one that was on the television!" the man exclaimed. Remi nodded politely at this assessment, glaring at the man who seemed to be oblivious to his disdain.

"Sit, sit!" he went on, beckoning Remi to take the seat next to him in front of the Arbiter's desk. "We were just discussing what we should do with you after that scene you caused yesterday!"

Something about the way the Mortal seemed to be acting as if Sylvia's office was his own made Remi's blood boil, but he resolved to keep his thoughts buried for the time being.

"Oh, are we?" Remi faked the biggest smile he could muster, adding a laugh he hoped would sound somewhat convincing. "Well, I think I should be a part of this conversation!"

Under his breath, he added a quick, "*Occulatio.*" The books in his hand were instantly made hidden to the Mortals by the light Glamour of Concealment before Remi walked further into the room.

"What's that you have in your hand?" Kensington asked, then upon seeing Remi seemingly empty hands, gave a puzzled look.

"What's that?" Remi cocked a brow at the mayor, feigning a level of befuddlement to match the Mortal's own. He gave a quick glance to Sylvia, setting the stack of things on her desk and catching her eye. He silently mouthed the word '*Glamour*' and winked so that she would be on board and not give him away. She inclined her head just slightly enough for him to see but said nothing in response.

"I could have sworn you were holding something when you came in just now," the Mortal said, scratching the back of his head and seeming more lost than ever. He looked back at his servicemen, furrowing his brow. "But I guess these two would have stopped you if that were the case."

"I should hope so!" Sylvia gave a curt laugh and Remi could instantly feel just how on-edge the Arbiter already was. "Now," she seated herself again, "back to the matter at hand, Mayor Kensington."

"Matter at h-" the Mortal squinted as if she were speaking a foreign language, before exclaiming, "Ah, yes! The matter at hand!"

The man turned to Remi and began speaking to him as if they were old chums that had gone to college many years ago.

"Now, look. I'm going to be entirely honest with y'all," he spoke with a somewhat sophisticated drawl, waving his hands about as he did so. "If I had any say, you'd all be lined up on a wall and shot. Because the way I see it, y'all Shiners are an abomination in the eyes of our Lord with your witchcraft and hocus pocus."

He paused here just long enough to hear a very audible sound of disgust from Sylvia, before going on as if he hadn't, "But the Board of Alderman won't let me have my way for that to happen. Damn liberal, Shiner-lovers, if you ask me."

Remi was almost shocked at the use of the term 'Shiner'. He had heard the slur for Warlocks used many times over the years, but never would have expected it from an elected city official.

"As is," the man went on, seemingly oblivious to the fact that he had offended both Remi and the Arbiter, "even if they refuse to let me get y'all out of this wonderful city, y'all know what you did was wrong. Just plain out, no use in pretending like it wasn't. Y'all are filthy in His eyes," the man paused here to point at the ceiling and Remi knew he was referring to some deity that governed Mortals. "Ain't no way around that. It's just proven fact."

"Yes," Remi began, keeping his voice level despite his overwhelming desire to deck the ignorant Mortal from his chair with his good arm. This was a feat he had not thought possible for him in the face of such bold ignorance. He was sure that the Arbiter must be just as furious as he was by this point. "We are quite aware, Mayor Kensington, of the nine Mortals and three Warlocks left dead in a crossfire that was started by *your* men. Yes," Remi repeated with a flat voice. "Quite aware, sir."

"I assure you," the mayor said, clearly flustered by such a blatant accusation from someone so unclean in his eyes as a Warlock. "It was *not* one of our officers! How dare you even suggest such a thing?"

"Oh, no," Remi admitted coolly. "I never said I was referring to your officers. I simply meant 'your men' as in Mortals. After all," he glared and the other man finally seemed to notice it this time, "all of us Shiners are the same in your eyes, so why not lump all of you Mortals together with some blanket statements as well and save some time for everyone?"

He paused just long enough for the words to sink in. He wanted to make it abundantly clear that he no longer had the patience to deal with Kensington's ignorance being spewed so willingly.

"The officers, I will say," Remi went on, "were under strict orders to use only non-lethal force in the situation. I must admit that I was very pleasantly surprised and impressed at their compliance with those orders."

"Well," the Mayor beamed pompously, puffing his chest out in front of him like a proud animal showing off its young to the world. "I do approve of the way that we train our law enforcement. The way they handled that situation, even in the face of such imminent danger from *your* people was simply beautiful. Even y'all have to admit that."

"*We?*" Remi mocked, not bothering to hide his amusement at just how ready the Mortal mayor had been to take credit for how the situation had been handled. "Oh, no, Mayor Kensington!" he reeled the man's attention back to him. "I'm the one that gave them those orders, sir. After one of your men by the name of Sanders waved his little toy in my face and then proceeded to stab it into my back. You might be proud to learn that at least *one* of your officers clearly shares your earlier sentiments about us 'Shiners.'"

Remi paused his explanation to revel in the shocked expression on the man's face. "I gave them those orders, just as I gave my own men the very same. All of them complied, on both sides, without any argument. And when all was said and done, you got the suspects responsible for the incident handed over to fill your cells and line your pockets on a silver platter, while our Infirmary got all of the bodies left in the wake of the events. I don't recall you or any of your men being there to comfort the friends and families of those who had lost loved ones in all the gunslinging, Mayor. I actually remember a distinct lack of cooperation on your part prior to calling us and making demands, sir."

No one else in the room said anything as Remi's words hung in the air like a cloud filled to the brim with accusation and defiance. "Now," he said in closing, "just what *are* we going to do about me, Mayor Kensington?"

The man's eyes skewered Remi now and he had to maintain composure, as he could easily feel the heat emanating from the Mortal that was directed at him.

"Mr. Caswell," he spat the name with a glare, almost like it was poison on his lips. "I do not like this power you have over whatever. Or what y'all seem to think y'all can do with that power whenever y'all so please. Now I am a God-fearing man! And I know for a fact, because the Good Book tells me so, that He don't like this devilry and witchcraft that you folks got cooking up behind that big, ole gate sitting out there!"

Remi glanced over to see that Sylvia's hands were in front of her. He noticed immediately that her fingers were laced together and white at the knuckles from trying to maintain a sense of composure in the face of the man's false propheteering. Remi was almost positive that she must have been making permanent indentations in her hands as she tried to keep herself together.

"Now," the mayor went on, his drawl thickening almost to a point beyond comprehension. "What's going to happen, is that you are going to apologize to the folks' families that were *devastated* by the *tragic* loss of life that took place here yesterday at *your* hands! You Shiners *know* that this whole mess was caused by *y'all's* tomfoolery during all this!"

It was becoming increasingly apparent that each line from the man's mouth beyond this point would be nothing more than unfounded accusations. He had clearly been so offended by Remi's previous statements that he could no longer form a thought that was not filled with hate toward them.

"Furthermore," he went on with his list of demands, "y'all are going to give them whatever they ask for. And y'all are going to give any information y'all have regarding this incident and that man's death over to our authorities. And, since I'm feeling just a bit froggy today," the man adjusted his glasses and puffed his chest out again as if to show dominance over them, "y'all gonna like it!"

The mayor sat back in his chair then, grinning pompously from ear to ear like a Cheshire cat as he awaited Remi and Sylvia's rebuttal on the matter.

"Mr. Kensington," Remi kept his tone calm through sheer and unbridled force of will at this point. "What, would you figure, is the worst part about your job as the Mayor of Oxford, Mississippi?"

"What does that have to do with anything?" the Mortal gave a confused look to Remi, before shifting his gaze to Sylvia.

"Humor the man," the Arbiter shrugged, finally unclenching her hands in front of her to cross them tightly just below her chest. She leaned back, almost as if she were already amused at the thought of what could possibly come out of this vile creature's mouth.

"Well," the mayor took a moment then to consider every detail about his position. The man seemed to be genuinely weighing out his response before saying, finally, "I guess it would have to be signing all those bills that come through. Gives my hand *real* bad cramps, y'know?"

"Oh, yes," Remi let out a hostile, single-syllabled chuckle. "Don't we all know how *strenuous* that must be for you! Would you like to know what just a few of my worst parts are about being a member of this Coven's Witch's Guard, Mayor Kensington?"

The man nodded eagerly, welcoming him to go on with a gesture of open arms.

"It's having a broken arm," Remi replied simply, glancing down at his sling just briefly enough for the Mortal to take notice of it before going on.

"It's having a broken arm," he repeated, "and sitting in an Infirmary next to one of your friends who might not wake up. It's knowing that the reason he might not wake up is because he was stabbed in the back so many times while protecting people he didn't even know. People who, much like you, Mayor Kensington, think he's just the scum of the earth and deserving of death just because he's a 'Shiner', as you so eloquently and repeatedly put it."

"The worst part about my job, Mayor Kensington," Remi let his silvery-blue eyes bore into the man fully at this point, not bothering to conceal his pure hatred for the man any longer, "is sitting in that uncomfortable, wooden chair and watching for hours as every single family..." he paused, then corrected, "The *actual* families, just so we're clear on who I'm referring to, you pompous piece of chicken shit. I don't mean some fake cover piece that a news station made up in order to increase its base of hate-spewing viewers."

He let the words hang in the air for a few moments before he went on, glaring across at the Mortal the entire time.

"It's watching *those* families," Remi continued, "that have lost loved ones come into a place that they're not comfortable with in order to collect the bodies and belongings of those same loved ones. It's watching them break down just across the room from you. Because I'm sure none of them knew that the last time they said 'goodbye' to those loved ones would be *the* last time they would see each other."

Remi glared whole-heartedly at the slimeball of a man before him, noting how increasingly uncomfortable the Mortal was getting as he went on and revelling in that small victory.

"The worst part about my job, Mayor Kensington," he punctuated his explanation with the other's name, "is having to watch a woman, who has outlived every single person in her entire family, pick up the last baby she had left. And knowing that she will be readying him for a funeral that she wasn't prepared for. Or telling a young girl that I know it hurts that she lost her best friend, but that the hole will heal in time. Because we both know that it won't. I say 'we' in that sense because I'm nearly positive that Mortals experience the same kind of grief as us sickly *Shiners*."

"But, yes," Remi stood now and propped himself against the edge of Sylvia's desk to get a better angle of the man's face. "I'm sure that signing papers must be just absolutely *dreadful*! I couldn't even imagine how much effort that takes on your part!"

"I didn't mean-" the man started to defend himself against the onslaught, but Remi quickly silenced him with a look that could have killed.

"No!" he shouted and the Mortal was shoved forcefully back in his seat. Remi could feel the room charge with the same static as if he had just cast. "I'm *sure* you didn't *mean* to piss me and my Arbiter off with your trivial, bigoted bullshit after the past few days the two of us have had, Mayor Kensington," Remi spat at the man, beyond the point of being disgusted. "But here we are! Now, would you like to know what's *actually* going to happen when you leave this office, sir?"

The mayor looked past him to the Arbiter, clearly speechless. He opened and closed his mouth several times and made sounds like he wanted to object, but couldn't find the words. Remi didn't need to check behind him to see what Sylvia's reaction was. He could feel her unfold her arms and shrug.

"Now, we'll agree to your little press conference," Remi said, feeling the shock from both Sylvia and Kensington. It seemed to permeate throughout the room and meet in the middle. "But we're going to be honest about a few things, first. Agreed?"

"Go on?" the mayor crossed his legs and knitted his fingers together to await the list of demands. It was plain to see that he was pleased with himself for having convinced the Coven to meet his requests.

"First off," Remi began, counting out on the fingers of his good hand, starting with his thumb. "The man that was hanged was not a Mortal. He was a Lycanthrope, which falls under our jurisdiction. This detail will be addressed during said conference so that we can alleviate all of the unnecessary confusion. Secondly," another finger, "we will not make any reparations toward families of any kind. The people masquerading as victims are lying for publicity and we all know this. If those true families of the deceased choose to request payment, they will do so through the city clerk's office and *you* will pay those out. Since it was Mortals that put them in those caskets, after all. I'm sure your press people can handle addressing that task without direct supervision."

The mayor clenched his jaw but otherwise remained quiet and attentive.

"Next," Remi went on, "at this press conference, we will have the Pack Alphas, as well as whoever they decide to bring. They will be scouting the crowd and surrounding area for any potential threats while the Witch's Guard watches the stage."

"Oh, no! I don't think so!" the Mortal fumed at the very idea of this demand. "Not on my watch!"

"You'll have your protection," Sylvia spoke finally, backing Remi's points so far. "We'll have ours. It seems reasonable so far. Go on, Caswell."

Kensington glowered at her but retained his seated position of silent acceptance.

"Lastly," Remi said, reaching his final digit and demand simultaneously. "Your office will accept all of the blame for what happened yesterday. And the officer that caused the ruckus that allowed our walls to be breached will be reprimanded for being an accomplice to negligent and willful manslaughter. This will be done publicly, whether by you or the chief, I really don't care right now. So long as it gets done. And if you decide to keep him on your force, he will be made to take sensitivity training as well as a course on how to effectively de-escalate a hostile situation. These will be offered at our Academy in Memphis, free of charge."

Remi finished with the last point and braced himself for the impact, which did not take long at all.

"Like *hell* he will!" the mayor was red in the face as he shot to his feet. "We will do no such thing! Who even knows what hocus pocus nonsense y'all'll try to fill his head with up there? You two!" he turned to shout at his servicemen. "Take this man into custody, immediately!"

The two men tensed, but remained at their post, not wanting to move from guarding the door. "I said *now!*"

Before either could make their move, there was a nearly inaudible voice behind Remi, "*Dormio.*" There was a soft thud as the two men fell back against the wood panelling of the office walls.

"I don't think you're in very much of a position to argue with us, Mayor Kensington," the Arbiter's voice was a soft warning, although she maintained a level of diplomacy with the Mortal that Remi had long since moved past. The mayor gawked at her with a positively horrified expression.

"Don't worry," Sylvia said, almost cheerfully. "They're only asleep until we get done with our conversation, Mayor. Wouldn't want any rash decisions now, would we?"

"But Sanders has got kids and a wife!" the man protested heartily, seeming more panicked than political. "What will they think when he comes back shooting sparks out of a stick like some kind of Shiner demon? He's a Christian!"

"Mr. Kensington," Sylvia dropped the Mortal's title and all forms of diplomacy she had held through the debate thus far as she addressed him this time. "Magic cannot be taught. You're either born with it or not. There is no learning of such things like this. We cannot teach something to someone who does not have the power within themselves."

The man appeared shaken and shocked, as if the very logic being presented to him was a foreign concept to everything he had been taught throughout his life.

"And as for religion," she went on before he could interject with his thoughts on the matter. "The reason our people are so militant and organized now is because of that very same religion. The deity and text that you, and so many others before you, cower behind are what started the initial war between our two groups almost four centuries ago. That very same being that you use to pillage and plunder and still feel justified in your actions. That book that you view as so sacred that you'll use it to explain away everything that you don't agree with."

"This is why we even have the social and political constructs that govern us as Warlocks. This is why we have the very Covenant that protects not only our kind, but every other kind; Mortals more than anything else."

"So in a way," Sylvia said in closing, "I suppose we should be thanking you for your people's ignorance so long ago. Feel free to educate yourself, Mr. Kensington. I'm quite certain that they still teach at least a few facts about Salem in even your Mortal history classes."

The mayor opened his mouth a few times to protest, just as he had moments ago, before hanging his head in a clear sign of shame and defeat.

"And if you still wish to protest any of these things like a petulant child," the Arbiter added hastily, finally letting her temper get the better of her for a moment. "That officer Sanders that caused this whole commotion with his ignorance? We can very easily take a play from your book and burn him at the stake in a public display as they did so many years ago to our kind, Mr. Kensington!"

The Mortal looked at her now as if she had suggested lowering a child onto a bloodied spike in the town center. It was clear that the Arbiter had his full and unbridled attention at this point.

"Now," Sylvia went on, certain that he would not make another peep as she did so. "The terms of our agreement with your desire for a press conference have been made laid out for you by Mr. Caswell. I see nothing too unreasonable with the requests made by our camp. Would you like to change any conditions to any of the points he has presented to you, Mayor?" She offered, to which the man shook his downturned head in refusal. "Then, will you accept the terms agreed upon by both parties?"

The Mortal mumbled something under his breath, which Remi imagined to be another slur or insult, but said nothing as Sylvia stood and came around her desk. She extended her hand toward him.

"Do we have a deal then, Mr. Kensington?" she asked, her voice ice. Remi watched as the man extended his hand reluctantly to grab hers.

"Deal," he replied, begrudgingly. The two shook to bind the agreement and the Mortal turned to his sleeping servicemen.

"*Gradiosomnus*," Sylvia said and the man's guards rose to their feet, although their heads remained at an uncomfortable angle. "I'm sure you'll see yourself and your men out?"

Sylvia and Remi watched as the horrified and defeated mayor left, not bothering to look back. Once he and his men had made their way completely out of the office, she turned to Remi with a stern glare, "This had better have been worth all that trouble."

"It is," Remi smiled excitedly. "*Aperio*," he muttered, uncovering the

Glamour he had placed on the books to conceal them. "Look at this. Ever heard of the Lacunaes?"

"No, I can't say that I have," Sylvia replied, returning to her seat and staring down at the volumes that Remi had presented her with. "Is this what you needed to make your case?"

"It isn't," Remi admitted hesitantly. "But at the same time, it is!"

"What do you mean?" she asked, seeming intrigued by this statement.

"So," Remi began, knowing his explanations tended to ramble on. "I haven't really had a chance to talk to you with all that's been going on in the past few days. But you remember how Finn and I were looking through that last book that I got from the archives?"

"Yes," Sylvia said. "And yeah, it has been pretty crazy around here recently. What did you find?"

Remi gave her a brief explanation of everything he and Finn had found in the book he had taken home the other day, leaving out the detail about how the page had been held open to a certain section, not wanting to worry her with that bit of information.

"So you're telling me that between that and your meeting with the Valerie woman at the morgue, that you think this Lacunae whoever might be the person related to all of these other cases?"

"I'm not sure on that just yet," Remi admitted, hesitantly. "It would make sense, though. It's someone that hasn't been on our grid for years, maybe even centuries. It's someone that has an intimate knowledge of both the Coven and the area around here. At least intimate enough that they still haven't even been seen by anyone working this case or any of the other ones that might be related to it."

"What about the killings?" Sylvia asked. "How are they all related to your findings in the archives?"

"Well, this is all speculation at this point," Remi explained earnestly. "But I think that this Dark Warlock that we've been searching for might be connected to all of the cases I've been working on these past few days. And if I'm right about other things, then there might be more cases that we either haven't found out about yet, or just haven't made the connection to this particular culprit."

"What do you mean?" Sylvia goaded. "You think there have been more murders around Oxford that we just haven't found out about yet?"

"Possibly," Remi replied. "I've been looking at some of these alchemical formulas in this other book," he opened to the first page that he had earmarked in the book he had presently been holding and set it down on the desk in front of the Arbiter. "I think that some of these rituals might be in a certain correlation to whatever this man is trying to accomplish. I just don't know exactly what that is at this point."

"Are you saying that you need more time upstairs, Caswell?" she asked, rubbing her temples as she stared down at the plethora of pages that had been placed before her. "I told you that you didn't have to come down until you had finished with your research."

"It's not that," Remi shook his head, searching for a better explanation. "It's like all of the pieces are there," he said finally, "but I don't have a clear image of what the puzzle is supposed to be when I'm finished. Does that make sense?"

"Elaborate," Sylvia replied, crossing her arms in front of her chest. "You need more time? Because I'm not entirely sure that anyone has more time to give us, given the current circumstances. You know the Mortals are going to get restless after we go to that press conference with Kensington. And there's no guarantee that he won't betray us once he has an audience he can manipulate for points."

"I know," Remi admitted, agreeing with her sentiments about the slimy Mortal mayor that had just left her office. "It's just that in that other book we had, it was almost like someone had purposely blacked out the name all throughout the pages, wherever it had been mentioned. Then, in that one," he indicated one of the tomes sitting on the Arbiter's desk, "there are only so many things that it says about Warlocks from that line. Even those seem to be only the important details. And I found what little I could on Blood Magic in that alchemy volume," he indicated the second book. "But this guy we've been dealing with is just so all-over-the-place that I can't hammer out a distinct motive."

"Well," Sylvia unfolded her arms, placing her elbows on the edge of her desk and interlacing her fingers. "Do you want the good news or the bad news first, Caswell?"

"Surprise me," Remi said, not liking the grim tone that his Arbiter had taken with him. "I'm sure I'm not going to like either one of them."

"Probably not," the woman admitted with a shrug. "While you were upstairs, the Trace came back on that wand you brought me from the campus. It links the recent string of murders together." She paused here and gave Remi a peculiar look.

"That should be a good thing, right?" he asked, cocking a single brow and squinting at her as if he were trying to decipher some abstract message in her words.

"It would be," Sylvia agreed. "But there are no other spells that could be Traced back past those particular spells. And here's the kicker," she held up a finger before Remi could interrupt. "We don't have that wand anywhere in our databases! Not in Oxford, not in Salem, not in a filing cabinet in the *entire* Coven or High Coven! So it's like this particular perp doesn't even exist to us."

"I've got to admit," Remi stared at the floor as he spoke, "that *does* complicate things a bit."

Neither of them said anything for a few moments, as Remi was sure both of them were trying to figure out where they might go from here. He watched as the Arbiter slowly closed each of the two books he had placed on her desk and stared at the third, which he still had tucked under his arm.

"What's in that one?" she asked him finally, reaching up to hand the other two back.

"A bit of homework for me," Remi shrugged. "The alchemy book only barely touched on Blood Magic. That's all that's in this one."

"You're not going to use any of that stuff, are you?" Sylvia seemed genuinely concerned now, to which Remi shook his head.

"No way!" he assured her with what he hoped was a convincing smile. When she didn't seem to buy this, he went on to explain, "I don't know what this guy is planning, so I want to be prepared. I'm not going to use any of this stuff myself as far as the Blood Magic aspect goes, but I did see some counterspells in here that I want to practice before I have to use them against someone who has probably been working toward this for their entire life."

"I hope so," Sylvia said, clearly not liking that Remi had brought something so taboo into her office. "I don't want to lose one of my best members of the Oxford Witch's Guard to Blood Magic."

"You won't," Remi assured her. Then, as he caught what she had said, he gave her a grin. "You think I'm one of your best?"

"Get out, Caswell," Sylvia glowered at him now, in a semi-playful manner. "I have to prepare myself for a press meeting with the Mortals, apparently."

Remi laughed and moved across the room to the Arbiter's desk from where he had been pacing as he talked.

"Let me know what you find, Caswell," Sylvia said. "Keep up the good work."

Remi nodded and tucked all the books beneath his arms and turned on his heel to leave, only stopping near the door as a darker thought than all of this occurred.

"What would you do if I did end up using one of these spells in this book?" he asked, staring at the door as he froze in place. "Purely hypothetical question."

"What do you mean, Caswell?" the Arbiter asked, sounding more-than-a-little concerned by the question he had posed. "I'm not sure I feel comfortable answering that at this time."

"What if I found something in here that would protect us all from those people that stormed our grounds the other day?" he asked. "Would you still treat it as if it were just some common, outlawed form of magic?"

"I know you care about him," the Arbiter said earnestly. "But that's not the way to go about it, Caswell. I'm sure I would be on your side, but I would have to do my duty as the Arbiter to this Coven. You know that better than anyone else here."

Almost as if on cue, the door to the office burst open at that moment, effectively putting an end to their sudden philosophical exchange. Finn stood in the threshold now, silhouetted in the light being cast from the chandelier behind him. The younger Warlock walked into the office timidly, his skin a pale shade of green and his expression just as gaunt.

"I feel sick," he announced to them, just before leaning forward to heave bile from his empty stomach all over the floor just in front of himself and Remi.

The Arbiter had been all too ecstatic at Finn's sudden and miraculous recovery from his temporary coma to be angry with him.

Remi had sprinted up the steps to the Infirmary to collect the few things the younger Warlock had had on his person during the battle, while Sylvia had cleaned up the mess that had been made on the hardwood of her office floor. Remi had brought Finn home with him and made soup while the other had showered.

Finn had hastily gulped down six full bowls without stopping, which was not a surprise after having been out of commission for nearly three full days.

"You sure you're cool with this?" Finn had asked, looking guilty even as he readied himself for bed. "I don't want to intrude on you."

"It's not a problem at all," Remi had insisted. "No one's used that room since I moved in. That's been roughly five years, now."

Finn had given him an expression of gratitude mixed with something else that Remi could not quite read.

Exhaustion, maybe? he had thought to himself in the moment.

Now the younger Warlock had gone to bed and Remi stood in the doorway of the guest room, watching him sleep and wondering how he could still be so tired.

It's just like having a puppy, Remi thought and laughed to himself as he closed the door behind him.

He walked down the hallway slowly, being careful to step around the creaky boards so as not to wake Finn. He moved his steaming mug of coffee into his sling arm so that he could hold it while he opened the door to his own bedroom.

As soon as he turned the knob and pushed, Remi could feel every single hair on the back of his neck stand on end. He looked to the bed and a phantom echo of the nightmare from the previous night flashed in his mind.

"*Detego*," Remi whispered, bracing himself for a second encounter that never came. He inched toward the nightstand, feeling very uneasy with each step as if he were being watched despite the detection charm having revealed nothing. Remi took a sip from his coffee and set it down on the nightstand, replacing it with his wand and making his way back downstairs.

He went through the entire first floor, making sure that both doors and each window were locked and bolted, respectively. Once satisfied with these, he made a few sweeping motions with his wand, muttering incantations with each movement.

"*Seromnis*," all of the locks were bolstered against anyone that might try to come in.

"*Claustromnis*," the window latches.

"*Occludo*," the air inside the house was charged with the static of a Glamour of Concealment.

"*Repello*," a curtain was cast over the house to deter any would-be intruders from even wanting to come close to it.

"*Defensiva lumen*," a network of minuscule spores of pale, white light fluttered to land on the front door. He repeated the charm for the back door.

Feeling accomplished with his work on the first floor, Remi reascended the stairs. A shadow of a tree coming through the window at the end of the hall caused him to nearly jump out of his skin. He laughed at how ridiculous he would look if Finn were to wake up anytime soon and focused his wand in the center of the hall.

"*Prospicio defensiva*," Remi whispered the incantation so that he would not wake his guest. He watched as the orb of blue-white light shimmered to life between his and Finn's doors.

Remi was now thoroughly content in his defenses. He went back into his room, only to find that he still felt shivers run through him.

He quickly tucked his wand into his pocket and grabbed his coffee, making his way back down to the living room, where he finished it off. Remi placed the freshly emptied mug on the table in front of him and positioned himself at one end so that he would not roll onto his injured arm if he were to have another restless night.

Thankfully, Remi did not dream that night and somehow managed to get the best sleep he'd had in the past week, despite being on his uncomfortable couch.

XV

"Any particular reason there's a Sentinel cast in the upstairs hallway?" Finn was standing on the middle landing of the staircase, looking down on Remi with arms crossed. He cocked a single brow as Remi rolled over to see him. "Or why I can't open any of the doors or windows to let in some fresh air?"

Remi grumbled and rubbed his eyes, before stretching and laughing from his spot on the couch, "You don't even want to know, kid."

Finn eyed him suspiciously, but said nothing.

"I hope you got a good night's sleep," Remi went on. "Because we're going back for round two today. You look a lot better than you did last night. Did you get sick at all after you fell asleep?"

"Not that I remember," Finn shrugged, before furrowing his brow and adding, "Round two?"

Remi thought back and remembered that the other had not yet entered the office until after Mayor Kensington had already left, so he had not been there to witness the heated exchange of words.

"We have to go to a press conference today," Remi explained, pushing himself into a sitting position and twisting so that his back popped from having slept on the couch. "It's being arranged by Mayor Kensington, but we'll be more prepared for anything that might go down this time. We'll have more of the Witch's Guard there this time and the pack Alphas, at least."

It was clear that Finn did not like the sound of any of this information, but the younger Warlock remained stoic despite it all.

"If something happens this time," he said, staring somehow through Remi, his emerald eyes suddenly having glazed over and looking very far away. "I refuse to incapacitate. I aim to maim."

Remi felt a mixture of tightness in his chest and the desire to laugh. He knew the other was serious, but the fact that the last line rhymed made him wonder, even if only slightly. He knew it would do no good to argue with him after what had happened the other day and, honestly, he did not want to test the limits in either direction.

Who can even blame him? he thought to himself. Remi secretly wanted to just sit back and let the kid work out whatever frustrations he might still have, with the Mortals or anyone else, until the hostility had passed through his system. *The Arbiter will never go for that brand of therapy, though*, he reminded himself.

Remi twisted his back in the opposite direction just as he had before until he heard it pop once more, before smiling at Finn still standing on the landing.

"Fine by me, kid," he shrugged. "If things go down, I'll just turn a blind eye, so as not to incriminate myself any further than I do on a general basis."

"What happened to your arm, by the way?" Finn asked, before realizing and nodding the question away in his mind. "Oh, right!"

"Yeah," was all Remi could manage, reaching in between the cushions where he had stashed his wand before falling asleep the night before. He would be glad when his arm was well enough to remove from the sling. His wand felt more like a crutch at this point than if he had actually been made to use one for his injured leg. He looked down at that point and realized that he had not taken off the bandages around the wound yet, despite the Healers having reminded him that it was okay for him to do so the previous day.

"Why don't you start the coffee while I work on disarming these charms?" Remi asked, pushing himself up from the couch with only relative difficulty.

Finn nodded a silent agreement before making his way into the kitchen while Remi trudged his way up the stairs, still half-asleep.

Once at the top, he made a dismissing wave with his wand, muttering, "*Exauctoro*." The wisp of a Sentinel dissipated like smoke and Remi went back down. "*Tenebrae*," he said twice. Both nettings of protective light at each of the main doors dimmed to nothing, disappearing with a barely audible snap.

"*Reseromnis*," he said and the doors were unbolted.

"*Patefaciomnis*," he muttered for the windows.

"*Apertum*," Remi held his wand above his head and brought it down slowly, like he was gradually pulling at a tangible string to draw back a large curtain from in front of a window. This act cleared away the Glamours he had cast on the entirety of the house to keep unwanted guests out as he and Finn had caught up on their lack of sleep the night before.

Satisfied that everything had been effectively reset to a blank slate, Remi tucked his wand into the waistband of his pocketless pajama bottoms and walked into the kitchen. Seeing that the coffee had not quite finished making, he took his wand back out and laid it on the counter, trading it for a stick of a different sort.

He went out onto the back patio, glaring at how bright the sun was in contrast to the magically-induced darkness he had plunged his house into via his Glamours.

"Here," Finn said just behind him, handing him a mug. "I didn't know how you took it."

"It's fine," Remi answered, lighting up and taking a sip of the scalding, black liquid. "I have a feeling it's going to be a black coffee kind of day today."

"If we have to deal with another Mortal mob of fools," Finn chuckled into his own mug, "it sounds more like a Bailey's and Joe kind of day to me."

Remi cocked a single brow and laughed at the very thought of the other drinking so early in the day, but kept this commentary internalized.

"Come on, kid," Remi said, flicking his butt down. "We had better get ready if we're going to get to the Coven House before they all leave us."

"This armor is so heavy!" Finn complained as he and Remi made their way up the steps to the Arbiter's office. "I would have been fine with just the regular, old hunting gear."

"Maybe so," Remi half-heartedly agreed. "But this just makes sure we don't have a repeat of last time." Finn sighed but argued no further. "Hey, you're not the only one who's going to have an issue today. I'm the one in a sling. If anything goes down, I'm an easy target."

"Fair enough," Finn sighed once more. "By the way, remind me to teach you a few Glyphs."

"Come again?" Remi cocked his brow, not sure if he had heard correctly.

"Glyphs," Finn repeated. "Instead of wasting time casting all of those individual defensive Glamours and charms, you could have just used a single Glyph and gotten the same effect."

"Is that so?" Remi laughed at the thought of the other, younger Warlock being able to teach him anything.

"Yeah," Finn replied, oblivious to the other's amusement. "Although, you might not get your security deposit back if you decide to move. It usually tends to scorch whatever surface you decide to draw it on." He averted his gaze, looking a bit guilty at this admission.

"And just how would you know all of this?" Remi asked, eyeing the other curiously now.

"Remember fifth year at the Academy?" Finn responded with a question, to which Remi nodded. "Where they make you take a vocational course for whatever field you're planning on going into? Well, I took Combat Machinations. Part of that was tactics and traps, which included offensive and defensive Glyphs. They're pretty easy to learn. I can teach you some time if you want?"

"I can use them," Remi informed him. "I just prefer casting. It feels more natural for me, even if it takes a little extra time on things like that."

"Oh," Finn shrugged. "Well, let me know if you change your mind!"

"Will do," Remi assured him just as Sylvia emerged from her office.

"*There* you two are!" she exclaimed, pleased to see the two of them already nearly to her. "We have a bit of a situation on our hands, at the moment."

Though she was glad to see them, she also seemed somewhat on edge. Remi and Finn exchanged quick glances as the Arbiter welcomed them into her office, closing the door behind them. Remi saw immediately what, or rather *who*, that situation was.

Propped against the Arbiter's desk was a rather slender man with pale skin. His pants seemed to have once been part of an expensively-tailored pinstripe suit, while his shirt was a plain, black V-neck t-shirt. His pitch-black hair fell loosely around his defined, angular jaw and had a greasy quality to it that seemed to purposefully reflect the light away from his face.

A small cross had been burned into the left side of his neck and the man wore it openly like a brand for all to see and know that he had escaped whichever fool had been unlucky enough to attack him. Remi had met this man only once before in his career and knew that he was the current Lord of Oxford's Brood of Vampires, Sebastian Kaine.

"How nice of you to finally join us, gentlemen," his voice was both slimy and sinister, a feat that Remi had forgotten was possible until hearing it again. "I understand that you have been consulting with one of ours on a certain case you have?"

"I wasn't aware that she was a part of your Brood," Remi said, knowing that the man must have been referring to Valerie. He supposed that he should have figured that she might at least have come into contact with them, living here for any prolonged amount of time. "It was never mentioned in our conversations."

Not that it's any of his business, Remi thought to himself, watching the Vampire Lord closely, as he knew what the man was capable of when provoked.

"She is not," Sebastian admitted. "Which is quite piteous, as we would gladly welcome one of her age and wisdom among our ranks." He paused to make a single, disdainful click with his tongue before proceeding, "As is, Warlock, she prefers the company of Mortals; however brief their existence might be. And we would never wish to take that choice away from her, as we are not entirely unreasonable people. We do, however, keep tabs on those like her, who refuse to join us."

"For what purpose?" Remi asked, already having an idea of what the reasoning might be.

"Enemies closer than friends," the Vampire confirmed with a callous shrug. "Or however that saying goes."

"She's an enemy?" Finn asked, not seeming to grasp the idea of what the man was saying, to which the Vampire laughed.

"I have enemies even among my own subjects," Sebastian explained with a cold laugh. "All of whom would gladly see me dead for the seat of power alone!"

"Okay," Remi said, trying to keep the conversation moving along. "That's nice, but it still doesn't answer why you've shown up here this morning. I'm sure you would not be out in broad daylight if there wasn't a good reason behind it."

"Please do pardon my lack of manners, Witchguard Caswell," Sebastian said, a slight edge to his voice. "I just thought you all might like to know about something one of our scouts picked up while feeding earlier this week."

He knew they needed blood to survive, but the thought of a Vampire actually feeding made Remi's stomach do backflips in disgust even though he knew it was only on the wildlife in the surrounding area.

"Speak, Lord Kaine," Sylvia said, keeping an upbeat tone to her voice. "What is it your people have found?"

"A house," Sebastian answered, flashing them an unsettling grin.

"A house in the woods?" Finn asked. "Like a cabin?"

"That's nothing," Remi laughed at the false lead. "Several Mortals own cabin homes on the outskirts of town. I'm sure some are further out into the woods than others for the sheer privacy."

"Not a cabin, Warlock," the Vampire's grin widened then to reveal his retracted fangs. "A manor. One that is surrounded by what feels like several heavy Glamours."

The two Guards shared quick glances with the Arbiter, waiting for her cue to follow.

"Where is this manor you speak of?" Sylvia took no time in asking the important question.

"I can show you better than tell you, Madame Arbiter," Sebastian explained. "The Glamours make it hard to find and I wouldn't want any of you to get lost in my Brood's feeding grounds on my account. I just don't think I could bear the thought."

He grinned a second time and his fangs seemed to have descended slightly more than previously.

Something about the way he delivered the last line gave Remi a chilling feeling in the pit of his stomach. The three Warlocks exchanged a second look of approval before Sylvia gave a slight nod.

"Finn," she said. "You will accompany Lord Kaine into the woods to locate this manor that he speaks of."

"But," Finn hastily objected, "what about the press conference?"

The thought of the younger Warlock venturing away from civilization with Oxford's Brood Lord so soon after his recovery gave Remi an overwhelming sense of doom, but he knew what the Arbiter was trying to do.

"We'll be fine," he chimed in, trying to sound nonchalant about it. "This might help us find the guy we've been looking for."

"Recon mission," Finn said begrudgingly. He understood what they were trying to do and did not seem to like it one bit. "Got it."

"If we're not back before you are," Remi said, trying to think of something else to keep the younger Warlock busy. "You can go talk to the Healer that's in the dungeon. See if you can get any more information out of him, now that he's had a day to detox from whatever hold he's been under. I'll expect a full report when I get back."

Finn gave a fake smile and Remi could swear he saw the slightest flash of resentment in his emerald eyes.

"Right," he replied in a disappointed tone, then to Sebastian, "After you, Lord Kaine." As the pair reached the door to leave, Sylvia turned to them.

"Oh, and Lord Kaine?" she said coolly, driving her point home as she spoke. "That's the son of a Magister. Should any harm befall him while under your care, you'll have the full wrath of the High Coven brought upon your head. I wouldn't be able to help you if that happens. Even I can't save you from that."

The Vampire gave a curt nod of understanding before turning and escorting Finn down the stairs. Remi and Sylvia watched until the pair had fully exited the House.

Finally, Remi asked, "Are you ready?"

"Do I have a choice, Caswell?" the woman replied tiredly.

The two of them arrived in the Grove on Ole Miss campus, where Mortals had already started gathering. Remi had been directed to park in a spot that had been reserved for those that would be speaking at the event. The anticipation for the press conference that would soon be underway hung in the air, filling Remi with a dreadful pride.

As soon as they stepped onto the sidewalk that ran along the edge of the area, Remi took out a pair of mirrored shades that he had bought just for the occasion. He put them on, having gotten the idea from seeing the mayor's own two servicemen the day before. They saw that a single Mortal was running toward them, full speed. Remi immediately tensed, readying himself to strike out at the last second when the boy shouted in their direction, "Sylvia Ashcroft?"

Remi and the Arbiter shared a quick, puzzled glance before confirming her identity. The boy was holding a clipboard and wore an earpiece in one of his ears, which was connected to a box of some sort that had been attached to the back of his belt.

"Oh, good," he sounded relieved and gestured for her to follow him. "We need to get you fitted for a mic feed."

Sylvia looked like she did not want to go, but followed obediently.

Remi watched them disappear into the crowd and reached into his pocket, pulling out a cigarette.

"Hey, sir!" a security guard yelled at him as soon as he lit up. "You can't smoke on campus!"

Remi exhaled and pulled his shades up to make sure that the man had been talking to him. The man, upon seeing his moonstone eyes glinting in the sunlight, tipped his cap in apology.

"Never mind," he said politely, moving on and leaving Remi to stare confoundedly after him. Remi shrugged to himself and began surveying the area.

Oxford's Grove was a decent-sized expanse of greenery in the middle of Ole Miss campus. Situated just between the Student Union and the campus library, there were almost always a few handfuls of Mortal students huddled somewhere beneath the shade provided by the many, massive oak trees dotted throughout the area. During football season, it was littered with tents and parties full of kegs and grills, especially on home game weekends.

Remi had learned early on to keep up with those home game weekends, as that was when he worked from his kitchen table and caught up on paperwork. He refused to let himself get caught up in the traffic that accompanied the influx of so many Mortals if he could help it.

Currently, the Grove was filled almost to the brim with camera crews, students between classes, and townspeople who were generally curious to see what was about to unfold. Even in such a crowd, Remi easily spotted the Oxford Pack Alphas, thankful that they stood out among the Mortals.

He flicked his butt out and started toward the small group, noticing as he drew nearer that Davis from the Oxford Police Department was talking to one of them. Seeing that the argument was seeming to get pretty heated between the two, Remi moved faster, dancing through the crowd as best he could and trying not to stumble into anyone with his still-injured arm.

"Hey, guys," he greeted them all. The Lycans were not as formal as the other magical creatures Remi had dealt with. Davis noticed who he was and instantly lit up.

"Hey, man!" the officer exclaimed, grinning from ear to ear.

"Everything cool over here?" Remi asked. All but one of the Alphas turned toward Davis. One kept his gaze locked on Remi with a barely noticeable effort, giving him the feeling that he had intruded on something important.

"We were just settling a Pack dispute," the man said. "Nothing of major concern to you, Warlock."

The Alpha that had addressed him had sandy blonde hair with a beard to match. His brown eyes were warm, but remained strong and demanding of respect. Remi glanced past him to see the other four Alphas. One was ginger, slightly shorter than Remi, with the stature of a wrestler. Another was an older, grizzled man that had gone completely silver and seemed to be the senior-most of the group. The third was a burly, man the color of light coffee with striking, green eyes.

There was only one female Alpha, and next to the four brutish men, she looked quite tiny by comparison. The scar that ran down the left side of her face told Remi that she had earned her title in battle. As this was custom among the Lycans, she had pulled her brunette hair back to show it proudly, like a badge of honor.

"Well, I needed to talk to you all before we get started with this thing, anyway," Remi informed them. "Maybe I can help. What seems to be the issue?"

"The pup doesn't want to patrol with us," the ginger man was the first to speak. "Afraid some of his friends might find him out."

Davis's face turned a bright red and he turned away as if he had been slapped by a parent in front of his friends. Remi thought back to how Valerie had mentioned him being the only one at the Oxford Police Department who knew about her, then it dawned on him.

"You're a Lycan?" Remi asked and Davis refused to meet his gaze, as if he were ashamed of the fact.

"Ha!" the ginger Alpha laughed. "He doesn't even tell the Warlocks?"

"Allen!" the Alpha directly in front of Remi gave the other a harsh glare of warning, which effectively silenced him. "Enough! He is a member of my Pack and, as such, I will deal with him."

"You're all here to watch the crowd," Remi pointed out. "Does it really matter who Davis patrols with?"

"In all honesty," the sandy Alpha began, "you're probably right for the situation at hand. But," his voice trailed off as he tried to find the right words.

"It's a matter of pride," the female Alpha finished for him, her voice much calmer than the men around her.

"Normally, if a Lycan refuses their Alpha," the dark-skinned Alpha explained, "they refuse their entire Pack. For that, they should be cast out."

"That is for me to decide," the first repeated, reminding them all of whose Pack Davis belonged to once more.

"Well," Remi tried to reason it out in his head and find a neutral solution. "Isn't he on duty with the OPD right now?"

"He is," the man acknowledged. "Your point, Warlock?"

"Don't you think it would be a good idea, then, to have an inside man?" Remi suggested. "On the off chance that the Mortals spot something that your men don't?"

"Not likely," he laughed. "But I see your point, Caswell. Davis!" the man looked over at Davis, who picked his head up immediately as a sign of respect to his Alpha. "You'll be our leak, pup. Anyone sees anything suspicious or changes plans on us without giving us a heads-up, you come to me first. You got that?"

"Yessir!" Davis answered proudly, shooting a quick thankful smile over to Remi before marching off in the direction where the bulk of the crowd had formed.

"You're as soft as a pup yourself, Kit!" Allen laughed heartily. The sandy Alpha snarled in response. Even in his human form, it was formidable enough to silence the other once more.

"What is it that you needed to speak to us about, Warlock?" the oldest of them, who had remained silent up until this point, asked. This managed to pull everyone's attention back to Remi at once.

"Oh, yeah," he stuttered, gathering his thoughts once more. "About patrolling the crowd. Would you all remain in your human forms unless absolutely necessary?"

The five looked at him in a unified state of befuddlement, and he went on, "I don't want to give these Mortals any reason to act foolishly or hastily, as they tend to do. Most of them are already on edge after what happened the other day with us, and if they were to see you all Shift, it might cause them to retaliate. I don't want a repeat of the Coven House incident here."

"Fair point, Caswell," the silver Alpha replied. "You have my word." The others agreed silently.

"We don't need to Shift to deal with a bunch of weak Mortals," Allen gave a hearty guffaw, as if the very thought of being overpowered by any size group of Mortals was beyond him. "If they're truly that stupid, let them make the move!"

The female Alpha, in a move like lightning, caught the ginger by the scruff of the neck and kicked her boot in front of his leg, flipping him to the ground impatiently. The others laughed and Remi had to hide his own amusement.

"Thank you for that," he inclined his head in a sign of gratitude, turning away to head toward the stage.

"Dammit, Jill!" Allen cried out as Remi walked off, chuckling to himself.

Just then, his phone buzzed and Remi fished it out of his back pocket. "Hello?" he answered.

"Caswell!" the Arbiter's familiar voice came through the receiver. "Where are you? Get back to the stage as soon as you can!"

Remi hung up and rushed to see what was the matter, not knowing what to expect once he got there.

The Arbiter spotted him and waved him over, kneeling down at the edge of the stage. She covered a small microphone that had been pinned to the lapel of her jacket and asked in a harsh whisper, "Where have you been? I turned around and you were nowhere to be seen."

"Everything's fine," Remi assured her. "I just needed to touch base with some of our guys before this thing got underway."

"And?" she asked expectantly.

"Everything is under control," he said. "Have you heard from Finn yet?"

"No," she seemed nervous and fidgety as she spoke, leaving Remi to wonder if she had ever stood before a crowd this large before. "Have you?"

"Not yet," he replied. "What did you need?"

"Find a way up here," Sylvia instructed. "There should be a set of stairs around back that leads up unless they've already moved them."

Remi complied, making his way around to the rear edge of the stage that had been set up just for the occasion. There, he was halted by one of the mayor's servicemen.

"He's with me," Sylvia said, and the Mortal stood down, moving aside for Remi to pass.

"I don't think we have another microphone for him, ma'am," the boy that had spirited the Arbiter away only moments ago, reappeared seeming flustered at the idea of fitting Remi with a feed as well on such short notice.

"Oh, he won't be needing one," Sylvia assured him with a polite smile.

"Okay," the boy seemed slightly relieved to hear this. Then to Remi, he added, "There's the camera. Try to stay out of the shot." With that, the Mortal flounced away to busy himself with what Remi assumed were other projects.

When she was positive that the Mortal was out of earshot, Sylvia covered her microphone once more and got so close that Remi could smell her gardenia perfume.

"I need you up here so you can get a better vantage point over the crowd," she whispered directly into his ear. "If you see anyone who seems even remotely suspicious or out of place, you know what to do."

"Right," Remi whispered back giving a tight nod. "I've had a word with the Alphas, Madame Arbiter. They're under strict orders to remain as they are unless absolutely necessary."

"Good idea. And what of our men?" she asked.

"I already addressed them on the way over. They're only using casting as a last resort, and even then, only stunning charms," Remi assured her.

"Looks like all of our bases are covered then. Hopefully, we won't have another scene like we had on our hands the last time. And let's try for no storms today," the Arbiter added with a sly smile. She gave him a reassuring pat on the shoulder and turned to make her way to the media podium at the front of the stage where she could wait for the conference to begin.

Remi looked down at the area just in front of the stage and saw that the news crews were finishing setting up their equipment before things kicked off. He scanned the faces and saw that most of them had been the ones on the scene when the gate had been shot open a few days ago.

They're like dogs with bones over a story, he chuckled to himself. *I wonder which one had the fake story about the families that lost members.*

"There you are!" Mayor Kensington's overly enthusiastic voice directly behind him made Remi jump involuntarily. "I was wondering if I'd see you here today!"

The Mortal walked up to Remi and extended his right arm. In an act of defiance, Remi extended his left, glancing down at his other in its sling as an explanation. Rather than bother with the simple act of readjusting himself, the mayor simply dropped his own back to his side to avoid the gesture altogether.

"Well, it's so good to see you here!" he beamed, seeming overly proud. Remi knew what it looked like when someone was plotting something, and this man exuded that aura as he extended his arms to draw the Warlock into a tight embrace.

The man was just as close as Sylvia had been literal seconds before and Remi found himself both extremely uncomfortable and unable to escape without drawing attention to himself from both the servicemen and the crowd that was close enough to the stage at this point. The Warlock could smell the faint scent of alcohol that had been masked, unsuccessfully, by cologne as the man spoke directly into his ear in a not-so-hushed voice.

"Now," the mayor whispered, much more harshly than the Arbiter had. "I just wanted you to know that if you try any of your little Shiner shit today, I'll make sure to put you down like the sick dog that you are myself before those damn aldermen can stop me. Do I make myself clear, you little shit?"

Remi was about to wonder how such a bigoted man had been elected into a position of power in such a progressive town by Mortal standards, when he saw the faces of a few members of the crowd.

Remi was starting to question why they all had varying expressions of appallment when he noticed that they all seemed to be intently focused on him and their mayor. That's when it dawned on him that Kensington had not covered his microphone as Sylvia had before whispering.

"I said," the man made to repeat himself, "Do I make myself clear, you stupid Shiner son of a bitch?"

The crowd gradually erupted into a low roar of boos and heckling then, which rapidly swelled as it began to register with more people what was being said by the Mortal that had Remi in a locked grip.

The tech supervisor that had been talking to Sylvia was now staring, slack-jawed at Remi and Mayor Kensington, horrified as the man's voice echoed through the speakers.

The oblivious mayor seemed not to notice at all as he let go of Remi and went on, "Now, I done said what I think of y'all's kind. And if y'all think y'all are about to run this show, I can assure you that this ain't my first rodeo, *boy!*" He spat the last word at Remi like an accusation of inferiority and the Warlock had to bite his tongue not to reveal his hand at that moment.

The crowd was almost deafening by this point and Remi was wondering just how drunk the man in front of him must have been not to hear them by now, when he finally did. It took a few more seconds for him to register that it was all being directed at him. He turned toward the audience, confounded at what could possibly be causing this sudden outcry from his constituents.

"What the-" he began, but seemed unable to find the words to convey his anger. His face became bloodshot with rage as he turned on Remi. "You did this!"

He started toward the Warlock, hands outstretched like claws meant to grab at him. Kensington lunged forward and the crowd inhaled collectively as Remi ducked out of the way.

The audience watched as the man tumbled onto his stomach and rolled at Remi's feet. The Mortal clutched at his pants leg and Remi quickly snatched it away from the man. He pushed the man over onto his back with little effort from his foot.

"Your mic's still on," Remi stared down at him, almost feeling pity for him. "It's been on this whole time. They all heard what you had to say."

The audience had become eerily silent as they watched what might happen next in the exchange. Remi figured this must have been because most of them had seen what he was capable of under pressure during the altercation on the Coven grounds, Sure enough, the mayor struggled to his feet and pounced in Remi's direction. The Warlock saw it before it happened and launched a preemptive counter.

"*Consedo*," he muttered, feeling the static charge of the spell. Instantly, the mayor was suspended in the air. "*Extuno*."

The mayor was thrown to the far end of the stage where he remained in a crumpled ball.

Disapproval collectively and nearly instantaneously shifted to laughter. Remi could see even from this vantage point that the Mortal's face was now flushed the deep, red shade of embarrassment. He regained himself, only to point an accusatory finger at Remi. Sylvia's voice on the loudspeakers quickly put an end to whatever his tirade might have been.

"Mayor Kensington, everybody!" the Arbiter spoke. "Give him a round of applause!"

She led the round and those in the crowd quickly followed suit. "I believe he was just telling Mr. Caswell that he was feeling a bit ill and would be turning today's proceedings over to me?"

Remi knew that she was giving Kensington the opportunity to bow out gracefully. Thankfully, the Mortal saw this as well and turned his head away in shame, letting his servicemen lead him off and away from the stage.

When they had completely descended the staircase that led off the rear edge of the raised platform, Remi gave a thumbs-up for the Arbiter to continue.

"Sorry for that," Sylvia paused and blew out a sharp breath, "technical difficulty we were having there."

Remi could see that she was trying to salvage the conference and keep the mood upbeat. He knew that she wanted to avoid the mob mentality that had overtaken the Mortals and led them to storm the Coven earlier in the week. It seemed to be working, as many of them seemed to be genuinely laughing at her light-hearted attempt at humor.

"Big hand to Mr. Caswell over there for remaining calm," she went on, momentarily turning attention to Remi and making him glad that he was wearing shades to hide his discomfort at being the sudden center of everyone's attention. "I'm sure most of you have seen how 'tempestuous' his temper can be sometimes!"

Remi waved as he saw himself being broadcast on a big screen behind them on the stage, noting that more Mortals seemed to be laughing now.

Keep it up, he thought to himself. Sylvia seemed to be winning over the crowd with relative ease.

"Now that the entertainment portion of today's conference has been concluded," Sylvia continued her opening statement, "it seems to me that we have some serious business to attend to."

Remi let the Arbiter's voice fade out from his consciousness as he surveyed the crowd, scanning over the faces briefly enough to see if anything seemed to be out of place before moving along. He located each of the Alphas who, as if upon sensing his gaze, gave subtle shakes and nods.

He moved on to find the few other members of the Witch's Guard, garnering similar responses from each of them as well. Lastly, Remi found Davis, who was staring intently at something in the crowd. Remi trailed his gaze, expecting to find a person aiming a weapon at the stage toward the Arbiter.

Instead, what he found was a Mortal girl who had abandoned her shirt somewhere in the exchange between himself and the mayor to reveal her leopard-print bra underneath. Remi's gaze darted back across to see an open-mouthed Davis, eyeing the girl like he had never seen a shirtless woman and clearly distracted.

Remi sought out Kit in the crowd and, upon finding him, pulled up his shades to reveal his moonstone eyes. There were a few Mortal attentions that locked onto him in that brief moment, but most remained focused on Sylvia as she spoke.

Seeing Remi, Kit gave a questioning look, to which Remi whipped his eyes back to focus on Davis. The Alpha almost instantly found what Remi was signalling to him and began making his way toward the young Lycan officer.

Remi quickly let his shades drop back into place and watched as the scene played out, feeling almost like he was witnessing a short television drama.

The Alpha grabbed the surprised Mortal girl by the back of the arm and lead her toward a nearby campus security guard, who then escorted her away from the crowd. Remi observed as the friends she had come with gave chase to keep up with them. The security guard put the girl in the passenger seat of a waiting golf cart and sped away before the girl's friends had a chance to object and Remi assumed that he was taking her to wherever the campus security building was.

Kit had already made his way back to where Davis stood and seemed to be in the middle of scolding him for losing his focus during their current situation. Just as Remi relaid his eyes on the two of them, the Alpha made a gesture toward the stage.

Slowly, Davis's gaze shifted to lock onto him and Remi gave a slight inclination of his head. The officer blushed visibly even from where Remi stood on the raised platform and hastily turned on his heel, rushing into the crowd and busying himself with patrolling the area once more.

Remi frowned, stifling a laugh internally at how juvenile Davis seemed in the moment and allowing himself to tune back into the Arbiter's speech just in time to hear her issuing a mandatory, city-wide curfew.

"Now, this is only until we find the person responsible for this incident," she explained. Her words were coming increasingly faster and Remi could feel that she was in fear of losing the crowd at this point in her speech. "This will not affect those who work overnight for whatever reason, nor will it affect anyone who has emergencies that justify being out past the designated hours."

There were a few minor sounds of protest from the members of the audience, but before they could grow, Sylvia added a hasty, "Hey, it's cheaper to drink your wine at home anyway. And *those* guys close at ten!"

The sounds of discontent that had begun were quickly restored to laughter and she went on.

"We're really not trying to be unreasonable here, folks! We don't want to infringe upon your basic rights as citizens of this great city," she assured them. "This curfew just makes it easier for everyone all around while we continue our investigation and hopefully, it won't be in effect that long. If you could all just find it in you to bear with us until that time, it would be greatly appreciated by both us and your local officers. Sound like a plan?"

To Remi's delighted surprise, Sylvia's requests were met with cheers and applause as far as he could see. Then, just as he was ready to bask in the small victory, he noticed one of the trees at the far end of the Grove was shaking violently despite there being no wind.

He removed his glasses and saw that several of the Alphas had noticed before him and were already moving toward it. Then he heard Sylvia's voice suddenly commanding them all over the speaker system, "Get down!"

Everything after that seemed to become simultaneously slowed and thrown into an adrenaline-filled state of hyperdrive. There was a deafening crack that echoed in the air above the Mortals as the crowd collectively ducked and the tree was uprooted completely, flying directly at the stage. Remi felt himself spring into action and he was suddenly running toward the Arbiter. He tackled her to the ground on the other side of the podium just in time for the oak to topple down, crushing the media stand and ripping the screen from the hooked chains and wires that had held it in place above the stage.

There was the loud sound of metal being bent and torn apart as the tree crashed through the posts at the rear of the stage where the wind curtain had been strung and wrenched the bolts from their iron pillars.

The backdrop fell, blanketing the tree in its pale folds and Remi felt the surge of familiar, white-hot pain as his arm had struck the stage floor when he had pushed the Arbiter out of the way. He did not have time to acknowledge this feeling as one of the pillars that had been struck by the formerly aviated oak came crashing down. He pulled the Arbiter to himself and forced her into a barrel roll with him just as the large bar fell, cutting a chasm into the stage in the very spot where they had just been.

The two regained themselves jointly and looked out into the shady knoll, finding that the applause that had filled the Grove just moments before had been replaced with an overwhelming sense of terror. Mortals were now running in every available direction, trying to escape, and horrified screams filled the afternoon air.

"Are you alright, Caswell?" Sylvia asked, to which Remi grimaced.

He righted himself as quickly as he could and saw that two of the Alphas had Turned and were currently charging at a single figure in a black, hooded robe. He watched with a sort of detached horror as the figure lifted both arms casually and the two wolves were sent flying in the opposite direction.

"You have to help them, Caswell," Sylvia's voice was surprisingly calm, which was somewhat reassuring to Remi.

"Right," he agreed, pushing himself to his feet. "Set up barriers around the stage. I'll work on getting the Mortals to run this way."

The Arbiter nodded, pulling her wand from a pocket inside the jacket of her suit, which had been torn at some point during the initial chaos. She wasted no time in casting several defensive spells only seconds after Remi had leapt from the stage. He landed just in time for the ground to tremble and shoot up at different angles all around him, blocking his original path.

Remi heard a tiny cry somewhere off to his left, "Mommy! I'm scared!"

The earth was being pulled apart and crumbling away as the woman reached helplessly across the growing void. Remi could see that even as the Mortal stretched her arm, she was unable to reach the small, panicked girl as the ground fell constantly away between them with each second.

Remi did the only thing he could think to do then and ran toward the girl, jumping just before where the hole was forming to land where the girl was standing with her arms outstretched toward her mother. He picked her up from behind with his one good arm.

Remi tucked the tiny Mortal against his body and moved in the only direction that was still attached, lunging forward as he did so. He used his momentum to spin himself so that his back was the first thing to make contact as they crashed onto the new patch of ground, just as the old fell away.

The Warlock winced and glanced down to see the earth behind them crumble away into the circular fissure that had formed, knowing that they had made it off with only seconds to spare.

"Mommy!" the girl's shrill voice rang out in Remi's ear then.

He looked up just as the woman who had been reaching for her climbed toward them. The girl was lifted from his chest and he saw that her mother stood over him, clutching the girl to her chest now.

"Thank you!" she cried, staring into his moonstone eyes with an expression that simultaneously tied together her underlying feelings of fear and admiration.

"Get to the stage!" Remi commanded breathlessly, trying to inhale deeply through the pain that was shooting from his sling arm.

The woman asked no further questions, taking her daughter and obeying his order. Remi watched her run away and toward the group that was currently clamoring over each other to get onto the stage and make their way behind Sylvia.

He sucked in as much air as he could manage from his position and yelled at them all, "Help each other!"

A few seemed to have heard him and began pushing the women and children first up onto the stage.

Remi righted himself as quickly as he could and took a brief assessment of the turmoil that had fallen on the conference. The Grove had become an interweaving network of fissures, from which flames shot up menacingly, during the few seconds he had spent saving the girl from inevitable doom. There were Mortals all over, trying to get away in whichever direction had not been closed off by the fiery chasms or falling debris.

"Get them to the stage!" he called out to the Witch's Guard and Mortal officers who were within earshot. "To the stage!" he repeated. "Now!"

Those immediately around him acknowledged his orders only briefly before they began fanning out and shepherding the Mortals in the direction of the others. Remi watched as he saw two more Alphas charge at the hooded figure, only to see them thrown away in the same manner as the previous duo.

"Caswell!" Davis's voice roared off to one side of him. Remi turned to see that the Lycan officer was pointing to where the tree had been uprooted.

The wolf forms of Kit and Jill were making a second charge at the Warlock, only to meet the same invisible force that sent them flying through the air even further this time. They landed near the foot of the stage and Remi was truly surprised that they did not crash into the Mortals that were scrambling to make their way onto the platform.

"Davis!" Remi called back. "Help the others get the Mortals behind the Arbiter!"

The other man nodded and began charging through the crowd at an incredible speed, throwing people over his shoulder with ease and rushing them up to the stage. Remi saw that most of the Mortals had found their way out of the Grove already and still more were flocking to get behind Sylvia's barrier even without the help of the officers.

He turned back to face the hooded figure, freeing his wand from its holster strapped to his thigh.

"*Orbis Incendium!*" he shouted and a ball of white-hot flames shot from his wand. The Dark Warlock deflected it with ease.

"Surely that isn't your best, child?" he laughed mockingly, amber eyes flashing. The sound sent chills through Remi's entire body.

The Dark Warlock was clad in black robes and despite the fact that they billowed in an invisible wind, Remi could only imagine that the man must be suffocating in the stifling summer heat. The fires he had created served only to amplify the intensity of this unseen breeze.

His face was covered by a tighter hood that was attached to a steel faceplate that glistened in the nearby flames, reminding Remi of a gladiator's helmet. The only things visible were his amber eyes that were glowing with a bestial ferocity that caused Remi's blood to grow cold.

The Dark Warlock snapped his fingers and his own fireball shot at Remi.

"*Reditum*," the Witchguard said, with a wave of his wand.

The molten globe was instantly ricocheted back to its original caster. The Dark Warlock parried with just as much casual grace as before, setting a nearby oak's branches ablaze.

How is he doing all of this without a wand? Remi wondered to himself, keeping his own at the ready in front of him.

"I do so love a challenge!" the Dark Warlock exclaimed gleefully, golden gaze flashing with a violent passion that seemed to mirror the destruction he had caused thus far.

"So do I," Remi goaded, lifting his wand higher out in front of him and spreading his feet apart into a defensive stance.

"Why do you protect them, boy?" the Dark Warlock seemed genuinely puzzled by Remi's willingness to defend the Mortals that were by now mostly behind him. "What could you possibly seek to gain from these ants?"

"Why would I seek to gain anything?" Remi countered. "I am sworn to protect those who are innocent. Nothing to be gained from that."

"*Innocent?*" the Dark Warlock howled with laughter, clicking his tongue in distaste. "Their sins are woven into their very being, child. Our blood is on their hands even if they have never lifted their own against us. They must be punished for this. They must be made clean and ruled over by us. We must teach them the error of their selfish ways in a baptism of redemption and flame. Cast your ignorance aside and join me, youngling!"

The man extended a single hand toward Remi, who stared at it as if it was some sort of false offering on the other's part.

"Bit hypocritical, don't you think?" Remi refused the gesture. "You're not exactly spotless, yourself. Are you, Lacunae?"

"It seems that someone has done their homework," the Dark Warlock spoke in a conversational tone, as if he was not the one responsible for the Grove crumbling around them both. "The tricky thing about history though, and you must know this by now, child: it is nothing more than a whimsical construct that is so often written by those who deem themselves 'victors.' Therefore, can it's bias ever truly be trusted?"

Without warning, he hurled a bolt of lightning toward Remi with an unspoken curse. The Warlock barely had enough time to dodge out of the way as the thing went hurtling past him and split a tree in half vertically as if it had hit from above.

"Do you even know why these things are done, child?" the Dark Warlock went on as casually as if he had not previously tried to kill Remi. "Why would you seek to hinder me, when I offer new life?"

He's buying time for something, Remi thought to himself and wondered what that 'something' might be.

"Because whatever you're doing is wrong!" Remi shouted at the hooded man. "You shouldn't have to kill to accomplish whatever it is that you're after!"

"*Kill?*" the Dark Warlock repeated questioningly. "Oh no, child! You do not understand! I do not seek to kill anyone just for the sake of it. Why would I seek to do something so callous?"

He laughed as if the very idea of it were absurd to even consider. "No, no. To do that would be nothing short of futile on my part," he went on to explain, "I simply wish to elevate us above the peons that we were rightfully meant to rule over. I seek for us to walk this earth once more as the gods we truly are! Why would you and your Coven want to stop such a beautiful dream from being made into a reality, when it is our destiny?"

He offered his hand once more and once more, Remi refused the very idea of it.

"We were never 'destined' to be gods," he protested against the Dark Warlock's flawed logic. "We were meant to be nothing more than equal to the Mortals."

"I see that you cling to your ideologies," the Dark Warlock mused aloud, shaking his head with a sense of something like disdain. "While that is commendable, I simply cannot condone such a ludicrous notion, child."

He clapped his hands together and three spears of ice materialized before him, suspended in the air awaiting his command. "You will soon join the rest of the fools to fall before me. Perhaps then, you will see the error of your ways, youngling. Do send my regards, won't you?"

Without waiting to hear Remi's response, the Dark Warlock snapped his fingers and the ice spears were sent whizzing through the air in the direction of the other.

"*Parietas Pyros*," Remi said, feeling a sense of calm wash over him in that moment, seemingly from nowhere.

A wall of inferno sprung to life in front of him like geysers and melted the frosty javelins before they could reach him. He lifted his wand to touch his lips and he blew the flames out.

"*Adamas Pulvis*," Remi whispered the second charm.

A strong gale of frost and crystallized ice shards blasted the Dark Warlock, cementing him to the spot where he stood in a thick, glacial sheet.

The other man lifted his arms as he had done with the Alphas and a boulder-sized chunk of the earth rose into the air, before being forcefully thrown at Remi.

"*Discutio!*" he shouted and the massive piece was effectively shattered so that he was only lightly dusted with particles of mulch and grass.

"You seem to have the skill," the Dark Warlock complimented him, melting the sheets of ice that had formed from his waist down and held him in place. "I will admit that much. But it seems that you lack the will to do anything deserving of merit with that skill."

"Our versions of what constitutes as *great* are very different, sir," Remi said, sounding much more polite than he had intended.

"Clearly," the Dark Warlock muttered, his amber eyes flashing once more. "Truly a piteous decision on your part, youngling. With the help of those in your Coven, we could have reshaped this world together. Alas," he bowed here, making Remi wonder if he was mocking his unintentional cordiality, "you won't be one of the Warlocks to follow me into the new dominion. Truly unfortunate, as your heart seems to be fiery enough."

"There won't be a new *anything* if I have a say in it," Remi spat at the man.

"Ah," the Dark Warlock retorted, seeming to contemplate the threat. "You see, child? That's the beauty of the situation we have here."

As the man spoke, Remi found that he could no longer move, no matter how much he struggled against this newly unseen force.

"So that is where you are both wrong and right, Witchguard," the man explained this part as Remi came to the realization that his lips could not part to form a counterspell that might get him out of his current situation.

"You see," the Dark Warlock went on and Remi tried desperately to form some sort of charm in his mind, only to find that there was some sort of fog within his brain now that prevented him from performing even this simple task. There seemed to be nothing that would be strong enough to free him of this hold the Dark Warlock now had over him.

"You say that there won't be a new dominion if you have anything to say about it. But there *will* be because you don't have a say. Don't you see how beautiful the irony of that is?" the man's eyes flashed with a frightening sense of self-satisfaction.

Remi tried fervently to free himself from whatever curse the Dark Warlock had cast over him, becoming increasingly panicked with each second that passed.

"As I've said before," the man went on with his speech as Remi was helpless to object. "Many before you have tried to stop me and failed. They also tried to stop the plans that my ancestors set into motion and left me to tend. All they managed to do was prolong the inevitable only long enough for everything to be perfected, as it eventually came to be. And now, sadly, you must be the last to fall so that I may complete their glorious works."

The man was on top of Remi quicker than he could blink, with his hand clenched around Remi's neck.

"Do say hello to the others when you get there, won't you, Caswell?" the Dark Warlock hissed in his ear, in an act that felt both intimate and vile.

Then Remi saw a flash of silver and felt a blinding pain searing into the skin at his left collar. He tried to let out a scream, but the sound became instantly trapped in his throat. He felt a tear escaping his eye as the blade began to move across, cutting its way deeper into him. He could taste the blood forming in his throat as a tear rolled down his cheek and in that instant, everything changed.

There was a sudden explosion and a dazzling, silvery-blue light overtook the two of them, sending each of them flying in opposite directions. The Dark Warlock was thrown into the base of the same tree that had been set alight by his jinx earlier, making contact with a loud crack followed by a thud as the freshly ashen trunk collapsed onto him.

Remi was tossed back into the chasm that had formed behind him, as if he were nothing more than a ragdoll. He watched as the world rose up and around him, swallowing him in a darkness so thick that it pierced through his very being. He tried to call out any sort of spell that might propel him back to the surface, but he could not get enough oxygen in him to force out the words as he dropped with increasing momentum.

Remi felt the chilling grip of Death closing around him, pulling him into the depths of the earth. He could almost have sworn that he heard his name.

"Remi!" a woman screamed out a second time as he was cast down into the void.

The Warlock felt his heart skip a beat and seize in his chest as the world around him became suddenly painted by an overwhelmingly inky blackness.

XVI

Remi regained consciousness only to find that he was lying facedown on a cold, hard surface. There was no way that he could have survived that fall, yet here he was. His head was pounding and he couldn't remember what had happened to bring him down here.

Am I under the Grove? he wondered. His voice inside his own head seemed to have an echo to it now that it had never had before and he wondered if this was a side effect of his migraine. Remi stared up from where he had landed on his back and saw that the area above him was enveloped in a pure, impenetrable blackness. It was like the land was a giant beast that had swallowed him up and then closed its gaping maw so that he could not escape.

His head throbbed again and he suddenly recalled the blade at his neck. He reached up then, fully expecting to feel blood trickling from an open wound, only to find that there was no such injury. The skin around the area where the knife had sliced into him wasn't even raised, making Remi wonder if it had happened at all.

Was it just a dream? he asked himself, confounded by his current situation. *Is this what purgatory feels like?*

Remi rolled over and pushed himself up into a sitting position so that he could have a better look around, not letting his eyes focus on anything in particular.

He could barely make out shapes a few feet in front of him as the area was completely devoid of any light, save for a soft white glow several yards ahead. He felt the hardness beneath him and determined that it was some sort of stone.

But why would there be stone down here? he wondered. *And if I fell this far, how did I not break my back?* Each new detail he found only served to confuse him even more than the one before.

Remi decided that he couldn't stay in this solitary space, so he pushed himself to his knees and rose to his feet. It was then that he realized his sling was no longer there and that his right arm felt just fine.

That's it, he resolved to himself. *I'm dead. The bastard up there killed me and threw me down here and now I'm freaking dead.*

Remi swallowed against the bundle of nerves that had formed at the back of his throat and moved forward, inching closer toward the white light with each individual footfall. As he trailed along, he found that there was a certain aroma that was wafting through the air above him now.

Lavender? he wondered as he inhaled deeply. He couldn't be sure, but that's what he imagined it to be. *But why would it smell like flowers down here?*

Before long, he found that he was gradually becoming engulfed by the light at the end of the tunnel and thought that this must be the end of the line for him. He closed his eyes and continued walking, subliminally accepting his fate.

Then, as his hands trailed out beside him, he found that they were now knocking against what felt like stalks. He opened his eyes again and glanced down, his gaze landing on a field of towering sunflowers that stretched on as far as he could see in every direction.

This is definitely not a real place, Remi's internal commentary continued.

He felt the soft surfaces of the tall flowers, wondering how this area connected to the one he had just left. He checked behind him and saw that there was nothing more to greet him than another side of the expansive field. This caused him to question if the dark, stone room had been anything but his imagination playing tricks on him. He looked above to see that the sky had a lavender-tinted hue to it.

The hazy purple overhead was interrupted only by the low-hanging clouds and reminded him of the unfiltered moment just before dusk when all of the stars became visible to the naked eye. He searched around and saw that the path he was on seemed to have been carved out in between the rows of flowers and went on ahead of him to snake around a weeping willow. As he stared, it looked to Remi that the tree was nothing more than a decoration that had been carved from glass.

It seems so familiar for some reason, he thought to himself, though he could not quite place why this was.

As he questioned this, he heard a low, constant buzzing sound just behind his right ear. Remi turned and saw that a ruby-breasted hummingbird was fluttering beside him. The tiny creature was so close to him that he could feel the wind coming off of its rapid wing beats as it darted to each side as if it was studying him intently.

I'm definitely dead, he ruled. *There's no way any of this is real.* Remi then noticed that he could hear his voice echoing around him now as clearly as if he had spoken the words aloud.

"Not quite," a familiar voice laughed behind him.

Remi whipped around to see the galaxy-adorned phantom from the archives standing there, watching him with her blue moonstone gaze that so closely matched his own. Her hair billowed out behind her, caught up in a breeze that was unfelt by Remi and looking very much like the tail of a comet shooting across the night sky.

Remi looked on as the hummingbird fluttered to encircle the spectre, almost like it was her pet. He found himself puzzled as the woman stretched out a single arm toward him, offering her hand for him to take.

"Come," the spirit said. "We must get you out of here. You do not belong in this world and there is still work you must finish before you can stay."

Remi took the ghostly hand and felt an icy shiver surge through his entire body as he let the woman lead him further up the pathway. They walked between the towering stalks of the sunflowers until they stopped in front of the glassy willow.

Now, Remi could see that there was a shimmering window at the base of the tree, which seemed to be simultaneously part of and separate from the willow itself. As he peered into its undefined dimensions, Remi surmised that it was a sort of portal that looked in onto another scene.

"Where will this take me?" he asked, to which the spectre shook her head. He got the feeling that she either could not or would not explain anything to him, the only problem he had was that he did not know which of the two was true in this case.

"Go on!" she laughed playfully, causing Remi to wonder if this lady of nebulas was something that could be trusted. "I'll be waiting for you on the other side."

Remi eyed her warily, swallowing against the dryness that had taken over his throat. Finally, he took a single, cautious step through and the portal shut behind him like a closing window, becoming impossible for him to reopen. He turned and felt something inside him resonate from within as he knew this scene that he had entered. Though he could not quite put his finger on it, it was almost as if he were looking at it through a filtered lens that had shifted everything around him to a time in his distant past. He knew he had been here at some point before in his life, but he just could not bring himself to remember when that time had been.

But why? he wondered to himself, trying to piece it together in his mind. His head was still throbbing and foggy and he secretly wondered if that feeling would ever fully subside. *Why does everything feel so familiar?*

There was a small group of people a few feet ahead of him, huddled around in a clearing a then-empty field. An elderly man addressed them all in a heavy tone, his face turned down and his eyes skimming over the pages of a book he was holding as he read aloud. Remi searched each of the faces surrounding the man and saw that everyone in the group was a Warlock and that they all seemed to be sharing the same state of mourning, for some reason.

Remi moved closer to see that the man leading the service was standing between the heads of two black caskets with silver trim. Remi found the humanoid galaxy easily enough among the rest of the crowd. She had her hand resting on the shoulder of a child that reminded him of someone.

But who? he questioned, feeling almost guilty that he could not bring himself to remember. He moved closer and asked aloud, "Why did you bring me here?"

It seemed that no one had heard him, as not a single face turned to acknowledge the fact that he had spoken. He guessed that this must be some sort of scene that had already happened without him and that he was merely a spectator now. This should have been reassuring to him, but Remi felt like he was an intruder on someone else's intimate moments now.

The boy that appeared to be with the spectre was slight and wiry, with an unkempt mess of brown hair. When he turned to meet Remi's gaze, he felt as if the boy could actually see him. The Warlock could see now that the boy had striking, pale blue eyes. Although the boy's gaze had not yet shifted and did not shine as it would later in life, as his magic had not come in fully yet, Remi got the strangest feeling that he knew this child.

But how would I? he wondered. *I don't even know where I am right now.*

Something about this place made Remi feel a certain sense of heaviness and as the man at the head of the crowd drew his statements to a close and people began placing white roses on each of the caskets, it struck a chord somewhere deep within him.

This is their funeral, he remembered suddenly and with a harsh throbbing in his head. *My parents.*

They had both been killed in the field while working a case, as both been part of the Witch's Guard. This was nothing new, as there was a long line of Caswells who had met very similar fates in battle.

But why am I seeing this? he questioned. *Why can't I remember any of these people? Because I'm dead now, too. Aren't I?* The thought felt wrong, but Remi did not know why.

He could not make sense of any of it and, as he watched the boxes being lowered, he felt pangs in both his chest and his head.

"Come on," the spectre bent down and whispered into the boy's ear and Remi could hear the voice just as clearly as if she were just behind him. "We can go back home now."

"Hey!" Remi called out, trying to get the woman's attention. Again, not a single person in the emptying field looked up at the sound of his voice. It was strange for him, even though he already knew that no one could hear him.

Can they not see me, either? he wondered. Before he could test this theory, the scene changed around him.

Just as quickly as it had originally come about, the scene began to shift. Colors and shapes whipped past him in a rapid succession, each moving too fast for him to focus on as they flew by. Remi could feel himself getting dizzy and tried to pull himself down into a crouching position on the floor to combat the feeling of weightlessness that had overtaken him.

Now the wiry boy, a few years older in this scene, was sitting at a table. Remi took a brief assessment and gathered that he was currently standing in what looked like the center of someone's dining room. The spectral woman stood in front of a stove, stirring the contents of a skillet and humming old doo-wop songs as she worked.

I remember that song, Remi hummed along inside his head, taking a lower tone of notes as he could not hit the same ones as the woman, even in his mind. He inhaled and his mouth began to water as he got a strong whiff of homemade biscuits and gravy.

The boy had his hands lifted up in front of him at the table and had scrunched his face together as he concentrated on whatever he was doing. His expression was a thing of intent focus and Remi wondered what sort of feat he could possibly be trying to accomplish that would require this level of determination.

Remi trailed along the boy's gaze to land on a cookie jar that had been sitting on the counter. The thing was budging ever-so-slightly with each forceful grunt that emanated from the boy. He watched on as slowly, but surely, the jar inched closer and closer to the edge until it fell from the counter. The glass shattered, sending pieces of itself and its contents scattering across the linoleum floor in every conceivable direction.

The ethereal woman ceased humming momentarily and brought her moonstone gaze to rest serenely on the boy. Though he could not see her expression, as her face and body looked to be comprised entirely of stardust and gaseous clouds, he recognized the voice and the pale-silver stare.

But who is this woman? Remi questioned himself, furious that he felt such a familiarity to her but could not place her in his mind.

"Just a little harder next time," she told the boy gently, snapping her fingers so that the jar repaired and replaced itself on the counter for him to give it another try.

The scene shifted once more, albeit less violently than it had before.

Now, Remi found himself watching the ceremony of another funeral. They were in the same field as they had stood in before, where the woman had planted the sunflowers just two summers ago.

How do I know these things? Remi's voice inside his head growled the question, which caused his it to pound again as the sound reverberated off the walls of his mind.

This time, however, there was no crowd to be seen. It was only the woman and the boy in the field with him. Remi watched as the woman shed silent tears, feeling like he should go up and console her but remembering that it would do no good on his end. She did not bother hiding them from the boy and he averted his eyes out of an unspoken respect.

The woman lowered her husband's casket herself with a heavy wand and heart. There was a quiet resolve in her that Remi felt oddly comforted by. There were no other Warlocks to grieve with her this time, as she had already left the Oxford Coven.

She buried them all in the pasture, Remi remembered with the second dual pang he'd felt since this slideshow of memories had started. *Right under the tree.*

As Remi stared silently on, he saw nothing in the field besides the stalks of everly-budding sunflowers that somehow still managed to tower over the pair of them. There was nothing else besides the flowers and the two people he had been observing this whole time. The woman made a sweeping motion with her hand and the mound of dirt replaced itself over the man's casket, and became tightly compacted beside the others that had only just begun to regrow their grass.

"*Salix*," the boy said quietly then, lifting a single hand out in front of him.

Both Remi and the woman watched as a sapling sprouted up from the freshly packed grave dirt, taking no time at all to grow into a looming willow tree that wept over the mounds more openly than even the boy or the spectre. The woman knelt to pull the boy into an embrace, water running from her moonstone eyes to stain the shoulder of the boy's crisply pressed shirt as he stared unfeeling at his work.

The scene swirled around him rapidly, changing once more as it did so; this time, into the only one he had hoped he would not have to relive in this world between worlds.

I'll be really glad when this can stop, he complained to himself as he attempted to steel himself against the gamut of emotions he knew he was sure to feel in a moment.

When the room came into focus again, Remi saw that it was only the boy sitting at the dining room table. By this time, the boy's irises had shifted from a pale blue to a more silvery shade to match the moonstones of those who had come before him. They also had the same glow that they would retain for the rest of the boy's time, as his magic had come in fully now and this was the mark of a maturing Warlock.

Across from the boy was the same somber man from the first vision Remi had been made to endure; Franklin Ashcroft, the Oxford Coven's former Arbiter. The man looked like he was full of sorrow as he broke the news to the thirteen-year-old, whose eyes were downcast as if he did not want to hear anything the man had to tell him. Remi already knew what that *something* was.

His last remaining guardian had passed on, leaving him fully orphaned now. The boy would now be forced to go live at the Academy of his choosing for the next eight years of his life as a ward of the Oxford Coven.

But I don't want to go! Remi objected in his mind, knowing that neither of the characters in this tragic play of memories would hear him.

He knew deep down, however, that the boy needed to go to the Academy. It was there that he could learn how to wield his magic properly.

But I already know all about how to cast spells! Remi protested. *She taught me how.*

"I'm sure she did," Frank had said genuinely, as if he had heard him. Remi had to remind himself that the boy had actually been the one to speak, even though the voice seemed to be inside his own head. The Arbiter and his wife had been family friends for as long as the boy could remember, but right now that was not important to him. The boy felt too betrayed at this time by the hand he was being dealt to pay much attention when Frank went on, "But you just can't stay here, RJ. I wish I could change it, son."

But you can change it! Remi thought, wishing desperately that the scene would play out differently this time than it had before. He watched helplessly as Frank pushed a long, thin leather box across the dining room table toward the boy.

The young Warlock pulled the box to him and took the lid off to reveal a slender, black stick that had been nestled into a pillow made of blue velvet and covered in the same shade of satin trim. The boy pulled the thing out of the case to examine it.

The wood was easily the same pitch as the night itself, if not darker. The shaft was made of two seperate parts of the same wood, twisted so that they spiralled around each other to form a single piece. The grip of it was a bit thicker around and more sleek in its appearance than the main part, with a silvery filigree of vines and leaves snaking their way around the hilt, giving it a sort of ridged grip for whoever was wielding it.

There was a black gem fixed into the base of the hilt that seemed to be almost onyx, except where the light hit it and it glimmered as it reflected the same silvery-blue as Remi's own eyes.

Remi knew that it was a moonstone, albeit a darker version than the pale sheen his irises now possessed. But it was a moonstone, just the same.

This was the same wand that he had used for the past fifteen years.

"It's a piece of the willow you made," Frank informed the boy. "She left it to me to give to you, should something go wrong."

"Can I at least wait until after the funeral before they take me away?" the younger version of Remi asked, admiring the gift that had been left by the woman. The Arbiter hesitated for a moment as the young Warlock traced his fingers along the filigree, letting the black moonstone catch and reflect the light of the ceiling fan in the dining room as he did so.

After a heavy pause, Franklin Ashcroft let out a deep sigh and said, "There won't be a funeral, RJ. There was nothing to be recovered. I'm sorry, son."

Nothing, Remi repeated the word in his head several times over as the scene went on. *Nothing recovered.*

He felt his chest tighten as he watched the ghostly version of himself take the wand and run out the back door of the house, toward the field of sunflowers and regret, to the place where the willow mourned over the graves of his parents and grandfather.

The young Warlock aimed the ornately decorated tool at the tree it had come from and whispered, *"Vitrius."*

The tree began to crystallize at this command, shifting gradually from a thing of natural beauty into a glasswork ornament to lament over the resting places for eternity. It started at the roots, working its way up and throughout the base and trunk, until finally reaching the low-sweeping vines of the tree.

The wind whistled through then, causing the crystal teardrops to chime whimsically as the vines rustled like an angelic rhapsody. It was then that the Arbiter came to rest his hand on the boy's shoulder.

"It's beautiful," the man said simply.

Then I shouldn't have to go to the Academy, Remi hoped, though he already knew the answer.

"Now it won't die," the spectral Remi spoke in a voice barely above a whisper. "Now, it can't die."

The scene swirled away once more and Remi suddenly found himself in the stone room he had been in upon his arrival in this realm. He still had no clue where he was physically, but he had the strangest feeling that there was something here that he was meant to see. He just didn't know what that *something* might be this time.

There was the sound of movement behind him and Remi turned in the dimness to see that the galaxy woman was standing there. She looked to be in a battle stance with her wand upraised and as his gaze trailed along the sight of her weapon, Remi saw why.

There was another figure in the room with her and while Remi couldn't quite make out who it might be in the shadows, he did see the unmistakable golden glare. The same glare that had put him in this dimension. Remi did not know what to think as he watched this Dark Warlock trade casts with the spectral woman, both managing to look like they were using no more effort than it would take to tie one's shoelace.

It was a flurry of neon sparks and frozen flames, all the while, neither of the two seemed to be exhibiting any signs of slowing down. Finally, the two let out a simultaneous cast from each of their wands that collided in the center of the room. There was a loud explosion and suddenly all air seemed to be sucked out of the space at once. Remi turned to run, but found that his feet were no longer making contact with the floor. Instead, he was being forcibly pulled backwards and toward the area where the two spells had made impact behind him.

There were screams on one side of him and guttural growls on the other, as Remi imagined the two Warlocks must be in the same situation as he was. All at once, the sound stopped and Remi found that he could not move. Everything felt cold and hollow and as he tried to escape the crystallized prison he was now in, Remi felt something stroke his cheek.

Just as suddenly as the last scene had played out, Remi found himself in the field once more. It was just as it had been upon his initial arrival and the celestial spectre stood beneath the willow tree, seeming like she was waiting for him.

"Do you understand now?" the woman asked as Remi walked toward her. "Do you understand why you must leave this place?"

"Yes," Remi said, surprised at how powerful his words sounded in this world of hers. "I understand. But I'm not even sure how I got here, let alone how I'm meant to get out of this place."

"You have become broken in this place," the woman answered, somewhat mournfully. "You must Prove yourself again to be allowed to leave."

"Simple enough," Remi shrugged, sounding way more confident than he actually felt at the moment. "How do I do that?"

"I cannot help you this time," the woman replied. "You must remember for yourself if you are to stand any chance at toppling the Dark One's tower."

Tower? Remi wondered if he had heard her correctly in his current state. *When did the bastard get a tower?*

Before he could verbalize his confusion to the spectral woman, she had vanished, leaving only traces of stardust in her wake.

"Of course," Remi sighed. "How very on-brand of her, to leave me alone in a place where I have no clue how to move on from here. Thanks, grandma."

Remi had had his suspicions of who the woman was since his time spent in the archives, yet somehow verbalizing it felt simultaneously right and terrible. Right, because it was; terrible, because he felt he had wasted his opportunity to commune with the woman who had taught him so much.

Remi concentrated on himself then and on finding his way out of the mysterious place he had become trapped within. The woman had mentioned Proving himself again, but had she meant it literally?

"Surely she can't mean that I have to go through that entire process again?" Remi spoke aloud to himself now, as there were no witnesses to be seen that might consider him crazy for doing so. Remi closed his eyes as tight as he could, trying to remember how he had Proven himself before when he was trying to join the Witch's Guard. When he opened them this time, he was in the same sort of stone room that he had been in previously only this time it was comprised of slightly different dimensions.

The room was still bare, so Remi thought to start with the basics and hope some unseen force was watching him that would let him leave this place when he had met the requirements. It had not been as his prior Proving ceremony, as there had been no instructors around to pull him out this time if something went awry.

"Let's start with Creation," Remi decided aloud, figuring it would be best to kill two birds with one stone during each of his tasks. He faced the direction he imagined to be the north and raised his hands out in front of him, closing his eyes as he did so.

"*Terra labrum*," he said, feeling the earth shifting beneath him to bring forth a pedestal from the stone floor of the room which had been topped with a bowl of the same material.

For his second task, he would take on the element of water and Protection. Remi moved his right hand in a clockwise motion and uttered, "*Clypeus aquatem*."

At once, a large bubble of water began swirling itself around him to shield the Warlock from any would-be assailants in this empty room. Before the aquifer could make itself scarce, Remi let the wind carry some of it into the bowl in front of him. This allowed for the element of Air to be out of the way as well.

"Now, for Transmutation and Fire," he went down the list, feeling like he was making greater time than he had during his previous Proving ceremony as now he had a better idea of what to offer. Remi aimed his open hand at the basin that had become full of liquid and concentrated as he spoke, "*Factignis*."

With little more than a few small ripples to show his effort, the water in the bowl ceased to exist and became replaced with a roaring flame that cast its light on every corner of the circular room.

When he felt that the fire had burned long enough, Remi moved on to the Proving of Reversion. "*Reverto*," he spoke the simple incantation and watched as the bowl was once again splashed full of water.

"*Secare*," Remi said and a small indentation formed at the base of the pedestal, Proving his skill of Infliction. "*Excindo!*" he exclaimed the charm, feeling the static this time as everything he had materialized before him instantly became nothing more than a memory.

Remi had done it once again; he had gone through every aspect of the Proving ceremony. Creation, Protection, Transmutation, Reversion, Infliction, and Destruction had been demonstrated in the stone room where he now stood. He had even gone so far as to cover each of the four elements just in case whatever silent judge was watching him decided to count their omission against him. Remi then remembered that there was the fifth element of one's Spirit, which was used to weigh a Warlock's light and dark tendencies against themselves.

Before, this part of the ceremony had been conducted by the Arbiter of the Coven as a Warlock could not do it for themselves. As there was no one in the room with him now however, Remi was unsure of just how he would accomplish this final feat to make his way back into the land of the living.

"Any advice would be greatly appreciated right about now!" he called out, hearing his own voice echo off the walls that surrounded him on every side. There was no answer from anyone else. Then he heard it; a slow clapping that came from the shadows behind him. Remi spun around and was immediately greeted with the same set of golden eyes that he had been expecting. "Come to finish the job?"

"Not this time," the figure spoke without moving from the darkness. "I wouldn't get my hands dirty like that on such hallowed ground."

Hallowed ground? Remi repeated in his mind. Before he could ask what the Dark Warlock meant, there was suddenly a force tightening all around his neck and cutting off his oxygen.

Just as it had in the Grove, his mind went completely blank as if the Dark Warlock was using some sort of magical fog on his brain. Remi tried, unsuccessfully, to pry at the invisible constraint that was working against him, even as he fell to his knees with a hard thud.

The golden eyes glared at him with a sickening sense of accomplishment. Remi tried to call out, hoping that the galaxy woman might somehow hear him from wherever she had gone this time, but there was no sound.

Everything began fading to black around him and Remi was resolved to believe that this would definitely be the end, as he felt like he was somehow dying in a dream. He felt the rest of his body collapse onto the floor and suddenly there was another bright, white light. He remembered seeing one similar to this in the Grove and wondered if it was coming from the same source. However, when he tried, Remi could not open his eyes to look around him. There were footsteps then and Remi imagined this to be the Dark Warlock coming to make sure that he had finished the job this time.

"Go to sleep, young one," it was the soothing voice of the galaxy being. "You have done well in this place. All will reveal itself in due time."

Remi was still unsure of what the apparition meant for him to do, but he decided to follow her guidance. He imagined himself in the field of sunflowers they had been in before. He strode over to the tree where the woman had stood, watching his every move. He put his back to the trunk of the tree and let himself slide down until he was level with the base.

"Close your eyes and rest," the woman said, turning to leave him even in his imagination.

Figures, Remi thought. Only this time, he could feel a smile breaking its way across his face, even as he drifted off.

As she walked away, the sky began to tear apart, swirling away in a similar fashion to how the scenes had shifted moments before. The woman disappeared finally in a flash of silvery-blue light, and it was like Remi was watching a star die before him. The lazy imagery of the meadow around him slowly fell away and this time, it was not replaced by another. This time it simply faded to black, almost like the world he was in had become too tired to form another memory for him to walk through.

Remi felt himself drifting into nothingness while propped against the base of the willow tree, being pulled further and further into a dreamless sleep that he had become too drained to fight off by this point. He remained in this state for the next few days as the others tried to wake him from it.

"Do you think he can hear us?" Finn's voice was just beside the bed. "Do you think he'll remember any of this when he wakes up?"

"No way to know for sure," one of the Healers answered.

"Will he wake up?" Sylvia's voice. The Healer was silent, although Remi could hear him.

"I should have been there!" Finn sounded furious.

"You were on an important assignment," Sylvia's voice remained calm. "We had no way of knowing that this would happen. Besides, if this had been you again, your mother would have killed me for letting you put yourself in harm's way so soon after the last time."

"We should let him rest, now," the Healer told them.

"Come on, Finn," the Arbiter sounded exhausted. Remi could hear her turning to leave.

"You go on, Aunt Syl," Finn yawned. "I'll stay here just in case he wakes up."

Sylvia seemed to acknowledge this and Remi listened as her heels clicked away. He heard the Infirmary door open and close, followed by silence.

He could feel Finn's head rest against the foot of his bed and smiled to himself at how dedicated the other was. Remi slowly opened his eyes and looked down at the younger Warlock.

"What's that smell?" he asked groggily.

"You've been out for three whole days," Finn's head shot up with an expectant smile. "I've been here waiting for you to wake up the whole time."

"That explains it," Remi laughed, and instantly regretted the decision as a wave of pain pulsed through his ribcage.

"How does it feel?" Finn asked, his face full of concern.

"Like I just got hit by a bus," Remi grimaced. "And knocked over a cliff."

"Do you need a bowl or something?" the younger Warlock asked. "Do you think you're going to get sick?"

"Nah," Remi waved the concern away absentmindedly and was relieved to see that his sling had come off while he had been under. "I just need a shower."

"There should be some upstairs in the barracks. Do you need help getting up there?"

"You go ahead," Remi grunted his reply. "I'll make it up eventually."

Finn seemed briefly like he wanted to protest, but thought better of it. Reluctantly, he stood from where he had been seated for the past three days and walked out of the Infirmary.

Now, to get myself up there, Remi thought.

He pushed himself gradually and with some effort into an upright position and pulled back the sheets of the cot he had been resigned to, assessing the damage. As he had seen seconds ago, the sling had come off but as he was seeing now, it had only been replaced by more gauze and bandages in different spots.

His ribs ached as though he had been kicked in the side. He saw that his body had been wrapped to resemble a mummy from the middle of his chest to his navel and he found it hard to move. An image of him falling backwards into a gravelly abyss flashed through his mind and his head throbbed. He placed his fingers to his head and felt that it, too, had been covered all around by bandages. Remi felt very heavy in the bed and struggled to even dangle his feet over the side.

What happened during the explosion? he wondered. *Why can't I remember?*

His head was throbbing at the moment and he couldn't even remember most of what had happened the other day, let alone what had happened since he'd been in the Infirmary.

Remi pushed up on the bed and as his feet made contact with the cold, stone floor, his knees buckled. He fell back onto the bed, catching the attention of one of the nearby Healers across the way. As the man came toward him, Remi held up a hand to stop him.

"I'm fine," Remi lied. He knew he was simply too stubborn to accept the help even if he needed it. The Healer, who had already had dealings with Remi, knew this to be the case as well and threw his hands up in a gesture of frustrated acceptance.

Remi made a second attempt and was quickly reminded of just how strong gravity could be when you had been relatively free of its constraints for an extended period of time.

He thought of an old stop-motion clay movie he had seen one Christmas many years ago and chuckled as he repeated the mantra to himself.

Just put one put in front of the other! he chanted over and over in his head, laughing at how much effort such a seemingly miniscule task was now taking on his part. *This must be how babies feel.*

His entire body was stiff as if rigor mortis had set in and he was only now trying to shake the effects. Remi found himself silently grateful that the majority of the Coven had gone home for the night, leaving the grand staircase devoid of all of its usual traffic.

After a relatively brief bout of difficulty on his part, Remi finally made it up the single flight of stairs between the Infirmary and the House's training barracks. He could immediately hear the shower being used at the far end of the room.

The barracks had a similar design to the Infirmary, with the only major exceptions being that there was wood panelling in this room, darker mortar, and showers at the end of the room to accommodate any potential guest Warlocks that might come through, whereas the Infirmary only had a dry storage closet for herbs and other ingredients.

Remi trudged forward, beyond ready to rid himself of the god awful smell that had been allowed to fester with the grime that had accumulated on his person. He felt sticky and nasty, but was simultaneously thankful that no one had attempted a sponge bath during his sleep.

When he reached the showers, he found the entire area to already be filled with steam. He picked a stall nearest the door and began disrobing, grimacing once when he bent to pull his jeans down and again when he stripped away the bandages that clung to his body. He wedged his index and middle finger tightly between his skull and the wraps of concealment, unravelling those around his head and saw that they were crusted over with blood. He hastily checked and found that only dried bits of coppery red flakes had come away when he had pulled the bandages off. There seemed to be no new blood. Then he remembered the blade and felt his collarbone. There was a small area where the skin was slightly raised and he wondered just how deep the wound had been initially.

Once he had completely finished unwrapping himself from the bandages, Remi sucked in a sharp breath to refill his formerly compressed lungs, feeling both pain and delight at this simple act.

Remi turned the shower handle as hot as it would go, letting the steam build up for a moment before letting his boxer-briefs drop to the floor and stepping into the scalding downpour.

He stood there, unmoving as he allowed the water to burn away the dead skin and not bothering to use the soap just yet.

When Remi finally did grab the bottle, he could feel the heat being drawn out of his ribs as the water cascaded over him. He started with his hair, before using the suds created there to lather up the remainder of his body.

Remi stood there, staring at his feet while the bubbles rinsed themselves from him and down the drain, and long after. He did not move until he felt the first cold droplet that let him know he had drained an entire water heater of its contents. He turned the knob in a clockwise motion and stepped out, grabbing a towel and drying off before grabbing one of the plush, white robes that had been provided for visiting Warlocks.

It was at this point that he realized he had not brought any other clothes than the ones he had just taken off, and he simply refused to even consider putting those filthy things back on. He gathered his belongings and made his way back out the way he had come, feeling like a weight had been lifted from him afterward.

"Hey, wait up!" Finn's voice behind him caused Remi to tense involuntarily. "You feeling any better after that?"

"Loads," Remi admitted, almost as if he had suddenly become lighter than a feather. "I figured you had already gone back down."

"I thought about it," Finn shrugged. "But then I thought you might need someone here to make sure you didn't need any help getting back down there."

"Thanks," Remi said. "Did you find anything with the Vampire Lord? Or was it all just a wild goose chase?"

"Yeah I did, actually," Finn said, surprising Remi. "It looked like it had been abandoned for awhile, but there was definitely a manor. And it definitely had some pretty heavy Glamours cast on it. There was a strong presence there, and I'm not sure if it was just from so many of them in one spot, or if it was something else. We barely found it, to be honest."

"If it had been abandoned," Remi mused aloud, "why would it still have Glamours on it? Wouldn't they have been undone whenever the owner left?"

"That's what I'm still trying to figure out," Finn admitted. "I've been looking through every book and old record I can find to make sure no one lives there, but I've come up with a series of blanks so far."

"Did you try knocking on the door?" Remi suggested the simplest thing he could think of, knowing that sometimes that was the most overlooked.

"We did," Finn replied. "We tried every unlocking charm I could think of, a few bombardment jinxes, and Glyphs on all the different doors. Lord Kaine even managed to break into one of the windows on the second floor, but then something cast him out almost as soon as he had made it in."

The younger Warlock paused then, only briefly enough to let out a frustrated sigh, before going on, "Whoever it was that lived in that house before, did a very good job of hiding it from anyone that wasn't invited. It was very clear that it was done intentionally."

"Sounds like it," Remi observed, scratching his chin as he pondered and realizing that he needed a shave desperately. "Did you get a chance to talk to the Healer they took to the dungeons?"

"Not yet," Finn replied, looking a bit ashamed that he had forgotten, though it was understandable with everything else that had occurred in the past few days.

"It's fine," Remi hastily assured him. "Is he still down there?"

The younger Warlock nodded and Remi said, "Good. I'll talk to him in the morning. You just keep looking for any other clues and finding a way to undo those enchantments. And keep me posted on anything that you or anyone else finds on the place."

They had made it back to the Infirmary now, and as Remi opened the door to go in, he felt his heart instantly shattered into a billion tiny pieces.

"I thought you might want to see for yourself," Finn's voice sounded ignorantly excited, but the sound just fell hollow on Remi's ears.

Sitting there on the bed he had so recently been unconscious in, was someone he had not seen in fifteen years. Someone that he never, in his wildest dreams, thought that he would ever see again in this lifetime. It was someone that, put quite simply, he had thought to be dead.

The woman's silver hair had been pulled back into a tight bun, with a few tiny braids tied in on either side. Her frame was slight but strong, much like his own. Her skin had sunspots from years spent working outside in her personal garden and field.

She still wore the wedding band of the only man she had ever truly loved in her lifetime. Even from here, Remi could still smell her lavender perfume that had been caught on the breeze caused by him pulling the door. Her expression was remorseful and ecstatic, all at once and her moonstone eyes mirrored his own like a terrible joke from the universe.

This time, however, she was not a phantom created by his need for answers. This time, she was just as real as the indentions left on the cot as she stood to greet him. This was truly Nona Caswell; his grandmother.

She stood in the Oxford Coven's Infirmary, unchanged by the past fifteen years, as if they had never happened.

"Remi?" Finn's voice echoed somewhere off in the back of his mind for what felt like the third or fourth time. Remi felt his body moving slowly forward of its own accord.

He was moving toward her, at first; then suddenly past her.

"You're not going to say anything?" Nona said, as if she could feel the jumbled thoughts that were currently forming within his head.

Remi paused to acknowledge her voice, before grabbing the keys to his Jeep, accompanied by his wand and his phone from the nightstand. He simply could not make his mouth move after such an overdose of shock had been administered.

"Not even a hug?" the woman asked. It was then that Remi's voice found itself and worked for him.

"Don't you fucking touch me," the words came out like a dagger-sharp accusation and he saw that they had hit their mark. He pushed past the regretful Nona, then a stunned Finn.

He left the Infirmary and the Coven House altogether, not stopping until he was at his Jeep in the parking structure.

Remi opened the door and climbed into the driver's seat, letting the door slam shut behind him. He sat there for a few minutes, resting his head on the wheel and breathing deeply to calm himself before he did anything else.

"*Praeligo*," he muttered and heard a distinct whoosh of air as all sound left the cab. "*Umbra*," he called forth shadows of concealment to hide him from any potential onlookers.

Then, and only then, did Remi allow himself to cry. It was the first time he had done so in fifteen years and he had made himself a promise that he would never do so again; this day that promise had been broken just like everything else.

He yelled at the top of his lungs then, to the point where he was almost worried the windows might shatter and was glad that no one would hear or see him. He beat his hands on the wheel, dash, passenger seat; any solid surface he could find to hit. Remi did this until he could feel a line of blood trickling down his knuckles and his throat began to close, his voice becoming strangled and his lungs burning.

When he had finished, he wiped his dried tears from his face and climbed through the cabin of the Jeep to the very back. Being part of the Witch's Guard, he always carried a few spare changes of clothes as one could never predict the outcome of a certain case or when they might need them. He sat in the back section of the vehicle for a few moments as he sifted through things he could change into, shoving the dirty ones into a mesh bag and pulling on some fresh underwear. He shrugged the robe off and pulled on some jeans, a grey tee, and some socks.

Remi moved back to the driver's seat and cranked the engine, pulling some old, black-and-white Converse from the passenger seat and slipping them on.

"*Lumen*," he muttered, lifting the shadows.

"*Sonitus*," he dissolved the muffling charm.

Remi rolled the window down, put the Jeep in gear, and struck up his first cigarette in days. He sat there for a few seconds before pulling off, just letting the smoke fill his lungs and billow out of the cabin. There was no real destination, so long as wherever it was got him away from this place.

XVII

Remi found himself in the cornermost booth of Autumn's Bloom, drinking his fifth glass of Jack straight. He was beginning to feel numb and to him, that was the goal for tonight. He did not want to feel good or forget what had happened. He had come here as someone solely seeking a sense of disconnected complacency.

There was a live band tonight, which was not much of a shock as it was a Friday night in a bar on the Square. He was unsure of the other members, but he knew that the vocalist was a Fire Fae, as he had seen her perform before.

The Fae's hair was blonde and every part of her body was curved in the right spots. She reminded him of Marilyn Monroe, or some other unnamed pin-up girl as she crooned out her sultry covers of songs. The current selection was an old one he had heard before by the Ink Spots and Remi found himself chuckling under his breath at the irony of the lyrics as she sang about not wanting to set the world on fire.

He figured she must have been an Embodiment of Lust or something similar, as he felt things just from watching her perform that he knew he would normally never even consider which were only amplified by the whiskey that was coursing through him.

That was one thing he had always found fascinating about the Fire Fae; they could personify human emotions much more easily than the Fae in some of the other Courts.

"That's the one," he heard a stranger's voice say somewhere off to his left. "The one that's been on all the news stations over the past few days."

Remi shot the man a menacing glare and he quickly fell silent, averting his gaze to the floor.

"This seat taken?" a gruff voice just beside him pulled him out of his small feeling of victory against the Mortal man.

Remi looked up to see Davis hovering over him hopefully, looking much scruffier than Remi had ever seen him since the two had met. It was like he had gone from chiseled specimen of perfect manliness into grizzly lumberjack in just three days.

Must be the Lycan genetics, he thought to himself. He suddenly realized that this was also the first time that he had seen the other in street clothes. Remi took a quick glance and noted that he could see every muscle the officer had. He noticed a gaggle of college girls staring and smiled at how ridiculous they all looked.

He must not have had a chance to go buy new clothes since his New Moon, Remi chuckled to himself, then out loud, "Go ahead."

Davis joined him and ordered a Jack as well. "So," he said. "I guess everyone knows now."

"You told the guys on the force?" Remi asked, knowing that the other was referring to the Lycanthropy that he had been keeping secret for however long. Davis nodded, giving a somewhat timid smile. "And how'd that go?"

"A bunch of hell," Davis blew out a sharp breath. "But I guess I kind of deserved it," he said, then to Remi's questioning look, explained, "Most of them were cool about it after the whole thing that happened the other day, because they all got to see Kit and the other Alphas working just as hard as we were on the force. A few of the ones I'm a bit closer to just felt kind of left out, I guess, for not telling them sooner. Two of the older ones have completely refused to work with me, but they're both pretty close to retirement, so I don't think anyone is too worried."

"That's kind of shitty," Remi commented. "Understandable I guess, but still..."

"Yeah," Davis laughed. "Damn guys think it's contagious!"

"Well, they're not wrong," Remi cocked a single brow and smirked. "It kind of *is* contagious." The officer gave a shrug and a nod to agree. "How are Kit and the others?"

"They're as good as ever, man," Davis waved off the concern with a laugh. "A few broken bones and bruises, but nothing major. We heal up pretty quick, what with the condition and all. How about you? I saw what happened out there."

"I'll live," Remi said, a bit more harshly than he had intended. He added to the statement, trying for humor, "Unfortunately. But I guess that's my curse. I'm too spiteful. It'd make too many people happy if I kicked the bucket, and I just can't have all that."

Davis let out a laugh that turned into a sort of inhuman howl, which made Remi laugh and wonder just how many drinks the Lycan had had before coming to join him at the table. After the laughter had subsided and the two had slammed back their drinks and ordered another round, Remi asked, "Mind if I ask how you got it? Turned, I mean."

"Ex," Davis answered simply, with more than a little bitterness finding its way into his voice. He threw up his hand to order another round before the next had even made it to the table.

"I'm sorry," Remi said guiltily. "I didn't mean to dredge up a bad memory."

"It's fine, man," the other smiled now. "Things got pretty heated in the bedroom and the claws came out. I thought it was pretty kinky in the heat of the moment. So I left with a smile on my face that night. And the other two times we did it after that," he paused reflectively and seemed like he was reliving the moments with fondness before going on. "It wasn't until after that third time that they decided to tell me what was going on. But my First Moon was the next night, so I didn't have many options."

"There's a serum to prevent that sort of thing," Remi offered in vain.

"Yeah, I know that. Or at least I do now," Davis admitted. "But this happened way back before I had any Warlocks in the family, so I didn't know that was a thing. I didn't even report what had happened." He saw

Remi's look of disbelief and hastily added, "For other reasons we won't go into right now. Maybe when there's not so many prying ears."

"Even if you didn't want to report them, it shouldn't have been an issue, to begin with," Remi was drifting back into furious territory. He could almost feel himself fuming as he went on, "The fact that they concealed something life-changing like that, outright goes against our Covenants, Davis! And that's *my* job to look into things like that."

"Look, man," Davis pleaded with him. "It wasn't intentional on their part. I've moved past it. It only happened because I'm pretty good at what I do in that department." He gave a cocky chuckle and flashed a grin, of which Remi was not falling for. "I understand wanting to do your job, but I just think it would be stupid to go after something that happened so long ago. There are bigger fish to fry, man. I was at the Grove. Y'all seem like you've got enough shit heaped on your plate without someone like me adding to it. Even with just that one guy, you've got enough problems of your own."

It was at that very moment that Nona Caswell walked through the front entrance of the bar, framed by the light that poured into the dimly lit establishment.

"You don't know the half of it," Remi downed the rest of his drink in a single swig as the woman started making her way toward the booth they had taken up.

Remi could already hear the whispers from Warlocks in some of the other booths. Some of them had turned to gawk openly, while others seemed almost afraid to acknowledge the new patron.

"You want me to go?" Davis asked as Nona Caswell came to stand at the end of the table.

"I *want* you to shoot me in my face," Remi snarked. "Because I'm pretty sure that the nightmare is too real to wake up from without some Freddy Kreuger style death scene."

Davis laughed politely, before standing and inclining his head to Nona. "Ma'am," he said, and made a beeline toward the girls that had been ogling him from across the bar floor.

"How does he even fit into those jeans?" Nona turned her head to the side like a curious dog, as if trying to get a better view as Davis walked away.

At this comment, Remi held up his hand and waved the nymph behind the counter over. She came holding a bottle of Jack that seemed to have just been opened. Remi slipped her a hundred-dollar bill and flashed a smile, "Leave the bottle. The rest is yours."

The girl looked curiously from him to Nona, before doing a double-take and giving a slight tilt of her head.

"A bit steep for one bottle, don't you think?" Nona mused, cocking a single eyebrow at him.

"The stores are closed and if I go home, I'll have to be sober," Remi kept his tone flat. He poured himself another glass of the brown fire and glared, "How'd you find me?"

"You're not the only Caswell to drown their problems," she replied, taking up the vacant seat in the booth across from him where Davis had just been. "And you're not the first to come to Autumn's Bloom to do that, either.

Nona picked up the bottle and took a swig straight from it, her face scrunching up in disgust. "Been a minute since I talked to Uncle Jack," she coughed. She waved to the bar for a glass of soda and a highball glass with ice.

"So," she said, mixing her own drink as the items were placed before her. "I guess we've got some catching up to do."

"No," Remi said, maintaining a casual decency. "*We* don't have anything. You abandoned me, so as far as I'm concerned, you're just a ghost. Now, if you're a ghost that can keep up with me, that's up for debate. I'm five drinks in, straight. Your move."

"Yes, you are," Nona chuckled. "And fair enough on the other. I guess a simple 'I'm sorry' won't cut it?"

"I know you're sorry," Remi delivered in a harsh slur. "But what about an apology?"

"Your mother's drawl used to come out real bad like that after she'd had a few too many, as well," Nona noted, running one of her fingers over the rim of the glass in a contemplative manner. "Just like you have right now."

"Fockowf," Remi slurred then, catching himself and glaring. "I meant, *fuck off*," he enunciated more clearly this time.

Nona laughed at this casual slip of the tongue and took a sip from her own glass. "What do you want to know?"

"Shut up and drink, lady," Remi sneered. "Drunk men tell no lies, dead men tell no tales."

"What are we now?" Nona gave him a sardonic smirk. "Have we gone from a redneck to a pirate? I'd just like to know who I'm dealing with tonight."

"I wonder if they'd send another of the Witch's Guard to bring me in for re-killing a newly animated corpse?" Remi mused. "Or if they'd just expect me to turn myself in and save them the hassle of it all..."

He stared contemplatively into his own glass for a brief moment as if weighing his options, before upending it and slamming it down onto the table between them.

"Six," he belched, punching his chest to get a smaller gas bubble to come up before he continued drinking.

Nona called for another soda and when it arrived, she took the bottle and upturned it for six straight seconds. She returned the bottle and quickly chased the whiskey with the soda, with a full-body shake as she did so. "There," she laughed. "Now, we're even."

"What's wrong with you?" Remi asked quietly, not daring to look up from his glass.

"What do you mean?" Nona looked confusedly at him. "Talk to me, baby."

He had not expected it to sting so much, but something about the last word triggered something deep within Remi that he had been successfully keeping in check up until that point.

"Don't you 'baby' me!" he shouted across at her. There were a few concerned glances from other nearby patrons and he quickly lowered his voice to a harsh whisper before, leaning in before continuing, "Don't you *dare* try to waltz in here now after everything and act like nothing has changed. You have been gone for fifteen years; *fifteen*! And all you have to say when you come back is 'Oh, by the way, sorry about that?' No, you don't get to wipe your hands clean of that, lady. You just don't!"

"If you knew why I had to do it, you would understand," Nona replied calmly. "If I could have avoided leaving you like that, I would have."

"Bullshit!" Remi spat at her again, every emotion he had ever felt over the past decade suddenly welling up within him. "Let me guess: your excuse is 'because reasons', right?" He pulled out a cigarette and lit it in his usual fashion. "*Nova Caeli*," he muttered before ending with, "Because if that's all you've got, then I call bullshit right here and now."

"Give me one of those," Nona said, taking a single stick from the box.

"You don't smoke," Remi exhaled. "Or have you forgotten that in your absence?"

"Must have," the woman put the cigarette to her lips and sparked the tip in a similar way to how he had lit his own. She inhaled deeply, letting the smoke come out through her nose and drift up into the small vortex Remi had created above the table. "Don't forget who taught you how to do that in the first place."

"Yeah," Remi muttered under his breath. "A dead woman."

"She," Nona began in the third person, then corrected herself, "*I'm not dead.*"

"Might as well be," Remi shrugged. "For all the good you've done me over the years."

He saw that there was still a single Mortal staring at them after Remi's earlier outburst and shot the man a menacing glare, similar to the one he'd given the other man just seconds ago. The Mortal man quickly turned his attention back to the drink in front of him.

"You'll regret all this in the morning, Remi," Nona spoke through a cloud of smoke. This reignited the dormant fury that had been lingering just beneath the surface of his skin.

"How would you know what I'll regret?" he asked, sounding surprisingly calm given how he felt at the moment. He stared into the glass before him as if it held all the secrets of the universe, his blue moonstone gaze reflected back at him. This time Remi did not care who might be listening in and went on with whatever came to mind, somehow managing to keep his voice at a relatively low whisper.

"You know who was there when I finished fifth year and made the decision that I was going to join the Witch's Guard just like Mum and Dad?" he asked, and when Nona tried to respond, he threw up a hand to stop her. "No," he said. "You don't know."

"Do you know who was there when I started sixth year and started actually training to do just that? Or when I had to stay at the Academy during every single break when all of the other students went home to be with their families? No, you don't."

"How about when I finished eighth year and graduated from the Academy and decided that I was going to come back home? Who was there when I rejoined the Oxford Coven as a proud member of the Witch's Guard in the very last Proving ceremony that Franklin Ashcroft ever oversaw as Arbiter before he died? Who was there–"

Remi felt his voice crack then and heard the eerie silence that had befallen Autumn's Bloom. All eyes were on him by now despite how composed he thought he had been. Some were concerned and clueless, while others remained silent and pained as they watched his tirade against the woman across from him. Remi pushed all other thoughts away from him as he went on.

"Who was there when I went out on my first case and had to take a Mortal girl to Trial before the Coven for trying to bring her best friend back from the dead with Blood Magic just because another Mortal had shot her in the back of the head after raping her? Who was there when I broke down after that because I thought I couldn't do the job after she had been sentenced? Who was there, then or during any other important part of my miserable life?" Remi was speaking at a level somewhere between conversational and vehement whisper. Everything around him seemed to have paused and he was crying now, but he did not care.

"Do you know?" he spat at the woman sitting across from him. "No. You don't. Because you were just too busy having everyone believe that you were dead for fucking 'reasons!'"

He took the deepest, shakiest breath he could to calm himself bring his focus back to center.

"I've been the *only* one who was there for me during every part of my life," he said with a grim finality as surrounding Mortals looked on, almost eager for the conclusion to his monologue.

"When I crystallized that damn willow tree, I hardened myself against everything. Because of that act, not you or anybody else can come into my life and break me. I'm made of steel now and, yeah, I'm bitter about it. But if I am, it's because you and every other shit stain on this planet have pushed me to that point. So thank yourself, you self-righteous hedgewitch, Nona Caswell."

Remi upended his seventh and final drink, taking the final drag of his cigarette and stubbing the butt into the bottom of the empty highball glass.

He grabbed his keys and made his way out of the bar, every set of eyes trailing his movement in an audible and shocked state of hesitation.

He made it out into the street, ignoring the onlooking faces of everyone and stumbling against the side of the building. Suddenly, there was a strong arm around his waist, holding him up and steadying him so that he would not completely topple over.

"Don't!" Remi snarled and punched the person's chest with his full force, only to find that it was like trying to punch a brick wall.

"Come on, Caswell," a voice said. He looked up to see that it was Davis who was holding him and was suddenly acutely aware that he might get taken in for public intoxication. "Let's get you home, bud."

The Lycan kept one hand tucked around his waist and hastily pulled one of Remi's arms over the back of his own neck. The man half-guided, half-carried Remi down the sidewalk and across the parking lot to where his truck was parked. Once there, he lifted him into the cab as if he were as weightless as a sheet of paper.

"Don't," Remi repeated weakly just before curling over and heaving onto the floor of the passenger seat. "ImsosorryDavis!"

He was beyond mortified, but the Lycan only smiled gently down at him.

"It's cool, Caswell," he laughed reassuringly. "Let's just get you home before it happens again."

Davis buckled Remi's seatbelt and rolled the window down to let the drunken Warlock get some fresh air as they drove, before hurrying around to get into the driver's seat.

Remi felt the truck shift into gear with a brief lurch forward, before finally succumbing to the alcohol and letting it swallow him whole.

Remi was awakened the next morning by the sunlight coming through the slits of the blinds in his bedroom. He looked down and found, with a start, a nude-save-boxers Davis sprawled out across the foot of his bed on top of the covers. He lifted the sheets and was horrified to see that he was in a likewise state to the Lycan.

As if he had felt the covers tug underneath him, Davis stirred and rolled over to see Remi watching him with a rabid curiosity. With a stretch and yawn that Remi had to avert his gaze from awkwardly, the Lycan grinned across at him.

"Oh, hey," he laughed groggily. "You're awake!"

"Yeah," Remi managed awkwardly. He took another look at Davis's semi-nudity and then a brief second glance under the covers at his own, before beginning, "Um, did we-"

As if reading the thought, Davis laughed more whole-heartedly this time.

"Oh no, bud!" he assured Remi with a shake of his head. "You threw up on me and yourself coming up the stairs," he explained. "I got you out of those dirty clothes and into bed and took a shower. I didn't want to struggle with getting your drunk ass into more clothes, so I just left you like that. I mean, we're friends and all, but I don't think we're quite on that level in this bromance, bud. Plus, you tried to fight me several times."

"That does sound very on-brand for me," Remi said, feeling himself turn red with embarrassment.

Davis didn't seem to care and let out another laugh that turned into a wide yawn. "I hope you don't mind that I crashed here last night? I really shouldn't've driven, but someone needed to get you out of there before you hurt yourself or someone else."

"Oh, no," Remi laughed, feeling immensely better since his friend had cared for him. "And thanks for that, by the way. But why didn't you just borrow some clothes for yourself?"

"You're about two sizes smaller than me, bud," Davis laughed, smacking his stomach for emphasis. Remi noticed, with slight envy, that even as he did this, not a single muscle moved in reaction.

"Gotcha," he nodded. "Well feel free to use the washer and stuff downstairs while you're here. I really don't need my Mortal neighbors seeing a cop leaving my house wearing only his underwear."

"For sure," Davis gave a thumbs up and another deep full-body stretch, before getting up and grabbing his pile of dirty clothes from the floor beside the bed.

Remi watched until the other man was fully down the staircase before getting up and rushing into the bathroom, where he got sick in the toilet a final time and stepped into the shower to quickly wash last night's adventure off.

Once he was clean and freshly clothed, Remi made his way downstairs to find himself enveloped in the intermingling aromas of coffee and food being made. He rounded the corner to see that Davis was standing in front of the stove in his boxers, stirring something while the pot to his right was going through its final percolations.

Remi watched silently while the Lycan danced around the kitchen, listening to some 70s soul playlist on his phone, completely unaware of his audience. The Warlock could not help but let out a loud guffaw at how uncoordinated the other man's movements were. At this, Davis jerked around with a guilty grin.

"You laughing at me?" he cocked an eyebrow, as if this was such a ridiculous thing to find out. He laughed at himself and went on, "Sorry, bud. Hope you don't mind. I just need some substance after a night like that."

"Help yourself," Remi threw his hands up with a shrug, making his way to the fridge, where he pulled out the milk. He fixed his first cup and watched with a curious eye as Davis sprinkled some cheese into the skillet, before folding the contents over into a half-moon shape. "Omelette you make another one before I cut you off from the supply."

"Oh!" Davis shouted, covering his mouth and waving the spatula around in front of him like he was about to start spitting out a diss track he had rehearsed in the shower. "Someone's got mad yolks, bro!"

"It's what I does, son," Remi chuckled with a slurp to punctuate. "It's what I does." He took another, slightly fuller sip of the brown liquid and set his mug on the counter. He opened the window above the sink and lit up a cigarette. "You smoke?"

"Sure," Davis said, cracking another few eggs into a bowl and whisking them before pouring the mixture into the skillet. He made a puckering face, to which Remi inserted an unlit cigarette. "Got a light?" Remi snapped his fingers absently and Davis exclaimed, "Watch it! That's my face!"

"Did I burn you?" Remi laughed, knowing he hadn't and blowing smoke into the air just above him. "Shut up and turn on the vent." He pushed himself up onto the counter as Davis flipped a switch on the hood of the stove, crossing his legs and picking his mug back up. "Thanks for last night, by the way," he said. "If you hadn't brought me home, I probably would have done something stupid."

"It's no problem, man," Davis shrugged it off, stirring the contents of the skillet before adding a few more. "I know you would have done the same for me if the situation was reversed."

The washer buzzed to signal that the final cycle had just finished. Remi leapt from the counter to switch the clothes over to the dryer. "For sure," he agreed. "But still, thanks anyway."

"It's cool, bud," Davis said, sprinkling cheese into the second omelet. He folded it just as he had the one before, turning the stove eye off and sliding it onto a plate. He brought both to the end of the bar counter. The two hastily finished their cigarettes and Remi grabbed some forks from the drawer beside the sink, handing one to Davis. They dug into their plates, quickly devouring the omelets like neither of them had eaten in several days. Now that he thought about it, Remi actually *hadn't* eaten in several days.

Just as Remi had set the empty plates and silverware into the sink, he heard the sound of a key turning in the knob and Finn's voice calling out, "Remi?"

"In here!" Remi called back.

"Oh, good!" the younger Warlock sounded relieved as he came into the house. "I heard about last night and didn't know where you had run off to. Then, I didn't see your Jeep. Whose truck is that, by the way?"

Finn rounded the corner to see Remi and Davis standing in the kitchen, the latter in nothing but his boxers. "Oh," he blushed, making to turn back the way he had just come. "I didn't realize-"

"Hey," the Lycan waved, looking very much like a deer caught in the glare of headlights. He looked briefly between the two Warlocks, adding, "I'm just waiting on my clothes to dry."

"Oh," Finn managed, just as the door opened and closed a second time.

"Remi?" Nona Caswell's voice called. Clearly seeing Finn under the open archway that led to the dining room, she came to stand beside him. She took in the sight of Davis and fixed her hair, "Well, hello there, young man!"

Davis and Remi shared a brief glance before bursting into a joint fit of laughter at the reactions of the other two.

I needed that after last night, Remi thought to himself as he wiped tears of laughter away and doubled over trying to catch his breath.

The pair finished their guffaw as Finn and Nona looked on as if they had both gone suddenly mad.

The dryer buzzed and Davis grabbed his clothes, hurriedly tucking himself into his jeans and pulling his shirt on.

"So *that's* how he does it," Nona recalled her question from the night before in Autumn's Bloom.

"Looks like I'm out, bud," Davis said, pulling on his boots with only a few grunts.

"Cool, cool," Remi said. "Let me know when you get home."

Davis gave a nod and a thumbs-up, excusing himself past the other two Warlocks to leave. They all heard his truck engine rev to life as he pulled away. This left both Nona and Finn to stare at Remi intently for an explanation, which he did not give.

"I found something I think we can use," Finn said finally, moving on after realizing that Remi was leaving an air of mystery about his night with the Lycan.

"I brought your Jeep," Nona explained, handing him the magnetic slider box with his spare key inside. "Do you have any kudzu and honey?"

"Should be in the cabinet," Remi replied. "Grinder should be next to the jar with the kudzu. Teabags are on the shelf below those."

"Do you need any?" Nona asked.

"Nah," he replied with a wave of his hand. "I actually think I hurled up all of the whiskey I drank from last night."

"Kudzu and honey?" Finn gave the two of them a puzzled look as Nona went about gathering the materials.

"With hot tea," Remi explained, putting on a fresh pot of coffee for his new guests. "Best thing for a hangover."

"Seriously?" Finn looked impressed. "I never knew that."

"And who taught you that?" Nona asked over her shoulder as she searched the cupboards for something to put the water in, a sly tone in her voice.

"A dead woman," Remi replied, but without the venom that the statement had taken on last night. "Kettle is in the bottom, to the left of the oven."

"Just what I was looking for," Nona acknowledged the unspoken apology with a smile.

"I thought so," Remi sighed into his second cup of coffee.

"We'll talk later," the woman assured him with a wink.

"Touching," Finn eyed the pair of them curiously, clearly not understanding the hidden sentiment behind their words. "But we've got battlements to make."

The young Warlock set the satchel he'd had slung over his shoulder in one of the chairs and pulled out a long, rolled-up tube of paper, which he proceeded to roll out across the dining room table. He pulled out several thick tomes, placing them at each corner to hold the edges down.

"What's all this?" Remi cocked a single brow curiously, staring down at his table that had been converted into a workstation.

"I couldn't find out who owned that house that Sebastian led us to," Finn explained. "But, I did manage to find the blueprints for it in the Coven's records."

"What are these?" Remi asked, pointing to one of the various handwritten scrawls that had been marked on the blueprints. "It looks like... are these all Latin dictionaries?"

"They are," Finn confirmed. "Apparently, when you put any sort of permanent enchantments or Glamours on a house within any particular district, the High Coven requires you to send them a list so they can Trace it and send the records to wherever the local Coven is."

"So they can Trace the use of magic?" Remi was slightly taken aback by this information. "I never knew that."

"They started that way back before I was even born, some seventy-odd years ago," Nona reflected from across the kitchen, just as the kettle started to whistle. She removed it from the stove, turning the eye off and pouring the tea into a mug, where she sprinkled in her ground kudzu leaves and honey before joining them.

"It had something to do with the Mortals being at war with each other," she went on, taking a tiny sip of her hangover remedy. "They started policing their own citizens and putting them into internment camps if they had ties to one of the countries they were fighting with or something along those lines. Naturally, when this brand of patriotism went over without much opposition, they decided to get bold and try the same thing with us."

"They put Warlocks into internment camps?" Finn sounded as appalled at the idea as Remi felt.

"Are you kidding?" Nona let out a brief chortle and went on. "They tried it and, of course, they had no means of keeping us there because it's very easy to cast a bombardment charm and blast your way out when you have the power. Of course, this sent them into a frenzy because up until that point, Warlocks had been so off-the-grid as far as the Mortals were concerned. And we all know Mortals can't stand not having their hand in something that involves power."

Remi and Finn exchanged quick glances and nods as the woman continued with her explanation, "So the Mortal president at that time traveled all the way to Salem to meet with the seated Magisters on the High Coven and discuss what could be done to make the Mortals sleep better at night. Hence, the Trace was born."

"But, why would the High Coven not just overturn something like that after the Mortals were done with their war?" Finn asked.

Nona took another sip of her tea, before closing, "Because, it actually ended up helping us more so than the Mortals. Because we started using it on stuff like what you were saying, with the permanent enchantments, and rogues that had broken the Covenant for minor enough infractions where they were only sentenced to be monitored for a time afterward. It's easy enough to undo the Trace, but doing so without prior consent from the High Coven results in the rogue being marked for immediate elimination. It works essentially the same as the Mortals' bondsmen; you skip bond, your sentence gets revoked."

"Why did we never know this before?" Remi asked, finding himself wondering what else he did not know about the High Coven. "Why did they even let that happen in the first place?"

"There was nothing that could be done at that time," Nona shrugged. "Sure, we could avoid the internment camps with our magic, but we didn't have anything that would protect us against something like the threat of a nuclear attack. Sure, now we have Glamours made specifically for things like that, but back then, there was nothing stopping the Mortals from nuking us besides the fact that they might actually do more damage to their own people. It was essentially the choice between a rock and a hard place."

"I see," Remi said thoughtfully, taking a sip from his own mug and turning to Finn. "So, what else did you find out about this house, kid?"

"Well, actually," Finn began, pulling out some notes he had taken down while researching. "Apart from the Coven House, this manor is the *only* one in Oxford that has even a single permanent Glamour protecting it. And the funny thing is, between the two of them, not a single one of them are the same."

"That's odd," Remi noted, and the three exchanged looks of concern at the idea.

Someone doesn't want anyone to get in that house for some reason, he thought to himself.

"I've seen some of these before," Nona informed them, staring down at the paper and moving her index finger across one of the lines of scrawled text.

"Great!" Finn exclaimed, pulling out several pens and stenography pads from his satchel. "Do you think you can work on the counterspells for those while Remi and I take on the others?"

Nona agreed, taking one of the pens and placing stars on the blueprints beside the ones that she would be working on. They all took the materials that Finn had provided, taking seats around the dining room table and getting to work on breaking the code.

By the time midnight had fallen, the trio of Warlocks had finally managed to decipher every single spell that had been placed on the manor at any given time. Nona had taken the task of working on the Glamours, while Finn had worked on how to dispel the Glyphs that would be in place, and Remi had worked on the actual charms and jinxes that would work against them when the other two had finished their work. In the several hours they had been huddled around the blueprints, they had collectively gone through 4 pots of coffee, three and a half packs of cigarettes, two pizzas, and an entire twelve-pack of sodas, all while managing to only get up during that expanse for the occasional bathroom breaks in between.

When they had all been finished, the three rose from the table in unison, seeming to be satisfied overall with their work. Each gave their own groans, grunts, and stretches as they agreed to be done for the night.

Remi grabbed another cigarette and opened the back door, stepping out onto the back patio and letting the house air out. Finn went to grab another soda and leaned over the bar counter in the kitchen, checking for any messages that had been missed during their brainstorming session. Nona gathered all of the notes they had taken, flipping through them and counting them up.

"Twenty-three spells, seventy-two Glamours, and fifteen Glyphs in total," she announced to the room, sounding impressed with what they had accomplished.

"Good lord!" Remi sighed out a large cloud of smoke, stretching again as it drifted up. "Is it really that many?"

"Yep," Nona recounted. "A hundred and ten protections, altogether."

"I'll call Aunt Syl," Finn said, coming back to the table and grabbing a cigarette for himself. "I'm sure she'd love to know what we found."

"Good idea," Nona agreed, filing through the pages in her hand once more before setting them back down in a neat stack. She grabbed a cigarette of her own before joining Remi outside, where she lit it and inhaled deeply, clearly glad to be done with the project they had just finished with. "I guess now, we finally have a chance to talk. Without either of us drunk yelling at the other."

"I make no guarantees about that," Remi retorted, accidentally blowing smoke out of his nose. Nona chuckled but was cut off before she could begin.

"She's not answering," Finn said, coming outside and staring at his phone. "I guess it'll just have to wait until in the morning."

"It's late," Remi mused aloud. "With the week we've all been having, she probably went to bed before anything else could go wrong for us." They each forced out a half-hearted laugh.

"You're right," Finn agreed. "I'm probably going to turn in for the night, myself. Night, guys."

"Good night, sweetie," Nona kissed the younger Warlock on the forehead and both she and Remi watched him walk back inside and up the staircase, to the spare bedroom he had taken over.

"Good," she said, finally. "We're alone now. There's so much I have to tell you, I don't even know where to start."

"You'd better find a place to start soon," Remi chuckled, striking up another cigarette before he had even thrown the other to the ground. "I think I'm about ready to turn in myself. Right after this last one." Nona checked the face of the watch strapped to her wrist and nodded.

He caught a whiff of her lavender perfume in the breeze and a thought occurred to him then. He Remi took a drag off his cigarette as he mulled the question over in his head, before finally asking, "Weren't you working a case just before you went missing?"

There was a brief flash of something across Nona's face. It was gone too soon for Remi to get a good read on what it might have been and if he hadn't been paying such close attention to the woman standing before him, it might not have even registered to him that something was amiss.

"I was," Nona answered carefully, clearly thinking out what words to use at the moment. "But that's been so long ago that I don't recall any of the details."

"Right," Remi eyed the woman suspiciously now. She didn't seem to notice, as she simply glanced down at the watch on her wrist.

"You're right," she agreed. "It's late tonight. We'll have time tomorrow. For now, we should get some rest." She finished her own cigarette and let it fall to the concrete where she stepped on it.

"Good night," she said, turning away and walking into the house and up the stairs.

Remi found himself somewhat torn as he watched his grandmother ascend the stairs to where she had taken over his second spare bedroom. On the one hand, he was pleased overall with what had been accomplished at his dining room table just since Davis had left this morning. At the same time, he couldn't help but feel that there was something Nona was keeping from him about the last case she had been working on before she had gone missing.

Is it that she doesn't want to tell me? he wondered to himself. *Or is she just afraid that Finn might overhear something he shouldn't?*

He resolved himself to interrogate her further on the matter in the morning, whenever he could get her alone. As he thought of Finn, he made a mental note to question the Healer that was still in the dungeons of the Coven House as soon as he got there in the morning.

It did not take much longer for him to finish his last smoke before stepping back inside the house. He locked the doors and bolted the windows, adding the Glamours to each as he had become accustomed to doing over the past few days and eventually making his way up the stairs. He had let Nona take over the room directly across the landing from Finn's and knew that she would be reading for a few more hours before turning the lights out. He had resolved himself not to disturb her during this time, choosing instead to make his way to the end of the hall where Finn was already asleep.

Remi turned the knob and peeked his head just inside the door. It had taken no time at all for the younger Warlock to pass out in his bed and Remi briefly wondered just how long he had been working to find the blueprints and information about the mysterious manor in the woods.

Probably went straight there after I stormed out of the Infirmary, he guessed himself, feeling only slightly guilty at the event.

He closed the door as soundlessly as he could, hearing Finn's phone vibrate on the nightstand as he made his way back down the hall to his own room.

Must be Sylvia responding, he assumed. Then another thought occurred to him. Remi peeked his head back into Finn's room to ensure that the younger Warlock was still asleep. Upon seeing that this was, indeed, the case, he moved across to the room where Nona was. He knocked lightly on the door.

"Come in," his grandmother's voice answered, so he did. "What's wrong?" she asked upon seeing him framed in the doorway.

"I have some questions before I go to sleep," Remi replied. "Mind if I come in?"

"It's your house," Nona said, placing her book on the table and removing her glasses. "What is it that you wanted to ask?"

Remi walked across the room to take a seat at the foot of the bed. He wondered how to go about with his questioning, as he genuinely did not want to start another fight. Finally, he decided to just be blunt, "I know about the case you were working on. I looked into it when I first joined the Witch's Guard at Oxford because I had this overwhelming need to know. But certain things were marked in the case file as classified information that I wasn't allowed to see without taking on the case myself."

There was a long pause in which neither of them spoke, with Remi staring at the floor and Nona adjusting her glasses as if she were searching for a way to respond.

Remi had always admired her and her casework since he was young, as he knew that his grandmother was a rare breed when it came to the Witch's Guard. As far as he was aware, women were seldom inducted as members or even allowed a Proving ceremony. But Nona Caswell had changed that when she was very young. Even after she had broken with the Oxford Coven in favor of training Remi when his own magic had first started manifesting itself, she had been allowed to work cases for them at her leisure to earn a bit of extra money. The Ashcrofts and the Caswells had been friends for generations, which might have had something to do with this, but Remi liked to imagine that it was simply due to Nona's own skill in the field.

Finally, she said, "So then you know how the case you're working must look to me?"

"No," Remi answered earnestly. "I really don't. Could you tell me?"

Nona said nothing for a few moments, then let out a heavy sigh and replied, "You know we're not supposed to talk about cases like this unless it's with someone else who is working on the case. But I guess I really don't have a choice in this particular case."

"What do you mean?" Remi asked, overwhelmingly curious by this point.

"The last case I was working on before everything changed," the woman spoke as if each syllable was its own labor, "was *the* case. The case that killed your parents. The one that took your grandfather as well."

"You think it's the same Warlock?" Remi asked, an image of the golden eyes flashed behind his own as he thought of what this meant if everything connected like Nona was suggesting.

"I know it is," she replied. "I saw him that day in the Grove when he attacked the press conference Sylvia was holding. There's no mistaking that golden glare."

"So then he has a vendetta against our family?" Remi asked, suddenly remembering the sinister voice telling him to greet the 'others'. "But why?"

"Because of who we are, I would imagine," Nona suggested. "I know you saw the story of how the Witch's Guard came to be. I made sure of it."

"So that *was* you!" Remi said, louder than he had initially intended. "How long have you been watching me then?"

"Fifteen years," Nona answered, taking him slightly aback.

"And you waited until I was almost killed to make your presence known?" Remi was starting to feel the same resentment he'd felt last night but tried to push it back down until he had more answers from his grandmother.

"Not exactly," she replied. "I couldn't let myself be seen outright while I was guarding him in that place. But I sent you signs when you needed them. Like in the archives. And I had my Familiar watch your house every night when he broke free."

"Guarding?" Remi repeated. "Broke free? What are you even talking about?"

His head was swimming with unbridled emotions and questions at this point, but Remi was so unsure of how to move forward with the conversation.

"The Dark Warlock," Nona said. "Alexander Morrigan. When we met in battle, I only succeeded in locking him in a crystal stasis. I couldn't physically leave him, as I was unsure of just how many others might have been on his side, waiting for me to leave so they could release him and finish what he started."

"So you just sat there watching him for fifteen years while your spell wore off?" Remi asked. Then, catching what else the woman had said, he went on, "What do you mean by 'what he started'?"

"Some sort of Blood Magic ritual," Nona explained. "I could never figure out just what he was attempting to accomplish, but I do know some of what he had already done."

"So he's done this before then?" Remi asked, becoming increasingly mortified at the thought that no one had stopped this Dark Warlock before.

"Not before," Nona corrected. "It's a continuation of sorts. I only managed to stop him before he finished."

"And you didn't get rid of what he had already done up until that point in fifteen years?" Remi asked, sounding disbelieving that he was hearing such a thing.

"I tried, RJ," she used her pet name for him. "I really did. The thing about Blood Magic is that it takes a lot to perform, but it takes all that and even more to undo what has already been done. I would have had to make a payment of my own in order to undo his work up until that point."

"You had him in crystal stasis," Remi said slowly, trying to sift through the expositional overload that was being hoisted onto him. "Why didn't you offer him as payment since it was his crimes that started it all?"

Nona said nothing for a while, and Remi was unsure if it was due to him suggesting her using Blood Magic herself or if she simply did not have an answer to give at that point. Finally, she replied, "He had somehow made himself a part of the ritual. Even if I had done as you suggested, it would have only served to complete his infernal workings."

There was another long pause in which neither of them spoke, each seeming to mull over the possibilities in their heads. After a few minutes of this, Remi was the first to speak, "I think it's time for me to go to bed. I suddenly have a lot to think about."

"I think that might be best," Nona agreed. "We're both tired. We can figure something out in the morning over breakfast."

Remi nodded and made to leave the room. When the door had closed, he walked down the hallway to his own room. As his hand touched the knob, Remi found that he still did not want to risk sleeping in his bed after his nightmare earlier in the week. He went downstairs and took his place on the couch. His mind was still racing when his eyelids began to droop and it took no time at all for him to succumb to the tired feeling that had been hanging over him for the past few hours.

In a way, they had wasted an entire day pouring over all of the information that Finn had presented, but at the same time, at least now they could revisit the manor without fear of getting attacked by whatever enchantments had been placed upon the house.

However, with everything that Nona had just told him, Remi felt an overwhelming sense of dread bubbling through him as he drifted off. Finally, they had a name and some form of lead on the Dark Warlock known as Alexander Morrigan.

But does that make anything better? was Remi's last conscious thought before he finally fell asleep.

XVIII

The smell of food being prepared in the kitchen woke Remi up the next morning. He eagerly arose from his place on the couch and made his way around the corner. There, he saw Nona Caswell standing in front of the stove, humming softly to herself as she stirred what he already knew was gravy. He could smell the biscuits in the stove and wondered how she had gotten them.

"Did I have the stuff to make all this?" he asked, startling her out of her humming.

"Don't sneak up on me like that!" Nona exclaimed with a laugh. "And no, you didn't. I had to run to the store when I woke up. Breakfast is an important meal."

"Where did you get the money to go to the store, ghost lady?" Remi cocked a single brow at the woman, already knowing the answer.

"Maybe I borrowed it," she replied with a sly grin. "Maybe you just shouldn't ask so many questions about things."

"Fine," he sighed, moving to the fridge, where he pulled out the milk. He fixed his first cup of coffee and took a sip to wake himself up. "Has Finn not come down, yet?"

Nona shook her head, "I wasn't going to wake either of you up until it was ready. But it's almost there, so you can go get him."

Remi silently agreed and made his way out of the kitchen and up the stairs to the guest bedroom. He knocked on the door before entering, just in case the other man was in the middle of changing. "You awake yet?"

He turned the knob and pushed on the door only to see that Finn was in an upright position on the bed, staring off into the distance. "Oh, good," Remi smiled. "You are. Breakfast is ready downstairs."

When there was no response from the other, he looked down to see that he was holding his phone in his hand and joked, "Breakup text? I know how that goes, kid. You'll be fine." Again, no response.

Remi moved closer to the younger Warlock and looked down at him, seeing that the screen on his phone had been unlocked to reveal a single message. He took the device from the unmoving Finn's hand and immediately saw why he was in such a despondent state. He felt himself blanche as he read aloud:

I have her.
Come claim her.
-AL

The contact was saved in Finn's phone as 'Aunt Syl', so it had come from her number. The timestamp revealed that it had been received this morning, shortly after they had all gone to sleep. Remi felt the dread filling him as he knew what that meant.

"Shit," he said breathlessly, tossing the device back onto the bed where it landed just in front of its owner. "Finn, come on. We have to go now."

The younger Warlock continued staring at the wall in front of him, emerald eyes blank and his face slack-jawed.

"Finn!" he slapped the other man to get his attention. "Now!"

"I've contacted the High Coven," Nona told them roughly thirty minutes after Remi had informed her of the situation.

She had made the two eat while she had gotten on the phone, with the reasoning that they could not start what was sure to be such a hectic day on empty stomachs. Shortly after they had finished, the three of them had made their way over to the Coven House. Once there, Remi and Nona had stood in the Arbiter's office while Finn had been taken to the Infirmary to find some kind of mixture to calm his nerves.

"They have been made aware of the potential crisis we now have on our hands regarding Sylvia and this Dark Warlock," Nona finished, staring down at the rotary phone on the desk as if she expected it to ring at any minute.

"How did they react?" Remi asked.

"Not well," the woman's voice was grim. "They have deemed it necessary to place the entire city under a protective barrier. No new people in or out until this has all been sorted out."

"They can do that?" Remi asked. "I mean, without contacting the Mortal authorities?"

"I'm sure they saw the broadcast of what happened at the Grove," Nona said. "I highly doubt that they are finding themselves very concerned with what the Mortal authorities have to say on the subject of magical well-being at the moment. And after that, who can blame them?"

Remi thought back to the chaos that had overtaken the stage and the Mayor of Oxford whispering slurs against Warlocks into his ear. It had only been a few days ago, but it felt like an eternity had passed since the press conference.

"You should go talk to Finn," Nona went on. "I'm sure that he must be pretty shaken after that and I'm certain he could use a friend right now. Meet me back here within the hour. I need to speak to you."

"Right," Remi agreed with a nod. "I'll go check on him and then we'll come straight here."

"No," Nona's voice was stern. "I need to speak with you, alone."

There was something about the way she said this last part that gave Remi a feeling of unease in the pit of his stomach. He gave her a puzzled look, but did not speak as he turned on his heel to leave the office. He could feel Nona's eyes on the back of him as he walked away and sped up the pace.

Remi did not stop moving his legs until he had reached the Infirmary, where he found a clearly shaken Finn was sitting in a chair just inside the door. His gaze and thoughts still seemed to be in some faraway space that Remi could not quite peer into, but the other man looked up from the spot he had been staring at when he heard Remi's footsteps on the stone floor.

"What's that?" Remi asked, indicating the cup in his hand. There was a chocolate bar in his other hand, but Remi already knew that was merely standard protocol that the Healers often used to pep patients up.

"Whiskey," Finn explained, sounding just as glum as ever. "Supposed to make me feel better about everything, I guess."

"Whiskey and chocolate?" Remi made a face. "How's that coming?"

"Great!" Finn lied and faked a smile. "Now I feel like shit with a buzz!"

"Well," Remi chuckled. "At least you're talking now. That's a start." He pulled up a chair next to the younger Warlock and sat in it with his legs straddling the back, resting his elbows on the edge of it to prop his chin up.

Finn took another large bite from the candy bar and spoke around a mouthful of chocolate, "What if we don't make it in time? What if he's already done whatever it is that he's going to do?"

Remi pondered this for a moment before answering, "Then he wouldn't have sent the message. I think he wants us to at least think that we have a chance to stop him, otherwise he wouldn't have bothered."

He spoke with much more certainty than he felt and was glad that Finn did not seem to notice any doubt that might have slipped into his voice.

"What if it's a lie?" the younger Warlock pointed out something that Remi had been thinking all along. "A trap just to get us there and then kill us, too?"

"Could be," Remi answered honestly with a shrug. "But I highly doubt that in this case. From what I've seen, he's only targeting those that he needs for whatever ritual he's going to attempt."

"Yeah," Finn agreed with a sigh. "But, what if–"

Remi cut the young Witchguard off by bringing the cup in his hand up to his face and tipping it to his lips.

"What if you stop worrying about what could happen and start helping me come up with a plan to get her and us out of this mess?" he chuckled as he forced Finn to chug the drink. "If we get there and it's worse off than we thought, then we adjust and bring his body back and save the High Coven a Trial."

Finn pushed the empty cup away, and let out a hiccup and a squeak that Remi took to be a laugh. Then the sky flashed a blinding white and it sounded like all of the sound had been sucked from the room in an instant.

The two of them, along with everyone else that was currently in the Infirmary, stared out the window just as a silvery-white curtain began to fall from the sky, as if being drawn straight from the clouds themselves. Remi knew this to be the High Coven's doing and watched in quiet wonder as the barrier was cast, descending and trapping the town of Oxford under a shimmering dome of what they thought would be protection.

He could feel his stomach knotting itself together as the curtain cascaded down, knowing that this would only serve to set the stage for a final battle with Alexander.

Remi grabbed the empty cup from Finn's hand and waved to get one of the Healers' attention.

"Barkeep!" he shouted, feeling suddenly very dizzy with anticipation. "Another round!"

The dungeons of the Oxford Coven House were a stark contrast to the rest of the structure. Whereas, the entrance hall below them was lighted by a large chandelier that hung from the center of the ceiling, these chambers were so poorly illuminated that Remi could barely see his hand outstretched in front of his face. Most of the other floors even had some form of the same dark-stained wood panelling throughout to give a semblance of uniformity.

It was plain stone here, and even though it was on the tenth floor of the house, it had the appearance of being underground. There was next to no natural light apart from the few grates that revealed the sun shining onto the dusty floor. There were a handful of magelight torches that hung in sconces along the walls. Other than that scarce amount of illumination, the cells were dank and humid from the rainwater that often flooded the bricked corridors. Remi felt himself sweating, despite the stagnant breeze that seemed to be flowing steadily throughout the halls from the grates carved into the wall.

It was well above and the ground floor of the house and was where rogues were held to await their Trials after they had been brought in for whatever charges they might be facing. It was also where people served their sentences, although there had not been the need for this in recent years, as the previous few Arbiters had been very harsh in their punishments. The entire floor had been Glamoured so that no sound would escape once the door had been sealed. On the off chance that a rogue did manage to escape, there was a jinx in place that would cause them to want to run up the staircase instead of down, where they would leap from the highest floor they could reach.

Remi made a conscious decision to breathe through his mouth while he was here, as the smell was almost too foul for him to stand when he inhaled through his nostrils. There were at least twenty cells on the floor, but there was only one being occupied at the moment. The Healer looked up from the floor when he heard Remi's boots falling on the stones.

"You may leave us," Remi told the Witch's Guard who had been stationed to the cell as he came into the light. The man gave him a suspicious look, to which Remi assured him, "I need to speak to the prisoner alone."

The man glanced at the Healer in the dark cell behind him a second time, before giving a slight nod to Remi and walking past him toward the staircase that would take him into the main part of the House.

"What do you want, Caswell?" the Healer asked after a moment of silence passed between them.

"Do you remember what it was like being under his control?" Remi asked when he was sure that the other Warlock had made it out of earshot.

"Vaguely," the Healer watched him curiously now. "Why? What's it to you?"

"I need you to tell me everything you can remember," Remi answered, still keeping his voice low on the off chance that the other had returned. "The Arbiter might be in danger and I need to know everything you can tell me about that Dark Warlock. What can you remember?"

"Honestly," the man began, "not very much. It's all kind of a blur until the Infirmary incident. Sorry about that, by the way."

Remi gave a slight nod of acknowledgment and the other went on, "I remember going home the night they brought the Magister's son in. I can remember getting to my house and going to sleep. Then, the next thing I know, I'm being pinned on a bed and thrown in this cell."

"So you can't remember anything between those two times?" Remi asked. "Nothing at all that might be relevant to this case and finding the Arbiter?"

"Well," the man said hesitantly. "That's the thing. I can remember some things, but it all feels like a dream. Like I don't know what's real and what was been put there."

"Put there?" Remi repeated, furrowing his brow in confusion.

"It feels like someone went into my head and messed around with my memories," the Healer explained. "I mean, I can tell you everything I remember, but I can't be sure what's really me and what that Dark Warlock added to it."

"Okay," Remi nodded, understanding somewhat. He pulled a chair from beside the cell bars and took a seat in front of the Healer. "Start from the top," he said. "Tell me everything you can think of and we'll both try to sort through them to figure out which ones are your true memories and which ones aren't. Does that sound reasonable?"

"Will it get me out of here?" the Healer asked, slumping back against the wall of the cell.

"I make no guarantees on that," Remi answered honestly. "But I can tell you that if you choose to withhold information from the Coven, you could stay here until we forget about you. It's completely up to you which route we go down today."

He pulled out a cigarette and offered one to the Healer, which the man took. Remi snapped his fingers to light them both and took out a pen and pad.

"Start from the beginning," Remi said. He crossed his legs so he could have a makeshift rest for the pad as he wrote. "First off, what's your name?"

"Seriously, Caswell?" the Healer choked and Remi wondered if this was due to too much smoke on his last inhalation or simply out of his own disbelief. "You know my name!"

"No," Remi replied with a stony expression. "I really don't. Just because you've treated my wounds before does not mean we're automatically buddies. Now, name?"

The man seemed hurt by the comment but informed Remi that his name was Daniel.

"Okay, Daniel," Remi said, scribbling the name down on the top line of the page. "You said that you remember getting home the night before the incident. Did you do anything out of the ordinary that night?"

"Not really," Daniel replied, trying to think back. "I left here after the graveyard crew showed up. Then I went to go get some groceries to take home. And something to eat, because I wasn't feeling up for cooking once I made it to my house."

"Was there anything out of the ordinary once you actually did make it home?" Remi asked, writing as they conversed. "Had the door been left unlocked or anything of that nature?"

"No," Daniel shook his head, before adding, "There was a note about inspections at the end of the month, but other than that, nothing different than usual."

"Inspections?" Remi repeated, to which the Healer nodded. "Do you rent your home?"

"Well, yeah," the man answered. "I live over at Taylor Bend."

"So you live in an apartment, then?" Remi scratched over the word 'house' and replaced it in his notes.

"Yeah?" Daniel seemed confused. "Is that important?"

"Maybe not," Remi admitted. "But the more accurate we are on your details, the more likely it is that we'll find something."

"Right," Daniel agreed, flicking his ash on the floor of the cell. "Well, what else would you like to know?"

"I'm assuming that living in a complex, you must have neighbors. Correct?" Remi asked, to which the Healer nodded. "Are most of them Mortal?" Another nod of confirmation. "So you don't think any of them could have done this?"

"I mean," Daniel replied, seemingly imagining the other tenants in his building. "I've met everyone around my apartment. It's possible that there are other non-Mortals in some of the other buildings, but I haven't seen anyone that would jump out at me as someone who might attack me, no."

Remi jotted down the words 'maybe a neighbor' and clicked his pen a few times while he tried to think of another question. "Do you think someone jinxed you while you were out? Maybe without you realizing it?"

"I can't really say, if I didn't realize it," Daniel shrugged. "I guess it's always a possibility. I just think it's highly unlikely, given that I remember going to sleep."

"Okay," Remi nodded slowly. He took a few silent puffs of his cigarette before going on, "So you distinctly remember crawling into bed and falling asleep?"

"Yeah, Caswell," Daniel seemed to be getting annoyed with the repetition of the questions. "I went to sleep."

He paused then and focused intently on the opposite wall of the cell. Remi watched him curiously for a few seconds before asking, "What is it?"

"I keep getting flashes of a weird dream, but I don't know what it means," Daniel said.

"Are you sure it was a dream?" Remi asked, suddenly very interested in what type of images were flashing in the other's mind.

"Not really," Daniel admitted, shaking his head slightly. "It's like I went to sleep and then I was suddenly looking through someone else's eyes. And they were looking at my apartment from the outside."

"Are you sure it was your apartment?" Remi asked, taking notes as the Healer went along.

"I've been there long enough to know what the outside of my apartment looks like, Caswell," Daniel said. "I'm sure it was mine."

"What else happened in the dream?" Remi asked, lighting a second cigarette before letting the first drop to the floor. "Did you just stand outside?"

"It wasn't me," Daniel replied. "I'm not sure who it was, or even how I know it wasn't me, but I just do. And no, they got into my apartment and the next thing I know, they're standing over me and watching me sleep."

"What happened once they were standing over your bed?" Remi asked, getting a sinking feeling in the pit of his stomach. It felt almost like he was reliving the other night at his own house.

"That's when everything starts getting fuzzy for me," Daniel answered. "I remember a large house in the middle of the woods. I remember being given something to bring to the Coven House. I remember doing everything of a volition that was not my own, almost like I was being puppeted by someone. Then, there was a flash of gold and I was down here."

Remi said nothing for a moment, jotting down notes as he went over the details in his own mind and tried to link them up with the case he was working on. Finally, he asked, "Can you describe the house? The one from the dream?"

"Yeah," Daniel said, trying to remember. "It was somewhere in the middle of the woods. And it was this big, black manor. It wasn't even really a house. It was more like a mansion."

Remi suddenly felt a cold chill run down his spine and knew it had nothing to do with the air that was coming in through the grate just above them. He tucked the pad and pen into his chest pocket and stood from his chair.

"What is it, Caswell?" Daniel asked. "What's wrong with you?"

"I have to leave now," Remi explained. "I'll send someone down here to make sure to let you out when this is all over."

"What do you mean 'when this is over?'" Daniel looked at him, clearly confused by his words. "What are you talking about, Caswell?"

"I've got to go," Remi said, turning on his heel and breaking into a jog. "I can't explain!" he called back over his shoulder.

Remi did not know where he was going exactly, but he had a feeling his feet would lead him to wherever it was that he needed to be.

Alexander Morrigan watched as the Oxford Coven's Arbiter gradually came to. He had given her a sleeping draught after taking her from the House, to stop her from squirming and potentially escaping as he brought her to his lair.

"I trust you slept well, Madame Arbiter?" he asked as her head lolled about in a groggy haze.

Sylvia opened her eyes to see, with a start, that she had been strapped to a plush chair atop a circular stone pedestal. Her hands had been left to rest in her lap and as she struggled to remove the rope around her wrists, she discovered that a mark had been carved into her skin on her forearm. She knew it to be a Glyph that bound a Warlock from casting until it either healed or was removed, though she had never seen one that had been cut so deep into someone's skin.

"What is it you expect to accomplish from this?" Sylvia asked, craning her neck to get a good look at the Dark Warlock that had been causing so much havoc for her and her Coven over the past few days.

He had hair the shade of open flames and pale skin. Sylvia got the impression that he had not been above ground in many years, but there was still something almost regal about it.

It was almost as if she were staring directly into the face of the moon just as it caught fire, where there was not an absence of sunlight but, rather, a reflection of it.

He wore robes the color of obsidian, with silver embroidery on the breast and trim of a deep purple hue. This gave her the impression that he might be some sort of royalty among Warlocks.

His jaw and face were chiseled like the man had been made from marble and Sylvia could tell, even beneath his robes, that he was physically powerful even without his magic.

Above all, the most notable thing about the Dark Warlock, however, were his glowing, amber eyes; where there should have been white, there was only black. This made them even more striking and although they seemed to be warm and welcoming now, Sylvia had already seen what this man was capable of and could almost feel them bore into her very soul as his gaze rested upon her.

"What do you seek to gain from this senseless killing of so many?" she asked again, pulling herself out of her assessment of the man.

"So many?" Alexander stared blankly at the Arbiter. "I am only taking that which I need; nothing more, nothing less. And as for 'senseless', I've seen many before me strike down entire nations on a whim and difference of opinion, Madame Arbiter. So who is to truly say that which I do is any more wrong than the Mortals you seem so intent on defending?"

Sylvia remembered the books that Remi had shown her from the archive and had an idea. "We both know that it won't work," she bluffed as if she knew what his plan was already.

To her surprise, Alexander laughed heartily at this accusation as if it were the funniest joke he had ever heard before.

"You don't even know what you speak of, dear!" he trailed off and began clapping mockingly. "I must applaud both you and your Coven, my dear Arbiter. You were all so close to finding the answer. But no cigar, I'm afraid."

He began walking around the cavernous room they were in as he spoke. Sylvia watched silently as he moved to other platforms, much like the one she was on.

"I do hope you don't mind the little affliction my dagger left on your arm," he indicated the Glyph that had been carved into her. "I had to ensure that you would not try to escape during your visit."

Sylvia looked down at her arm and wondered if it would ever heal once she had been rescued from her confinement.

"I suppose I should explain a bit about what it is that I seek here," Alexander went on casually, as if discussing the weather. "Before I begin, are you comfortable, Arbiter? Would you like some tea? I know how long-winded I tend to be, but I'm nothing if not a gracious host."

The Dark Warlock snapped his fingers and to Sylvia's surprise, a table appeared just before her, complete with tea and crackers along with an assortment of other foods and jams.

"Now let's see," he went on. "Where to begin? I suppose I should tell you why I am doing what I am doing. It's because of the affliction we Warlocks were cursed with at birth, you see."

"Affliction?" Sylvia repeated, not sure if she had heard him correctly. "What do you mean?"

Yes, affliction," Alexander confirmed. "You see, we need only look at the Fae to see how mirrored our own society is to theirs. They have Courts and High Courts, we have Covens and a High Coven. They can control the very fabric of nature, so can we. Do you know the one thing they possess that we do not, Lady Arbiter?"

"I'm not sure I do," Sylvia answered honestly, not sure where he was going with this.

"Immortality!" Alexander answered and his eyes flashed with the words, sending a strange feeling through Sylvia. "Surely you must have known that by now?"

"Yes," she replied. "But what does that have to do with what you're doing here?"

"I seek to bring that blessing unto us, Lady Arbiter!" the Dark Warlock explained. "To bring us to a level that is equal to the Fae that are so like us. Perhaps even more than that, depending on how the spell works."

"Why kill so many if you're after immortality?" Sylvia asked, pointing out what she thought was the flaw in the logic.

"I do not look at it as killing," Alexander explained. "I simply look at it as payment for something that will make our people greater than they already are. The magic I work with requires payment equivalent to that which must be done. Rest assured, for the crimes I have committed, I will be judged eventually. But if that means making my people greater than they were before I left them, then I am willing to make that sacrifice, Lady Arbiter."

Sylvia stared at the man before and something in her almost felt sorry for him. He seemed to know that he was in the wrong for what he had done, but he also seemed genuine in his wish to bring about change that would make the Warlocks better as a whole.

"Surely, if you seek to make us greater as a whole," she suggested, "then there must be a way to do so that does not require the payment of another's life?"

"There is," Alexander admitted. "But even that comes with its own problems. Surely you must know the stories of the Lycans and the Vampires, do you not?"

"I'm not sure I do," Sylvia said. "At least not in the sense that you are suggesting."

"There was one before me who sought to do the same," Alexander explained and his voice seemed almost sorrowful as he did so. "That someone did not want to make the payment required that would have assured his success. So as she finished the ritual, her own magic became volatile and forced the payment from her body. She became tainted and cursed from that day forth. Sure, she had acquired the boon of immortality, but it had transformed into a curse. One that she would pass on to anyone who came into contact with her. Do you know who that individual was, Lady Arbiter?"

"I do not recall the name," Sylvia admitted a bit shamefully. "But I believe that you are referring to the first known Vampire?"

"Correct," Alexander smiled at this as he continued. "From that individual, we can also blame the affliction of the Lycans."

"They created the Lycans as well?" Sylvia asked confusedly. She definitely did not remember this from her history lessons at the Academy. "Surely you don't mean to imply that on top of the other?"

"Not quite," Alexander laughed slightly at this, as if it was one of the more ridiculous things he had heard. "But they were the cause for it. I'm sure you've heard tales of the Fae changing Mortals into animals throughout the years?"

"Vaguely," Sylvia agreed. "It was so rampant in the days before the Covenants were drawn up that there are several bylaws forbidding such a thing from taking place."

"Correct," Alexander seemed pleased by her partial knowledge on the subjects he had been speaking on thus far. "Before the Covenants were put in place, however, it happened many times. One such time was a Mortal in search of a way to defend his family against the Vampires that had ravaged the land. I believe it was somewhere in Scotland, if I'm not mistaken."

"So you mean to tell me," Sylvia spoke slowly as she tried to piece together what the Dark Warlock was telling her, "that *we* are responsible for Vampires and that the Fae created the Lycans?"

"Precisely!" the man exclaimed and there was another golden flash of passion in his eyes as he spoke. "I'm sure it must seem far-fetched, but it makes perfect sense when you really think about it. Those two have a blood feud of their own, much like the one between our people and the Fae."

"We don't have a blood feud," Sylvia said. "I think you must be mistaken."

"It isn't quite as outright as that between the Vampires and the Lycans," Alexander agreed partially. "But the Fae have always been slightly better than the Warlocks. And there have been several of us over the centuries that have coveted that one thing they have that we could never attain. But you see, Lady Arbiter, I have found a way for us to achieve that which could not be done before. Even if it means giving myself up to make it so."

"You truly are mad," Sylvia said before she could catch herself. Luckily, it did not seem to phase the Dark Warlock as he continued with his explanations.

"Perhaps," he seemed to agree with her on the state of his own mentality. "Although I must also inform you, that had I not been thwarted before, your Witch's Guard might have saved you from the fate I must deliver upon you."

Sylvia felt her heart seize in her chest but remained attentive so as not to alarm the Dark Warlock.

"As you must be well aware by now," he went on, "the ritual that I am attempting to perform has been in the works for many years."

"Yes," the Arbiter replied, maintaining a steady voice with ease as she had for so many years dealing with Mortal officials. "I am somewhat aware of this."

As Alexander began pacing back and forth and stopped paying attention to her, Sylvia began looking at the table that had been set before her. She located a sharp knife that she was sure must have been intended for slicing open the bagels. While the Dark Warlock was still otherwise occupied, Sylvia took the knife and tucked her hands under the table and out of view.

"Had I not been thwarted so many years ago," Alexander went on, moving toward a small dais much like the one she had been seated on. "I might have finished my work long before you had to become involved in such a way."

"What do you mean by that?" Sylvia asked, using the knife to saw against the thick ropes that bound her hands under the table as she spoke.

"It had almost been completed before the Caswell woman interjected herself," Alexander replied, pulling a small phial of red liquid from somewhere inside his robes as he spoke. "I suppose it would be fitting that one of her spawn should take up the mantle where she could not finish the job herself."

Sylvia knew that the Dark Warlock must be referring to Remi and Nona, but she was not sure she had the full story just yet. She decided that it would serve her best to keep him talking until she had freed herself from her bindings.

"What is it you mean by 'thwarted'?" she asked. "You told me your end goal, but you never truly explained what the killings had to do with accomplishing that."

"Ah, yes!" Alexander exclaimed, as if he had simply gone off-topic during his explanation before. "The ritual I must perform to achieve that which I wish is a rather extensive one. It seeks to change the very fabric of being for an entire people. As such, it requires quite a bit of sacrifice from all different walks of life."

He uncorked the phial he had retrieved and held it high above the dais, emptying the contents of it into a stone basin below. Sylvia realized, with a lurch of her stomach, that the scarlet liquid was blood.

"How large of a sacrifice are you talking about?" she asked, trying to take her mind off what would soon be in all of the basins.

"There must be four from each of the races," Alexander explained. "It starts with a single Fae from each of the Courts. Then that is matched by each of the other races."

"So you've killed sixteen people?" Sylvia asked. "Why have we only heard about three of them? And why was one of those a Mortal?"

"I assume that you mean the boy at the lake?" Alexander asked, to which the Arbiter confirmed. He then went on to explain, "I, too, was under the impression that he was nothing more than one of the plague children you refer to as Mortals. Upon further review, he had been newly Turned. So he fit in perfectly with my plan."

Sylvia said nothing as he went on, though the news of the boy having been made into a Vampire Fledgling was noteworthy to her.

"You see," the Dark Warlock went on, "I already had all of the blood I required from the Lycans from the last time I attempted this before I was sealed away. I didn't even have to get my hands dirty for that, as they fight amongst themselves so much that I only had to wait and collect."

There was something callous about the way he used the term 'collect', but Sylvia remained silent as the Dark Warlock continued.

"I only had half of the toll required from the Vampires," he said, pausing briefly to laugh. "They thrive on the stuff so much themselves, it is actually quite ironic that it has to be taken by them so forcefully. One would imagine them to be more understanding. The Fae and our own people were slightly harder to select, as I had to be sure of the power that was given when I took my payment for the ritual. That being so, I only managed to take three of each before I was halted in my efforts."

"So that explains the two Vampires," Sylvia seemed to be following along thus far, given the new information she had received about the boy at the lake. "And the naiad. But what of the final Warlock? Where are they?"

The Dark Warlock's eyes flashed a deeper golden then than they ever had before and Sylvia instantly regretted asking such a foolish question in her current situation.

"That, my dear," Alexander said, "is where you come in. I shall use you as bait to lure in the final piece of my puzzle before I take his life as well."

While he had been talking, Sylvia had been too preoccupied with freeing herself from the ropes around her wrists that she had not noticed him walking around the room to a second basin and emptying the contents of another glass phial into it.

"Just how do you intend to do that?" Sylvia asked, not liking the sound of what the Dark Warlock was telling her.

"Ah, yes," he seemed to catch himself. "I suppose there is no harm in telling you, as you will soon become a catalyst."

The Arbiter swallowed hard against the rope that was binding her.

"You see, my dear Sylvia," he spoke in a voice like silk. "I am a visionary man. I see us as the divine beings that we truly are." He threw up his arms in a gesture of grandeur to match his own delusions.

"I see us as equivalent to the Fae that, by happenstance, created us all. We have the power to create and destroy at will, just as they. But there is one glaring imperfection that sets us apart from them. And by design, this makes us somewhat lesser than those beautiful creatures. Since we are both Fae and Mortal, we have all of these godlike power, but the same lifespan as those whom we should be ruling over. As a man who searches for equality in all things, I, Alexander Morrigan, seek to remedy our kind of this affliction that has plagued us from the very beginning!"

"That doesn't answer my question" Sylvia pointed out, effectively ignoring his rantings.

"Yes!" Alexander shouted and his face became contorted into a grimace of both excitement and madness as his voice bounced off the walls of the cave.

"You see, Lady Arbiter," he went on, quickly regaining his composure, "I know that the Witch's Guard along with the descendant of the Caswell woman will soon come to the conclusion that it is I who have taken you. When that time comes, I am certain that he and whatever makeshift army the boy can muster will come right to me in an attempt to reclaim you. And when *that* time comes, they will have you, but I will take the final payment from the boy!"

Sylvia was now not only fearful for her own life, but that of Remi's as well. As she sat there, searching for an answer, that fear quickly became mixed and eventually replaced with fury at the thought of it all. How had she let herself be caught by this supposedly visionary Dark Warlock in broad daylight, surrounded by a Grove full of witnesses?

Alexander was suddenly right beside her as if he had teleported across the entire length of the cave without her noticing. She had to quickly tuck her hands further under the table so as not to be found out just yet.

"It will all be over in due time, Lady Arbiter," he said, stroking her face and sending shivers down her spine. "Just remember, do not look at this as me simply 'killing' the boy. Look at it as a welcome, albeit unknowing, sacrifice on his part in the name of something greater which he simply does not understand."

His eyes seemed to have been filled now with a blazing passion that waited just beneath the surface to lash out and consume anything the man touched. Slyvia was suddenly more terrified than she had ever felt before in her life. "And you, my dear Arbiter," he whispered against her ear, "get to be a tool in that sacrifice."

"It is done!" a voice from the shadows echoed around the cavern. "They will come."

"Are you certain?" Alexander turned in the direction of the voice, suddenly very interested in what its owner had to say.

"Am I ever anything else?" the voice was a soft warning, like venom-laced satin.

The woman stepped out from the shadows and smirked up at Alexander as if he had just insulted her by asking such a benign question. Her skin could have been made of ivory and her blood-red locks cascaded around her shoulders and down her back like sanguine rivers.

She wore robes the color of the night sky just after sunset with a corset over them to reveal her ample bust. All of this paired with her angular features in the dim lighting of the cave made the woman appear as some dark and sinister variant of an angel.

The heels of her stilettos clacked across the stone floor of the room as she moved closer to them and as she stared at this new addition to the conversation, Sylvia was horrified to see the same glimmering amber irises of Alexander in the woman.

When the woman smiled, the Arbiter imagined that she had seen fangs but could not be entirely sure about this.

"Of course not, my darling girl!" Alexander beamed down at the other from the dais on which he hovered over Sylvia. "How very careless of me to ask, my dear, sweet Venus! Do forgive me?"

"As you wish," the woman sighed, unamused by his pleading. "Now, if you are quite done revealing the bulk of your plan to such a common hedgewitch," she spat the insult at Sylvia, "I thought you might like to be informed that everything is now in place with the Oxford Coven."

"Oh, but Venus!" Alexander laughed at the insulant girl. "This is no mere hedgewitch! This is the Arbiter of the Oxford Coven; one of the originals and the crux on which the rest of my plan now rests!"

"Her blood and title mean nothing unless she can grant us the power we seek," Venus gave him only a callous, monotonous cackle. "She did, after all, manage to let herself be captured by you. And you haven't been all that well-thought-out in your plans, thus far."

"You will see, my dear," Alexander protested. "Soon, they will all see."

"They have already brought down their barrier," Venus said, and Sylvia felt her heart leap in her chest with anticipation. "We have a limited time to work now, due to your carelessness. Do not disappoint me, old man."

"Then let them come!" Alexander lost his composure for an instant and Sylvia's fear resurged. She looked from the Dark Warlock to his blood-tinged accomplice and realized, with a grim start, that the woman was holding a phone.

Sylvia knew instantly that the device was her own and was forced to swallow against the bile that had crept into the back of her throat with this realization. She sent up a silent prayer to the universe that the Warlocks of her Coven would not come.

But she had known them all long enough to realize just how stubborn they all were and knew better than to even hope that they would ignore her and save themselves.

She felt herself drifting, once more, out of consciousness to the sound of the two Dark Warlocks' paired, maniacal laughter.

XIX

"What did you want to talk to me about in Sylvia's office?" Remi asked, not bothering to turn around to face her. He had semi-drunkenly stumbled his way out to the stone garden behind the Coven House, leaving Finn alone upstairs to gather his thoughts in the Infirmary.

He had found his way through the surrounding maze of hedges and flowering trees, knowing that no one would bother to search for him out here. So many of the other Warlocks in the House often found themselves lost and desperately avoided venturing into the center, so they generally avoided it altogether. But Remi had learned to always stick to one side or another throughout the trek and would always eventually find himself in the center of it until he was ready to face whoever he was hiding from at the time.

It had always been one of the more beautiful parts of the grounds, in his opinion.

The area was dotted with several knock-off versions of famously sculpted works of art, and covered with greyish gravel. There were no flowers of any kind toward the center, save for the few small bushes that marked different options to leave the maze. The place where Remi had come was primarily grey, framed by green. However, it was this absence of what one might expect to find in a garden that gave the place its unique charm.

"How did you know it was me?" Nona Caswell said from somewhere behind him.

"I knew we didn't have any lavender bushels out here," Remi replied, referencing her perfume that had been taken up by the breeze.

"What makes you think I wanted to deal with them any more than you?" she asked, sounding tired already.

Just as Remi had predicted, the High Coven's barrier had sent the Mortals up-in-arms. Their authorities had deemed the act of placing an entire city on lockdown without prior knowledge and agreement on their part was unconstitutional. To which, the Magisters had collectively laughed, explaining that magical law trumped the Mortals' feebly-made constitution. There was really nothing the Mortals could do to combat the Covenant, as it governed all magical creatures and this was definitely a situation that specifically involved Warlocks.

The whole thing had put most of the townsfolk at a loss, as many of them had no clue of their own rights as citizens and this had never happened before.

Now, the entire sky around the city of Oxford had become illuminated by the shimmering, silvery curtain of protective magic, and there were no signs of it coming down anytime soon. It was a state of chaos that Remi was not currently prepared to deal with.

The rocks crunched under Nona's shoes as she came to sit down on a bench just across from where Remi stood. She patted the spot beside her for him to join, which he declined.

"I guess it was just too much to wish for that I get five minutes to myself?" he joked.

"If I don't, why should you?" Nona countered. Then, "How is he?"

"Getting there," Remi replied, knowing she was referring to Finn upstairs. "So, we're alone now. What is it you needed to discuss?"

Nona hesitated, as if trying to think of a polite way to put whatever she was about to say into words.

"You remember," she said finally, "how we were talking about that last case that I was working on last night just before bed?"

Remi nodded and she went on, "And you remember how I used the term 'guarding' when I was talking about Alexander?" He nodded again. "Well, that wasn't entirely accurate."

"So you ran off to Cancun for the majority of my life?" Remi jested to keep himself from being furious.

"Not funny," Nona's tone was flat. "I had been searching for the person behind your parents' murder. And your grandfather's. And when I found him, I let myself become careless." Remi said nothing and could not bring himself to look over at his grandmother just yet.

"I knew it couldn't have been just any typical rogue Warlock, because your parents and grandfather weren't any typical members of the Witch's Guard. I knew there had to be more than what the Coven was willing to explore," she explained. "Even after I took on the case, I never expected to find everything that I did. It took about five years of my own research, paired with what I already had available within the file itself to find out who was behind it all."

"Morrigan," Remi answered the name he already knew and felt her nod beside him.

"Yes," Nona agreed. "And while I was searching for him, I managed to find all of his victims and tie them together. I was so proud when I finally did that and found his hideout, I went in blindly, knowing that after all that time that I was going to finally be the one to bring him to Trial in front of the Arbiter."

"So, what happened?" Remi was very curious now, although he still could not make himself look over at her.

Nona explained, "When I found him, I confronted him. It was foolish to go on my own, but I was so overcome with rage by that point that I wasn't thinking clearly. There was a long and drawn-out battle between the two of us." She paused then as if she were reliving the event with her retelling.

"I didn't realize what I had gotten myself into until it was too late," she went on. "He was surely going to kill me if I didn't kill him first. But I couldn't do that. Not after everything he had done to so many of our people. So I did the only thing I could think to do at the time; putting us both in permanent stasis."

"So you sacrificed yourself as well," Remi realized with a sudden feeling of admiration. "You sacrificed yourself so that he wouldn't escape.

But if that's true, then why have both of you returned? Putting someone into a state of permanent stasis like you're saying takes a lot of energy. Doing it to yourself and another person, there should be no way for either of you to escape. Something went wrong."

"Something did," Nona replied, admitting an unforeseen error in her plan. "There was someone that found us and let him out. I don't know who or what, but I know that they were there for him. The fact that I escaped was nothing more than a miscalculation on their part. I stayed there for days while he escaped and whatever spell they used slowly melted my own away until I could cast myself out of it. Even then, I couldn't risk him seeing me leave. So I waited still, until I was alone. And I came into this world and saw the news about the press conference. And I knew that would be where he would strike."

"So that's why you were there," Remi surmounted, to which Nona laughed. Then a thought occurred to him and he couldn't resist asking, "But you said that you had been sending me signals over the years… What about that?"

"Both times that I mentioned were while I was still trapped, but enough that I could conjure a Familiar to send to you," Nona explained, causing Remi to furrow his brow in confusion as she spoke.

"So your Familiar can take on the shape of you?" he asked. "I thought they always took on the form of an animal."

"They can take on whatever form they need to, depending on the Warlock that conjures them," Nona explained. "I had only ever used one to send messages to others within the Coven before. I'm not sure what might have caused it to take that form in the archives, unless it was somehow responding to your own thoughts."

"It was in my dream, as well," Remi pointed out. "After I got thrown back into the chasm. It kind of helped me go through a second Proving and guided me back into my body."

"That doesn't sound all that uncommon," Nona mused. "When conjured in dreams, Familiars tend to do whatever it takes to protect a Warlock while in such a vulnerable state. Maybe mine followed you into your dreams and knew that I could not protect you there."

"Well," Remi sighed. "I haven't seen it since I woke up in the Infirmary. So let's hope that's all it was. I think we've got enough problems to deal with, without having to worry about some sort of celestial being that we know nothing about."

"Another thing," Nona said then, causing Remi to finally turn to look at her, letting out a somewhat exasperated sigh. "The house we were working on with the barriers last night. I know for a fact that it's his house, RJ. I just couldn't bring myself to say anything last night, especially not in front of Finn. Not until I had talked to you first, at least."

"How many secrets are you keeping from me, woman?" Remi rubbed his hands hard against his face as if he were trying to rub it right off. "Because now would be the time to let it all out, while there are no witnesses around to hear your confessions."

"It's my fault that he's out, RJ," she said, suddenly and regretfully. "I should have destroyed him when I had the chance."

"I don't think that," Remi sighed once more. "But at the same time, we can't let Finn find out that you're connected to this in any way. We need him to trust both of us if we're going to get Sylvia out of there."

"You really think he won't figure it out on his own?" Nona sounded skeptical of what Remi was suggesting.

"I think we've got bigger things to worry about than who's to blame for all of this, right now," Remi replied, sounding suddenly callous.

"You're right," Nona agreed. "I just had to tell someone, because it was killing me being the only one that knew."

"I talked to Daniel," Remi said. Then, to Nona's confused expression, added, "The Healer that was upstairs in the holding cells."

The woman nodded and he went on, "He told me everything he remembered from the night before he tried to attack Finn."

"And? What did you gather from that?" Nona asked, seemingly fully concerned with what he had to say now.

"Well, his description of the dream that led to his temporary possession matched up with what happened to me. And his description of the house in the woods matches up with the one that the Vampire Lord informed us about. The one that you're telling me, now, is Alexander's."

"So you think that's definitely where he took her?" Nona asked, going along with his explanation.

"I can't be sure if that's where Sylvia is," Remi admitted. "But I think finding out what *is* in that house is our best bet at finding her and bringing her back."

"Right," Nona nodded her agreement. "I'll get to work on assembling a team."

"You realize they're going to hate us even more than they already do after this," Remi changed the subject, pulling out a cigarette and sparking a flame with his fingers. "You do know that, right?"

"Fear is often mistaken for hate," Nona said, serenely.

"Maybe," Remi shrugged, feeling almost contemplative. "But unbridled fear partnered with ignorance of an entire people is what breeds hate. And Mortals often fear that which they do not understand."

"Because fear is easier than questioning and understanding," Nona chuckled to herself. "You've gotten a bit wiser since I've been away."

"Fifteen years alone tends to do that to a guy," Remi laughed in a hollow tone, exhaling a thick cloud of smoke. "Would you say it's wiser or just that I'm more cynical than you left me?"

"You know you're not supposed to smoke out here," Nona lightly scolded.

"Who's going to stop me?" Remi laughed, genuinely this time. He jerked his chin toward the Coven House. "They've got bigger fish to fry up there right now than my vices."

Nona smiled at the small act of rebellion.

"Come on," she said. "I need someone with a strategic mind."

"And?" Remi inhaled deeply. "Why are you talking to me about it?"

"I've had time to read a few of your files," she smiled knowingly. "Enough to know that you can help me. Also, enough to know that your handwriting is worse than chicken scratch if the chicken were drunk, blind, and had a club foot."

"It gets the job done," Remi laughed at the colorful description, taking another drag.

"Come," Nona stood, smoothing down the seat of her pants. "I need someone to walk me out of this place."

"Just stick to the left," Remi took the final drag and stood as well, letting the butt fall to the gravel.

"And here I was, going to the right," Nona grinned back. "Shall we be off, then?"

"First," Remi said when they had made it back to the Arbiter's office, "we need to contact Vesna. See if she'll give us access to her portals. Maybe even a few sentry scouts, if she can spare anyone from the Woodland Court."

"Sounds reasonable enough," Nona agreed. "I don't see why she wouldn't."

"Then, we need Sebastian," Remi said, then corrected, "Lord Kaine, to have a few of his Brood members overhead. They found the manor to begin with, so they're our best bet to keep the area under surveillance. Then the Alphas," Remi thought aloud, pausing to figure out how to best handle the Lycans.

"We can't let them know that we're working with the Vampires," he concluded. "Otherwise, they'll drop out before we've even begun. But they're the best option as far as who to use for land units. I'll call Davis and have him talk to Kit. That's at least one of the Packs that'll help us."

"What about Warlocks?" Nona asked, clearly liking his plan so far. "You'll need someone to break through all of those defenses that are on the actual house."

Remi paused and pondered this detail, having not considered it before she had brought it up.

"Finn and I, for sure," he answered slowly, reasoning gradually with himself as he went along. "This guy obviously wants *us* there. Other than that," he shrugged in response. "I've got no clue about who to take."

"Surely, you must know at least one other Warlock who could accompany you on this mission?" Nona's blue moonstone eyes watched him curiously.

"You?" Remi guessed, to which the woman shrugged her head. "I'm a lone wolf kind of Warlock," he explained. "I don't know anyone else well enough to work with them, and I like it that way."

"Your grandfather was the same way," Nona laughed, understanding Remi's point. "Which is why I've already decided who will be accompanying you on this mission."

She glanced past him to the door of the office and he turned, just as it opened to reveal ten other Warlocks standing in the threshold.

The most striking of them was a brawny man with greying hair and orange skin. His right eye was a clear blue, like a diamond, and he wore a patch over the left. He was wearing a tweed jacket and jeans, which reminded Remi of Mayor Kensington, but somehow looked right on this man.

"Let's get down to business, Caswell," he spoke around a cigar. Remi was unsure if the man was addressing him or Nona.

"Robert!" Nona's eyes instantly brightened at the sight of this new Warlock. "How good to see you!"

She came around the desk and went to embrace the man in a long hug. He looked down at her and gave a curious smirk.

"I know I've only got one eye left," he laughed, pointing at the patch, "but you look purdy damn good for a corpse, Nona Caswell! This him?" The man glanced to Remi briefly, then back to Nona.

"It is," she said, letting go. The man extended his hand, which Remi shook, and laughed.

"If you're anything like your folks, we'll get along just fine!" Robert exclaimed, jerking Remi's arm around so violently, he was almost certain it would be popped out of its socket.

"Do you always work with so many people?" Remi asked, taking in the rest of the seemingly ordinary crew.

"Only when the need calls for it," Robert explained. "You can never befriend too many combat Healers in your life."

"Fair point," Remi agreed. "So if they're all combat Healers and I'm assuming former members of the Witch's Guard?" he peered over the ensemble, taking them all in and finally bringing his gaze back to rest on Robert. "What's your specialty?"

"Demolition," the man grinned in response. "I make things go boom!" He yelled the last word and laughed as everyone jumped.

"Is that how you lost the other eye?" Remi found himself asking before he could stop himself.

"Well, whaddya think?" Robert guffawed like it was obvious.

"Good," Remi regained himself, rubbing his hands together slowly as he formed a plan. "That means you can go first."

He turned to his grandmother with a sly grin, seeing now why she had chosen this particular group of Warlocks to accompany him.

"Great!" Remi was saying on the phone. "As long as we have one of the Packs there, that should be able to cover more ground than we could by ourselves."

He hung up with Davis, knowing that the Lycan would talk to his Alpha, who would hopefully talk to the others.

"Are you almost ready?" he called up the stairs.

"Yeah!" Finn called back down, descending soon after, donned in his full gear.

Standard field gear for the Witch's Guard was usually just a breastplate and bracers made from leather. This gear was more elaborate and functional for defensive purposes.

There were the pants that had been padded, much like those used in certain Mortal sporting events. Then, they wore steel-toed boots to protect the wearer's feet.

For the top, it was a chainmail shirt worn under a dragonskin breastplate that was meant to block both physical and magical assault aimed at the torso. There were arm and leg bracers, made from the same dragonskin as the breastplate, worn over the rest of the gear to add an extra layer of defense to the extremities.

Everything was black and had several Glamours woven into it to help the Witch's Guard move more freely and blend into the shadows better.

Remi wore his holster for his wand on his left thigh, while Finn had simply pushed his own into his left arm bracer.

"This feels so heavy," Finn complained, to which Remi laughed.

"You should work out more," he said. "Mine feels as light as a feather. Of course, I've had to wear mine a few more times than you have. Your Glamours might just be wearing off."

Finn glared, but said nothing in response.

"Come on," Remi leapt from the counter. "We have to get to Autumn's Bloom. I'm sure everyone is already there, waiting for us."

"Is this everyone that will be joining us, Witchguard Caswell?" Vesna asked as the rag-tag team stood in the office of the closed bar.

Remi gave a quick glance to encompass them all before answering, "I believe so, M'lady."

"Then let us begin," Vesna nodded approvingly, moving to the mirror.

They all watched as she touched its side and the image began to change. In a matter of seconds, the scene had shifted from the tiny office to a familiar scene that Remi recognized to be the Woodland Court.

"Will you be able to get us into the forest around the manor without passing through the Woodland Court?" Finn asked, to which Vesna smiled sardonically.

"All wooded areas, great or small," the Queen explained, "fall into my realm. Thus, to be in a forest of any sort is to find yourself inside my Court, young Ashcroft."

"Looks like you're still a bit green, kid," Robert slapped Finn on the shoulder. "Stick with us long enough and you'll learn a few things!"

Remi remained silent as the portal shifted through several wooded areas in rapid succession, some of which he knew, some he had dreamt about or seen in movies. It was almost as if Vesan was trying to pinpoint the exact location of the manor that the Vampire Lord had found.

Finally, the swirling series of images stopped on something that looked like a deformed version of a forest that sent a collective chill through the room, despite the thickness of the gear they were all wearing.

"This," Vesna spoke evenly, though Remi had a sneaking suspicion that she had been perturbed by the twisted and unnatural aura that this area seemed to exude, "is as close to the place which you seek as I can get you."

"This is fine," Remi said, adding hastily, "Thank you, M'lady." He looked at Robert, who awaited his command. "Are you ready?"

The older Warlock nodded, "We'll see you on the other side."

Without another word, he and the others in his party filed through the portal, one after another until only Finn and Remi remained. The younger Warlock was on the precipice of the portal when Remi pulled him back.

"What is it?" Finn looked puzzled.

"I just want you to be prepared," Remi replied. "We don't know what we'll find when we get there."

"You think he's already killed her," Finn's voice and expression were solemn.

"I don't know what he's done yet," Remi admitted. "But I just want you to be ready to face down whatever is waiting for us, and that is a possibility."

"I know, Caswell," Finn's emerald eyes had clouded over with an emotion that Remi couldn't gauge, even from this proximity. "I know what could be waiting out there. But I also know what will happen if we don't go at all, and so do you."

Remi felt sorry for breaching the subject in the first place as Finn stared off into a determinedly different direction.

"Look," he went on. "We're wasting time by just standing here. If you want to turn back, go right ahead. But I'm going through this portal and I'm bringing Aunt Syl back even if it's the last thing I ever do in this lifetime."

With nothing so much as a glance back at him, Finn charged through the mirror into whatever was on the other side. Vesna eyed him pensively, her leaf-colored gaze fixed on his own silvery-blue moonstones.

"Don't wait up," Remi said and the Woodland Queen smiled.

With that, Remi dashed through the portal himself, landing flat on his face in the foreign woods.

Remi quickly regained his footing just in time for an ice spike to come flying through the air past his head, burying itself in a nearby tree.

"*Contego!*" Finn shouted, just as another flew at Remi's head with more precision than the first. The thing shattered, dusting Remi's gear with bits of frost. "Get down!" Finn shouted as a third spike came hurtling through the woods.

"*Reditum!*" this time, it was Remi. he watched as the projectile was reversed in midair to pin its original caster against one of the trees. There was a sickening crunch and satisfying scream of pain as the thing lodged itself inside whoever was responsible. "Come on!" Remi shouted to the younger Warlock.

The forest was covered in a dense fog that left only the outlines of the trees that were directly in front of them visible. Even those were barely so, which meant running was strictly out of the question.

The other Warlocks that had come through before them were nowhere to be seen, but the sounds of battle off in the distance let the pair know that someone else was definitely out there, besides themselves.

Remi searched the treetops above, where the mist was thinner, and grimaced as he saw that bodies had been spiked onto many of the tree limbs. Some were all together, while others were only an arm or a headless body with a leg. He choked back the bile and felt guilty, glad that he did not recognize any of the contorted faces that had been left.

He resolved himself to only staring ahead, knowing the dizzying effect of looking up while walking, paired with the canopy of carnage above them would only serve to make him sick if he continued.

The fog seemed to thicken the further in they walked and Remi found it increasingly disorienting. He lifted his right hand in front of him while keeping his wand arm steady and whispered, "*Lumen.*"

Instantly, a small orb of bluish-white light jumped to life in his hand. It did not seem to do much in the way of combating the impenetrable fortress of mist.

"*Nova Caeli*," Finn said and they were greeted with the familiar whoosh of air. Instead of helping, however, this only seemed to make the fog grow thicker.

The two moved forward at a snail's pace, keeping as quiet as they could to listen for any sign of the other Warlocks that had come with them, along with anything else that might be lurking just beyond the fog and waiting for them. They found nothing as they trailed along until they heard a loud explosion a few yards ahead. The two shared a quick, hopeful look, knowing that it had to be Robert.

Remi took off sprinting, running into trees as Finn tried to keep up somewhere behind him.

The two quickly reached a clearing in the thicket of pines and saw that the fog had lifted around this small, open area.

Robert and two of the other Warlocks were casting at the front of the manor, while one of the Healers tended to a wounded party member.

Remi gazed up at the house and saw that it was, indeed, a rather intimidating structure. It looked much more like a warped version of the Coven House than he had been expecting, looming over them like an unspoken threat. It was a black two-story, Antebellum-style house with granite pillars and rust-colored shutters on the windows.

He looked up to the second story and saw where the Vampire Lord, Sebastian, had managed to break through before being ousted by the enchantments, just as Finn had said.

"Get over here!" Robert shouted back at them, having heard their separate footfalls on the grass. Remi and Finn obeyed, raising their wands to aid the onslaught of charms being cast at the towering structure in front of them.

"Where are the others?" Remi called out as he cast.

"This is all that made it!" Robert answered gravely. "Something was waiting for us in the woods!"

Silence about the subject fell over them as they continued throwing spell after spell at the manor before them. Remi thought back to Vesna's knowing face.

Did she know before she sent us through, he wondered to himself. *Surely, she would have told us if she had.* Perhaps, she merely thought they had already known. Or maybe, the fog of the Glamour had somehow clouded even the Woodland Queen's vision of her own Court. Remi could not be entirely sure either way, but he remembered how wrong each of them had felt as soon as the image had come across the mirror.

Finally, after what felt like an eternity of throwing everything they had at the manor, there was another thundering boom and all of the Warlocks were knocked back onto the ground of the grassy clearing. Remi pushed himself up onto his elbows to see that the front doors had been blown from the hinges completely, almost as if the house was now inviting them in. Robert howled with delight, but as Remi looked over, he could see the older man's labored breathing. He rushed to the demolition Warlock's side and knelt down.

"Are you alright?" Remi asked, but Robert waved his concern away like it was an unwarranted question.

"Patches over there'll have me fixed up in no time," the older man answered, indicating one of his Healers. He pulled out a cigar and lit it with the tip of his wand. "I did what I came to do. Now it's up to you, Caswell."

"You're not coming with us?" Finn asked from over Remi's shoulder.

"Nah," Robert exhaled a puff of smoke. "You two take the others and go on ahead. I'll wait here."

Remi looked around and saw that the two Warlocks that had helped them break through the manor's barriers had been knocked unconscious in the final blast. Then there was the lone Healer of the group that had made it out through the woods. She was currently working on one of the fallen.

Remi glanced at Finn questioningly.

"There's no time," the younger Warlock answered his unspoken inquiry. "We have to go now!"

"Go ahead," Robert laughed with a cough and a wheeze. "These can help me with that Glamour out there once they come to." Remi nodded and stood, moving to join Finn before looking back over his shoulder.

"Robert?" he began. "Try not to make the entire forest go 'boom'. We're going to have enough problems when we get back without the Queen of the Woodland Court being on our asses, too."

"I make no guarantees, Caswell," the man laughed and gave him a wink.

"Let's go," Remi said, shaking his head and turning back to Finn. The younger Warlock gripped his wand, readying himself to go in.

Alexander felt the explosion shake its way down through the foundation of the house above them.

"Sounds like we have company!" he smiled gleefully to Sylvia. The Arbiter stared above them to where the cavern met the stone of Morrigan Manor, hoping that no one had been injured in the siege.

"I do hope they're alright!" Alexander clapped his hands together. "I wouldn't want them to miss out on the show."

XX

Remi and Finn inched their way forward into the vestibule of the manor. Remi could instantly feel the goosebumps rising on his skin and every hair on his body became charged with the static of the structure's dark ambiance the second he came through the door.

"I think I'm going to be sick," Finn said, all color draining from his face the second they had crossed the threshold.

There was a low humming sound emanating from somewhere beneath the front hallway's prismatic, black tiles that went up through the mahogany panelling of the corridor. The lamps along the walls were a jade color and cast an eerie green shade onto the already dark interior.

Remi glanced up to see a gilded brass chandelier hanging from the ceiling, where the candle flames were an ethereal turquoise that only managed to add to the heavy atmosphere. The whole house pulsated with an unspeakably vile energy as they trailed along.

"We need to find your aunt as soon as we can," Remi said, swallowing against the lump of nerves that had lodged itself at the back of his throat. "I don't like the feeling I'm getting from this place."

As they moved along, the walls of the vestibule themselves seemed to be almost vibrating with a sense of foreboding that he simply could not shake.

The sooner we get out, the better, Remi thought. *I don't care if we find that bastard, or not.*

The pair steeled themselves and pushed forward as slowly as they could, ignoring the creaks of the structure as it settled against itself. Both kept their eyes peeled, searching for any sort of clue as to where their leader might have been kept. Remi's nostrils flared open as he caught the unmistakable odor of burning flesh. He checked back to see if Finn had noticed, but the younger Warlock seemed to be oblivious to the stench. Remi decided it might be best not to alert him to this detail unless he brought it up himself.

"Do you see anything?" Finn asked, his emerald gaze darting around as they moved along.

"My eyes are still adjusting," Remi replied, letting his free hand trail along the walls and feel for some sort of a hidden door or latch. "You don't think she might be upstairs, do you?"

Finn shrugged and the two turned back the way they had come to make their way up the spiralling staircase on either side of the hall they were currently standing in.

Almost as if to answer the question, a door at the opposite end of the corridor creaked open, causing both Warlocks to freeze and tense. They waited for someone to come out and when nothing else happened, they exchanged nervous glances. It was like a silent invitation from the manor itself.

Yeah, Remi thought to himself. *Because that's not sinister at all!*

Remi gave a slight inclination of his head before moving to the front, wand stretched out in front of him and ready to cast.

Remi stared down into the overwhelming blackness that was being offered up to them by the newly revealed doorway.

"*Lumen*," he whispered against the cold darkness.

The tip of his wand burst to life just briefly enough for him to see a set of narrow stairs leading downward. It should have been a brilliant glow but, almost as if the very radiance of the light was being swallowed up by the shadows, his wand fizzled out like a broken flashlight.

Great, he muttered to himself. *Like I'm coordinated enough for this.* The halls of the manor seemed to mock him with their palpable silence.

"She could be down there," Finn said, his voice hardened against the dread Remi knew he must be feeling in that moment.

"Right," Remi nodded, descending first. He moved his feet like he was treading through water, keeping his right arm against the wall of the stairwell to brace himself on the off chance that he missed a step. It was only after the tenth step that he noticed the wood panelling of the manor starting to shift into something more coarse against his palm.

It felt less like the wall of a house and more like the wall of a cave. Finn seemed to have noticed this shift in texture as well.

"Is this brick?" he asked. "Are we in the basement now?"

"Maybe," Remi replied, unsure even as he said it. "We are going down, after all."

He noticed a bluish-white light coming into focus a little farther down, swelling up against the dimness of the torchless corridor. The illumination seemed to be pulsating as they drew closer to it, almost rhythmically.

That must be where that humming sound was coming from, Remi thought to himself.

The last handful of stairs became exponentially easier, as their eyes gradually adjusted to the serene glow of the radiance being cast before them. As they reached the bottom, the corridor fell away behind them and opened up into a rather extensive cavern.

There were torches hung in sconces along the walls, with the same ghostly, turquoise flames as the chandelier on the floor above. This light cast on the pale blue stone of the cavern made it seem lighter and much less daunting than that of the bleak atmosphere that had welcomed them into the entrance hall of the manor.

Remi craned his neck back to see the foundation of the house above them. Stalactites hung from the ceiling of the cavern, all pulsating with the same dark energy that had culminated itself in this place.

There was a single, immense orb in the center that radiated a sterile glow that, paired with the flames along the walls, seemed to be the source of the pale glow that had led them down here. Branching out from this, there were four stone platforms each holding a similar stone basin at its center; except for one.

"Aunt Syl!" Finn shouted and the Arbiter's head lolled drunkenly up to meet his horrified expression. Her own eyes widened with affirmation as it registered who she was looking at.

To Remi's absolute surprise, she did not appear to be tied up or in distress of any kind. From the looks of it, she had been enjoying a lavish spread of tea and sweets before they had entered and seemed to be just waking up from a nap with her head on the table.

I must be missing something, Remi thought to himself but did not speak aloud. *Is she his guest?*

As the Warlock studied her more closely, he noted that her ankles did appear to have been strapped to the front legs of the chair she was seated on. Her wrists were holding each other and Remi imagined that they, too, must have been bound. Then he saw a flash of silver between her fingers and it dawned on him that the Arbiter must have been planning something to get herself out of the situation.

"Get out of here, now!" Sylvia commanded them then, but it was already too late.

"How nice of you to join us!" a voice descended the stairs behind them. Both Remi and Finn jumped and turned to see the Dark Warlock casually striding into the cavernous room. "I was beginning to think you might never arrive."

Unlike their prior meeting, the man's amber eyes seemed almost inviting to Remi now. That did not change the unshakeable feeling of sickness that had formed in his stomach, weighing him down like an immovable stone. He thought of what his grandmother had told him about their shared stasis and quietly scanned the room for another person to jump out of the shadows at any given moment.

Alexander Morrigan, he thought to himself.

"We were just about to get started," the Dark Warlock threw his arms wide in a gesture of mock welcome to encompass the two members of the Witch's Guard that stood before him. "I would not want either of you to miss out on witnessing the greatness that is come!"

"Let her go!" Finn yelled out, casting blindly at the Dark Warlock.

The man quickly disappeared in a wisp of black smoke, reforming at

Sylvia's side nearly instantaneously as Finn's curse hit the stone wall of the cavern.

"How rude!" Alexander spat, momentarily losing his calm demeanor.

Finn raised his wand to cast again, but Remi grabbed his arm and jerked it down. He knew full-well what the Dark Warlock was capable of from their previous encounter.

"Do you want to hit her?" he whispered in a harsh tone, the scar at his collar burning in a phantom pain from the blade that had pierced through his skin in the Grove. Finn looked like a scolded child but did not resist. "What do you want?" Remi shouted at Alexander, who seemed to search through his mind for a way to explain his wishes.

"Let us start from the beginning," he answered finally. "I'm sure you have both heard my name by now and have grown to fear it. As you should," he began. "But do either of you know what it means?"

The two Warlocks shared a brief glance of confusion before shaking their heads in unison.

"Alexander," the man went on, "means 'one destined for greatness', much like the conqueror so many centuries ago. But Morrigan means 'one who brings about change'. Which, I suppose, is fitting with what I'm about to tell you."

Remi could feel Finn's tension beside him as the Dark Warlock explained himself but the two remained silent, each searching for some sort of distraction that would allow them to get Sylvia out of this place.

"You see, boys," Alexander continued his explanation. "What I intend to do on this day, is to bring forth a new age of magic. One in which we, as Warlocks, can walk about the Earth as freely as we did in the beginning before the Mortals reduced us into the shadows. An everlasting era where we are free to be the gods we were always meant to be. There will be no more minuscule Covens or silly Covenant laws binding our hands. I seek to grant our kind the freedom to create life and break the bindings of time that have constricted us for so many years!"

"Now," Alexander paused to lace his fingers together, as if contemplating how to further explain his plan. "I already know what the two of you must be thinking. 'Why seek to fix something that is not broken?'"

He shook his head and gave a condescending smile, "That is exactly my point. We were broken from the start! I seek to remedy our people of the human affliction known as Death by granting us immortality!"

He paused now, throwing his arms up above him as if waiting for a thanks or applause, which never came.

"If you're so godlike," Remi goaded, "then why do you require sacrifices to attain your goals?"

Rather than getting upset, Alexander lit up at the question. It was like watching a teacher who had baited a student into asking something just so they could go into an overly complicated explanation to answer.

"Blood," Alexander explained, "is the perfect conduit for my work. The perfect lightning rod that will spark my Gift that has remained dormant in our people for so long! It holds the very life essence of those creatures that I wish to, by nature of this ritual, change. Do not look at this as merely sacrifice, but an opportunity for them to usher in the new age of which I speak. After all, what better way to grant new life than in the death of the old?"

"You're insane!" Finn spat, trying to wrench himself free of Remi's death-grip on his arm. This only caused Remi to dig his fingers in deeper around the younger Warlock's wrist.

"I told you to wait!" Remi whispered through gritted teeth, squeezing so that the other buckled slightly under the pressure.

"You may think that now," Alexander admitted, looking down on them with an almost piteous tone. "But, perhaps someday in the future, you will be able to thank me properly and know that you bore witness to history being made."

The Dark Warlock vanished again, much in the same manner as he had before, almost instantly reappearing at one of the stone basins on its pedestal. The two watched as Alexander tipped the bowl upward so that the contents spilled down into grooves that had been etched along the floor of the cavern, connecting all of the stone platforms. Remi had not noticed these before and now watched as the stagnant blood trailed along, spreading out from the center of the pedestal to lap lazily at the edges of the other stone platforms.

"The blood of the Fae," Alexander said, his words seeming to be charged with the power of some sort of incantation, "that which has birthed all life as we know it to be." In a flash, he was at the second basin, repeating the process.

"The blood of the Vampires," he continued his chanting, "lest we become selfish in our ways." He arrived at the third basin, just as the blood from the prior two met and merged in the grooves along the floor.

"The blood of the Lycans," he tipped the stone bowl, "lest we lose sight of our humanity during our moments of near-sighted anger."

Alexander paused to watch as the third stream of blood trailed along and added itself to the others. He moved slowly toward the dais that held the chair on which Sylvia had been tied as if the act of walking itself had become too laborious for him to manage.

"And finally," he spoke measuredly, as though it pained him to do so. "I wish it were me, but I must be the one to complete the ritual. I do hope you will understand and forgive me in the next life."

He pulled Sylvia to her feet and stroked her face as an athame shimmered into existence, materializing in his opposite hand. Luckily, he seemed not to notice as the ropes that had been binding her to the spot up until that point fell away the instant she moved. Finn was struggling with his full force against Remi now, looking at him like he had suddenly gone stark-raving mad.

"Wait just a few more seconds," Remi whispered. "We need him to be completely vulnerable before we strike." The younger Warlock nodded a silent understanding and Remi dropped his hand finally, readying himself to cast out against the Dark Warlock.

He lifted the ceremonial dagger to Sylvia's throat and began to press it gently into her skin, speaking as he did so, "The blood of the Warlocks, who shall receive this gift of immortality and ascend into godhood!"

Sylvia looked on, unflinching, and Remi suddenly noticed that Alexander had not actually managed to draw blood from her with his weapon. Then, everything happened all at once.

In a move like lightning, Alexander spun on his heel to throw the athame full-force at Remi's chest. Simultaneously, Sylvia drew the knife she had been hiding up until that point and stabbed it through the back of the Dark Warlock so deep that it ripped the front of his robes open as they became stained a deep red. The man let out a howl of pain and rage as Remi ducked out of the way and Finn began sprinting toward the Arbiter to help her.

Sylvia kicked Alexander away from her and ran as he became nothing more than a crumpled mass on the floor of the cavern.

"Your arm!" Finn exclaimed as he reached his aunt, grabbing her wrist and pushing up her sleeve to get a better view.

"It was done so I couldn't cast my way out of here," Sylvia explained, adding hopefully, "The Healers will be able to patch me up in no time once we get back to the Coven House."

Remi regained himself from the floor of the cavern where he had landed as he avoided the athame flying at him. "Is everyone alright?" he shouted at the other two, who both nodded in confirmation. "Call a cleanup crew. We need to get all this blood cleaned up so no one else stumbles on it and tries to finish what this lunatic started."

Sylvia nodded in agreement, borrowing Finn's phone to make the call as she did not have hers at the moment. Remi searched the cavern floor around him to find the athame that Alexander had thrown but did not see it anywhere.

It should be around here somewhere, he thought to himself. *I'm sure I heard it land right behind me.*

Then, his color drained as he came to a chilling realization in that moment. He spun on his heel and shouted at the top of his lungs, "Run!"

In an instant, Alexander was suddenly looming over the two Ashcroft Warlocks with a maniacal grin carved onto his face. Finn made to cast at the Dark Warlock, but Sylvia pushed him out of the way with all her might. In a movement that was almost too quick to register, Alexander pierced the ceremonial dagger through her with such force that it slipped out of the Arbiter's back with sickening ease.

His golden eyes flashed triumphantly as Sylvia cried out in a manner similar to how he had when she had done the same to him seconds earlier. Finn shouted in denial, but it was too late. Alexander pulled the blade from the Arbiter, letting her body slump down onto the floor with a sickening thud.

Remi watched in abject horror as the Dark Warlock brought the dagger down to pierce the stone floor and let the blood trickle down the blade to congeal with that of the other races. As they all met along the grooves, the atmosphere of the room changed in an instant, becoming suddenly much heavier. Sparks of static electricity were suddenly arcing along the grooves almost like chain lightning as the spell began to take effect.

Then there was a thunderous boom that knocked all of them, Alexander included, forcefully off their feet and threw them forcefully against the walls of the cavern in different directions.

Remi grunted painfully as he pushed himself up onto his elbows and caught his breath. He looked across to see Finn, only a few feet away, picking himself up off the floor of the cavern.

"Go!" Remi shouted, barely able to hear himself over the ringing sound that had filled his own ears.

He wasn't sure if the other had heard him or if he was running on pure instinct, but Finn charged forward regardless. Remi took a quick survey of the area and saw that Sylvia had been flung from the dais and pinned somehow between two of the stalagmites at the other side of the cavern from where he was.

Alexander had been knocked across the room by the blast and Remi could see that the athame was now skewering his heart and keeping him in place.

Remi hastily brought himself to his feet and moved to where Finn was trying frantically to mend the wounded Sylvia, reciting every healing spell he could possibly muster.

"No, Aunt Syl!" he shouted between spells as he tried to stop the red liquid that was pouring out of her. "You do not get to do this to me! You do not get to leave me like this!"

The blood continued to pool through his fingers from the tear the

Dark Warlock's blade had left in her stomach, effectively staining Finn's hands as he tried to save her.

Finn looked up at him, emerald eyes full of tears and panic.

"Help me!" he screamed desperately, his hands having been painted red and the floor beneath Sylvia's body becoming increasingly drenched with her life force. Remi knelt down beside him and placed his own hands over the fearful Warlock's.

"Move," Remi told him, as gently as he could while trying to keep his voice as level as possible. He pushed the flaps of skin on either side of the gash together, not caring that his Arbiter's blood was rapidly overflowing and covering his fingers. "*Consarcio*," he muttered, remembering a spell he had picked up from one of the Healers over the years.

Immediately, stitches began sewing themselves across the wound, pulling the skin tight with a shimmering layer of string. He checked to see that Alexander was still unmoving against the wall of the cavern.

"Do you know any replenishment charms?" Remi asked Finn, who nodded as he choked on his sobs, while he rolled Sylvia over to do the same with the exit wound. "Stay calm and try some of those," Remi commanded. "I'm going to go check on him and get the others."

Finn nodded in agreement, going back to speaking in a muttered and constant tone, using every bit of healing Latin he could manage in his current state. Remi stood and began walking toward the Dark Warlock's body, the fear in his gut slowly becoming replaced by sickness at the thought that Sylvia might die down here before they made it back to the surface. He dropped to his knees in front of him and placed his hand over Alexander's neck, feeling for a pulse; there was none.

Remi closed his hand around the hilt of the blade and began pulling, trying with all his might to pry it from the wall so they would be able to take the body back with them to present to the High Coven.

As he did this, Alexander's hand grabbed his suddenly and Remi let go of the athame, attempting to leap back in his shock.

"You won't," the Dark Warlock growled in a feral voice, "take this from me, Caswell!"

The next second, he and the blade were gone. Remi turned just in time to see him reform just behind Finn, dagger raised above him in a striking pose.

"Finn!" Remi cried out, but it was too late.

With one fierce swipe of his arm, Alexander knocked the younger Warlock against the wall of the cave with such force that Remi was sure his neck must have snapped.

The Dark Warlock then brought the blade back down on Sylvia several times, moving her so that she was hovering over the grooved patterns of the floor and letting the blood trickle down freely into them. He turned toward Remi then and he could see now that the man's face and the front of his robes had been stained red. Alexander grinned and his golden irises flashed like a beast in the heat of a successful kill.

"Let us see how you mend that, child!" he snarled and Remi found the fear lodging itself deep within him once more.

Remi lifted his wand and shouted, "*Orbis Incendium!*"

A ball of fire erupted from the tip of his wand, flying straight for Alexander. The Dark Warlock cut through it with the blade as if it was nothing more than a sheet of paper, letting out a spine-tingling laugh as he did so.

"Surely," he shouted, "you can come up with better than that! You are a Caswell, after all!"

"*Plasmas!*" Remi yelled, shooting a bolt of lightning, which Alexander used the blade to conduct and steer back toward him.

Remi leapt out of the way just in time for the bolt to cut a chunk out of the cavern wall, exposing the mineral deposits just beneath the surface. The Dark Warlock shot an ice spike at him then, which Remi shattered like glass with a quick wave of his wand.

"*Ventus Ignis!*" he yelled, causing a swirling pillar of flames to encircle Alexander.

The Dark Warlock growled as the fiery twister grew hotter with each rotation and began encroaching in upon him. In a moment of insanity, Remi aimed his wand at the ceiling that was the foundation of Morrigan Manor.

"*Fatisco!*" he shouted and immediately felt the strain as his spell carved several small fissures into the stone and caused a handful of the stalactites to fall toward the ground.

Remi waved his wand at the falling mineral spikes and sent them hurtling toward Alexander, just as the Dark Warlock doused his previous spell.

"*Deleo!*" Alexander shouted, dissipating the firestorm. He waved his hand casually and the formations that had been flying toward him crashed into each other, lightly sprinkling him and Sylvia's unconscious body with mineral dust. "For shame, young Caswell!" he made a disdainful clicking sound with his tongue and teeth. "You almost torched your very own Arbiter trying to get rid of me! What would the High Coven have to say about that?"

Remi looked past him to see that Finn was pushing himself to his feet just as he heard the house above them all cracking. This was the first sign that it had started to cave in on itself.

Just a few more minutes, he told himself.

"*Tempestas Veni*," he muttered under his breath so Alexander would not hear him.

"What's that?" the Dark Warlock shouted, lifting his free hand to cup his ear. "You'll have to speak up if I'm to hear you, Caswell."

A light flick of his wrist sent an invisible wall of energy into Remi, slamming him onto his back and dragging him across the floor of the cavern. Alexander slammed the dagger into the ground, causing the floor directly in front of Remi to erupt into a small sea of jagged stalagmites. It was like teeth formed from gravel and he could see the Dark Warlock's golden eyes glaring down at him with a volatile passion.

"You will not deny my Gift as the rest of your family before you have, Caswell!" Alexander jerked his arm back and Remi felt his body being pulled along the cavern floor, inching toward the menacing bed of spikes. "You will not shun this wonder for others! I will not allow it!"

Remi could now fully feel the strain of his hurricane pulling on him and imagined his heartbeat slowing at an alarming rate. He felt himself starting to panic as his pulse drummed against his ears, replacing the ringing that had been there before.

He could only faintly hear Alexander's maniacal laughter echoing off the walls of the cave somewhere off in the distance, but could not bring himself to do anything with all of the force coming down on him from his own spell.

Then he felt it; they all felt it. A low rumbling sound above them shook the entire house, dislodging rocks and sending them showering down onto the cavern floor.

The roof! he thought to himself, almost gleefully.

Small clouds of dust drifted up to where the rocks had fallen. Remi could now hear a constant, high-pitched whirring sound tearing through the cavern as he was slowly pulled nearer and nearer to the stalagmites and his impending doom.

Remi noticed that the entire room had started to glow an eerie blue-white now. He craned his head down to see that as the blood had pooled into the grooves and met, runes along the floor had sprung to life. Remi had never seen these types of markings before but was filled with a sense of foreboding. He did not know exactly why, but these runes felt instinctively wrong and perverse to him for some reason.

There was another thunderous boom above them, closer this time than the one before.

"Get her!" he shouted, forcing himself to move now as he knew what would come next. Aiming his wand at the rocky teeth just inches from him, he shouted, "*Discutio!*"

A single row of the stalagmites that had formed from Alexander's unspoken curse shattered before him and he stood to see that Finn had just made it to throw himself over Sylvia's body.

Alexander heard this and turned to strike.

"*Flagrum Ignis!*" Remi shouted and a chain of fire shot from the tip of his wand. He whipped it back and jerked his arm, watching as the chain wrapped itself around Alexander's neck. He pulled hard and the Dark Warlock fell to the ground just as the whip broke from the force.

With his strength rapidly dwindling and Alexander writhing in agony now the flames continued to lick around his neck, Remi aimed his wand at Finn, who had curled himself over Sylvia as if to shield her.

"*Praegero!*" he shouted. The two Ashcroft Warlocks were lifted up into the air and pulled toward him, both flying to land on top of him. "Cast a barrier, kid," he whispered to Finn, his breath having been knocked out of him by the impact.

"How touching that you wish to perish with your friends," Alexander's golden gaze glared down on them menacingly. He clutched at the burn mark that Remi had left around his neck. "I'll be sure that the history books are not unkind to you, Caswell."

"*Discutio*," Remi aimed at the remaining rock formations that stood between them. Instantly, they were disintegrated, throwing fractured bits of rock and dust directly into Alexander's eyes as well as his own. Remi blocked his line of sight as the Dark Warlock let out an inhuman howl of pain.

When he removed his arm, he watched in horrified amazement as Alexander was simultaneously struck by four different bolts of lightning, one from each dais. The Dark Warlock was enveloped in a cocoon of light and lifted from the ground by an unseen force.

There was a final, deafening barrage from the ceiling and Remi looked up just in time to see the foundation of Morrigan Manor being ripped away and engulfed in a swirling, obsidian vortex.

Why hasn't he cast yet? he wondered, looking down to see that Finn had been knocked unconscious by the force of being thrown into him. *Well, shit*, he thought, unsure if he could manage even a simple enough barrier to cover them all.

Remi saw the sky turn a dark purple as lightning clapped inside the black clouds he had brought down onto the house. A monsoon poured down into the cavern onto them and Remi hoped that Robert and the others had seen his spell being cast in time to find cover. He did not want them to be sucked up into it, but he did not know if he still had the ability to control it at this point. He could feel it pulling on him, etching his energy away gradually like someone carving images into stone.

"How fitting that you should call forth rain to wash away the sins of the past, Caswell!" Alexander called down to him. His voice sounded amplified and otherworldly, making Remi wonder just how this ritual was now changing him.

Remi shuddered to himself in the same instance that a bolt of lightning from his magical hurricane shot down. It hit Alexander's photon bubble and split apart, with arcs hitting against the cavern walls and shaking the ground with a thunderous rumble as another fork came crashing down almost instantly.

"*Contego!*" Remi shouted, just in time for one of the static fingers to bounce off of his Shield Charm. The very force of it knocked him and the two sleeping Warlocks back a few paces.

Remi felt himself becoming light-headed at the strain of casting while his hurricane continued to break off pieces of the manor. He could see his vision spotting over as a cyclone from his spell touched down inside the cavern, barreling straight toward the ritual stones and Alexander, pulling bits of the cave floor into it as it moved.

The Dark Warlock laughed and the cold sound somehow echoed around the now-roofless room.

"You still think you can stop me?" he cackled.

I have no control over this now, Alexander, Remi thought to himself. He was too drained at this point to even move his mouth, let alone stop his spell.

All he could do now was watch in a state of detached sort of horror as the hurricane he had created sent down even more cyclones to break apart that which it could not reach.

The spinning hands of Remi's spell swirled constantly forward, burrowing themselves into the ground throughout the cavern. He watched as the blood from the four magical races was drawn into the body of each cyclone, so that each towering vortex became tinged in a sanguine hue as they spun through the room in different directions. The rain became tinted red as well, giving the appearance that blood was falling from the clouds.

The blue-green flames along the wall were sucked into them as well. Instead of being put out, the independent storms were set ablaze.

Remi watched as Alexander, in his cocoon of blinding light, was pulled closer and closer by one of the fiery obelisks, until he was inside of it. That was when everything changed.

As Alexander's orb was drawn into the swirling spire of white-hot flames, lightning shot down and entangled itself around the single twister. His laughter, which had up until that point been triumphant, instantly became screams of agony.

Something is wrong, Remi bolted upright on the floor, pushing the other two to the side of him. From seemingly nowhere, Remi felt a sudden resurgence of energy. *Is my spell absorbing his?* he wondered. *Is it absorbing him?*

Remi knew he had to do something. *But what?*

As if his body was now moving of its own accord, Remi lifted his wand at the tornados he had created and shouted, "*Stabilis Mille!*"

Each vortex broke free from the clouds above and slowly came to a halt in its swirling.

"*Permadesco!*" he shouted and the rain, which had been pouring down all this time began rushing toward the dying cyclones, dousing the flames of them all almost immediately.

"Help!" Alexander cried out laboriously. "Help me, Caswell!"

Remi could feel himself becoming overwhelmingly ill now. With an effort, he lifted his wand further into the sky.

"*Serenitas!*" he yelled. He could feel himself being pulled forward from the floor of the cavern as the earth shook and the skies tore apart.

Sylvia was lifted almost lazily from on top of him, but Remi was quick to grab her and pull her back down to him.

"*Gravitas*," he muttered and felt himself becoming heavy along with the others. He watched as each of the tornadoes dissipated. His last spell had caused his hurricane to be undone and now, all they could do was wait.

Remi watched as Alexander fell to the ground, no longer being suspended in light or blazing winds. The Dark Warlock hit the ground of the cave with a satisfying thud and Remi could not help but equate it to a fallen god plummeting back to Earth after being ousted from the Heavens.

Remi looked up just in time to see Robert peeking his head over the edge of where Morrigan Manor had once been, only moments before his incantation had ripped it away in fragments.

"Look out, kid!" the older Warlock called down, just as a slab of the foundation came crashing down into the cavern. As Remi's storm had dissolved, there was no longer anything to keep the previously airborne pieces of the structure from falling back down and crushing them all. "Take cover down there!" Robert shouted.

The handful of other Warlocks that had accompanied them and made it through the treacherously Glamoured forest surrounding the house came to join Robert on the upper edge of where the mansion had been. Remi watched helplessly as they all lifted their wands into the chasm, not knowing what they would do next.

"*Parma Decrusto!*" the Warlocks shouted in unison.

A barrier of magic was instantly thrown over the mouth of the cavern, like a shimmering curtain. Remi watched as another, smaller piece of the manor's foundation fell into this freshly cast shield. There was a sound of drumfire, accompanied by a colorful display of sparks as the thing was disintegrated to the point that it was almost nothing but particles of dust. There was still a substantial portion of it that had been left intact, however, and this is what came crashing down through the barrier.

Remi could feel his vision blurring over once more as the pieces of Morrigan Manor fell back down into the cavernous hole they were lying in.

With the last ounce of energy that he still had left, he gripped his wand. He could not even lift it this time, but he had to do something to prevent them from getting crushed by the debris.

"*Absque Domus*," he managed, casting another type of shield over himself and the Ashcrofts so that whatever stray pieces of the house still came through would be repelled from them all.

Remi's entire body felt heavy now and he could hear the sounds of the house being pulverized in the distance, coupled with the shouts of Robert telling him to get out of the way.

But he could not move an inch, and finally let himself fall into a deep sleep as the fireworks display flashed behind his eyelids and Morrigan Manor crashed down around them in pieces and dust, effectively undone by his spell.

Remi awoke to find himself still in the cavern, only something felt very different about it this time. He looked down to see that Sylvia and Finn were no longer there and wondered where they had gone. He could not hear anyone from the crew they had brought with them into the forest and wondered if the others had left him in the cavern.

Did they think I was dead? he asked himself, his voice reverberating in his own mind. *Surely they would have brought me back even if that was the case.*

Remi checked down to see that everything had remained intact on his person. Upon seeing that it had, he pushed himself up and onto his feet. There was a low humming sound coming from within the walls of the cavern around him and he wondered if maybe the blasts from the house being reduced to dust had caused him to go temporarily deaf.

Wouldn't my ears be ringing if that were the case? he wondered to himself.

There was a light emanating from somewhere in front of him. It wasn't blinding this time, but felt somewhat warm and inviting.

What is that?

Remi inched closer to the source of the radiance and immediately felt his body become full of rage. Alexander looked up at him from the stone floor of the cavern. He had been bathed in the light and somehow seemed victorious even in his currently mangled state of being. His limbs were going in all the wrong directions and the athame had once again become lodged in his stomach, pinning him to the floor of the cavern. He wore a smile on his face and his golden eyes seemed to have lost their previous ferocity.

"Caswell," he spoke up toward Remi. "I see your Coven have left you to bask in my glory."

"How have you not passed on?" Remi asked, confused by what he was seeing. "Your blood loss alone should have killed you by now."

"Ah," Alexander nodded laboriously in agreement. "It seems that I have accomplished that which I sought to achieve. It is a shame that it was only bestowed upon myself, however, as I had hoped to share it with the world."

"And what gift would that be?" Remi smirked. "Immortality? Sorry, Al, but if every bone in my body is broken and I can't move from the spot I've been pinned to by my own blade, I'm not sure that I would want to live forever."

"This is but a mere flesh wound, Caswell," Alexander beamed. "These injuries can be fixed. Then I can adjust the ritual so that it includes every Warlock next time. With your help, of course."

"My help?" Remi guffawed at the very thought of it. "You *do* realize that I'm supposed to take you to Trial, right? Why would I help you?"

"Because you're not that unlike me, Caswell," Alexander laughed as he said this. Remi was unsure which was more absurd, the comment or the fact that the Dark Warlock was asking him to join him.

"I'll pass," Remi retorted, turning to leave and find the others. "And I'm nothing like you."

"You know if you leave me, I'll only do it again once I repair my body," Alexander said behind him and Remi suddenly found himself doubling back on his steps.

He was in front of the Dark Warlock in an instant and pulling the athame from the man's stomach, replacing it with his wand. The scene around Remi shifted then and he was now standing on the edge of where the mansion had once been. He lifted his wand out in front of him and spoke some words that he did not know he knew. He could feel that they were a spell of some sort, but he had no idea where they were coming from.

A string of inferno, fueled by the blood of the self-made god below him, erupted from the tip of his wand and consumed the remains of the house. They grew larger and larger until they reached well above the tops of the trees in the forest. Remi kept his wand in front of him and brought his free hand to the same height, effectively pulling at the flames as they threatened to dance away from him.

Remi could feel his own spell searing at his skin, but he could not seem to stop himself as the echoing laughter of the Dark Warlock rang out in the woods around him.

Remi woke to find himself in the Infirmary with no recollection of how he had gotten there.

Was it all just a dream? he wondered to himself. *Or another nightmare?*

He glanced down at his hands to see that they had both been covered in bandages that wrapped all the way around, like thick mitts made of linen.

Maybe not, Remi thought, now wondering if they had even made it into the forest around Morrigan Manor. He resolved himself to get some more rest and find out in the morning.

XXI

Remi sat on the kitchen counter, letting smoke billow up from his mouth to collect on the ceiling. He sipped his third cup of coffee and watched the sun rising over the misty morning in the silent city of Oxford.

He hummed along as he listened to the song playing in the background. It was 'Storms' by Fleetwood Mac. He'd always liked the simplicity of it, even though it rarely made its way onto anyone's 'Top 10' list from the band.

Remi laughed to himself at the lyrics, briefly letting his mind trail back to the cavern floor and Morrigan Manor falling all around him.

"Stevie Nicks," Nona's voice startled him out of his internal reflection. "You want to talk about it?"

"What do you mean?" Remi took another drag of his cigarette.

"I've heard 'Landslide' on loop more times in the past two days than I care to count or admit," his grandmother replied, opening a window to let the room air out. "I know when something's wrong with my babies."

Nona gave him a discerning look and he sighed.

Am I that transparent? he wondered to himself.

"Does 'everything' count as what's wrong?" he asked aloud.

Remi was letting his grandmother stay with him until she could speak with the Mortal family who had bought her house from the Oxford Coven when she had gone missing and ask them about buying it back.

"It does," Nona answered, pouring herself a cup of coffee and splashing it with milk. She pushed herself up onto the counter with him, her silvery-blue eyes searching his own that were so similar to hers. "But you and I both know that I can't fix everything."

"Davis is watching Finn," Remi began hesitantly. "He said that if his vitals remain stable that the Healers are going to let him out for the funeral." He took a sip of his coffee and another long drag.

"How are the High Coven reacting to everything?"

"As well as can be expected, considering everything," Nona replied, staring down at her mug as if it held all of life's answers. "I'm informed that Sylvia's brother, Virgil, and Dahlia Ashcroft will be in attendance."

"What about the barrier?" he glanced outside to see the wall of the dome glittering against the clouds in the morning sunlight.

"They're going to leave it in place until after the funeral," Nona informed him. "Better to bury one of our own without Mortal interference, I suppose." Her voice trailed off and Remi felt the guilt of it all tugging at his heartstrings for what felt like the millionth time since they had made it back to the Coven House. Even with everything that he and Finn had tried to do to save Sylvia just before Alexander had regained consciousness, the Dark Warlock had effectively sealed her fate during his second onslaught. By the time they had made it back, she had already lost too much blood to be saved. Remi had watched with a heavy heart as the Healers had tried the same spells he had used and then some, even resorting to drawing runes on her. But the Arbiter had been so far gone at that point that the runes themselves seemed to not even take or go into effect. Finn had passed out by the time the news broke, due to the sheer shock of it all.

Remi could feel hatred burning inside him as he thought of the man who had caused all of this pain. He looked over to see that Nona's moonstone eyes had become glazed over.

"What's wrong with you?" he asked, giving her a look of concern.

"Does everything count?" the woman mimicked with a smile. When he said nothing in response, she took a deep breath and went on, "They've appointed me as the new Arbiter of the Oxford Coven.

"That's good!" Remi exclaimed, throwing his hands in the air and nearly falling off the counter. "Isn't it?"

"Is it?" Nona let out a single, hollow chuckle. Her expression had clouded over with doubt and worry. "I'm not entirely sure that it is. She's not even in the ground yet, and they've already replaced her."

The two sat there on the counter, letting a few moments of silence pass between them. The lyrics of the Fleetwood Mac playlist were the only thing breaking through their absence of words. Remi reached for another cigarette as his first came to an end.

Finally, Remi spoke, "What's the worst that could go wrong?"

They both shared a brief glance and Nona answered, "Everything."

"I can try," Remi mimicked her earlier statement. "But we both know that I can't fix everything."

The pair of Caswells laughed briefly before the sobering reality of the morning hit them and brought them back down.

"I always told myself that I never wanted to be in a seat of power," Nona was the first to speak this time. "I guess I just didn't tell myself hard enough."

"I guess not," Remi mused, taking the last drag off his second cigarette. He stabbed it out in a shot glass he had pulled from the cabinet earlier that morning. "Is it permanent?" he asked.

"Only until they can hold a proper election to find a replacement," Nona replied.

"That's what they told Sylvia when Frank died," Remi said with a bitter smile. "That was five years ago. Here we are."

"Then I guess I've only got five years to live," Nona joked, but it fell flat between them.

"When are you going to talk to the Mortals about buying your house back?" he changed the subject to something lighter.

"Getting tired of me already?" Nona cocked a single brow at him and gave a sly smile.

"No," Remi shrugged and took a sip of his coffee. "I've just got a bunch of your things to give back."

"I'll keep you posted," she smiled weightedly.

"You're going to do it behind my back, aren't you?" Remi asked, shooting her a knowing grin.

"We should get ready," Nona spoke somberly, changing the subject.

"Yeah," Remi sighed, leaping from the counter. "I'll bring a change of clothes for Finn, just in case the Healers let him leave the Infirmary today."

"Something tells me," Nona gave him an empowered look, "that they'll let him out."

"Absolute power corrupts absolutely," Remi smiled, making his way from the kitchen to get dressed.

Venus Nevan's stilettos clicked across the stone floor of the cavernous dungeon, the sound echoing over the ruins that had been left in the wake of Alexander's spell. Morrigan Manor was nothing more than a pile of ash and rubble now that the battle was done. She had seen it all from the safety of the surrounding woods.

She had watched as the veteran and his company of retired members of the Witch's Guard had pulled the two Warlocks and the corpse from the ruins of what had once been her home. She had heard them shout to each other and proclaim victory over a dominion they could not have even begun to fathom.

Venus surveyed the area, seeking out her prize under the decimated slabs of what had once been Morrigan Manor.

"The boy does have a certain affinity for the art of destruction," she mused to herself with a sinister grin.

Then she heard it; a sound that was like an awakening to her. It was the sound of a phoenix rising from the ashes nearby.

Venus whipped her head, her auburn curls bouncing off her shoulders. It was there that she saw it; the outline of a hand rising up against the gravel and dust.

"Venus?" Alexander called out to her. "Daughter, have you come for me?"

She sprinted the length of the cavern floor, her heels twisting over the rocks, until she reached him.

"Father!" she cried, pushing back the debris with her bare hands. "What have they done to you?"

"I have done it, my dear daughter!" the Dark Warlock laughed against the pain, ignoring her question as blood spat from his mouth. "I have conquered Death and acquired the gift of immortality for us all!"

Alexander coughed now and his mouth filled with the bright, red liquid.

Venus positioned herself so that she could cradle her father's head in her lap. She shushed him and stroked his hair to soothe him while she rocked back and forth.

"You need to rest now, Father," she spoke against her tears. "Let yourself go to sleep. This will all be over soon." She ran her fingers over his ginger hair that had darkened from the blood to more closely resemble her own.

"Gods have no need for rest, my child," Alexander laughed at the very notion of it all. "And now, we shall be gods. Just as we were always meant to be, Daughter!"

Another crimson flood escaped his lips and his head lolled weakly over against her thigh.

"Yes, Father," Venus whispered, her fingers closing around the hilt of his athame that had been stabbed into the ground beside them. "Gods need not rest. But you are no god."

Venus brought the blade of the dagger to rest against Alexander's throat.

"But, my darling," the Dark Warlock smiled up at the vengeful goddess he had spawned so many years ago. "You do not understand! You do not know what you speak of!"

He tried to laugh it away, but Venus did not join in his pathetically panicked guffaw.

Instead, she gazed down upon her Father, her amber eyes flashing into those so much like her own. The same stare that she had known her whole life. An overwhelming wave of sorrow rushed over her and she had to breathe deeply to calm herself before she went on.

"Crowns," she said, "were meant to be passed along, Father." She swallowed against her tears.

"In order to keep dynasties from caving in upon themselves like the Romans, so long ago."

She gently began applying pressure to the dagger against Alexander's throat and felt her breath catch inside her.

"If you wish not to pass along the crown, Father," she went on, closing her eyes against the pain that was welling in her chest. "Then I must take what is rightfully mine."

"Venus, I-" Alexander spoke his final words as his own ritual dagger pierced through his neck just as it had so many others before him. Venus finally let out the sobs she had been holding in up until that point just as his body began to go limp. His eyes rolled back into his head and she knew he was gone.

When Alexander's head had been severed, she looked down upon the lifeless man that she had pulled across her only moments ago. She knotted her fingers in his hair and brought the head up to her own.

Blood dripped from his freshly exposed neck as she pressed his lips to her own.

"Forgive me," she whispered tearfully, kissing him gently one final time. She closed the lids over his glossed-over, golden eyes softly so that they would not see what she was readying herself to do. "Forgive me, Father; for I know what I have done."

Venus placed Alexander's head to the left of her and slipped her hand into the gullet of the Dark Warlock until she felt his still-beating heart. She laced her fingers around the arteries and closed her eyes.

"*Discedo Vita Indu Ego*," she spoke the words and instantly felt a surge of power rushing into her as her father's life force was drained and transferred into her through the incantation.

Venus felt the earth tremble beneath her as Alexander's heart gradually slowed to a halt in her clutch. It was almost as if the very world around her was reacting to the sin she had just committed and she could finally feel the weight of it all.

She looked down at her robes that had been stained the color of wine from the ichor of a false god. She unclenched her fist and removed her hand from inside the Dark Warlock. She pushed the body from her and stood, wiping the dirt from the back of her robes.

Venus could feel the drunkenness of the divine power coursing through her veins now. She nearly stumbled over the fallen angel as she made her way to the centermost dais, where her father had performed his failed ritual.

She looked to the heavens, basking in the gleam of the sun as it rose against the clouds.

Venus knew what must be done.

The grounds of the Coven House had been swarmed with people that morning. There were a few that Remi knew in passing, but most of the Warlocks here that he had never laid eyes on before in all his time with the Witch's Guard. Nona Caswell had made her way straight to the Infirmary upon arrival to bring Finn his change of clothes and inform the Healers that he would be in attendance for the funeral, regardless of what they said.

Remi stood back, leaned against the Jeep, and took notes of who all was there while he finished his cigarette.

He saw the Alphas, Kit and Julia, along with the rest of their Packs. The other Alphas had sent representatives in their stead since they could not all make it. He imagined Davis, who was there on behalf of his Pack and the Oxford Police Department, must still be upstairs with Finn until the Healers let him go. Valerie was there, as well as Sebastian Kaine, which surprised Remi as he had not expected any of the Vampires to show up today.

Then, there were the unmistakable Queens of the Fae. Rydia was in a toga, much like the one he had seen her in the last time, only this one was dark indigo and reminded him of a moonlit harbor at midnight.

Vesna had donned a flowing gown the color of petrified wood, a sign of mourning for her Court.

Enya, the Queen of Fire, wore a black, form-fitting dress that made Remi think of things that had been carbonized by flames and made her caramel skin appear almost bronze in the sunlight.

Aria, the Queen of the Wind Court, wore dark grey akin to a rain cloud and an anklet to anchor her to the ground as a token of her heaviness for today.

It did not take long for Remi to find the Magisters who had come to oversee the event. Dahlia Ashcroft and Virgil Henderson; Sylvia's sister-in-law and brother, respectively.

The pair saw Remi standing at his Jeep and immediately began making their way toward him across the front lawn, where everyone had gathered. He let his cigarette fall to the ground, crushing it into the gravel with his heel. Even from here, he could see the resemblances as the two talked amongst themselves.

Virgil looked almost identical to Sylvia with a darker complexion and stronger jawline. His white-blond hair had been pulled back into a ponytail for his sister's funeral and his peridot eyes gleamed with unshed tears for his fallen kin.

Dahlia Ashcroft could have easily been mistaken for a Fae if he had not known better. She had jet black hair and small, dainty features with porcelain skin that seemed to reflect the sun. Even from so far away, Remi could see that her eyes were not only the same shade of emerald as her son's but also had the same oval shape to them.

Maybe it wasn't his dad that was the Fae, Remi wondered to himself, thinking back to an earlier conversation he'd had with Finn about parentage.

"Remington James Caswell, I presume," Dahlia was the first of the two to speak. She extended her hand formally.

"You may call me Remi, Magister Ashcroft," Remi said, taking her hand and bringing it to his lips as he bowed. "Magister Henderson," he said, righting himself and inclining his head towards the man in question. "Forgive me, but I feel there is no need to be so formal on my behalf, given the circumstance."

"Yes," Dahlia gave a forlorn half-smile. "I do wish our first official meeting could have been under different circumstances."

"I know you probably don't know it," Virgil spoke arduously. "But my sister was quite fond of you, Caswell. She raved about you almost every chance she got."

Remi felt his heart catch, "She did?"

"Sure! All the time!" Virgil threw his hands up as if it had been obvious all along. "When you brought down a hurricane to protect the House, it was all she could talk about for days after. I felt like I was there, even though I only saw it on the television."

"I-" Remi felt himself choke and had to swallow several times so that he could go on. "I never knew. I thought she hated when I did those things."

"I figured," Virgil nodded. "She rarely let people know how she really felt about them. Always thought of it as unprofessional to mix Coven business with personal feelings."

Remi was unsure how to take that bit of information. Before he got a chance to decide, Dahlia had wrapped her arms around him and squeezed.

"I just want to thank you for keeping my son safe," she spoke into his chest, muffling her tiny voice so that she was barely audible. She sounded mournful and obliged at once. Remi did not know what to think, as he had always imagined the High Coven as a single, domineering entity. It seemed to him, at least in this instance, that the individual Magisters had hearts and personalities when not surrounded by their peers.

The small woman released him and opened a compact mirror to make sure she had not smudged her face off onto his chest during the embrace. Remi stood there for a few moments, questioning how he should process the situation.

"He," Remi began, trying to form a coherent sentence that would get him away from their stares. "I didn't know he had told you about me."

"Only the important things," Dahlia said. "That he had been partnered with you and that you were letting him help on the big case with you, even though you essentially had no prior knowledge of him or his skill level. He also told me that you let him stay with you and had cast a Sentinel charm to keep him and Sylvia safe in the Infirmary."

"He was awake for that?" Remi was slightly taken aback to find this out. "I never knew. He never said anything to me."

"He thought it might have just been a hallucination from the medicine," Dahlia admitted. "But then, you cast another when you brought him home and he knew it must have been real."

"I don't know many Warlocks that can leave a spell like that overnight!" Virgil slapped him on the back of the shoulder with a smile.

"I only did what needed to be done," Remi answered earnestly. "I suppose he'll want to leave now, though. After everything that's happened in the past few days."

"He hasn't said, one way or the other," Dahlia replied. "I'm sure he will have a lot to think over before he makes a decision. I'm just glad he found a friend in the Oxford Coven.

"Me, too," Remi swallowed against the lump that had formed in the back of his throat. Then, a thought occurred to him. "How long before we hold the election?" he asked.

"I'm sorry?" Virgil looked confusedly at him.

"For the seat of Arbiter," Remi went on. "My grandmother said you all appointed her temporarily. I was just wondering when the election would be held. No offense meant, but your sister was only supposed to fill in until an election could take place and that was five years ago."

The two Magisters shared a glance with each other, seeming as if Remi's brief explanation had only served to puzzle them further.

"What happened to Sylvia was a mistake and a tragedy on our part, as representatives of the High Coven," Dahlia was the first to speak. "But I'm not sure you know quite everything about the situation with your grandmother, Mister Caswell."

"When it was discussed," Virgil took over, "there was no mention of the position being temporary. There won't be an election, as the position has already been filled. Besides, there would be no one to run against her, and I'm sure not many would disagree with her appointment as the Head of this House."

Remi stood there for a moment, certain he had misheard the two of them.

But what reason would either of them have to lie to me about something so trivial? he thought to himself. *Neither of them knows me well enough. But she does. And she's the one who didn't tell me.*

"Come on," Virgil said, giving Remi a soft pat on the shoulder and breaking him out of his personal commentary on what he had just been told. "I figure they'll start the ceremony pretty soon."

"You go on ahead, sir," Remi said, with a polite incline of his head. "I'd like to talk to someone before we go out."

The Magister nodded his agreement and both he and Dahlia began making their way down to where the ceremony would take place. Before they had made it too far down, Dahlia turned and called back, "Mister Caswell?"

"Yes, Lady Magister?" he replied. The woman was staring at him curiously and Remi was suddenly very nervous about what she might say.

"Would you care to tell me why one of your Coven's Healers is still in the prisons of this House?" she gave him a sly smile as her emerald eyes bore into him.

"To be honest, ma'am," Remi answered, "I'm pretty sure we all forgot about him with everything that's going on."

"Would you mind going to un-forget him?" she gave him a smile that was both light-hearted and commanding of his respect. "I wouldn't want to attend another funeral from this Coven so soon after this one."

"Yes, Madame," Remi fisted his right hand over his chest and bowed. "I'll go have him released before the ceremony begins."

When they were far enough along and he could no longer feel Dahlia's piercing emerald eyes, Remi turned his attention to the crowd and made his way directly toward the one person he had questions for.

Vesna turned as she saw him coming, giving him a sort of mournful smile as he neared where she and the other Queens had huddled together.

"Witchguard Caswell," she spoke first. "To what do I owe this pleasure on such a sad occasion?"

"I need to speak with you," he replied. Then, upon the other Queens focusing their attention on him, he bowed and added, "Alone, if you would not mind, M'lady."

"As you wish," Vesna agreed, sending the others away with a wave of her hand. "What seems to be the problem, Warlock?"

"What did you see before we went through the portal into your domain?" Remi asked in as hushed a tone as he could manage.

"Whatever do you mean?" Vesna gave him a coy look.

"I mean," Remi tried to find the right wording. "Did you know what we were walking into before you let us go?"

"Are you implying that I would send you to your death?" the Woodland Queen's eyes seemed to flash. "That I would be so bold as to not weigh the repercussions of such a blatant disregard for your Covenant Laws?"

"No, M'lady," Remi backtracked. "I just meant... It seemed like you knew something was waiting for us, but you didn't say anything."

"That much is true, Caswell," Vesna admitted with a slight inclination of her head. "I did know something was waiting in the woods. As, I'm sure, did you all as you prepared to go."

"Yes, M'lady," he said. "But I know that the Fae can see through the Glamours cast by Warlocks more easily than other races. And that forest was very heavily enchanted by someone."

"I can only tell you what I saw, Caswell," Vesna eyed him warily. "What you choose to do with that information is entirely up to you and your Coven."

"What did you see?" Remi was suddenly very curious now.

"Each Warlock has a sort of trail that they leave behind when they cast even the simplest of spells," the Woodland Queen explained. "Most do not notice it, but we Fae are not like most. We see even the most primitive signs left behind by the use of magic, Warlock."

Remi had never known this, so he remained silent as the Queen went on.

"This is why I have such a strong relationship with Death," she explained. "It is not simply a matter of feeling her presence, but because she is such a noticeable embodiment of magic in its purest form."

"Did you see her there in the woods that night?" Remi asked, feeling strange to be referring to Death as an individual being. "Was she waiting for us?"

"She was," Vesna admitted. "Although, when I see her beforehand, I can never tell if she has already done her work or if she is merely waiting for who she will call to join her. That is why I did not mention it that night, Caswell. I did not wish to alarm you of something if it could be avoided. That is all."

"I see," Remi let out a sigh he had not realized he had been holding in.

"But there was something else there that night, as well," Vesna's tone had turned very grim now. "Along with the overwhelming presence of Death in the forest, there was something darker. The enchantments cast upon Morrigan Manor were similar to those that were cast on the trees. They had an almost identical trace of magic. But there were slight differences."

"What does that mean?" Remi asked.

"I am not positive," Vesna said, before going on. "But I believe that there was at least one other waiting for you that night. Though, I cannot say who that might have been."

That doesn't sound very promising, Remi thought to himself but remained silent.

"I hope that you can find whoever this person may be," Vesna said in closing, giving him an ominous stare. "I shudder to think what it could mean for all of us, Magical and Mortal alike, if they were left to their own devices. I'm sure you will not disappoint me, Witchguard Caswell."

"I'll try my best, M'lady," Remi confirmed, giving a slight bow. He hoped desperately that the Woodland Queen would not be able to read all the thoughts that were currently rushing around inside his head, as she tended to do.

When Remi recovered from the vulnerable stance, Vesna had already moved on to other things, leaving him standing there to wonder who this 'other person' could possibly be. Now, however, was not the time for that. He could see everyone who was in attendance gathering near the seats that had been placed at the edge of the lawn for them and decided he should make his way down to join them.

But first, he needed to get down to the dungeons.

"Next time you find yourself in the Infirmary, Caswell," Daniel said in a voice that would have been threatening, had he not looked like he had been left out to dry for a week on the line, "I will make sure I repay this whole thing to you, ten-fold!"

"Go ahead and get down to the Infirmary, yourself," Remi fought hard not to laugh at the man's misfortune. "I'm sure they can plump you back up. At least a bit, if not all the way."

"You just mark my words, Caswell," the Healer made a second attempt at a threat. "This is not the end of this discussion. I'll make you all remember forgetting me down here."

Remi kept his head down to hide the fact that he was snickering under his breath as the pair of them walked down and out of the Oxford Coven's prison cells. They parted at the landing to the third floor, Daniel going toward the Infirmary for nourishment while Remi made his way back out onto the grounds of the Coven House.

The funeral was held on the outer edge of the hedge maze that surrounded the Oxford Coven's stone garden. The dreary feeling was made even more prominent by the rain that hammered against the shimmering circumference of the barrier that had been put in place by the High Coven only days ago.

Feels like ages, Remi mused to himself as he watched the individual droplets fall and congeal in a sort of melancholy pitter-patter. *Fitting for the occasion, I suppose.*

It was a closed-casket affair, as the Healers had not been able to cover the multiple scars that had been left across Sylvia's body, despite their best efforts. Understandably and as her closest living relative, Virgil had decided that he had not wanted the people of Oxford to remember the former Arbiter that way.

Instead, they had placed a portrait of the woman and Franklin Ashcroft standing in front of the Coven House, at the head of the casket. Remi could remember when the photo had been taken, but all he could picture in the back of his mind when looking down at the black box was Alexander's golden gaze flashing like a beast as he sliced through her repeatedly like she had been little more than butter with the blade of his athame.

Remi turned his gaze to focus, instead, on the portrait beside the casket and tried to push away any negative thoughts. He remembered that he had just been gone through his Proving ceremony to join the Witch's Guard and that following winter it had snowed, which was a rare occurrence in Mississippi, even this far north. There had been several people there that day, some visiting family for the holidays while others had simply been stuck in town to work on unfinished cases.

There had been snowball fights and teams between all divisions of the House. He could not remember which team had won, but he did remember a big dinner before everyone had left to be with their families.

In the midst of all of the throwing that day, someone had taken a picture of the two former Arbiters; right before a renegade snowball had plowed into the side of Frank's head and dusted his coat in snow.

That was the picture that was being used, and Remi could not help but wonder if the happy memories he was feeling had been why Virgil had chosen that particular one. He let his eyes dart quickly through the audience and found himself realizing just how many lives Sylvia had touched in her comparatively short run as the Arbiter.

I wonder if some of these people are here out of respect for the family name? he thought to himself, not daring to mention anything out loud.

There were the Alphas and Davis, who was there as a liaison for both his Pack and the Oxford Police. The Vampire Lord, Sebastian Kaine and

Valerie, whom Remi was almost sure had never met the Arbiter. There were all four of the Fae Queens.

There were the two Magisters of the High Coven, Dahlia and Virgil; both of whom were there as family to the deceased. But on top of all of these that Remi could name, the grounds had been filled with at least two hundred other people he had never seen before this day.

Remi felt a pang in his chest as fingers interlaced with his own. He glanced down to see Nona Caswell's hand and followed the arm up to meet her knowing moonstone gaze.

Nona placed her free hand on his shoulder and gave him a reassuring smile.

Does she know I already know? he wondered. He quickly put the thought to the side, resolving himself to ask her later, when the crowd had died down and he could get her alone.

Remi turned his attention to the front of the crowd, where he half-listened to the chaplain drone on in a monotonous voice, waiting for the man to finish speaking of a woman he did not know. He took a quick survey of the crowd and was relieved to see that he was not the only one there who shared this sentiment.

Finally, after what felt like hours of his talking, the man took his seat and Virgil took to the stand. He briefly recounted all of the troublesome situations he and his sister had gotten into as children and young adults, before she had met Franklin Ashcroft. Then he went on to talk about all of the things that the loving couple had done, both in Frank's time as Arbiter and her own. Virgil had come to a close in tears and had to be led from the stage to compose himself away from the crowd.

After he had finished, Dahlia had stepped up and remembered how wonderful it had been to finally have a '*Sororcula*'. Then she had said that she had always considered Sylvia a sister and treasured her as such, even after the passing of her brother, Frank. Though she did not break down, Dahlia had become choked up more than once during her section of the eulogy and her words had seemed to become heavier each time this had happened.

The woman had powered through and eventually gone back to her seat so that the funeral could be brought to a close.

Everyone had watched silently as the casket was lowered and a concrete angel, which had been Sylvia's favorite statue from the garden, had been placed over the fresh mound. Remi felt remorse wash over him like a flood and had bitten the inside of his cheek so hard that he could taste blood.

He had remained this way as the members of the crowd had said their individual goodbyes and eventually dispersed. He knew that if he could focus on the pain, then he would not be at risk of crying in front of so many people that he did not know. Even though he would probably never see most of them again, he did not want to take the risk in any case.

"I think I'm going to go make sure that Finn's okay," Remi told Nona after the ceremony had concluded and most of the people had made their way onto other things that needed to be done.

His grandmother nodded her silent understanding and gave him a pat on the shoulder. He turned as it dawned on him that he had forgotten to ask her about what Dahlia and Virgil had told him earlier. Remi watched, not wanting to yell to get her attention for fear of causing a scene, as the woman made her way over to converse with the two Magisters.

Remi continued to stare with a stone jaw and though he did not know exactly what was being said, he did see the slightly horrified expression on Nona's face as she turned back to see him watching the three of them.

So it's true, then, he thought to himself, having all the confirmation he needed for the time being.

Remi walked over to where Finn sat unmoving, staring at the broken patch of ground where Sylvia now rested. He took a seat beside the other and stared at him intently, although the younger Warlock seemed not to notice the new presence.

"How you holding up, kid?" Remi asked in a soft voice, so as not to startle him.

"I keep hoping I'll wake up eventually and that this'll all be just some messed up, extended dream," Finn replied, a haunted shadow covering his normally brilliant emerald eyes. "I guess hoping just isn't enough anymore, though."

"I'm not going to tell you that it gets any better," Remi admitted, though he was not quite sure where the words were coming from. "Because it doesn't. You just learn how to cope a little better each day. The void you're feeling can't be filled. But it can be patched up as time goes on, until it doesn't hurt as much anymore."

He rested his hand on the man's shoulder to offer support. "I just want you to know that you're always welcome to stay. However long you like or need to, my door's always open for you."

"I don't want to put you out like that," Finn objected.

"You're fine," Remi assured him, pulling his friend in for a hug. "Just know that you've always got family here, bud. Always."

Remi felt Finn starting to cry into his chest and pulled the younger Warlock tighter to him, trying to conceal him from anyone who might still be around to see this moment of weakness.

When it had all been let out, Finn untucked himself from Remi's embrace and quickly righted himself, taking a handkerchief out of his pocket to wipe his face of tears and snot. Remi did not dare to look down at his shirt, knowing that it had been ruined for the day and feeling that it was not important.

"Thanks," Finn choked out. He coughed to clear his throat of any sort of phlegm that might have been dislodged during the minute-long episode and repeated, in a more level tone, "Thank you."

"Have you decided where you're heading, yet?" Remi asked, trying to change the subject to something lighter.

"Not yet," Finn admitted. "I like it here but after all this, I'm just not sure."

"Well, you know," Remi gave him a reassuring pat on the shoulder. "You've always got a place to crash if you're in town, even if it's just a visit."

"Thanks," Finn nodded, looking slightly less burdened than he had when Remi had come over. He glanced back over his shoulder to where Dahlia and Virgil were still talking to Nona. "I'd better go say goodbye before they leave."

"Yeah," Remi agreed as the younger Warlock stood up. "You probably should." He watched the other disappear into the throng of people that still remained on the lawn.

"Seems like he's feeling better," Nona Caswell's voice was suddenly behind him.

"I guess," Remi kept his voice as level as he could.

"How are you holding up in all of this?" she asked, taking a seat on the row behind him. It was almost as if she knew Remi would lose his nerve if he had to look at her right then.

"What do you mean?" he played coy.

"We both know you were there that night," she said. "I know what Robert told me before you went in and after you cast that hurricane. What happened while you were down there?"

"A woman died," Remi said bitterly. "Read my report. It's on your desk."

"That's not what I meant," Nona sounded annoyed at his petulance, which gave him the extra nerve he needed.

"When were you going to tell me?" he asked. There was silence and he pressed further, before she could object.

"What? Did you think I wouldn't notice after a few years had gone by and you were still Arbiter?"

Still, Remi was greeted with more silence.

"How many lies are you going to tell me now that you're back?" It was deafening now. "Are you even really back? Or was the stasis thing and you breaking out just another lie, too? You know what, I don't even want to know the answer to that one."

"I see," Nona's words sounded choked now as they finally came. "I believe I'll take my leave, then."

He felt her stand behind him and instantly knew he had gone too far this time, but Remi could not bring himself to care at that moment.

He listened as her footsteps slowly faded out across the grass and were replaced by much heavier bootsteps.

"How come," Davis's voice was suddenly beside him, "every time I see that woman walking away from you, she's on the verge of tears?" The Lycan took the seat two chairs down from Remi. "Are ya really that big of a jackass, Caswell?"

Remi's head lolled to the side to encompass Davis in a look that he hoped was nonchalance.

"Jury's still out on that one," he replied casually, to which Davis shook his head in mild disbelief.

Remi pulled a cigarette from his pocket and offered one to the officer beside him. They lit up and as Remi blew out his first puff of smoke, he went on, "Y'know, I think I will take you up on that drink offer."

"Oh, gawd," Davis laughed in a thick drawl. "You're not going to puke in my truck this time, are you?"

The two shared a brief chuckle and that was when Remi heard it; a sad sort of laughter. It was almost as if someone had lost everything, but there was still a maniacal sense of underlying victory.

The haunting sound grew in both volume and intensity, until it was impossible to hear anything else. Remi turned to see, with a slight feeling of relief, that he was not the only one on the lawn that was hearing it. Then something that paralyzed them all with dread and fear happened.

Everyone turned their gaze upward just as the silvery lining of the High Coven's barrier shimmered brighter against the clouds

Remi quickly looked over to where Virgil and Dahlia stood, only to see them staring up, clearly just as befuddled as everyone else. Then there was a sharp sound like glass being shattered with a hammer and all of the air came crashing back in on the city of Oxford, like a vacuum that had been set in reverse.

Remi watched in a helpless sort of wonderment, along with everyone else, as pieces of the broken sky fell away to reveal the pinkish-red hue of sunset lying underneath. The rain came pouring into Oxford now, marking that the High Coven's enchantment had been completely undone. All the while, the haunting and melodic laughter echoed throughout the city.

CPSIA information can be obtained
at www.ICGtesting.com
Printed in the USA
LVHW101319061022
730102LV00001B/22